THE HEAD OF GOD

THE HEAD OF GOD

The Lost Treasure of the Templars

Keith Laidler

Weidenfeld & Nicolson
LONDON

First published in Great Britain in 1998 by
Weidenfeld & Nicolson

© 1998 Keith Laidler
The moral right of Keith Laidler to be identified as the author
of this work has been asserted in accordance with
the Copyright, Designs and Patents Act of 1988

A CIP catalogue record for this book is available
from the British Library.

ISBN 0 297 84129 7

Typeset by Selwood Systems, Midsomer Norton

Set in Stone Serif

Printed in Great Britain by Butler & Tanner Ltd,
Frome and London

Weidenfeld & Nicolson

The Orion Publishing Group Ltd
Orion House
5 Upper Saint Martin's Lane
London, WC2H 9EA

Contents

Acknowledgements

This book is founded upon the work and studies of a multitude of authors and researchers, whose books and manuscripts stretch back for more than three thousand years. The conclusion presented in this book would have been impossible without this enormous catalogue of scholarship. Certain modern texts have had a profound impact on my thinking, chief among them the seminal *Holy Blood and Holy Grail*, the origin of my interest in this subject, Ahmed Osman's books on ancient Egyptian/Hebrew connections, and Andrew Sinclair's *The Sword and the Grail*, an enigmatic book which suggests far more than it reveals.

I was helped during my researches by a number of individuals who gave freely of their time and knowledge. Robert Bryden proved an invaluable store of information on the Templars, which he graciously shared with me. Stuart Beattie and members of the Rosslyn Chapel Trust were kind enough to allow filming access to Rosslyn Chapel. Dr Joe Zias was a mine of information on aspects of the Cult of the Head and Dr Malcolm Smith provided genetic and population information I would have been hard put to find elsewhere. To them, and to everyone who helped with this work, my heartfelt thanks.

Illustrations

The barrelled roof of Rosslyn Chapel.
A head of the 'Green Man'.
The Rosslyn Crucifixion scene.
The 'Veronica' or perhaps a representation of a sacred head.
The head of the Apprentice.
The Apprentice Pillar.
The top of the Apprentice Pillar showing Isaac and the ram.
Detail showing the damage (thought to be deliberate) done to the Pillar.
The Nidhogg serpent winds itself around the base of the World Ash.
Apollo's head on the cross.
The sun's 'head' on the cross.
The Head of God crucifix.
The head of Sarah, Abraham's wife.
Templar head painting bearing an impressive resemblance to Jesus.

1

The True Nature of the Templar Treasure

The French king's soldiers came in the early hours of Friday 13 October 1307. Just before dawn, when men sleep most soundly and guards are least vigilant, the seneschals of Philip IV descended simultaneously on the most renowned military order in Christendom, the Knights of the Temple. Every member of the order found was arrested, including the grand master. The accusation against the Templars was stark and terrible – a charge of heresy. In the words of the royal order for their arrest, the Knights of the Temple had 'abandoned God their maker and sacrificed to demons ...' It was 'a bitter thing, a lamentable thing, a thing which is horrible to contemplate, terrible to hear of, a detestable crime, an execrable evil, an abominable work, a detestable disgrace, a thing almost inhuman, indeed, set apart from all humanity'.[1] But amongst all this high-flown hyperbole there was not one word of what was most probably the real reason behind Philip IV's unprovoked attack – his desire to acquire the fabulous treasure of the temple for himself.

Yet ironically, the base motives for Philip's assault on the Templars brought to light the presence of an even more valuable treasure within the Order of the Temple – a forbidden relic of inestimable worth.

Despite their full title, 'The Order of the Poor Knights of the Temple of Solomon', by the early fourteenth century the Templars were possessed of immense power and wealth. In just under two hundred years, from their inception in or around 1112 until their dissolution in 1307, the Knights Templar gathered land, gold and property in abundance. At his reception into the order, a postulant had to take vows of chastity, obedience and poverty, and he was required to turn over all his wealth to the temple.[2] Their land holdings were extensive, their possessions divided into eight *langues* (linguistic regions) and ten provinces which ignored national boundaries. Preceptories, castles and vast estates stretched over most of Europe, from Scotland in the west to the eastern outposts of Outremer (Palestine). They owned a fleet of galleys, shipyards and ports such as La Rochelle. Unlike other military orders, the Templars lent money and over the course of time became bankers to most of Christendom, with many kings heavily in their debt. Added to this was booty, the fruit of spoil gathered in battle from the Holy Land and elsewhere. They even received tribute from Muslim potentates and from their Islamic counterparts, the warrior-mystic Assassins.[3]

The Templar's enigmatic beginnings in the Holy Land lent a numinous aura to their wealth, and with reason. At its inception, the first knights of the order had apparently remained sequestered in their quarters on the Temple Mount in Jerusalem, on the former site of the Temple of Solomon, for more than nine years.[4] Recent research has confirmed that the knights of the fledgling order had undertaken excavations beneath the Temple Mount, fuelling speculation that they had found at least part of the fabled treasure of Solomon, thought to have been hidden beneath the temple just before the legions of Titus had laid siege to and finally destroyed the edifice in AD 70.[5] Tradition also asserted that something else, something of great importance, had been found beneath the temple, with suggestions ranging from the Ark of the Covenant, sacred writings or even the Holy Grail, which later legends connected with the Templars.[6] Whatever the truth of these tales, by the beginning of the 1300s the organisation had become the antithesis of its original name. 'Poor Knights' they were not – the sum of Templar wealth was almost past counting.

Yet strangely, when Philip le Bel, King of France ordered the destruction of the order and sent his armed gangs into the Templar estates and preceptories, little in the way of gold, jewels or specie was discovered. This was all the more curious because the suppression had been well planned by the king and his henchmen, with an extraordinary level of attention to security. The pope's help and acquiescence had been sought. Sealed orders were issued to the king's officials, with instructions that they were not to be opened until a set time, after which the king's commands were to be put into effect immediately, the intention being to prevent any prior word getting to the 'Militia of Christ'. The commentary contained in the orders underlined the seriousness of the charges levelled against the Templars: 'Like beasts of burden deprived of reason, in fact exceeding the unreasonableness of beasts in their bestiality, they have abandoned God their maker.' A detailed list of indictments had been drawn up, which included sodomy, denial of Christ and the crucifixion, spitting and urinating on the cross, and the reverencing of idols – especially the worship of a severed head.[7]

Even more compelling than the lack of treasure was the almost complete absence of evidence of this Templar 'idol', the head they were accused of worshipping. That a head or heads of some kind were revered by the order is beyond dispute: the confessions of Templar captives are too consistent to be ignored. Many who refused to admit to sodomy, worshipping cats or any of the other litany of 'satanic practices' listed by the Inquisition, nevertheless confessed that a severed head formed part of the Templar ritual. The name of this relic was most often given as Baphomet, which translates as 'Father of Wisdom', a term that was to recur in startling circumstances later in our story. A brother of the order, Etienne de Troyes, gave the Dominican friars of the Inquisition a most vivid description of his first view of the head. He had seen the relic when it had been brought out at the annual chapter of the order, in Paris. The inquisitorial record states:

> He was in the chapter for three days ... and at the prime of the night they brought a head, a priest carrying it, preceded by two brothers with large wax candles upon a silver candelabra, and he (the priest) put it upon the altar on two cushions on a certain tapestry of silk, and the head was, as it seemed to him, flesh from the crown to the shape of the neck with the hairs of a dog without any gold or silver covering, indeed a face of flesh, and it seemed to him very bluish in colour and stained, with a beard having a mixture of white and black hairs similar to the beards of some Templars.[8]

Other Templars gave different descriptions of the head they had seen. The head 'seemed to be white with a beard', or it was '... red in colour and as large as a human head'. From the Templars' statements to this Inquisition, it is clear that, although the Baphomet was accorded special reverence, more than one head was in the possession of the Templar hierarchy and used in rituals. A series of heads was involved. In one account the head was described as 'an old piece of skin, as though all embalmed and like polished cloth'. This statement raised the first suspicion in my mind that what was being related by the Templar captives, perhaps all-unknowing, was the shadowy presence of an ancient tradition. 'An old piece of skin', which was nevertheless 'a head', suggested to me that this particular relic was the last sacred vestige of a previously intact head, perhaps of untold age.

The discovery of such an 'idol' by the king's men would certainly have

3

condemned the Templars in the eyes of most of their contemporaries, and vindicated Philip le Bel's persecution of the order. However, although no effort was spared in the search for 'Baphomet', no trace of the relic was found. There is good evidence that the Templars had prior warning of the suppression and that the treasures of the order, along with its written records, were spirited away just days before the king's crackdown. At least one Templar spoke of the treasure being removed under cover of darkness from the Paris preceptory a day or two before the onslaught on the temple by Philip le Bel's officers. It seems likely that the sacred relics were removed at the same time as, according to all the evidence, they were held in high reverence and would have been accorded even greater importance than the order's temporal treasure. But where did they go? To what safe haven were they taken?

These were important questions, but there was another of far greater import as far as I was concerned. Until now, the preserved heads of the Templars had always been spoken of in passing. Never a part of the main plot, they were simply 'props' to the central characters, the Templars and their oppressors. The heads the Templars worshipped have come to be regarded by present-day researchers in exactly the same way that the medieval inquisitors looked upon them – simply as 'idols', inanimate items, cult objects. But if they truly were preserved heads, then they were the remains of someone who had actually lived and breathed in times past. Someone who had suffered the common lot of humanity; who, like ourselves, had been elated and downcast, had walked this earth and schemed and fought and loved and dreamed.

A life once animated each embalmed skull. Whose life? Whose heads were being worshipped? The question became more and more of an obsession. I wanted to know their identities, to speak the true name of Baphomet. I needed to understand why they were chosen for this grotesque form of immortality. And there was more to consider: if these heads had been part of the treasure discovered by the Templars during their excavations beneath the Temple of Solomon, then they were ultimately Judaic in origin. How could this, and their ritual worship, be reconciled with the Templars, the Militia of Christ, men whose foolhardy bravery in the service of the Cross was renowned, knights who willingly gave their life in defence of the teachings of Jesus?

There was one clue. After the Templars were suppressed, the inquisitors who inventoried their possessions discovered a single sacred head – or rather a beautifully wrought silver reliquary in the form of a female head: 'inside were two head bones, wrapped in a cloth of white linen, with another red cloth around it ... the bones inside were those of a rather small woman'.[9] The reliquary was marked 'Caput LVIIIM'. Some researchers have read the 'M' as $\mathcal{M}$, the astrological sign for Virgo, and believe the bones to be those of the Virgin Mary, Jesus' mother. Whatever the truth of that theory, the tiny remnant of what had once been a head was another tantalising clue. It reminded me irresistibly of the 'old piece of skin' that was also a 'head', suggesting once again that the worship of certain heads was a tradition of immense age. But what really captured my attention was the rest of the caption. LVIII is the Latin rendition of the number fifty-eight. Why fifty-eight? For me, it was confirmation that the relic was one of a series, a line of sacred heads that had been held in great reverence. But what was their origin? And where were they now?

The Knights Templar's beginnings were in the Holy Land, and they were known to have been steeped in occult lore, much of which originated in the eastern Mediterranean and especially in Egypt. At this initial stage of the investigation, this region seemed the most productive area of enquiry. It appeared reasonable to assume that the preserved heads, and the origin of the worship of these macabre remains, should derive from somewhere in the Middle East and, given the fanatical faith of the Templars, that they were linked in some way with Christianity, though not necessarily orthodox Christianity. Caput fifty-eight, whoever the remains belonged to, seemed to point the way: it spoke mutely of a tradition, a hidden religion, stretching back far beyond the beginning of the Christian era, and on some calculations, to at least the time of Moses.[10]

2

Moses the Pharaoh

In 1937 the father of psychoanalysis, Sigmund Freud, published his last major work. It was quite unlike anything he had previously written, and was entitled *Moses and Monotheism*.[1] Freud had been fascinated by the discrepancies in the biblical account of Moses and had developed a startling new hypothesis, in its way just as epoch-making as his more famous psychological theories. In the book, Freud gives his reasons for believing that Moses was not a Jew, but an Egyptian, a follower of Akhenaten, the 'heretic' pharaoh. This was a revelation for me: if true, it was another tantalising link between the Templar sacred heads and the time of Moses.

Akhenaten is an accepted historical figure. He was the world's first monotheist, the pharaoh who broke with the old gods of Egypt and who attempted to introduce the worship of a single deity – the Aten. But more especially, occult tradition credits Akhenaten with originating many of the precepts that govern mystical orders. The Rosicrucians, for example, trace their origins to Akhenaten, who is said to have created a great brotherhood, a mystery school whose beliefs have since spread across much of the earth. Templar philosophy is known to have marked similarities to Rosicrucianism, suggesting a common origin for at least some of the teachings. It was arguable, therefore, that both groups were, ultimately, following the precepts of the Pharaoh Akhenaten. This line of thought intrigued me greatly, as I was myself a member of the Rosicrucian Order and had recently participated in an initiation during which I had had a most singular experience. Although it is forbidden to make public the secrets of the order, during the ritual I had personally experienced the appearance (in a mirror) of several disembodied heads. Could this vision be in some way linked to the very heads the Templars worshipped?[2]

As a presumed disciple of Akhenaten, the story of Moses and the Exodus provided a plausible link between the lands of Egypt and Israel. The Order of the Temple had been founded in Jerusalem, the capital of the Israelite nation. And it was the Templars' excavations at Jerusalem, beneath the ruins of the Temple of Solomon, that seem to have led to their ritual adoration of embalmed heads. Was there perhaps a connection between these different peoples and events? Could the worship of the severed head have begun with the 'heretic' Akhenaten? And had it then been carried, first to Judea and the Temple of Solomon and finally, via the Templars, into France? The possibility seemed remote, but I decided to look more closely into Freud's seemingly eccentric claims. To my surprise, not only did they turn out to be well founded, but the research also revealed potential routes by which the sacred head tradition reached the West, and it was eventually to shed new and altogether unthought-of light on the antecedents of Jesus.

The Moses Story – The Early Days

As recounted in the Bible, Moses was a Hebrew, born in Egypt in the land of Goshen. His father, Amram, was a member of the house of Levi, as was his mother Jochebed. The Hebrews at this time had been in Egypt for several generations, having come down from Canaan at the behest of Joseph (of the coat of many colours) who had been appointed pharaoh's vizier and had prevailed upon the Egyptian monarch to allow his kinfolk to settle in the eastern delta lands. The Hebrews had grown in numbers and 'waxed exceeding mighty, and the land was filled with them' (Exodus 1: 7). A new pharaoh ascended the throne and became increasingly afraid of these now-powerful immigrants. He considered them a threat, afraid '... lest they multiply, and it come to pass that, when there falleth out any war, they join also unto our enemies, and fight against us ...' (Exodus 1: 10). The Egyptians tried to curb the power of the Hebrews by enslaving them and setting them to build the cities of Pithom and Raamses. When this failed to hold down their numbers, pharaoh ordered the murder of all new-born male children. The purge was brutally and efficiently carried out. If mothers were suspected of hiding their infants, the Egyptians brought their own babies into the Hebrew homes and made them cry, in the hope that the Hebrew children would take up their wailing and reveal themselves.

According to the Bible, Moses' Hebrew mother hid him for three months until, in desperation, she placed him in a basket, waterproofed with tar and pitch, and placed her infant among the reeds on the bank of the Nile.

Here he was found by pharaoh's daughter when she went to bathe. On opening the basket, the Egyptian princess was filled with compassion for the little child, who was crying piteously. Moses' elder sister, Miriam, had been charged with watching over the child from a distance. Now she approached pharaoh's daughter, suggesting that a Hebrew woman be appointed to nurse the child. This idea was taken up, and Miriam fetched Jochebed, Moses' own mother, who joyfully carried the child off to care for him, safe now under the protection of Egypt's royal house. When Moses was weaned, she took him back to the palace, where pharaoh's daughter adopted him as her own son. It was then she bestowed on him the name Moses 'because I drew him out of the water'.

So runs the story; but even in my teens I had found it hard fully to accept the tale. Pharaoh's daughter was the heiress, and because the royal bloodline of Egypt ran through the female descendants, a princess was even more precious to the Egyptians than a male heir to the throne.[3] It is inconceivable that she was not heavily protected, surrounded by body-guards and courtiers who would have effectively isolated her from contact with ordinary Egyptians. And yet we are asked to believe that Miriam, a young woman of the despised Hebrews, could somehow break through this circle of protection and speak directly with the princess. To my mind, Miriam could never have even got close to the Egyptian princess, and if she had she would have been whipped out of the royal presence as soon as she opened her mouth.

Freud was also suspicious of this version of events, but for several more learned and technical reasons. Firstly, Moses is not a Hebrew name. Pharaoh's daughter's brief explanation that it derives from an Hebraic term meaning 'he that was drawn out of the water' simply does not stand up to scrutiny. The active Hebrew form of the name 'Mosche' can at best be translated as 'the drawer out'. To translate in the sense given in the Bible, 'one who has been drawn out', the name would have to be Moshui. Clearly, the old Hebrew scribe who edited the early biblical texts was attempting to gloss over the problem, to massage the truth to fit an orthodox explanation.[4] In addition, as Freud pointed out, to credit an Egyptian princess with a knowledge of Hebrew etymology is clearly non-sense. And yet this explanation has been accepted for centuries, by both Jew and Christian. As Freud noted: 'Perhaps the awe of Biblical tradition was insuperable. Perhaps it seemed monstrous to imagine that the man Moses could have been anything other than a Hebrew.'[5]

Moses is, in fact, an Egyptian name. 'Mose' means child in Egyptian. The final 's' has been added in the Old Testament's Greek translation (the

Hebrew has 'Mosheh'). The word crops up with impressive regularity in Egyptian compound names, such as Amon-mose, which translates as 'Amon (a god of the Egyptian pantheon) has given a child'. The Egyptian king lists are filled with mose-s, and the word features in the names of many of the best known of Egypt's pharaohs, e.g., Ah-moses, Tutmoses and Ra-moses (Rameses).

The Moses story is notable for a further anomaly. Like many other hero myths, it expounds an idealised version of the hero's life. But its storyline is very different. Other myths tell of a high-born infant (usually a king's son) being brought up by humble foster parents. Later, after many adventures, the royal child attains his rightful place as leader of the community. The stories of Remus and Romulus (founder of Rome), of Sargon of Agade (founder of Babylon), of the Greek heroes Perseus, Amphion, Telephus and many others, all correspond to this pattern.[6] The most probable explanation for such myths is the self-glorification of the hero who, in real life, was actually of low-born status. The humble family of the story are his true kin, but the hero/king needs to deny this unfortunate fact. To legitimise his claim to the throne, he needs to demonstrate that he is not simply an ordinary mortal who, by guile and cunning and perhaps even murder, has assumed the kingship, but that this exalted position is his by right of his true (and long-hidden) royal birth.

So, we have a stock plot of abandoned royal infant, found and cared for by peasant family, and finally returned to his royal status. What is unusual about the Moses story is that it is the exact opposite, a mirror image, of the standard version: Moses is born of humble parents, his foster parent is of the royal house of the pharaoh, and he eventually ends up back with his own humble folk, the Hebrews. For Freud, the conclusion was obvious: the Bible story is a cover-up, an attempt to hide the fact that Moses' true parentage lay with the Egyptian line. Moses was an Egyptian of high rank whom his 'adopted people' (the Hebrews) needed to make into a Jew. Strangely enough, as we'll see in Chapter 8, this conclusion is only half true, and for a remarkable reason.

There was another question, one that struck at the very heart of Freud's Judaism – that of circumcision. Although it is now universally regarded as a Jewish custom, the origin of circumcision is undoubtedly Egyptian, as Herodotus, 'The Father of History', claims in the first volume of his *Histories*.[7] The examination of numerous mummies (and the occasional explicit wall painting) proves that Herodotus was right. The Canaanites of biblical times are called 'uncircumcised' in the scriptures, so we can be sure that the custom was generally not practised by the Semitic tribes living on the eastern Mediterranean, whereas in the case of the Egyptians, males of both high and low caste submitted to the procedure. If the orthodox interpretation of Moses is correct, and his overriding ambition was to bring about the Exodus, to liberate his people from the hated Egyptian yoke and take them to a new land where they could be free from all Egyptian influences and worship their own god, why should he impose upon them a custom – circumcision – which was quintessentially Egyptian? As Freud says: 'If Moses gave the Jews not only a new religion but also the law of circumcision, he was no Jew but an Egyptian, and the Mosaic religion was probably an Egyptian one...'

Freud's logic is compelling, but his conclusion creates a new and seemingly insoluble problem. By virtue of his own personality, Moses imposed monotheism – the belief in one omnipotent god – upon all the Hebrews. While it is possible that certain Hebrews did possess monotheistic beliefs even before their descent into Egypt, it was Moses who gave monotheism to the mass of the people and who brought them back to it when, as they did more than once, they strayed after other gods. But, if we are to accept Freud's thesis, there is a problem – monotheism was not an Egyptian tradition. On the contrary, the nation was renowned for its wealth of gods, among them Osiris, god of the dead; Isis his wife; Seth, god of evil (who was said to have murdered his brother Osiris in a fit of jealous rage); and Thoth, god of wisdom, sometimes seen as the demiurge who created the world by the sound of his voice. The god Amun (almost unknown until the twelfth dynasty, around 1800 BC) eventually became known as the king of the gods, and rose to the highest position in the pantheon when he was associated with Ra, the sun god, as Amun-Ra.[8] In the eighteenth dynasty Amun-Ra was regarded as the state god of Egypt, and the pharaoh as his physical son, from whom pharaoh received the authority to govern.[9] Each of these gods was worshipped in its own temples, with its own priests according to its own rituals and incarnations, which could vary from place to place (e.g. Amun was worshipped in human form at Thebes and as a ram-headed man at Karnak, where a sacred ram was cared for as the living incarnation of the god. At Karnak there was also a sacred goose, another animal considered holy to Amun).[10]

How, then, could monotheism be considered an Egyptian religion that was passed on to the Jews? And how could Moses be identified not as a Jew, but as an Egyptian? The theory would be stillborn, were it not for a brief twenty-five-year period in Egyptian history. Only at this one time in Egypt's long history did a man appear who worshipped a single god as the creator of all things and the god of all men, and who pursued his vision with unswerving determination. Only once was the magnificent Egyptian pantheon swept away in a monotheistic religious revolution of breathtaking compass – in the time of Akhenaten and the Armana kings.

Akhenaten

The pharaoh we know as Akhenaten began his life as Amenhotep IV, a prince of the eighteenth dynasty (see fig. 1). His father was Amenhotep III, and his great-great-grandfather Tutmoses III, whose conquering sword had created an empire from Nubia in the south to the Euphrates river in the north, and had made Egypt a world power. This ancestor of Akhenaten was to play a key role in our story, and in the story of Jesus and the House of David.

Thanks largely to the Bible and biblical epics, we tend to see the story of Egypt and its pharaohs as unchanging, almost as a Golden Age: the pharaohs ruled and built their pyramids, the priests prayed and the peasants ploughed and irrigated their fields beside the Nile. Nothing disturbed the even temper of the times. The truth, however, is more prosaic, and a lot more interesting. Egyptian court life was as full of intrigue as any royal circle. Courtiers vied for position, preferment and royal patronage and pharaoh himself, the lord of the 'Two Lands' (as Egypt was anciently named), sat by no means easily upon his throne. This was especially true of the Armana kings, whose turbulent rule began with Akhenaten.[11]

The prince who was to become Akhenaten was born Amenhotep IV around the year 1396 BC. His birth is shrouded in mystery and danger; his older brother Tutmoses had disappeared in suspicious circumstances some time before, and the young prince's life is thought to have been at risk from the time he was born. The reason for this danger involves his bloodline and an intriguing love story.

As we will see in Chapter 8, there is considerable reason to believe that Akhenaten's mother, Tiye, was the daughter of a Hebrew who had risen to high position in the court of the Pharaoh Amenhotep III, Akhenaten's father. Because royal descent passed through the female line in ancient Egypt, the daughter of pharaoh held a position of extreme importance. Only through her children could the sacred royal line be continued. The only way the male heir to the throne (pharaoh's son) could accede to the kingdom was by joining with this bloodline and siring offspring. This is the underlying reason for the series of royal brother-sister marriages that so intrigue and puzzle our modern minds. Once married, the sister-wife was called the Great Royal Wife (pharaoh had several other wives) and it

11

was her children, and hers alone, who succeeded to the throne of the Two Lands. But, in the time of Amenhotep III, this tradition was shattered. Having dutifully married his sister Sitamun, it appears that the pharaoh became besotted with Tiye, the daughter of Yuya, his Hebrew vizier. Tiye's mother was an Egyptian (Yuya had married a daughter of one of the Priests of On, worshippers of the sun god), but she would nevertheless have been regarded by most Egyptians as a foreigner. Amenhotep III appears to have disregarded this; he married Tiye and, breaking with all tradition, named her, and not Sitamun, as his Great Royal Wife. This provoked an unprecedented constitutional crisis. The Priests of Amun were responsible for the inauguration of the pharaoh, and they regarded any male offspring that Tiye might produce as a threat. She was not of the royal bloodline, worse, she was part-Hebrew and yet, as Great Royal Wife, she could conceivably assert that her son was a legitimate claimant to the throne. In the eyes of the Egyptian establishment this was completely unacceptable. Tiye was a foreigner, a Semite and (to their minds) a 'descendant' of the hated Hyksos, the Semitic 'Shepherd kings' who, less than a hundred years before, had stormed across the eastern border and subjugated Egypt for more than a century.[12] They would never allow the child of a despised foreigner to rule them as pharaoh, to become the 'Son of Amun', their exclusively Egyptian god.

The pharaoh Amenhotep III appears to have taken drastic action to remedy the problem he himself had created. In an echo of the Moses story of the killing of the Hebrew children, orders were given to Tiye's midwives that any male offspring should be stifled at birth (some scholars believe that this was the likely fate of Akhenaten's elder brother, who had disappeared). But in some way Akhenaten escaped his fate and survived, later giving himself the soubriquet 'he who lived long' in apparent memory of his escape. To counter the danger he still faced from the protectors of Egypt's sacred tradition, he spent his early years away from court, probably in Heliopolis and the eastern delta land city of Zarw, which belonged to his half-Hebrew mother Tiye, and where many Hebrews had settled.

The Origins of Akhenaten's Beliefs

It was at Heliopolis that Akhenaten began to mould his new and, until then, unique conception of the deity, whom he called Aten. The Aten was the god of all mankind and indeed of every living creature, the unseen force that had made the universe, and whose power sustained creation.

For Akhenaten, the myriad gods of Egypt were shams, shadow figures without substance. There was no god but Aten.

Aten was, in fact, an old name for the sun god, and the new deity was symbolised as a sun disc whose rays gave life. However, it is plain from the texts that have come down to us that the new religion had appropriated only the name and the symbol of the old god. Akhenaten had gone beyond simple sun-worship – the sun was not being honoured as a material object, but as a symbol of the great being whose energy suffused creation.[13] The *Great Hymn to Aten* – written by Akhenaten himself almost 3,500 years ago – vividly expresses the pharaoh's reverence for the deity and for all his works. At the same time, it reveals that the 'heretic' was a man of great sensitivity and a poet of no small talent:

Thou arisest fair in the Horizon of heaven, Living Aten, Beginner of Life.
When Thou dawnest in the east, Thou fill'st every land with Thy beauty...
Thou art remote, yet Thy rays are upon the earth.
Thou art in the sight of men yet Thy ways are not known...
How manifold are Thy works!
They are hidden from the sight of men,
O Sole God, like unto whom there is no other!
Thou didst fashion the earth according to Thy desire
When Thou wast alone.
All men, all cattle, great and small,
All that are upon the earth that run upon their feet
Or rise up on high, flying with their wings...
Thy beams nourish every field and when Thou shinest
They live and grow for Thee...
Appearing in Thy aspect of the Living Aten
Rising and shining forth.
Thou art in my heart, but there is none other that knows Thee
Save Thy son Akhenaten.
Thou hast made him wise in Thy plans and Thy power.[14]

The last three lines of the poem emphasise Akhenaten's belief that he had been chosen by God. Like Moses, he was convinced that he had experienced the presence of God, and the secrets of the deity had been revealed to him, and to him alone.

The two main elements upon which Akhenaten seems to have drawn to form his new idea of godhead were both present in Heliopolis. It was in this 'City of the Sun' that the young prince came under the tutelage of the Priests of On, devotees of one aspect of the Egyptian sun god and, as we have seen, he chose a sun symbol, and an old title of the sun god for his new deity. It is probable that the new religion he instituted had its roots in the fusion of the teachings of the Priests of Heliopolis with a second main factor: the Hebrew concept of an unseen creator god. These teachings may well have been first introduced into Egypt when Akhenaten's Hebrew grandfather, Yuya, was brought from Canaan. Such fusion or syncretism is not uncommon; indeed it is very much the rule in the development and evolution of all religious movements. Egyptian religion was no exception – that Semitic beliefs influenced those of the Egyptians (and vice versa) is well known to students of this era. George A. Barton, Professor Emeritus of Semitic Languages at the University of Pennsylvania and Director of the American School of Oriental Research in Baghdad, has shown that Semitic vegetation gods 'were carried to Egypt by one of those prehistoric waves of Semitic immigration' and that they developed into two of the major deities in the Egyptian pantheon, Isis and Osiris.[15]

Such syncretism may have also combined a third, more esoteric, element in Akhenaten's religion. It is possible that Yuya, or some other Hebrew, was also responsible for introducing the aspect of Akhenaten's religion that I believed was held as a secret teaching – the cult of the head.

Evidence for a cult of the head in this region stretches back a very long way. At Cayönu, one of the most ancient settlements in the Near East, head worship has been shown to have existed from 7000 BC. A 'Temple of the Skull' was discovered at Cayönu containing more than seventy human crania. Metin Özbek, Associate Professor at the Department of Anthropology of the University of Hacettepe in Ankara, has made a special study of this site and believes that 'the neolithic inhabitants of Cayönu celebrated a "cult of human skulls" and built a special structure in order to carry out their ritual ceremonies'.[16] A cult is known to have existed in this general area for most of the Neolithic period (i.e., the epoch just prior to the Bronze Age of Akhenaten). Just to the south of Cayönu, in the Levant, there have been many finds of severed heads, usually in caches buried beneath the ground, e.g. in Jericho, at 'Ain Ghazal and at the cave site of Nahal Hemar in the Judaean Desert.[17] In some cases these skulls have been covered with plaster (with asphalt in the case of the Nahal Hemar finds) in an attempt to recreate the soft tissue of the face.[18] Because of the lifelike appearance of these plastered heads, Kenyon believes they represent actual portraits, possibly in an attempt to recreate the features of the individual 'spirit' that once animated the skull.[19] One leading researcher in this field has suggested that the practice may be linked to a cult of heroes, with individuals of exceptional worth chosen to have their heads removed and subsequently plastered.[20] As heroes were often believed to be the favourites of the gods, it is just as likely that this special treatment was reserved for 'holy men'. Or perhaps for both.

It seems clear that the head was very important to the people who performed these ceremonies and that they tried to reconstruct the dead person as he was in life. If such a belief had reached Egypt during the reign of Akhenaten, it is very likely that Egyptian embalming techniques would have been incorporated into the system, as embalming would achieve the very effect sought: the preservation of the soft tissues of the face. So, instead of plastered skulls, the cult would have evolved into a religion of the embalmed head.

The Road to Power

Akhenaten (Amenhotep IV as he then was) left Heliopolis in his early teens and was brought back to Thebes, the royal seat of his father and home to the state god Amun-Ra. Tiye's power had increased during his absence in the delta, and Akhenaten now found himself acknowledged as heir to the royal line. As was the custom, in order to establish his right to the throne he married his half-sister, the famous Nefertiti (the offspring of Amenhotep III's marriage to his sister, Sitamun). It appears that very soon after his return to Thebes he began to rule as co-regent with his father Amenhotep III, a sharing of power that lasted for over eleven years. During this period he nurtured and developed his 'heretical' beliefs, building temples to his new god, Aten, at Karnak and Luxor, and inspiring great enmity in the established priesthood. From the beginning, he seems to have actively challenged the guardians of Egypt's religious traditions. Akhenaten's temple to Aten at Karnak was built within the temple precincts of the Temple of Amun, a calculated snub to the priests who still saw him as a usurper of the throne.

The city of Thebes was the headquarters of dissent against Akhenaten's new religious ideas. It was the nation's capital and the centre of worship for Amun-Ra, the state god, whose religious hierarchy was vehemently opposed to Akhenaten both on religious and political grounds. The Priests of Amun-Ra had long been the most favoured recipients of the former pharaohs' largesse. Amenhotep III, Akhenaten's father, had added a massive mortuary temple, dedicated to Amun-Ra, to his own palace in Thebes, and the Amun priesthood had grown in power and influence until it functioned in many ways as an arm of the state. Such power brought great wealth, with generous gifts of gold, land and slaves. The influential Priests of Amun-Ra were a dangerous group to offend, and they were determined to hold on to their privileges.

But Amenhotep IV proved equally determined to advance the interests of his new god. Throughout his reign he revealed an implacable, stubborn streak to his nature which brooked no compromise with the devotees of other gods. The stage was set for confrontation between the priesthood and the new king. The situation in Thebes became increasingly tense and, in order to defuse a possible insurrection, Amenhotep IV decided, or was persuaded, to leave his father's capital and to found a new city over two hundred miles downriver, at a site now known as Tel el-Amarna. This city, which was to be Amenhotep IV's new capital, he called Akhetaten – 'The city of the horizon of the Aten' – signalling his intention that only the Aten was to be worshipped there.[21] And it was here, at Amarna, that he changed his name to Akhenaten (The Glory of Aten) in honour of his god.

Religious Revolution

Following the death of his father in year twelve of the co-regency, the young king, now sole ruler of the Egyptian empire, returned to Thebes and instituted a comprehensive programme to eradicate the old gods of Egypt. Their statues were smashed, and the bas-reliefs depicting them disfigured. All temples were closed, except those for the worship of the Aten, and their riches were given to the new god. Funding for the priesthood of Amun-Ra (and a host of lesser gods) was suspended and the sacerdotal rituals proscribed. Later, teams of workmen (probably supported by soldiers) were sent into every known temple and tomb, where they excised from inscriptions and wall paintings the names of the old gods of Egypt, and especially Amun.[22] The name of Amun was chiselled from all the royal tablets, even from those of Akhenaten's father Amenhotep III. So thorough, so extreme, was Akhenaten's monotheism, that not only were the names of Amun, Seth, Osiris and all the other gods removed, but even the word 'gods' had to be erased from ancient records. It was a quite unprecedented religious revolution. Such inflexible, uncompromising action provoked bitter opposition, not only from the priesthood but also from the common people who had worshipped the old gods for generations; and especially from the military who were charged with helping in the destruction. On the one hand the army owed allegiance to pharaoh, on the other they were for the most part believers in the ancient

Egyptian pantheon whose images they were ordered to destroy. Their loyalty was sorely tested by the new king's orders.

The policy was bound to fail. Opposition grew steadily until, in Year 15 of his reign, in an attempt to head off disaster, Akhenaten was forced to instal his brother Semenkhare as co-regent. It was at best a stop-gap measure, for the persecution of the old gods continued apace. The religious establishment, the Priests of Amun, stayed their hand for a while longer but it was an uneasy peace. Two years later they acted, and Akhenaten was toppled from his throne. There is no contemporary record of what happened to the 'heretic pharaoh'. We do not know from Egyptian sources whether he was killed, or was simply deposed and fled the country. However, it is noteworthy that no body was ever found and his tomb was never occupied. Akhenaten simply disappears from history. His successor, Semenkhare, died soon after, perhaps within days of Akhenaten's disappearance, and was probably assassinated. Unlike Akhenaten, Semenkhare's tomb, complete with his body, was discovered in 1907 by an American lawyer and amateur Egyptologist, Theodore M. Davis.[23]

Tutankhamun – The Boy King

It seems that Aye, Akhenaten's uncle, whose many titles included Commander of the Chariots, Master of the King's Horses and Chief of the Bowmen, still retained sufficient power over the army to raise Akhenaten's son, Tutankhaten, to the throne. The young king (he was just ten years old when he became pharaoh) was another compromise candidate. He continued to worship his father's god, but in a gesture of reconciliation he permitted the worship of the old deities alongside the Aten. And he altered his own titles, removing the provocative Aten from his name and substituting the old state god, Amun. It is with this name that he has become known as Egypt's most famous pharaoh, the Boy King Tutankhamun, whose opulent tomb was excavated by Howard Carter in 1922.[24]

Tutankhamun reigned nine years, in an atmosphere of increasing rancour. The change of royal name, the opening of the old temples and, in the fourth year of his reign, the removal of the royal court from Amarna to Memphis, could not heal the rift. Even the restoration of priestly incomes and refurbishment of the old temples (which Tutankhamun instituted later in his reign), failed to placate the priesthood. They still saw him as a scion of the line of Akhenaten. Tutankhamun was married to his sister Ankhsenpa-amun, herself the third daughter of the 'heretic' pharaoh. Any children born of this union would mean a continuation of the hated 'foreign' bloodline upon the throne of Egypt, which was anathema to the Priests of Amun. For them, nothing would suffice but the total annihilation of the hated religion of the Aten and of the man who had masterminded the abhorred cult of the one God. They bided their time and nursed their grievances, slowly consolidating and expanding their power base. The priests' animosity was probably well founded, for, despite the outward show, the Boy King remained at heart an Atenist. An inscription from Tutankhamun's tomb, while mentioning several Egyptian gods, ends with the boast that the King was 'the eldest son of the Aten in Heaven'. Further evidence comes from the beautifully decorated back panel of the throne found in his tomb. Covered with gold and silver foil, this shows the sun disc of the Aten displayed in a central position, its rays ending in hands which hold the ankh, the Egyptian symbol of life, to the faces of the king and his sister-wife Ankhsenpa-amun.

Tutankhamun died very young, at the age of nineteen, and there is considerable evidence that he met a violent end. The most detailed examination of his body, by Professor A. B. Abdalla, of Cairo University's Anatomy Department, and R. G. Harrison, Professor of Anatomy at the University of Liverpool, found no signs of fatal disease, but revealed a catalogue of horrendous injuries:

> When the bandages ... were removed, it was immediately obvious that the mummy was not in one piece. The head and neck were separated from the rest of the body, and the limbs had been detached from the torso ... Further examination showed that the limbs were broken in many places as well as being detached from the body. The right arm has been broken at the elbow, the upper arm being separated from the forearm and hand ... The left arm was broken at the elbow, and in addition at the wrist ... The left leg was broken at the knee. The heads of the right humerus and both femora (thigh bones) had been broken off the remains of the bone ... The head and neck had been distracted from the torso at the joint between the seventh cervical and first thoracic vertebra.[25]

The opulence of Tutankhamun's burial could not hide the harrowing facts. Though he was laid to rest with magnificent honours and in great reverence, the king seems to have been subject to physical torture before being put to death. The Priests of Amun had had their revenge.

The End of the Amarna Kings

Using his high position in the army, Tutankhamun's great-uncle, Aye, now laid claim to the throne. One of his first responsibilities was to arrange Tutankhamun's burial, as Howard Carter noted: 'Aye ... buried our monarch, for there, on the inner walls of Tutankhamen's tomb-chamber, Aye, as king, has caused himself to be represented among the religious scenes, officiating before Tutankhamen, a scene unprecedented in the royal tombs of this necropolis.'[26] But despite his high position, Aye himself was now vulnerable; he was a man well past his prime, and his efforts to protect the heretic king must have left him with a greatly reduced following. As the son of the Hebrew vizier Yuya, and brother to Tiye, Amenhotep III's Great Royal Wife, in Egyptian eyes he was simply another of the line of foreigners who had usurped the throne. Four years after taking power, he himself was overthrown, almost certainly murdered by his successor, the army strong-man Horemheb, who usurped Aye's powers and even took over the old king's tomb for his own sepulchre. The rule of the fourth and last Amarna king was over.

The Priests of Amun were not long in exacting a full measure of vengeance. As Akhenaten had tried to wipe out every vestige of their gods, so they erased all record of him. With the active connivance of the new Pharaoh Horemheb, the Amarna kings were anathematised; it was to be as if they had never existed. Their names were excised from the king lists; Horemheb's name was placed immediately after Akhenaten's father, Amenhotep III, and the glaring 'gap' of over twenty-five years was simply ignored. The Amarna kings' names and images were removed from monuments across the country, in what appears to have been a carefully planned operation to erase them from history. The chief 'rebel' (as some Egyptian authorities called Akhenaten) was singled out for especially draconian treatment – even to speak his name was forbidden.[27] The conspiracy succeeded for more than three thousand years – it was not until the late 1800s, when a French mission copied the texts from the tombs at Tel el-Amarna, that Akhenaten's name was once again given its due prominence in the history of Egypt.[28]

Akhenaten and Moses

But what happened to that single-minded instigator of religious revolution, Akhenaten, the man who Freud argued had inspired an Egyptian believer to 'adopt' the Jewish tribe, to give them the monotheistic belief

of his king and lead them into exile? For many years there was no answer –
Akhenaten appears, promulgates the Aten religion, then disappears
without trace, his tomb empty and unused.

Perhaps Freud's thinking, bold though it was, was not bold enough.
Perhaps, even for him, 'the awe of biblical tradition was insuperable'.
Because, having laid out such strong arguments in favour of Moses' Egyptian antecedents, and having pointed to the fact that the Moses story was
a mirror image of the usual hero myth, he failed to take the tale to its logical
conclusion. Instead, he identified Moses as a member of Akhenaten's
entourage, a high official named Tutmose. But, if the 'inverted hero myth'
is taken at face value, and Moses is not of Hebrew but of Egyptian blood,
then we have to accept that Moses was not simply an Egyptian, but a
blood member of the same family as his 'foster parent', pharaoh's daughter.
In short, Moses was a son of the blood royal of Egypt, the House of
Pharaoh. And as such, he was an heir to the throne.

Freud died six months after his book was published, at the age of eighty-
three. Although it caused something of a stir at the time, *Moses and
Monotheism* was largely ignored by scholars. The Second World War intervened and the horrors of the Holocaust made the subject of Moses' origins
a sensitive topic for Jew and Gentile alike. And so the subject languished,
forgotten by mainstream Egyptologists until the 'Moses problem' was
raised anew, and given a new slant, by Egyptologist Ahmed Osman. An
Egyptian by birth, Osman moved to Britain in the mid-sixties, to continue
his lifelong study of Egyptian and Hebrew texts. He realised where Freud's
theories should lead and, largely as a result of a close reading of both
biblical and Egyptian texts, came to the apparently astounding conclusion
that Akhenaten and Moses were different names for the same man.[29]

The Name of Pharaoh

The Old Testament is not very forthcoming on the names of the various
pharaohs who appear in the course of the biblical narrative. Almost all of
them, from the pharaoh who received the patriarch Abraham to the
Egyptian king who hunted the Israelites on the Exodus, are unhelpfully –
and somewhat irritatingly for historians – known as 'pharaoh'. This has
made pinpointing the date of the Israelites' Descent into Egypt, and their
Exodus, a thorny problem that has led to longstanding disputes between
Old Testament scholars. Attempts have been made to marry the broad
outline of the biblical story with ancient Egyptian records, thereby ident-
ifying the relevant pharaohs and dynasties, and thus dating each scriptural

story. Several authorities have followed the Jewish historian Flavius Josephus, whose *Antiquities of the Jews* (written in the first century AD) related the Israelite Descent into Egypt to the time of the Hyksos.[30] These 'Shepherd kings' were Semitic nomads who invaded Egypt around 1659 BC and usurped the power of the pharaoh (in Lower Egypt) for over one hundred years. They despoiled the temples of the gods, persecuted the native inhabitants cruelly, and were consequently greatly hated by all Egyptians. The Hyksos were finally expelled by Ahmoses, the founder of the eighteenth dynasty.[31] The fact that the Hyksos and Akhenaten were both of the same stock (at least in Egyptian eyes), and both had attacked the old religion, could not have strengthened Akhenaten's position when he began his religious crusade for the Aten.

Although Josephus specifically denies that Moses and Akhenaten were contemporaries, this seems to be in a fit of racial or religious pique, as he castigates an earlier chronicler, Manetho, for making such an assertion in his writings, and for daring to assert that the Israelites were associated in the Exodus with certain Egyptian elements, including 'unclean' priests (for which we should read priests who did not conform to the established gods of Egypt, and were therefore defiled).[32] However, other ancient authors have agreed with Manetho. In addition, we have in Horemheb (who took over as pharaoh following the death of the last Amarna king) a likely candidate for the pharaoh of the Oppression, and in his successor Ramses (who reigned for only one year and may have died in pursuit of the Exodus) a very probable contender for the pharaoh of the Exodus. Looked at objectively, the time of the demise of the Amarna kings fits rather well with the available facts. Such a reading brings with it another problem: the gap of over twenty years between Akhenaten's disappearance and his hypothetical leading of the Exodus, which in this scenario occurred on the death of his uncle Aye and the usurpation of power by Horemheb. If Akhenaten *is* Moses, then he must have escaped his enemies in Egypt and found refuge elsewhere before returning to Egypt a second time. Moses, of course, did exactly that in the biblical tale, fleeing the land after killing an Egyptian slave-master, and returning much later to lead the Exodus.

Akhenaten Abdicates

There is indeed now much evidence that Akhenaten was not killed at the time of his disappearance, but that he abdicated and left Egypt, only to return over a score of years later in an abortive attempt to reclaim his throne.

Akhenaten's tomb was never used. The grave was discovered in 1891 by an Italian archaeologist, Alessandro Basanti, at Wadi Abu Hassan el-Bahri in the hills to the east of Amarna. When opened, it was found to have been entered twice before, most recently by local tribespeople in search of treasure and, much earlier, by the anti-Atenists intent on destroying all memory of Akhenaten's name and religion. The burial chamber, 9.6 metres square and hewn from the living rock, had originally been plastered, but this covering was utterly destroyed by Akhenaten's foes. The entrance of the tomb was blocked with rubble and a large dump outside (seventy metres long and between five and ten metres in depth) was composed of tomb debris. Several expeditions – from 1894 to the early 1930s – mapped the tomb and took recordings of its surviving inscriptions (a daughter of Akhenaten, Meketaten, was buried in a side chamber of the main tomb and the decorations here were left largely untouched). They also collected the small fragments remaining in both the tomb and the dump in the hope of piecing them together for clues as to what really happened to the heretic pharaoh.

The results of the restorations, published in 1974, were very revealing.[33] They showed that the only objects in the king's tomb had been a large granite sarcophagus belonging to Akhenaten, ushabti figures (used as substitutes for the dead person to ensure resurrection even if the mummy was destroyed) and a canopic chest, in which the canopic jars (containing the embalmed organs of the deceased) were normally placed. All these objects were traditionally deposited in the tomb some time before burial, while the tomb's owner was still living. No evidence of a canopy or shrine – the usual accoutrements of a burial ceremony – was found. Nor was there any indication in the tomb of items normally placed there after death: chariots, chairs, amulets, papyri scrolls, boxes or magic bricks. The last were devices placed at four definite positions in relation to the body of the deceased, and were believed to offer mystical protection to the mummy. Akhenaten's magic bricks were eventually found, but in a location that furnished further evidence of his having survived his fall from power.

Akhenaten's magic bricks were discovered in the tomb of his brother, Semenkhare, who, as we have seen, survived for at most a few months after Akhenaten's disappearance, and seems to have been buried in great haste. As Ahmed Osman has argued, had Akhenaten died at the time of his disappearance, his burial rites (which, according to Egyptian tradition, would have taken seventy days to complete) would either have been over or still in progress when Semenkhare's own burial began. If Akhenaten was dead, his magic bricks, which were essential for the funeral rites, could never have been found in Semenkhare's tomb as they would have already been used for Akhenaten's own burial. The most likely explanation of this conundrum is that Akhenaten was not dead, and that his magic bricks could then be used for the (hurried) burial of his brother.

Supporting this evidence that Akhenaten's tomb had never received a body, the pharaoh's canopic chest had not been drenched in bitumen or resin, an invariable part of the traditional burial ceremony, once the canopic jars had been placed inside. In addition, the canopic chest was inscribed with an early glyph for the Aten, indicating that it had been made early in Akhenaten's reign, before the time the Aten received his new name (in Year 9 of Akhenaten's rule), and while the king still ruled Egypt. The Egyptologist Muhammad Hamza (who restored the canopic chest) was of the opinion that no burial ceremony had taken place in the tomb. Hamza wrote: 'As the box is quite unstained by the black resinous unguents to which those of Amenhotep II, Tutankhamun and Horemheb were subjected, it seems probable that it has never been used for the king's viscera.'[34] John Pendlebury, who led the British expedition to Akhenaten's Amarna tomb concurred, 'In addition there were found parts of Akhenaten's magnificent alabaster canopic chest, with protecting vultures at the corners, together with pieces of the lids capped with the king's head. The chest gives evidence of never having been used...'[35]

Further evidence of survival is revealed in dockets used by court bureaucrats of the Amarna period. These are invariably dated with the regnal Year of the incumbent pharaoh, regnal Year 1 being the first year of his reign. One docket in particular has provoked heated debate among Egyptologists, and has even led to accusations of tampering with evidence. The controversy centres around whether the docket, from Akhenaten's reign, specifies regnal Year 11 or Year 21. This latter reading is unacceptable to many scholars, as Akhenaten is 'known' to have ruled for just seventeen years. Nevertheless, the clearest and most legible evidence of the docket we have is a facsimile, published by the British Egyptologist Battiscombe Gunn in 1923 under the auspices of the Egyptian Exploration Society, and this apparently shows Year 21 in hieratic script, a later form of Egyptian writing which was less complicated than hieroglyphics.[36] On the basis of the facsimile, American academic Keith C. Seele was quite certain that 'the hieratic date is ... Year 21'.[37] The number ten in hieratic is written as a single upturned V, while twenty is two upturned Vs, one above the other, and Seele was adamant that two of these marks were present on the docket. This position, accepted by several scholars, was fiercely opposed by H. W.

Fairman, who had also worked at the Amarna ruins. Fairman maintained that he had examined the docket personally, and that it had also been seen by three other Egyptologists, all of whom had unhesitatingly read the docket as 'Year 11'. He also pointed out that Battiscombe Gunn had concurred with the 'Year 11' reading.[38] At first sight this seemed to bring the weight of evidence down firmly against Seele's arguments for a reading of Year 21.

But Fairman weakens his case when he admits, in the same article, that when he examined the artefact 'the docket had faded seriously'. In light of this, any modern reading is suspect, and the best record we have is Battiscombe Gunn's 1923 facsimile published almost forty years prior to Fairman's examination, *before* the fading had occurred. That original facsimile supports a reading of 'Year 21'. And Gunn's own decision to accept a Year 11 reading can be seen as a result of his wish not to break ranks with the Egyptological establishment. In *The City of Akhenaten*, Gunn states quite openly that 'In the absence of other evidence as to the reign extending beyond Year 17, no one will want to read the dating of (the docket) as "Year 21".'[39]

Several other authorities have been reluctantly persuaded by this argument. Professor Donald Redford of Toronto University, who at first agreed with the 'Year 21' reading, eventually returned to the orthodox fold, but not without admitting that the facsimile published by Gunn demanded a reading of Year 21: '... those who have only Gunn's facsimile before them will be forced to admit that the prima facie probability lies with the reading "21". If the present writer returns to the reading "regnal Year 11" it is solely because of his awareness of the increasing weight of the *argumentum e silentio*: if Akhenaten did attain a twenty-first year it is inconceivable that Years 18, 19 and 20 should be entirely absent from the Amarna dockets, especially in view of the large number of dockets dated to Year 17 and before.'[40]

But is evidence of these years 'entirely absent'?

William Bennet, who had worked at the Amarna site between 1930 and 1931, found an ostracon (a shard or broken remnant carrying an inscription) with the date 'Year 18' of Akhenaten's rule. Fairman, unsurprisingly, disagreed with this conclusion, and claimed that the reading was 'untrustworthy'. This judgement turned out to be unverifiable as Fairman, later in the same book, states quite unapologetically that 'the ostracon was not kept'. This is odd, to say the least. The 'Year 18 ostracon' was obviously a very contentious, and therefore important, find, as it could have provided new information on the Amarna king. The question immediately arises: why was it not kept? If the reading was disputed, it was all the more necessary to keep the ostracon safe so that it could be examined by independent experts. Instead, we find that it was 'not kept', that is, someone took the conscious decision to throw it away. Faced with this bland statement, Keith Seele's belief that evidence that did not fit the orthodox view was suppressed seems all too likely.

Nor is this the only artefact to have gone astray. Hidden away in the annals of the recondite journal *Annales du Service des Antiquités de l'Égypte* of 1931 is an article by D. E. Derry in which he notes that Akhenaten's rule 'has been extended to the nineteenth year by Pendlebury's recent discovery at el-Amarna of a monument bearing that date and with the further possibility that this may be lengthened to the twentieth year.[41] Mr Pendlebury has very courteously permitted us to make use of these hitherto unpublished facts.' Unfortunately the discoverer died before publishing a detailed account of his find, and no trace of this important (and for some, embarrassing) monument has ever been found.

A second docket, no. 279, also points to Akhenaten's survival. It is unique in having two dates, 'Year 17' and 'Year 1', placed one beneath the other. There is no argument among scholars that the 'Year 17' refers to Akhenaten's reign and 'Year 1' to Tutankhamun. However, as there is no evidence that there was a co-regency between these two monarchs, most Egyptologists have been content to assume that the double date occurs because Tutankhamun recorded the end of one reign (his father Akhenaten's) and the beginning of another (his own). This interpretation is highly unlikely, as the custom of dual 'dating' has never been recorded on any other Egyptian document. Some researchers, perhaps realising the weakness of the conventional argument, have tried to bolster it by convincing themselves that the Year 1 'overwrites' or 'partly overwrites' Year 17, the underlying idea being that Year 1 is deleting Year 17. This is quite simply not the case; the two numbers are definitely separate, and this fact alone makes a nonsense of the orthodox theory. But rejecting the standard explanation creates its own problem: in the Egyptian scheme of history, each king began his regnal years *after* the end of the previous ruler. Why then, if there was no co-regency, are two years inscribed separately on the docket?

The only likely explanation stems from the ancient Egyptian view of their pharaoh as a sacred king whose rule was sanctioned by the gods. In Egypt kings took their authority from the gods and ruled until death. If we assume that, although Tutankhamun was the new king, Akhenaten was still alive, then he would still be, in a constitutional (or rather a theological) sense, the ruler of Egypt. The unusual dual nature of the times was recorded on the docket as a double date (Year 17/Year 1), an occurrence which (like Akhenaten's abdication) had never been seen before in Egypt.[42]

The chronicler Manetho, whom we met above, also provides written evidence of Akhenaten's survival. Manetho correctly lists four kings as missing from the 'doctored' king lists authorised by Horemheb and his successors. However, the names of the 'lost' kings are given as Achencheres, Rathosis, Achencheres and Achencheres. Wolfgang Helck, a German philologist, has demonstrated that Achencheres is derived from Akhenaten, while Rathosis is thought to derive ultimately from Tutankhamun.[43] But why the odd repetition of Akhenaten (Achencheres) where we should have the names of the two remaining Amarna kings, Semenkhare and Aye? What we seem to have here is a confused account of actual occurrences. If Akhenaten was alive, he was, according to prevailing Egyptian beliefs, still pharaoh. And yet, three others of his line actually ruled after him, making in total the four Amarna kings. This is baffling enough to commit to writing, but it is easy to see how this occurrence, unique in the history of Egypt, could become muddled when transmitted orally. Because of this confusion, Akhenaten came to be regarded in folk memory as having ruled throughout the period of the four kings, hence the insistent repetition of his name in the list which, nevertheless, preserves the equally correct memory that the Amarna kings were four in number. If this reading is correct, these writings support the idea that Akhenaten did not die in Year 17 of his reign but instead outlived all the subsequent Amarna rulers.

So, Manetho's writings, the readings on the docket dates, and the evidence of the ostracon and monument, all point to a conclusion that Akhenaten abdicated the throne of Egypt in Year 17 and that he was alive at least four years after his fall from power. Where did he go? He is unlikely to have remained in Egypt at the mercy of his foes, and we must presume that he entered into voluntary exile. In an uncanny echo of the Moses story, his most likely place of refuge would have been the Sinai.

Moses in the Wilderness

The Moses of the Bible leaves Egypt twice. On the first occasion it is to escape pharaoh's retribution after he kills an Egyptian for beating a Hebrew slave. Wandering in Sinai, he meets and helps the daughters of a priest of Midian, is invited to their father's tent and stays with the grateful patriarch for an extended period, eventually marrying Zipporah, one of the daughters, and helping to herd his father-in-law's flocks. It is while acting as

26

shepherd that Moses sees a vision of God 'in a burning bush', and is ordered to return and free the Hebrews from bondage (Exodus 3: 2). At first reluctant, he is given two signs, a rod that can become a living snake, and an ability to change his hand instantaneously from a healthy to a leprous state and back again. God also promises that if these two wonders fail to impress the pharaoh, he is to take water from the Nile and to pour it out, when it will be seen to have turned to blood. Moses remains hesitant, complaining, 'I am slow of speech and of a slow tongue.' God rebukes him and suggests that Aaron, his brother, can act as his spokesman, 'And thou shalt speak to him and put words in his mouth.' Thus assured, Moses returns to Egypt with his wife and family and his brother Aaron (whom he meets along the way). Using the signs vouchsafed by God, they first convince the Children of Israel that they have come to deliver them out of slavery. Then, with Aaron, Moses seeks and obtains an audience with pharaoh. Moses demands that pharaoh allow the Hebrews to leave, but the Egyptian monarch refuses, saying that he has no knowledge of Moses' god, and shows his anger by ordering that the Hebrews be given no straw for the bricks they are to make, but that they should still produce the required number each day. When Moses repeats his demand, pharaoh replies by calling on Moses to show a miracle to prove himself. The rod of Moses is thrown upon the ground and turns into a snake, which swallows up the snakes of pharaoh's 'magicians' (for which we should read 'Egyptian priests') when they use their own staffs to emulate the miracle. Even so, pharaoh refuses to release the Hebrews. There then follows a series of ten meetings at which, each time, pharaoh refuses Moses' demands. On each occasion he is punished for his pride by the visitation of a disaster upon Egypt, which includes plagues of frogs, lice, hail, locusts and three days of darkness. Pharaoh's resistance is finally broken by the death of all Egypt's first-born, and the Children of Israel are allowed to begin the long march out of Egypt that we know as the Exodus, a trek that eventually took them (though not Moses) to the Promised Land of Canaan (Exodus 12: 29–41).

As in the story of his childhood, there is a similar series of remarkable correspondences between what we know of Moses the man, and the Pharaoh Akhenaten. So many that the biblical story of Moses' later life seems, essentially, to take up the tale of the man whom the Priests of Amun tried so assiduously to erase from history, the story of Akhenaten. Many scholars accept that the Exodus story has at its heart a kernel of historical substance – there are simply too many accurate indications of the workings of Egypt in the eighteenth dynasty for these to be the vain imaginings of a Jewish scribe writing over eight hundred years after the

27

event. So we can expect the story of Moses to be based on real happenings in Egypt and Sinai. If we attempt to look through the accretions and additions and distortions that overlay this text, the basic story relates that Moses was forced to leave Egypt, that he resided in Sinai for a considerable period, then returned to Egypt when a new pharaoh had been installed, carrying with him a magic serpent-rod. He disputes with pharaoh, often with magicians (priests) in attendance, and finally leads the Children of Israel out of Egypt to Canaan, where they follow the god of Moses, known as Adonai or Yahweh.

How does this basic story relate to that of Akhenaten?

As Ahmed Osman's research has shown, an account in the Jewish Talmud agrees with the Old Testament story that Moses had to flee to Sinai, but it does not give the murder of an Egyptian as the reason for his exile. Instead (while placing the story in Ethiopia, a country at times under the suzerainty of Egypt), Moses is said to have fallen from the kingship.[44] The Muslim Koran adds further details, saying that he fled when told of a plot to assassinate him by the nobility of the city:

> And there came a man,
> Running, from the furthest end
> of the city. He said:
> O Moses! The Chiefs
> Are taking counsel together
> About thee to slay thee:
> So get thee away, for I
> Do give thee sincere advice.
> (Sura XXVIII, 20)

The parallels with the story of Akhenaten are obvious.

If Akhenaten also left Egypt and went into exile, there are several good reasons why he should, like Moses, have made for Sinai. His mother's people, the Hebrews, were settled in Goshen, close to the eastern border of Egypt, and near to Sinai. Also hard by stood the town of Zarw, given to Akhenaten's mother by Amenhotep III as her own city. Akhenaten was almost certainly born at Zarw, and he spent his early life in the eastern delta. What is more natural than that he would have travelled first to this land for help and support from his relatives, before making his final departure? There are additional reasons why Sinai should be his destination: it was nominally under Egyptian suzerainty, but no military presence was maintained there. During Akhenaten's time Sinai was under the joint control of Neby, who was Troop Commander and Mayor of Zarw (the city of Akhenaten's mother), and Panahesy, whom Akhenaten himself had made Royal Chancellor, and both the Servitor of Pharaoh and the Chief Servitor of the Aten. Panahesy's family had been in control of the royal treasury for at least three generations up until the time of Amenhotep III and must have been close allies of the Egyptian royal family. The Sinai was also an important mineral resource for the Egyptians and, as the Royal Chancellor's responsibilities included mining expeditions to Sinai, Panahesy would have been in an ideal position to help the fallen king.[45]

Astonishingly, and of great support to the present scenario, in the early 1900s a temple was discovered at Mt Sarabit in Sinai (an important mining area for turquoise), containing the remains of a foot-tall statuette of Akhenaten's mother, Queen Tiye.[46] It had been exquisitely carved in the Amarna style, a technique which did not long survive the short reign of the Amarna kings. Even more surprising, a stela was also found (again in the Amarna style) in which Ramses I (the first pharaoh of the nineteenth dynasty and Horemheb's successor) describes himself as 'ruler of all that Aten embraces'.[47] No one has yet given a credible explanation for the inscription's attribution to Ramses, whose allegiance to the traditional gods of Egypt has never been questioned. But it is remarkable that the name of the Aten, forbidden for at least fourteen years during the rule of Horemheb, should resurface on this stela. That it was found in the very place of Akhenaten's supposed exile lends compelling support to the theory.

In order to follow the biblical story, Akhenaten, like Moses, would have had to return to Egypt from exile. But why should the 'heretic', 'the rebel of Amarna' whose very name had ceased to exist in Egypt, undertake such a dangerous journey? To understand the circumstances that would have led him to embark on so risky a venture, we must turn again to the genealogy of the pharaonic line. As we have seen, after the Amarna kings, the army generalissimo Horemheb sized power. In order to legitimise his claim to the throne he married Mutnedjemet, a sister of Nefertiti, and an heiress. Had this union produced children, it would have ensured the succession of the eighteenth dynasty that had begun over two hundred years before with the defeat of the Hyksos by Pharaoh Ahmoses. But Horemheb died childless and, with neither heiress nor heir, the eighteenth dynasty had finally run its course. Pa-Ramses, whom Horemheb had appointed Troop Commander and Mayor of Zarw, took over the throne as Ramses I, and founder of the nineteenth dynasty.

If the exile theory is sound, and Akhenaten had been hiding in Sinai, at the time of Horemheb's death he would have been the *sole* legitimate claimant to the Egyptian throne. It is very likely that he returned to Egypt on the death of the pharaoh (as the Bible says Moses did) not so much to free the Israelites, but to reclaim his lost patrimony. With him he would have taken the symbol of pharaonic authority that he would have carried into exile – a staff-like sceptre crowned with a coiled serpent of brass, whose resemblance to Moses' staff that 'became a serpent' is obvious. In fact, the Talmud is quite explicit concerning Moses' staff, calling it not a rod, but instead the very essence of royalty, 'a sceptre'.

Moses and his brazen serpent are also mentioned in a strange passage in the Second Book of Kings, in relation to Hezekiah who, we are told: '... removed the high places and brake the images, and cut down the groves; *and brake into pieces the brazen serpent that Moses had made*: for unto those days the Children of Israel did burn incense to it' (II Kings 18: 4).

'The Rightful Son and Heir'

Osman has added to Freud's analysis of the name 'Moses' by showing that in Egyptian times the word possessed a linguistic nuance which fits Akhenaten's position perfectly. Inscribed on the walls of a tomb at Sakkara is the story of an ancient legal battle.[48] In the inscriptions, the chief participant (a scribe named Khayri) is referred to only once by his given name, and thereafter is given the title 'Mos'. In the Sakkara tomb inscriptions, the sense to be drawn from Mos is that of 'rightful son and heir', which corresponds precisely with the heretic pharaoh's situation. We know that Akhenaten's name was proscribed in Egypt. If he did survive his removal from power and went into exile, his supporters in Egypt may well have used the name Mos in the same sense as the scribes in the Khayri legal battle, i.e., to indicate 'the rightful son and heir' of the Egyptian throne.

It would appear from all this that Moses' biblical confrontation with pharaoh is a distorted account of a meeting in which he (as Akhenaten) attempted to prove himself the 'rightful son and heir' by showing the brazen serpent staff, timeless symbol of pharaonic authority, to the assembled priests ('magicians') who were important participants in all questions of the royal succession in Egypt. The Koran adds to our information here, telling us that when Moses' staff 'swallowed up' those of the magicians, they bowed down before Moses, acknowledging his superiority (Sura VII). That the 'magicians prostrated themselves before Moses' reveals that his claim to the kingship was accepted by the priests. But Akhenaten's success was short lived. Just as Aye had used the army to keep Akhenaten in power, Ramses now used his own military position to maintain himself as pharaoh of the newly constituted nineteenth dynasty. Faced with overwhelmingly superior strength, Akhenaten had no choice but to retreat into the desert with his followers, who would have included those Egyptians still adhering to the religion of Aten, and the Israelites, his mother's people, who had been held at the fortress town of Ramses (Zarw) and used as corvée labour. This retreat is the biblical Exodus.

The Aten and Judaism

As we have seen, the chronology, events and main characters of the Moses story harmonise, with a high degree of correspondence, with the story of Akhenaten that we have been outlining. But the similarities do not end there. An examination of the Aten cult as promulgated by Akhenaten, and the religion bestowed upon the Children of Israel by Moses, reveals that they are essentially one and the same.

The Jewish creed, 'Schema Jisroel Adonai Elohenu Adonai Echod', uses Adonai as the spoken name of God and is usually translated as, 'Hear O Israel, the Lord our God is the only God.' As Freud was the first to suggest, Adonai is related to the name of Akhenaten's god; in fact it *is* Akhenaten's god, the Aten. Adonai (Lord) in English is really two words – the 'ai' at the end is a possessive pronoun in Hebrew, and Adonai is more correctly translated as 'My Lord', leaving 'Adon' as the noun 'Lord'. This is already quite similar to Aten, but the similarity becomes identity when standard transliteration protocols are used. Here the Hebrew 'd' and 'o' become the Egyptian 't' and 'e' respectively. And Adon becomes Aten. As Freud first proposed, the Jewish creed is, in reality, 'Hear, O Israel, our god Aten is the only god.'[49]

The indefatigable Ahmed Osman has unearthed additional correspondences between the two religions.

There were no statues to the Aten, a circumstance which finds its echo in the Mosaic commandments as, 'Thou shalt not make unto thee any graven image, or any likeness of anything that is in heaven above, or that is in the earth beneath, or that is in the water under the earth' (Exodus 20: 4). Akhenaten's god was worshipped in temples built on the model of the followers of the Heliopolitan sun god, facing east, open to the skies, with most rituals conducted in the open air. The tabernacle Moses set up in Sinai after the Exodus was of similar, if not identical, design and would have followed the temple constructed by Moses at Heliopolis in Egypt,

31

according to the ancient author Apion. Apion was a native Egyptian who lived around the time of Christ. He wrote a five-volume work, *History of Egypt*, which in book three states (as quoted by Josephus): 'Moses, as I have heard from old people in Egypt, was a native of Heliopolis who, being pledged to the customs of his country, erected prayer-houses open to the air in various precincts of the city, all facing eastwards, such being also the orientation of Heliopolis' (to face the rising sun).[50] By contrast, until the time of Moses, earlier Jewish hero figures such as Abraham had a tradition of building stone altars in sacred places where they had been granted visions, and giving offerings of animals, oil and probably wine to the deity (see Genesis 33: 20; 31: 54; 35: 14).

The sacrifice of animals points up another correspondence. When Moses speaks of sacrificing animals to his god, he refers to them as the 'abomination of the Egyptians', making it obvious that it is animals sacred to the Egyptian pantheon that he wishes to immolate. Creatures such as the crocodile, sacred to the god Sebek, were regarded as 'abominations' by the Hebrews and Moses is clearly aware that their sacrifice is offensive to Egyptian minds: 'we shall sacrifice the abominations of the Egyptians to the Lord our God: lo, shall we sacrifice the abominations of the Egyptians before their eyes and will they not stone us?' (Exodus 8: 26). This insistence on immolating animals held sacred by the Egyptians has direct parallels with Akhenaten's command to his followers that they offer the holy animals of the old deities to his new god, the Aten.[51] Another parallel arises from just who it was who sacrificed these animals. In the Aten religion, a select group of individuals, the priests, were responsible for making offerings to the god. By contrast, patriarchs such as Abraham sacrificed their own offerings – that is, there was no formal priesthood at that time. In Jewish history, priests (who possessed the same responsibilities and privileges as those of Akhenaten's – and other Egyptian – priesthoods) did not appear *until the time of Moses*.

Although not exclusively related to the Aten cult, that quintessentially Jewish object, the Ark of the Covenant, can also be shown to be of Egyptian derivation. Many gods (including the state god Amun-Ra) were carried in procession in stylised boats, or arks. They were, as it were, portable homes for the gods. This was a very ancient tradition. When Tutmoses III, the great empire builder of the eighteenth dynasty, went forth to do battle, his god went with him. 'Proceeding northward by my majesty, carrying my father Amun-Re, Lord of the Thrones of the Two Lands before me.' While he rejected many of the old ways, Akhenaten retained the ark as a 'home' for his god. That Moses introduced an identical concept to the

Israelites (who also used to carry the ark of their god Adon (Aten) before them when they engaged in combat) is quite compelling evidence of identity.

The number, significance and range of these correspondences made it impossible for me to reject the apparently unlikely suggestion that Moses was in fact the exiled Akhenaten, the heretic pharaoh of Egyptian history. He had not been murdered, but had instead abdicated the throne in the face of fierce opposition to his monotheistic religious crusade and fled into exile in Sinai. Later, after the death of Horemheb, he had returned to press his case as the rightful heir to the throne, only to be forced once more into exile, taking with him a band of followers (some Egyptian but mainly composed of his maternal kinfolk the Hebrews) who remained true to the Aten religion and who settled in the lands beyond Sinai. In short, Akhenaten was the true name of the prophet Moses.

This unexpected vindication of Freud's suggestion, and its link to Akhenaten made me very excited. I had hypothesised that the line of Templar sacred heads extended back to the time of Moses. If Moses was Akhenaten, this placed the origins of the sacred head cult in Egypt, at the very time that a 'heretic pharaoh' was attempting to institute a revolutionary religious 'uprising'. This seemed all the more likely after my discovery that a cult of the head had existed in Canaan for thousands of years and could well have been brought down into Egypt by Akhenaten's grandfather, Yuya the Hebrew vizier. In addition, Akhenaten was important for another reason: occult tradition credits him with having laid the foundations of the Great White Brotherhood, from whom the Rosicrucians and other occult societies claim descent. Although it is forbidden to discuss the teachings in detail, I knew from personal experience that certain Rosicrucian rituals involved the appearance of disembodied heads (though not of actual severed heads), so it seemed more than likely that the flowering of sacred head worship should lie with Akhenaten and the occult aspect of his Aten religion. This side of Akhenaten's philosophy would, as a matter of course, be hidden from the mass of the population that followed the Aten and the 'external' teachings. This is normal procedure in all occult schools (the word occult itself means 'hidden'). Progress would have been through staged initiation, each level revealing more and more profound aspects of the teaching's mysteries. Those secrets, like those of other mystery religions, would have been given orally and would never have been committed to writing.

But the religion of the Aten had been suppressed in Egypt as effectively as the Templars had been destroyed in France. To continue the research, I had to follow the track of the Atenists after they left Egypt. One trail, as we have seen, led via Moses/Akhenaten to Israel and the Holy Land. But there was another, which travelled to an altogether more surprising destination and had been taken, I discovered, by an heiress of Akhenaten's royal line.

3

Druids and the Cult of the Head

In Egypt, Akhenaten's Aten cult did not long survive the exile of its founder. One group, as we have seen, travelled with Akhenaten/Moses into the Sinai and eventually founded the Israelite state in what was to become Palestine. However, tradition records a second, far more unusual, emigration from Egypt at the time of the Exodus.

This tradition is very old. The earliest written record we have of it today is in the work of Nennius, a Welsh monk of the late eighth or early ninth century AD.[1] Nennius is thought to have based his writings on an even older manuscript, the (now lost) work of Sinlan, Abbot of Bangor, County Down, in the late sixth century AD. Sinlan, and all the ancient Irish chronicles, give as their authority an even older work, the *Chronicon Eusebii* (the *Chronicle of Eusebius*).[2] The eponymous author, Eusebius of Caesarea (*c.* 260–340) attempted the then unheard of idea of an overview of world history, setting the sequence of events in each of the world's known cultures in parallel columns (this idea is still with us: the Timeline in Microsoft's Encarta encyclopedia is simply the latest, silicon-driven update of Eusebius' concept). The *Chronicon Eusebii* gives a yearly sequence, year one being the date of creation, as divined from an analysis of the Hebrew scriptures, the central element of the structure Eusebius devised.

The information that concerns our story is found in Eusebius and other annals, but it is recorded in most detail in another ancient book, the *Scotichronicon*, or *Chronicle of the Scots*, compiled in the early 1440s by Walter Bower, Abbot of Inchcolm Abbey on the Firth of Forth.[3] The *Scotichronicon* deals with the early history of the race or tribe of the Scoti, the people who, originally Irish, later settled in, and conquered, most of Scotland. In this ancient book, the Scoti are said, quite matter-of-factly, to be descended from Egyptians – a group of people who left (or were forced out of) Egypt, at the time of the Exodus of the Jews. These emigrants, led by Scota, a pharaoh's daughter, and her husband Gaythelos, wandered by boat across the Mediterranean, sailing always westwards in search of a new home, and finally settled in Ireland. Unlikely as this sounds, new research findings have given this ancient story a credible scientific underpinning.

Language, Genes and Music

The ancient Egyptians were the result of an admixture of several races, but the predominant strain was Hamitic. The Hamites are believed to have originated in North Africa, along the Mediterranean coast. Today, the Berber tribe is the group closest to the original Hamitic stock – and strangely, Berbers are very Celtic in appearance. As early as 1901 Randall-McIver and Wilkin, in their book *Libyan Notes*, made the point that, suitably attired, many Berbers could be mistaken for Scotsmen or Irishmen.[4] The resemblance is apparently much more than skin deep. In a paper on blood group distribution, Morgan Watkin pointed to the correspondence that exists between the ABO blood groups of Berber stock of North Africa and the 'Celtic' populations in northwest Europe. In Watkin's opinion the evidence lends 'support to a view that a movement of people who might be described as ancient mariners occurred from the Mediterranean . . .'[5] While we should be wary of drawing conclusions from work based on a single genetic marker such as the ABO blood groups, it has recently been shown that genetic affinities and language are closely linked. Research has revealed that a 'family tree' based upon genetic similarities corresponds very closely to a 'tree' derived from linguistic studies.[6] In other words, there is some sort of parallel evolution occurring between genes and language. If this is so, do language studies corroborate the North African connection revealed to us by genetics?

Intriguingly, the answer is yes. Morgan Watkin quotes the linguist Pokorny as saying that 'the Celts show in the whole structure of their language a close affinity to the language of the White Mediterranean (i.e. Berber) people of North Africa'. In addition, recent studies by Irish musicologists have shown yet another link: the affinities of the rhythms of Irish traditional music are said to lie with the melodies of North Africa.[7]

An Ancient Migration

These new findings have made the idea of a migration from North Africa to Ireland a respectable hypothesis. In addition, there are a number of internal details in this ancient story of Egyptian migration that also point to its veracity.

We are told that Gaythelos was a Scythian (some versions say Greek) who, because of his warlike nature, had incurred the wrath of his own people and, with a number of like-minded young men, sought refuge in Egypt. Here he found favour with the ruling pharaoh, Chencres, and married one of pharaoh's daughters, Scota 'with a view to succeeding to his father-in-law's kingdom of Egypt'. At this point the narrative becomes confused, naming Chencres as the pharaoh who pursued the Jews, when they attempted to leave Egypt at the time of the Exodus. However, we are then told that, immediately following pharaoh's departure from the city of Heliopolis:

> Gaythelos remained behind ... in the city of Heliopolis, as arranged between himself and the King Pharaoh, with the purpose of possibly succeeding to his kingdom. But the Egyptian people who still remained, observing what had happened to their own king and at the same time guarding against their own inability to throw off again the yoke of foreign tyranny if once they had submitted to it, gathered their forces together and informed Gaythelos that if he did not speedily hasten his departure from their kingdom utter destruction would immediately attend himself and his men.

Several points leaped from the page when I first viewed this manuscript. The story is set at the time of the Exodus, in the days of Moses and Akhenaten. The name of the pharaoh, Chencres, is an obvious corruption of Achencheres, which, as we saw in the previous chapter, is itself a confused derivation of the name Akhenaten.[8] Gaythelos therefore married one of Akhenaten's daughters, a plausible enough scenario – the 'heretic pharaoh' is known to have had six female offspring. And Akhenaten, a foreigner himself, and champion of a religion whose deity was to be the god of all men, irrespective of nationality, is the *only* pharaoh likely to have countenanced the marriage of an heiress to a foreigner. The daughter of Akhenaten would naturally have been an Aten-worshipper and an initiate in the mysteries of the cult of the head. So, too, would Gaythelos (it is inconceivable that Akhenaten, with his single-minded devotion to his god, would have allowed his daughter to marry an 'unbeliever').

In the chronicle, Akhenaten's daughter and Gaythelos are said to have remained in Heliopolis during the Exodus, the same city that was the headquarters of the Priests of On, Akhenaten's religious allies, and one of the strongholds of Aten worship. This is exactly the place one would expect to find any of Akhenaten's relatives, especially a princess of the blood who (because of the matrilineal descent of Egyptian kingship), would be a priceless 'genetic asset' to the royal line. In fact, the leaving behind of a royal princess speaks very strongly of Akhenaten setting up a 'fall-back strategy' both for his line and his battered religion. If he and his followers were to be exterminated on the long and risky trek to their new home, there would still be a scion of the House of Pharaoh safe in Egypt, and able to carry on both the royal line and the worship of the Aten.

This hypothesis is confirmed by the *Scotichronicon*: Gaythelos (and pharaoh's daughter) stayed in Heliopolis 'as arranged between himself and the King Pharaoh, with the purpose of possibly succeeding to his kingdom'. The passage also confirms the confusion between Chencres and Ramses (the pharaoh who *did* pursue the Hebrews). If Chencres was Ramses, why should he leave Gaythelos in Heliopolis to 'possibly' succeed to his kingdom? This surely implies that both the life of the pharaoh and the succession were in danger, events that apply to a fleeing Akhenaten, but not to a pursuing Ramses (and especially not if he was merely pursuing fleeing Hebrew slaves). The passages which follow also have meaning only in terms of the Akhenaten scenario: the Egyptian people are said to wish to guard 'against their own inability to throw off again the yoke of foreign tyranny'. Why 'again'? This only makes sense if there had been an immediate, former 'foreign tyranny'. The time of the Hyksos, the hated 'Shepherd kings', was long past. But Akhenaten, as we have seen, was part-Hebrew and therefore regarded by many Egyptians, and especially the priests, as a foreigner. His forcing of a new god on the populace was certainly regarded by them as 'tyranny'. Akhenaten had been deposed and they wanted no more of the 'foreign' line. What seems to be recorded here is a memory of Ramses' death (which occurred just after the Exodus) and the people's (or rather the priests' and ruling elite's) fear that Akhenaten's daughter, who still resided in Heliopolis, would try to win back the throne for the deposed pharaoh. Akhenaten's daughter, her husband Gaythelos and all their retinue were given an ultimatum, and forced to leave under threat of imminent annihilation. Again, the *Scotichronicon* and other chronicles confirm this assumption: we are told that they 'fled in terror far from Egypt and their native land not just in fear of men ... but rather in fear of the gods'. The old gods of Egypt, the gods Akhenaten had suppressed, were baying for blood.

They seem to have been given time to prepare for their exile. Instead of following her father into the Sinai, Scota and Gaythelos decided to sail westwards and find uninhabited land to settle. This may have been an attempt to comply with Akhenaten's earlier plan to dilute the risk of the complete extinction of his lineage and teachings. Joining with him in Sinai would have made the royal line much more vulnerable: a single disaster would have been capable of wiping it out. Fleeing by sea was risky, but it still allowed for two chances of survival.

> When everything was finally ready, Gaythelos (with his wife and his whole household) and the other leaders were taken in skiffs and embarked on the waiting ships ... Then they made for the Mediterranean Sea between the southern bounds of Europe and Africa. As their prows cut through the waves of the sea, they headed towards the western regions of the world.

Suffering many hardships, the small fleet sailed past the Pillars of Hercules and turned north, hugging the coast of Spain until they reached a bay where they could land (one account names this as 'the vicinity of the islands of Cadiz', another near 'the river Ebro'). But whatever the location, the land was far from uninhabited and the immigrants were soon assailed on every side by the native peoples, striving by force of arms to dislodge the newcomers from their territory. Thanks to his 'warlike nature', Gaythelos and his men beat off every attack and gradually the small band of Egyptians established themselves in the land. The price of victory was high, however: 'Although he had been successful in inflicting heavy losses on the enemy on many occasions, yet he had never gained a single victory without some loss to his tiny nation, which he foresaw would grow smaller as a result of daily and unending decrease rather than increase [in numbers].' Gaythelos came to believe these hardships were the result of his not keeping to the original plan of finding an uninhabited land he and his wife could claim. With the consent of the nobles, he sent out small ships to reconnoitre 'the Boundless Ocean'. After some time, these scouts discovered an island lying to the west and north of Spain, and free of human habitation. On returning to Spain with the good news, they discovered Gaythelos dying of a sudden illness, but he urged his sons to act on the news and take possession of the island. Hiber and Hymec, both sons of Gaythelos, heeded the dying king's words and sailed with their people to the island, which they settled without trouble. Other chronicles support this account of an unopposed occupation, though one, *The Legend of Brendan*, differs in claiming that the island was inhabited and needed to be taken by force of arms:

> One of the sons of Gaythelos called Hiber, young in years but strong of purpose, was roused to war and took up arms ... He killed some of the few inhabitants whom he found and enslaved the rest, but he claimed the whole land as a possession for himself and his brothers, calling it Scotia after his mother's name.

Later, it seems the descendants of these Egyptian settlers called themselves Scoti for the same reason. They were also known as Gaetheli after Gaythelos, from which comes the Gaels and the language, Gaelic. The land, which we know as Ireland, was eventually named after Hiber, the warlike son of Gaythelos. It became, in Latin, Hibernia, and in English Iberland, later Iverland, and eventually Ireland.

The story therefore claims an Egyptian ancestry for the Scots. This is strange and, paradoxically, all the more believable because of it. There are a number of ancient traditions in European countries, which link their own history with the Bible story of Jesus and/or the Jews. Many of these were written during the Christian period and are thought by some researchers to be attempts to bring newly Christianised people into stronger association with the new faith. It has been argued such stories have no basis in fact and that they are nothing more than early Christian propaganda designed to forge mythic links to support the new religion. Whether or not this is true, the Gaythelos and Scota story is unusual because it ties the Scots not to the Hebrews, but to the 'bad guys', the Egyptians. Why should this have been done? Whose interests did it serve? Certainly not the Christian scribes who copied it. It is only in this century that anyone has suggested that Moses was an Egyptian, that Akhenaten might in fact be the man Moses, and that Akhenaten had at least part-Hebrew ancestry. And it is only now, in this book, that the link between Akhenaten and Scota has been established. It can have served no purpose for some ardent Christian missionary to invent a story that tells his wavering Dark Age converts that they are descended from the Egyptians, the nation that persecuted God's chosen people, whose inhabitants worshipped idols and strange gods and dealt in magic. Acting as it does against the best interest of the prevailing religious beliefs, this story only begins to make sense if it is true.

The chronicle tells us that the Scoti who remained in Spain continued to suffer from the depredations of their Spanish neighbours. One account speaks of them living in the '... desolate wastes and forests of the Pyrenees ... so that they were scarcely able to survive, supporting life on goats' milk and wild honey'. As word of the wonderfully fertile land beyond the sea reached them (Bede speaks of Ireland in terms of the Hebrew Promised Land, calling it 'an island rich in milk and honey'), more Spanish Scoti decided to leave the mainland and settle in the land of Hiber. A second major immigration is recorded, guided by Partholomus, son of Micelius, who was king of the Spanish Scoti. A third colonising wave followed, led by Simon Brecc (in Latin, Simon Varius), who is said to have greatly increased the number of settlers. Before he left on this expedition, Simon Brecc was presented by his father with a mysterious throne:

> ... a marble throne of very ancient workmanship, carved by a careful craftsman, on which the Kings of the Scottish people in Spain used to sit. Now this Simon Brecc set out for the aforesaid island and ... placed the aforesaid stone, that is the throne, in a place in his kingdom of some height which was called Tara ... and there the kings descended from his line used to have their seat throughout many ages, adorned with the insignia of royalty ...

In another part of the chronicle, further intriguing information is given about this ancient artifact. It is of Egyptian origin. And it is Gaythelos who is said to have brought the marble throne with him from Egypt to Spain. It was believed that the kingship of the Scoti would exist wherever the stone was located or, as an old verse had it:

> If destiny deceives not, the Scots will reign 'tis said
> in that same place where the stone has been laid.

So, according to this ancient book, after several decades, the remainder of Gaythelos' band of Egyptians, led by Partholomus and by Brecc (in two separate expeditions) made the journey to Ireland from their base in Spain, bringing with them certain Egyptian royal insignia, which included a throne originally carried into Spain from Egypt by Gaythelos. As this expedition from Egypt had been led by Akhenaten's daughter, these insignia could only have been the former possessions of the Pharaoh Akhenaten (whose own emblem of authority, the brazen serpent sceptre, appears to have been all he took with him into exile in Sinai). So highly regarded were these objects of royalty that Brecc brought them with him to Ireland and they became for the Scoti the essential emblems of kingship, the throne upon which each of their kings had to be crowned if they were to be regarded as legitimate rulers. All the high kings of Ireland were crowned upon it until, as the *Scotichronicon* states was recounted in the (now lost) *History of the Blessed Congall*, Fergus, son of Feredach, brought the throne with him to Scotland when many of the Scoti moved from Ireland and took up residence in Argyll.

What we have, in this ancient account, is nothing less than the origin of Scotland's most prized relic, the Stone of Destiny, and its identification as Akhenaten's throne.

The Stone of Destiny

When Edward I of England invaded Scotland in AD 1296, one of his main objectives was to secure for himself the Scottish Stone of Destiny, which was lodged at the time in Scone Abbey where, over two hundred years before, it had been placed atop a wooden pedestal before the high altar by King Kenneth II of Scotland.[9] The English king carried the stone back with him on his return to London and placed it in Westminster Abbey, under the seat of the Coronation Chair, which was specially constructed to house the relic. Edward mistakenly believed that possession of the stone would secure for him the crown of Scotland. In fact, as we have seen above, the prophecy did not state that whoever owned the stone would rule the Scots, but that wherever the stone was laid, the Scots would rule. Scotsmen are fond of pointing out that this prophecy did in fact come true. When Elizabeth I of England died in 1603, the English royal line failed with her. The Scottish King James VI became King James I of England and was crowned above the Stone of Scone in its resting place beneath the Coronation Chair. Whether believers regard the recent return of the stone to Scotland as presaging imminent political disorder and the break-up of the union of Scotland and England is debatable.

As appealing as this story is, there have been persistent rumours that the stone Edward carried back to London in triumph is not, in fact, the true Stone of Destiny. The stone (returned amid much pomp on St Andrew's Day, 30 November 1996 to its new 'home' deep within Edinburgh Castle, in the Scottish capital) is a fairly nondescript piece of sandstone, rectangular in shape, measuring approximately 66 × 41 × 27 centimetres and weighing over 135 kilograms. In no way does it correspond to the marble throne of Gaythelos described in the *Scotichronicon*. And medieval chroniclers, for example Robert of Gloucester, who saw the stone around 2,300 years after its supposed arrival in Ireland from Egypt, also describe it as marble-like, with carvings.[10] These medieval reports are a far cry from the present-day stone's appearance, but very like the 'marble throne ... carved by a careful craftsman' of tradition.

It has been shown that the inhabitants of Scone had three days' warning of the intention of the English king to plunder their treasure. Edward I had sworn an oath to conquer Scotland and his blood was up: when he left Berwick the entire population of that Scottish border town, some 17,000 men, women and children, had been murdered, their bodies left hanging in the wind as an earnest of the English king's determination to subdue his northern neighbour.[11] It seems inconceivable that no steps were taken to preserve the Stone of Destiny, and more than likely that the canny Scots placed a 'counterfeit' stone in the place of honour at Scone, and carried off the true stone to a place of safety. (As we'll see in the next chapter, the 'counterfeit' stone was not simply a quickly fabricated forgery. It was the Bethel Stone, another sacred relic, but one apparently expendable in the face of the threat to Scotland's ancient throne of power.)

But what happened to Akhenaten's throne, the true Stone of Destiny?

An intriguing report that appeared in the *Morning Chronicle* of 2 January 1809 gave a new twist to the saga of the stone, and added weight to the theory that the true Stone of Destiny had been hidden in advance of Edward I's sortie to seize the relic. The *Morning Chronicle* reported that, following days of heavy rain, a landslip had occurred at the site of Macbeth's castle, Dunsinane, in Perthshire:

> As servants belonging to the West Mains of Dunsinane-house were employed in carrying away stones from the excavation made among the ruins that point out the site of McBeth's Castle, part of the ground they stood on gave way and sank down about six feet, discovering a regularly built vault, about six feet long and four feet wide. None of the men being injured, curiosity induced them to clear out the subterranean recess when they discovered among the ruins a large stone, weighing about 500 lbs which is pronounced to be of the meteoric or semi-metallic kind. This stone must have been here during the long series of ages since McBeth's reign. Beside it were also found two round tablets of a composition resembling bronze...[12]

That the 'two round tablets' appear to be bronze is intriguing, as Egypt at the time of Akhenaten was a Bronze Age society. The *Morning Chronicle* reported that the stone had been sent to London, 'in order to discover its real quality', but there is no record of its arrival. The enigmatic 'throne' simply disappeared en route to the English capital. There has been no definite news of the stone's whereabouts since that date, but the throne of Akhenaten probably never made the journey south, and it is almost certainly still in Scotland. In a BBC Scotland TV programme, *The Stone of Destiny*, John Ritchie (who, significantly, was described as a 'Scottish Knight Templar') stated emphatically that 'The Stone of Destiny never left Scotland.' He went on to say that the stone's location was known to a few, and could be determined by 'an equation that spells out where it is'. In response to another question, concerning the Westminster 'Stone of Destiny' that Edward I had stolen, he was equally adamant that it was a fake, that it was a block of sandstone 'that had gone to England and done very well for itself ... There was never any Scottish King ever crowned on it.' Jamie Sinclair, owner of an estate around Dunsinane, and the descendant of a leading medieval Scottish Templar, was more guarded in an interview he gave for the same programme. He did, however, state that 'As a child I was certainly brought up to be led to believe ... that the stone might well have been hidden somewhere around here.' Asked if he thought the stone would ever be recovered, he gave a number of reasons why it should remain concealed: 'If it is brought to light again ... everyone will be arguing about it and wanting to pinch a piece of the fame ... If it did appear again where would it be housed? Would it be shipped off to Edinburgh like the Westminster Stone? I think it's better left where it is.'[13] This Scottish laird, heir to a long line of Templar tradition, undoubtedly spoke with authority, and I was inclined to believe him. The same family, the Sinclairs, had begun to figure strongly in my studies, and I suspected that they knew far more than they were prepared to say publicly. Moreover, my research had led me to another site owned by the Sinclairs and steeped in the traditions of the Scottish Knights Templar. It is even possible that the stone comprises part of the 'treasure' whose resting place I believe I have located.

Where to Now?

If we accept the underlying truth of the Gaythelos and Scota account, then around 1350 BC, an Egyptian princess of Akhenaten's line fled Egypt with her followers and settled in Ireland. Given their background, and that they were expelled from Egypt, 'in fear of the gods', their religion would have been that of Akhenaten, the worship of the Aten. We can expect that, over the centuries, local differences in the outward manifestation of the teachings would arise – in the same way that a Methodist church service bears little relation to a Greek Orthodox ceremony – but some of the underlying tenets should have remained identifiable. This would also have been true for the mysteries of the Akhenaten religion, which would have included, I believe, the veneration of the severed head, in occult ceremonies known only by the highest initiates of the religion. This ritual would therefore also have come to Ireland. In addition, these mysteries should have been more or less identical to that taught by Moses/Akhenaten to the Jewish initiates. And logically, if ties of blood linked Moses and the Jews with Scota and the Scoti, there should also be evidence of links between Ireland and Israel.

I realised that the new research areas had effectively defined themselves: was there any evidence of Akhenaten's religion in the customs of the ancient Irish? And could I find any ancient link between the Irish and the Jews?

Reviewing the facts, there seemed to be one obvious place to start. In the history of ancient Ireland there was just one group that offered the most promising line of research, a religious order that stood out like a beacon of intellectual rigour and accomplishment in a dark sea of West European ignorance – the druids. Their religion predated the Celtic invasions of Ireland and, in classical times, they were recognised through-out the known world as philosophers and teachers 'involved in the study of god and the mysteries of nature'.[14] If there was evidence, it was to be found in the story of these white-robed 'philosophers'.

The Druids

The stronghold of the druid religion was the British Isles, with Ireland the land least tainted by contact with the religions of Gaul and other European tribal groups. Ireland's special status seems to have always been recognised; to the ancients, Ireland was the *insula sacra*, the Sacred Island.[15] We first hear of the Irish druids from writers working just before the time of Christ. Even then the Egyptian immigration of Scota and Gaythelos was almost one thousand years in the past. The druids were the direct cultural descend-ants of these followers of Akhenaten, of the 'invasion' of Hiber and his followers, of Simon Brecc and the curiously carved marble throne. It is likely that they preserved at least some of the ancient wisdom that Scota had brought from Egypt, long after the pharaohs themselves had been consigned to their opulent tombs.

But we could not expect the teachings to have survived unaltered. Even a cursory view of the history of religion makes it obvious that beliefs of any faith move rapidly away from the original precepts of its founder. In

Christianity, Jesus' teachings of 'God the Father' and 'turning the other cheek' were speedily transmuted into belief in the Trinity and a pantheon of demi-gods, the saints, and to such hideous acts of violence as Charlemagne's forcible conversion of pagans by fire and sword, and the Roman Church's merciless suppression of 'heresy'. In the East, even the teachings of the Buddha, who emphatically eschewed all gods and emphasised man's own responsibility to escape the cycle of birth and death, were soon transformed into unrecognisable offshoots. Variants such as the Mahayana (Greater Vehicle) school taught that the work of salvation is initiated by a 'trinity' of the three bodies of the universal buddha, and that the boddhisattvas, a pantheon of benign higher beings, analogous to both the Christian saints and pagan lesser gods, stood between man and Ultimate.[16] It seems to be the way of things that all great religious leaders are doomed, upon their death, to have their high ideals usurped and corrupted by men and women who only vaguely understand the teachings that their revered leader attempted to promote.[17]

Akhenaten's monotheistic religion of the Aten could not reasonably be expected to have survived in its entirety in the intervening millennium between Scota's arrival in Ireland and our first written accounts of druidism. What we could hope for, however, were signs of its presence in the form of symbols or beliefs that were traceable to Akhenaten's ancient heritage.

The druids were the priestly class of the Celts, responsible for the wellbeing of their tribe by virtue of the rituals they performed. In Ireland the country was divided into five independent communities or districts, unified by virtue of the great national feasts and 'folk-moots', presided over by the druids.[18] More than any other historical or racial factor, it was the druids that gave the heterogeneous Celtic people their common identity. They acted as judges and arbiters of disagreements both in peace and war. The Roman historian Diodorus Siculus records that 'these men and their chanting poets' were obeyed by the Celts right up to the moment of battle. Even as two armies are about to join in combat the druids 'will step between them and force them to desist as one might charm wild beats'.[19] Given the ferocious, unrestrained nature of Celtic combat, where warriors whipped themselves into a frenzy of berserker rage, and fought naked to show their disdain of death, such peacemaking abilities serve to emphasise the druid's prestige in Celtic society. To an observer unaccustomed to the reverence in which the priestly class was held, they must indeed have seemed like magicians.

Allied to their judicial expertise was their role as teachers. Writing was known, but was reserved for the mundane affairs of public and private business. All instruction was oral (as is the case in most mystery schools), the druids taught verbally and their acolytes chanted back the verses until the performance was word perfect. Pupils of worth might spend up to twenty years in study, learning sacrificial ritual and almost endless genealogies by rote, and honing their skills in poetry and prophecy. Caesar confirms that verses were passed on orally, to keep their content secret. The great Roman's testimony is valuable here; Caesar not only held high rank in the Roman military, he was also a priest of the state religion, and therefore well versed in matters of faith and philosophy. So esteemed were the druid teachings that the Gauls of Europe sent their youth to Britain to be educated by the druids. The range of subjects offered by the druid colleges was broad and, according to Caesar, included 'many things concerning the stars and their motion, the extent of the world and of our earth, and the "nature of things", and the limitless power and majesty of the immortal gods'.[20]

Druidic philosophy is mentioned by Aristotle (fourth century BC), and their teachings must have been well established even at this early date. The parallels between druid theory and Pythagorean thought were widely noted in ancient times, with many commentators believing that Pythagoras had derived his teachings from the druids. Diogenes Laertius (third century AD), whose compilation of the lives of the philosophers was famous in its time, states that it was a common belief that philosophy was invented by 'the barbarians'. He includes the druids along with another esoteric group, the Gymnosophists of India, as '... teaching that the gods must be worshipped, and no evil done, and manly behaviour maintained'.[21]

Aside from such generalised statements, the precise nature of druid philosophy remains mysterious and a matter of scholarly debate. Two separate 'camps' exist. One, relying mainly on the traditions of Posidonius (a Stoic philosopher (c. 135–50 BC) who travelled widely in many countries and spent some time among the inhabitants of Gaul), stresses the barbaric nature of druidic activities, including human sacrifice.[22] The second, the Alexandrian tradition, seems oblivious of any trace of barbarism in the druids, and regards them primarily as high philosophers, concerned with the hidden things of nature.

The Posidonian camp has one advantage over the Alexandrian school: it draws on apparently first-hand accounts of druid brutality. Thus, the druids were said to stab a sacrificial victim from behind and read the future from the unfortunate victim's death throes, and the flow of blood.[23] The

Greek geographer and historian Strabo tells us (*Geography* iv: 4) that 'they would shoot victims to death with their arrows, or impale them in temples, or, having built a colossus of straw and wood, throw into the colossus cattle and animals of all sorts, and human beings, and then make a burnt offering of the whole thing'.[24] Pliny claims that the Romans did great service to humanity when they suppressed the druid faith and 'put an end to the monstrous practices by which to kill a man was a highly religious act, and even to eat him was very salubrious'.

However, when the motives of the 'barbaric druid' writers are examined critically, the position becomes less clear. Most are concerned with justifying the forced absorption of a free people, the Celts, into the Roman empire. Anything that rationalised Roman imperialism was useful to these writers and their patrons, and portraying the native religion as horrific, baleful, and in league with the dark forces, gave strong justification for the suppression of the malefactors and their nation. Caesar is an all too obvious exponent of this strategy, while a whole section of Strabo's *Geography* is effectively a diatribe against the Celts, and an apologia for Caesar's and Augustus's attempts to romanise the 'barbaric' western tribes. So, we must be careful not to take these accounts too literally. Although it is known that human sacrifice did take place, at least in European Celtic society, the frequency of such offerings is unknown. And more importantly, the role of the druids in such rites is by no means proved. Many of the stories told of druids immolating or disembowelling their victims may be no more than black propaganda, designed to salve the conscience, and extend the boundaries, of the Roman empire.

When we come to look at the other strand of evidence, the Alexandrian tradition, tales of bloody sacrifice are conspicuous by their absence. While the Alexandrian writers had no first hand knowledge of the druids, they were privy to ancient documents stored at Alexandria, documents that predated any sources used by the Posidonian tradition. One writer, Ammianus Marcellinus, gives as his authority Timagenes, who wrote around the middle of the first century BC and is said to have drawn on even older written documents.[25] Ammianus regards the druids as holding to the same doctrines as the Pythagoreans: 'The druids, men of loftier intellect, and united to the intimate fraternity of the followers of Pythagoras, were absorbed by investigations into matters secret and sublime, and, unmindful of human affairs, declared souls to be immortal.' The poet Lucan knew of the druidic role as repositories of arcane knowledge, and that their doctrines included teachings on the immortality of the soul and its rebirth. Even Caesar admitted this teaching as druidic: 'They desire to inculcate as their leading tenet, that souls do not become extinct, but pass after death from these present to those beyond . . .'[26] Valerius Maximus, writing around the beginning of the first century AD, mentions the druidic belief in life after death, which he again identifies as a Pythagorean tenet, and emphasises the point by describing how the Gauls lend 'sums of money to each other which is repayable in the next world, so firmly are they convinced that the souls of men are immortal'.[27]

Despite their seemingly diametrically opposed positions, it may be that the Posidonian and Alexandrian perspectives are reconcilable. The 'druid as brute' school (the pro-Roman Posidonians) were writing about Gallic, not British, practices, and at a time when druidism is known to have been in decline for several centuries. The Gauls were under increasing pressure from Rome and, unable to stem the Roman advance, many Gallic Celts must have considered whether the victorious Roman gods were not in fact superior to their traditional deities. Elements of Roman paganism are known to have been incorporated into some European Celtic societies. It is possible that human sacrifice became prevalent in these regions only at this late date, and was then reported by the Posidonians as evidence of druidic barbarity. And of course, there was always the propaganda war to win, which must have inclined these writers to exaggeration.

The Alexandrians, by contrast, seem to have had no particular axe to grind. They were reporters and researchers and as such are arguably a little more reliable than their propagandist 'opponents'. There could also be another reason for the discrepant reports. As we have seen, druidism was in decline at the time of Roman expansion, and probably had been for several centuries prior to that date. The Alexandrians' sources were older than the Posidonians', and were concerned with a time before the druids' decline. So, they were giving an account of druid society several centuries before, when it was at its apogee, and before the decline in status and power that affected most of the Celtic world with the coming of the Roman legions. Human sacrifice may well have figured not at all in druid teachings in this golden age of druidism. We cannot be entirely sure of this, however; the Alexandrians were primarily interested in druidic teachings, as opposed to their religious practice. So it is possible that details of sacrifice were quite simply irrelevant to them and, as such, went unreported.

The religion of the druids seems to have held sway over much of western Celtic Europe prior to Roman expansion. Strangely, although Celtic tribes existed in an almost unbroken swathe from Galatia in Asia Minor westwards to the British Isles, there is no mention of druids among the Celts of Italy and Spain, nor even among Celts east of the Rhine. It is now widely accepted that the druid order derives from a pre-Celtic institution of the far west of Europe which so impressed the invading Celts that they adopted the forms and tenets of this new religion when they settled among earlier-established tribes (although no doubt with some grafting on of their own, traditionally held beliefs).[28] Intriguingly, Caesar reports that druidism began in the British Isles and was exported from there to Gaul: 'The discipline of the druids was thought to have originated in Britain and to have been introduced into Gaul from there.'[29] In addition, it appears that Ireland was the heartland, the centre of the essential druidism, least tainted by contact with continental paganism.

I felt it was time to take stock of all this evidence: what we had was a pre-Celtic religion of high philosophical worth, which was taken over by the Celts from former inhabitants of the British Isles. The centre of this religion appeared to be Ireland, the *insula sacra* of tradition. Could it be, I wondered, that the origins of at least the rudiments of druid practices might be found in the Egyptian immigration of Gaythelos and Scota? This theory would accord well with what we now knew of the Scota legend: an Akhenaten-based religion of high cultural worth that had been forced by circumstances to carve a home from the wilderness of Ireland and to survive in an uncivilised and unfavourable environment.

Other facts also hinted at such an association. The matrilineal society of the Scoti resembled that of the Egyptian pharaohs, with the royal succession transmitted through the female line. So strong was this tradition that the Scoti are said in the *Scotichronicon* to have granted the wife-hunting Picts females of their own race as mates, but only on condition that the kingship of the Picts from then on descended through the female line. There was the association in both Ireland and Egypt of bulls, and the strange practice of Irish kings physically marrying the land they ruled, which seemed to hold echoes of the ancient Egyptian practice of the pharaoh masturbating onto the soil of Egypt, in emulation of the god's creative act. At an even more speculative level, the druids were said to be necessary at various rites, because 'only they know the language of the gods'. Could this, I wondered, be the language of the Egyptian priests, passed down orally through the line of their successors, the druids? It was all very suggestive, but hardly conclusive. If the Egyptian origin hypothesis were true, then we should find that at least something had survived of the Akhenaten religion, and the mysterious reverence of the head which I believed he instituted.

It was there, in an unmistakable form. Almost unbelievably, the teachings of the priestly caste of the Irish (and because of diffusion of the religion, other Celtic nations) had as its principal tenet the veneration of the very object I was attempting to trace – the severed head.

The Cult of the Head

Central to druidic teaching (and therefore, I suspected, to their Egyptian forebears and Jewish 'co-religionists') was the cult of the head. At its most basic, headhunting was practised by the Celtic warrior-elite; combatants took the heads of their enemies in battle and drilled the skulls so that they could be hung from their saddles, or from poles in front of their dwellings as a sign of martial prowess. Posidonius, cited by Strabo, mentions victorious Celts bringing home enemy heads from battle and nailing them to the entrances of their dwellings. Strabo states that Posidonius 'himself saw the spectacle in many places, and though he at first loathed it, afterwards, through his familiarity with it, he could bear it calmly'. The Roman historian Livy, in his *Historiae*, describes the fate of a Roman consul-elect, killed by a Celtic tribe, the Boii. They:

> ... stripped his body, cut off the head, and carried their spoils in triumph to the most hallowed of their temples. There they cleaned out the head, as is their custom, and gilded the skull, which thereafter served them as a holy vessel to pour libations from and as a drinking cup for the priest and temple attendants.[30]

But even in this grisly tale the symbolic meaning of the head is evident; it was taken to the holiest temple, gilded, and used by the priests as a sacerdotal chalice. Obviously, this head was not simply a trophy of war but a holy relic, an object of great veneration. Many sacred sites bear witness to this fact. At Carrawburgh in Northumberland, at the old Roman fort of Brocolitia, a well was discovered containing over thirteen thousand coins, and a human skull, all given as offerings to the gods.[31] A shaft excavated at Newstead in Roxburgh contained three human skulls and two wooden wheels, believed to be sun symbols. When real heads were lacking, stone or wooden effigies were often used as substitutes. One of the more spectacular finds was reported from France in 1963, when scores of carvings, including twenty-five miniature heads, were discovered in the neighbourhood of a Celtic sanctuary of the second century, set in former marshlands of the River Seine.[32]

For the Celts, the head was the religious object *par excellence*, venerated in battle, in holy sites, and in myth. The legend of Bran the Blessed gives us some insight into the Celtic perception of the attributes of the severed head. In the story, the hero Bran is struck in the foot with a poison arrow while fighting the king of Ireland. Realising his death is imminent, Bran orders his own men to behead him but, instead of dying, the head remains animated, speaking and prophesying for forty years while it feasts its followers. Afterwards, Bran's head was buried at White Hill, outside London, with his face turned towards France as a protective charm to defend the city and the island of Britain from evil.[33] Intriguingly, an almost identical myth holds that the head of Adam is buried on the northern approach to Jerusalem, to defend the Holy City from invasion.[34]

The myth of Bran illuminates the numinous qualities that the Celts believed imbued the severed head. For the Celts, it was the centre of the emotions and of life itself, to be venerated above all else as the seat of the soul, a magic talisman of inestimable worth. Diodorus Siculus, writing in the first century AD, says that when a great man died, be he enemy or ally, his head was embalmed 'in cedar oil and carefully preserved in a chest'. These heads were so highly valued that they would not be sold for their weight in gold, for they were said to possess powers of prophecy, healing, speech and fertility, motifs which prefigured those of the Templar embalmed head and which would continue to recur as our story unfolded. Researcher Ann Ross has given perhaps the best summary of the Celts' devout attitude towards the head, which I believe also epitomised the core of Akhenaten's religious legacy. The head '... was regarded as the essence of being, the seat of the soul, the symbol of evil-averting divine power'.

In short, the severed head symbolised divinity.

4

The Bethel Stone

The previous chapter established the strong possibility of a link between the Irish and the Egyptians, and provided a reason for the appearance of the cult of the head in Irish-Celtic society. Was there, I wondered, any evidence of a connection between the Irish and the Jews?

Perhaps the most striking indication of an Irish-Jewish connection concerns the sacred stone that Jacob used as a pillow to sleep on at Bethel. The ancient chronicles relate that this same stone was brought to Ireland five hundred years before the birth of Christ. Other tales confirm that a central stone in the most holy circle of the Irish druids was also named Bethel.[1] It is this stone, taken by King Edward I of England from Scone in 1296 and returned there in 1996, that is now mistakenly identified with the Stone of Destiny, the throne upon which, as we have seen, kings from at least the time of the Pharaoh Akhenaten have been crowned. The Stone of Bethel was never originally connected with royalty, but with the god of the Jews. It was a tangible symbol of the deity's presence on earth.

The Bethel Stone

The Bible relates that Jacob, the grandson of Abraham and father of Joseph (who was eventually to figure largely in our story), was travelling between Beersheba and Haran when night came on. He took a stone for a pillow and slept in the open, and there dreamed his famous dream of a ladder stretching to heaven with angels ascending and descending. In the dream, God gave to Jacob the land where he slept and promised him that his descendants would be 'as the dust of the earth'. When he awoke, the Bible tells us that Jacob was afraid and full of awe:

> How dreadful is this place! This is none other but the house of God, and this is the gate of heaven. And Jacob rose up early in the morning and took the stone that he had put for his pillow, and set it up for a pillar, and poured oil upon the top of it ... And Jacob vowed a vow, saying ... this stone, which I have set for a pillar, shall be god's house ... (Genesis 28: 17, 18, 20, 22).

So the Bethel Stone, Jacob's Pillar, was the House of God. It was therefore analogous in many ways to another House of God, the Ark of the Covenant, in which Yahweh/Adonai was said to dwell. And to the Egyptian arks, each of which housed a different god of the Egyptian pantheon. And it seems that, like these arks, the Bethel Stone was also designed to be mobile. Even today, in its most recent resting place in Edinburgh Castle, one can see the two metal rings, which hang from eyes attached to the stone, by which it could be transported. That it was moved from place to place is evident from the deep gulleys eroded in the body of the stone which are consistent with the use of a wooden pole (passed through the metal rings), to carry the sandstone block over long distances. An account in the Irish *Chronicles of Eri*, 'The Story of Lia Fail' says of the relic that 'in the early days it was carried about by [Hebrew] priests on the march in the wilderness. Later it was borne by sea from East to West – to the extremity of the world at the sun's going.'[2] This was, clearly, a stone of some religious power and importance, held in great reverence by both the Hebrews and the ancient Irish. Indeed, it has been considered of the utmost importance right up to the present day, as was evident in its recent ceremonial return to Scotland. During the Second World War, the stone was among a select group of relics chosen to be hidden in the grounds of Westminster Abbey in the event of a German invasion. Only ten or eleven men were privy to the secret of its hiding place. By contrast, there were no comparable plans to secure the Crown Jewels from potential Nazi occupiers.

Sir Compton MacKenzie, the literary critic and writer, believed that the stone was a fake, made from sandstone taken from quarries near Oban on the west coast of Scotland. However, while he could produce no proof for this assertion, recent research seems to bear out the Bethel Stone's authenticity, or at very least its point of origin. Professor Totten of Yale University has been a long-time student of the stone. His researches led him to conclude that 'The analysis of the stone shows that there are absolutely no quarries in Scone or Iona wherefrom a block so constituted could possibly have come, nor yet from Tara' (the three sites occupied by the stone since its arrival in the British Isles).[3] Another academic, geologist

Professor Odlum of Ontario University, explored the issue of the stone's geological origin. Professor Odlum claims to have discovered a sandstone stratum that is identical in every way with the composition of the Bethel Stone. The location of this geological formation is exactly where the Bible text says it should be – at Bethel, in Palestine, where Jacob had his dream of the heavenly ladder.[4]

That the stone was a relic of priceless importance is therefore beyond doubt. But is it the Stone of Destiny upon which the high kings of Ireland were crowned? I cannot believe that this is true. The evidence points against it and towards the marble throne that Gaythelos brought from Egypt, to Akhenaten's throne, an object whose connection to kingship was obvious and indisputable. The Bethel Stone was undoubtedly holy, but holy by virtue of its association with the patriarch Jacob, and because it was perceived as the house of his god, the deity that was to become the God of Israel. But there is no connection here with any royal line. Other stories concerning Jacob's Pillar point away from the concept of kingship and towards the stone's true origins. These tales claim that it was also at one time the cornerstone of the Temple of Jerusalem. The temple was built by Solomon as a 'house' for his god, and it is easy to see how the Bethel Stone, another 'house of god', came to be associated with the temple. It is not so easy to see the connection between this stone and kingship, and for a very good reason: there is none. Important though the Bethel Stone was for its connection with Israel, the original Stone of Destiny was the black marble throne on which the first kings of Ireland were crowned – the throne of Akhenaten.

Confusion has arisen because, during the long centuries of their existence, both Akhenaten's throne and the Bethel Stone have been given the title Stone of Destiny. This coincidence has confused many researchers and impeded a true understanding of the complexity of the story. Because there was one title, the Stone of Destiny, it was assumed that there could only be one object. Since the time of Edward I's invasion of Scotland, when the Scots allowed the less valued of the two stones to be seized by the English, no one has looked any further for the more precious relic: Akhenaten's throne.

It is easy to understand why the Scots sacrificed the Bethel Stone: if no relic had been found at Scone, Edward would undoubtedly have redoubled his efforts to find the stone, and could well have seized both holy relics. So, despite the evidence of the ancient accounts, and the witness of medieval chroniclers, that the Stone of Kingship was made of marble, the existence of the marble throne of Gaythelos was studiously ignored and, over the years, quietly forgotten. The Bethel Stone has been allowed to claim the ancient title Stone of Destiny exclusively. As we saw in the previous chapter, even the chance discovery of the carved marble throne at Dunsinane in Victorian times failed to dent the complacent edifice of tradition that has grown up around the Bethel Stone.

This is not to say that the Bethel Stone is unimportant, even from a historical point of view and especially not to our quest. The tale of its arrival in Ireland certainly testifies to strong links of religion and blood between the Jews and the ancient Irish.

The Stone Arrives in Ireland

The Bethel Stone was lodged at the capital of the House of Judah, in Jerusalem, during the early part of the sixth century BC, and it may even have been, as has been claimed, a part of the Temple of Solomon. The sixth century is a chequered and often violent period of Jewish history. In 586 BC the Babylonian army under King Nebuchadrezzar invaded Judah and assaulted the city of Jerusalem. After a siege that lasted over a year, and left the inhabitants starving and dispirited, the city fell, and its king, Zedekiah, the last king of the line of David, was captured as he tried to escape across the plains of Jericho. Nebuchadrezzar's revenge was merciless: all the nobles of Judah were executed. King Zedekiah, in chains, was forced to watch the slaughter of all his sons. It was the last sight he ever saw. With the image of horror still burning in his brain, Zedekiah's eyes were put out and he was taken, blind and helpless, as a captive into Babylon (Jeremiah 39: 4–7). For the Jews, it was a disaster of monumental proportions: the city was laid waste, and the House of David was extinguished. However, a daughter of Zedekiah, named Tamar Tephi, is said to have fled from Israel to escape the carnage and the subsequent deportation of the Jews to Babylon. She sailed to Ireland, carrying with her the sacred stone on which Jacob slept when he dreamed of a ladder extending heavenwards towards God. According to the legend, the prophet Jeremiah also went with her to the new land.

There is in fact considerable support for this story in the Bible. Jeremiah was in Jerusalem during the siege and he did survive the destruction of the city. He had fallen out of favour with King Zedekiah and was being held in prison when the city was taken by the Babylonians. King Nebuchadrezzar named Gedaliah as governor over Judah, and placed Jeremiah under the charge of Nebuzar-adan, the captain of the guard, ordering him to treat the prophet with respect and 'do him no harm; but do unto him even as he shall say unto thee' (Jeremiah 39: 12). Nebuzar-adan obeyed the command, and a little later set Jeremiah free with the words:

> And now behold I loose thee this day from the chains which were upon thine hand. If it seem good unto thee to come with me into Babylon, come; and I will look well unto thee: but if it seem ill unto thee to come with me into Babylon, forbear: behold, all the world is before thee: whither it seemeth good and convenient for thee to go, thither go.
>
> (Jeremiah 40: 4)

It is obvious from this that Jeremiah was placed under no constraints whatsoever. The whole world was before him, to travel as he willed.

But what of the princess? Why should she have been spared when all of Zedekiah's sons were put to death? It seems that the Babylonians' concern was only with the male heirs, for the Bible records that several daughters of the Jewish king survived the fall of Jerusalem. They were perhaps awaiting deportation along with the rest of the 'important people' of the kingdom of Judah, possibly they were destined for the Babylonian king's harem. However, a certain Ishmael, himself connected with the royal House of Judah, assassinated the governor Gedaliah during a meal at the town of Mizpah. In the ensuing confusion he seized '. . . all the people that were in Mizpah, even the King's daughters, and . . . carried them away captive, and departed to go over to the Ammonites' (Jeremiah 41: 11). Apparently, Ishmael was planning to use the princesses as 'bargaining counters' in his negotiations with the Ammonites. Fortunately, Johanan, a loyal war captain of Judah, came to the rescue with a remnant of Zedekiah's army. He overtook Ishmael and forced him to hand over all his captives, including the princesses.

They were all in great danger, with the Babylonian army scouring the land, mopping up pockets of resistance. It was decided that their safest course lay in retreating south into Egypt. Jeremiah counselled staying in Judah; he seemed concerned about the consequences of settling in Egypt and he prophesied that all who went into that country would die. But his warnings were ignored and the remnant of the House of Judah (which the Bible specifically states included the daughters of King Zedekiah) made their way by unused paths south into the kingdom of the Two Lands (Jeremiah 43: 6). They are likely to have carried with them whatever sacred relics they had been able to salvage from the destruction of their city, their temple and their nation. One of these relics was, I believe, the House of God, the Bethel stone. Why Tamar Tephi eventually made her way to

Ireland is not clear in the story that has come down to us. It may have been Jeremiah's certainty that staying in Egypt would lead to destruction that prompted her to set sail for Ireland. Or perhaps it was decided among the king's daughters that they should go their separate ways in order to maximise the survival of the royal bloodline.

There was one sea route that had been traversed before by people of her own race and beliefs – the path to the land of Hiber and the tribe of Scota. Given the close blood ties of the two groups (the people who followed Akhenaten's daughter to Ireland, and those who fled Egypt under Akhenaten himself), they are likely to have maintained contact with one another (as borne out by the fact that Tamar Tephi was eventually to marry an Irish king who, according to the chronicles, was himself of Israelite descent). It is possible that Jeremiah actively chose to seek out these distant cousins, and to convey a princess of the royal line to the island in the Western Ocean, seeing in it a place of ultimate safety from the shifting alliances and uncertain fortunes of war in the Middle East. Whatever the reason, the chronicles relate that Tamar Tephi and Jeremiah, carrying the holy stone with them, took ship for Ireland in or around the year 584 BC.

In Ireland, Tamar Tephi (who as Zedekiah's daughter possessed immense status as a direct descendant of the House of David) married Eochaid the Heremon, an Ardath or high king of Ireland and himself of Israelite blood, being closely allied to the tribe of Dan.[5] The Irish high kings (now carriers of the bloodline of David) kept the stone at the ancient palace of Teamhair Breagh through the reigns of fifty-six high kings, a period of over one thousand years. It came to symbolise the Davidic lineage and legitimised all who were crowned in its presence. It was also thought of as the keystone of the destroyed Temple of Solomon, which further enhanced its already exalted status.

Like the true Stone of Destiny, Akhenaten's throne, the Bethel Stone was carried into Scotland when Fergus Mor McErc (of the Irish Gaelic kingdom of Dalriada) invaded Argyll in western Scotland and won it from the Picts sometime in the fifth century AD. A further thirteen kings of Argyll held the holy relics until, in AD 843, Kenneth McAlpin united the Picts and the Scots and became the first true king of Scotland.[6] It was he who built the first church at Scone, where he had won the crucial victory against the Picts. Here the Bethel Stone remained, venerated in a place of honour before the high altar, until Edward I of England removed the holy relic to Westminster Abbey.

It was time to take stock of what I had learned. Here in the history and myths of western Europe was strong evidence of a web of affinity and influence. A connection between Egypt and the British Isles had been established, with Akhenaten's daughter Scota leading the first ships as a refugee fleeing the wrath of the Egyptian gods and the priesthood that served them. She had brought Akhenaten's religion to Ireland; it had survived in a modified form in druidic teaching, where the cult of the severed head had become a dominant feature of the religion of the Celts. In addition, in the story of the Bethel Stone and Tamar Tephi, a link between Israel and the western Celts had been demonstrated. But one major question remained unanswered – the Jews, as descendants of Akhenaten's exodus from Egypt, should also have been privy to the mysteries of the severed head. Was there, I wondered, any evidence of a cult of the head in Jewish history?

5

Sacred Hair, Sacred Heads

Unlike the early history of Britain, the severed head is not immediately apparent as a dominant theme in the history of the Jews. This was not entirely unexpected. My hypothesis was that Akhenaten had led the Jews toward the Promised Land and that he had given them, along with his monotheistic beliefs, a secret tradition of head worship, the head being viewed as a personification of the divine. This theory had been given great impetus by the discovery of just such a belief in Palestine 7000 BC, and also among the descendants of the Egyptian immigration to Ireland, led by Akhenaten's daughter. It appeared that, over the centuries, the Irish secret tradition became more overt and available (at least in a simplified form) to the population at large.

Because Akhenaten, as his *alter ego* Moses, came to be viewed as the greatest of the prophets, and his memory remained strong among the Jewish people, I believed that the traditions of secrecy he had instituted in the worship of the head remained intact. Of great interest was my discovery that, in Esoteric Judaism, the first emanation of the Divine 'which contained within itself the plan of the universe in its infinity of time and space, in its endless variety of form and colour and movement' is known, even today, as the White Head.[1] This concept of a head as the source of all wisdom was to recur later in my quest in quite astonishing circumstances.

While in Ireland and Britain it became acceptable practice to consider the head of almost any human being as worthy of preservation, in Israel the embalming of the head and its reverence was reserved solely for those who had shown great powers of leadership and mystical abilities. In addition, the secret teachings were never revealed to the mass of the Jewish people and remained the preserve of an initiated elite. This would make evidence of head worship particularly difficult to find. Nevertheless, the clues were there, scattered throughout the biblical sources.

Sacred Heads

An in-depth review of the biblical literature revealed that severed heads are mentioned in a number of contexts: David takes the giant Goliath's head after he has slain him in battle (I Samuel 17: 46ff); in his running fight with the Midianites, Gideon is brought the heads of two of their princes, Zeeb and Oreb; and when King Saul is killed by the Philistines, his head is cut off and carried in triumph to be hung in the temple of their foremost god, Dagon. While the last story does contain overtones of a religious or ritual use of the head, it is difficult here to separate worship of the head as a religious object from the simple taking of the head as a war trophy or symbol of one's victory over a hated opponent. It is equally hard to interpret the story of the beheading of the Philistines' god Dagon by the Jewish deity Adonai. When the Ark of the Covenant is captured by the Philistines, it is taken to the temple of their god Dagon and laid before his idol. The following morning the Philistines' 'false god' is found cast down before the Ark, and with its head removed (I Samuel 5: 4). Is this tale a simple nationalist folktale, or is a deeper symbolism involved?

There are, however, several biblical events that indicate far more clearly the existence of a religious reverence for the head and its ritual removal and storage.

Saul was the first king to be set over the Children of Israel. He was chosen by the prophet Samuel, and the story of his choosing includes a most intriguing verse. Samuel has berated the Children of Israel for asking for a king to rule over them (up until that time Israel had been ruled by a line of wise and holy men, the Judges). As far as Samuel was concerned, God should be the people's only king. However, he agrees to their demand and calls on them to present themselves before him and the Lord tribe by tribe. When the Benjamites approach, he asks for the family of Matri and for Saul, who is described as the son of Kish. But Saul is nowhere to be found, he is in hiding, not wishing the honour of kingship, and has to be brought bodily into the presence of Samuel. Then '... when he stood among the people he was higher than any of the people from his shoulders and upward' (Samuel 10: 23) This phrase bothered me: nowhere in the rest of the Bible is Saul described as being a tall man, whereas standing head and shoulders above everyone else would have made him a giant, comparable almost to Goliath, and his great stature would certainly have been commented upon in other contexts. Could it be, I wondered, that it was Saul's religious standing that was being described here? The phrase 'from his shoulders upwards' indicates his head; was Saul's head in some way higher or greater than any other person present? From a religious and symbolic point of view, this was quite clearly true. Earlier that day, Samuel had secretly anointed Saul king over Israel, by taking a vial of oil and pouring it over Saul's head, thus sanctifying it in the same way that, I was later to discover, a priest resanctified the holiness of a Nazarite's head if it had been accidentally defiled. Was Saul's head made equally holy by his anointing? Could this be the reason that, when he and his son Jonathan were finally slain in battle, the Philistines at first ignored his son's corpse, and the king's body, and carried only Saul's head to be hung before their god in the temple of Dagon? It may well be that we have here the reason that the head was sacred and preserved in the shadowy cult originated by Akhenaten. The heads of men who were inspired of, or anointed by, God were regarded as embodying the deity. The deity worked through them during life and, on death, could still be reached through the medium of the sacred head. If this was so, then the preservation of such holy heads would become a sacred duty, of the utmost importance to those who had been initiated into the secret tradition.

Saul was a Benjamite, and the prophet Samuel lived in the Benjamite village of Ramah and was almost certainly a Benjamite, a tribe that was to become increasingly important as my research progressed. Just after King Saul had been slain but before David was anointed king in his place, the Bible tells us of two of David's warriors, the brothers Baanah and Rechab. They were the sons of Rimmon, who was of the House of Benjamin (as was King Saul and all his sons). In the light of what I was later to find, this particular detail, the Benjamite connection, turned out to be of great significance. In the biblical account, the two brothers steal into the house of Ish-bosheth, one of the sons of Saul. It was noon, and Ish-bosheth was asleep on his bed. Under the guise of fetching wheat to the house, the two brothers get close enough to Ish-bosheth to stab him 'under the fifth rib'. With Saul's son dead, they behead their victim and set off for David's camp, expecting his approval for the murder.

Instead, David is appalled by their actions. In a particularly grisly scene he has them slain, their hands and feet cut off, and their mutilated bodies hung up over the pool of Hebron. In contrast, Ish-bosheth's head is treated reverentially and, significantly, his body is ignored by David and his companions. When Saul's head was taken and hung up in the Philistines' Temple of Dagon, its rescue or return was out of the question, and David took great pains to find the remainder of Saul's body in order to bury it with due honour (II Samuel 21: 14). But here, with the head safe, he ignores the rest of Ish-bosheth's remains. Ish-bosheth's head is, however, handled with great respect. We are told that David and his men 'took the head of Ish-bosheth, and buried it in the sepulchre of Abner in Hebron' (II Samuel 4: 12).

What intrigued me, apart from the value that is obviously placed upon the storing of Ish-bosheth's head underground, in a sepulchre, is that it was placed in *Abner's* sepulchre. Abner was the captain of Saul's army, but because of an argument with one of Saul's sons, decided to throw in his lot with David. Abner was another Benjamite, and in the previous chapter of the Bible story he had been slain by Joab, who smote him 'under the fifth rib, that he died . . .' This was an odd coincidence. Both men, both of the House of Benjamin, had apparently been slain 'under the fifth rib'. Why, I wondered, in this particular way? Was the fifth rib of any ritual significance? As I researched, the 'coincidences' continued. Abner had himself slain another man, Asahel, who was chasing him after a battle. Again, Asahel is slain 'under the fifth rib'.

The biblical redaction of the King James version places rib in italics, indicating that this is a 'best guess' by the editor of a word that was omitted from the original text. I began to wonder if 'rib' was indeed the best guess. Smiting anyone under the fifth rib is not a guaranteed killing blow: there is a chance of hitting a lung and, if the blow is on the left side of the trunk, a small possibility of connecting with the heart. But in combat, the idea is to finish the opponent as quickly as possible. The emphasis on the fifth rib did not make sense, and its appearance on three occasions in the space of two chapters seemed to me a guarantee of its ritual significance.

Could the word, I wondered, be something other than the non-lethal fifth 'rib'? But what other part of the human anatomy possesses five or more 'parts'? With the exception of the fingers and toes (once again, hardly lethal killing points), the only other possible structure is the human spine. Could the missing word have been the Hebrew equivalent of vertebra? Striking 'under the fifth vertebra' would certainly ensure a very speedy demise of an opponent or captive. And it was the ideal point to strike in one particular ritual. The act of beheading. If this is accepted, then we have in the biblical stories several accounts of ritual beheading by, and of, members of the tribe of Benjamin.

Salome and her dance before King Herod Antipas provides an even clearer insight into the cult of the head in Israel and the reverence in which the head of great men was held. The story is well known. Herod is so pleased with Salome's dancing that he offers her anything she might ask, up to and including half his kingdom. As the story makes plain, this is no idle proposition – once Herod has made the offer, he is bound to comply with whatever the girl requests. Salome rushes off to seek the advice of her mother Herodias and gets an almost instantaneous reply. Instead of requesting gold, or land, or a position of power, Herodias tells Salome to ask for the head of the prophet, John the Baptist. Salome does so, and Herod is portrayed as being aghast at the request. This is strange, because the Bible does not shrink from painting Herod in the most horrific colours, as a sadistic beast, a monster with incestuous and murderous tendencies. But here, for some reason, Salome's request leaves him utterly dismayed. However, as he has sworn an oath to give Salome whatever she requests, he agrees to her demand and '... immediately the king sent an executioner and commanded his head to be brought: and he went and beheaded him in the prison. And brought his head in a charger and gave it to the damsel: and the damsel gave it to her mother' (Mark 6: 28).

In this part of Mark, John the Baptist is portrayed as being still in prison and still alive when Salome's dance is performed. But, just thirteen verses prior to this account (Mark 6: 14) Herod is described as being alarmed when he hears of Jesus and his preaching and healing of the sick. Herod's response to these reports is revealing: 'And King Herod heard of him ... and he said, that John the Baptist *was risen from the dead*, and therefore mighty works do show forth themselves in him.' Here, we have a clear, definite statement from Herod that John the Baptist was dead long before Salome performed the dance that got her the prophet's severed head. Why Herod was holding the head is a matter for conjecture: it may be that he was aware of the existence of an Israelite cult of the head and felt that the head of John held occult powers. Or perhaps for Herod the head was more a symbol of political rather than religious power. Whatever the reason, it is obvious that when Herodias ordered her daughter to request the head of John the Baptist, she did not do this simply out of hatred for the prophet and a desire for his death, as is commonly supposed. The prophet had already been executed. What she craved was not John's death, but his severed head. And Herod's dismay at the request can be for no other reason than that his hurried oath had forced him to hand over a valuable relic, one for which Salome and Herodias had refused half of Herod's kingdom.

There did now seem to be a very real indication that a cult of the head had existed in ancient Israel from at least the time of Saul until the birth of Jesus. And there was something else that emerged from the detailed overview of scriptural texts that I had undertaken, something that once again pointed to the importance of the head. This was the regular appearance of one particular attribute – the ritual importance of hair, and especially long hair, to one group of Jews, the Nazarites.

Samson

The Nazarites were a sect specially dedicated to the service of the Hebrew god Adonai. Unusually in the Jewish world, a Nazarite could be of either sex. They were not allowed to drink alcohol, and were especially forbidden the grape, either fresh or dried, or as wine. All aspects of the vine were taboo, 'from the kernels even to the husk', so it seems that it was not just the intoxicating properties of this plant that were shunned but, for some obscure reason, the plant itself. Nazarites were not allowed to come close to any dead human body, even those of their parents or siblings. And Nazarites were forbidden to cut their hair, which seems to have been regarded as sacred.

Although in Jewish legend, the strength of Judah, one of the sons of Jacob, was said to reside in his hair,[2] the first biblical mention of the sacredness of hair is in those chapters of the Book of Judges which concern Samson. He was a member of the tribe of Dan (the tribe from whom the Irish husband of Tamar Tephi was later descended), and he became the twelfth judge of the tribes of Israel, wielding power for twenty years in the days before the Hebrews came to be ruled by hereditary kings.[3] The story of this Jewish hero's strength, his betrayal by Delilah (who cut off his hair and so rendered him powerless) and his final suicidal act of vengeance on the Philistines by using his god-given strength to topple their temple, is well known. Less well known are the circumstances of Samson's conception and birth, and that he was promised to Adonai/Yahweh, the Jewish god, by his parents while still in the womb. His mother had been incapable of having children, but was told by an angel that from the time of their meeting she must abstain from alcohol and any 'unclean thing'. This was essential as she was about to conceive and bear a son. It is then that a specific prohibition is mentioned concerning the coming child 'and no razor shall come on his head: for the child shall be a Nazarite unto God from the womb' (Judges 13: 5).

Samson's strength was said to be dependent upon his hair, and he used it to strike terror into the Philistines, who at that time were overlords of the Jews. At first, Samson seems to have been drawn to the Philistines' way of life. He chose a wife from among them, and lived with her family, much to the chagrin of his own parents. However, Samson soon fell out with his wife's people and, having tied firebrands to three hundred foxes and released the animals in their corn fields, he fled back to the land of his birth. But his own people, in fear of the wrath of their overlords, came in strength to capture him and send him back to face the justice of the Philistines. After extracting a promise from the Hebrews that they would not kill him themselves, Samson allowed himself to be bound and delivered up to the Philistines. But no sooner had he been made captive than he used his great strength to burst his bonds and with only the jawbone of an ass as a weapon, he fell upon his erstwhile jailers and slew one thousand of their number.

It was only when Samson became besotted with Delilah that his secret became known. Delilah was in the pay of the Philistine nobles, each of whom had offered her eleven hundred pieces of silver if she could entice Samson and learn from him the source of his power. Acting on their orders, she pressed him three times for the secret of his strength. Each time Samson replied with a lie and was able to drive off and kill the Philistines whom Delilah allowed into the house to try to seize him. Eventually (and rather stupidly, given the fact that she had betrayed him so many times to the Philistines), Samson informed Delilah that the true source of his strength was that he was a Nazarite, and that his power resided in his hair which from birth had never been cut. Having at last won Samson's secret, Delilah persuades him to sleep resting on her knees. While he slumbers his hair is shorn and he is unable to resist the next onslaught of his foes. Captured and blinded by the Philistines, he is forced to work the prison mill until, at the time of a great ceremony to Dagon, he is brought out into the temple to be baited by his captors. However, by this time Samson's hair has regrown sufficiently for some of his power to return. After asking God to give him his former strength just once more so that he can take vengeance on his enemies, he pushes down the central two pillars of the Philistine temple, crushing himself and his enemies in the process.

The biblical story that has come down to us has undergone the usual 'rewrite' by at least one editor, but the redaction has not masked a number of important points. The story may well record the exploits of a historical character named Samson, but there is certainly an additional mythic dimension to the tale, especially in the cyclical nature of parts of the story. This is emphasised by Delilah's repeated requests to know the cause of Samson's power, in his repeated false replies and in his incomprehensible decision to tell her the truth. It is also worth noting that Samson's name means 'Man of the Sun'.[4] This has prompted some scholars to suggest that the origins of the story lie in a myth from some unknown cult of the sun. Given the association of Akhenaten's god, the Aten, (known to the Jews as Adonai) with the disc of the sun, it suggested to me that the hero's name may well be an indication of his initiation into the Aten religion. This seemed especially likely in view of his membership of the Nazarites, whose taboo on the cutting of head hair provides a further suggestive link with the cult of the sacred heads.

The Nazarites

Further research revealed that a number of important Old Testament characters are also named as Nazarites. Apart from Judah and Samson, Joseph of the coat of many colours (whose ancestry is pivotal to an explanation of the mystery – see Chapter 9) is also given what appears to be a Nazarite consecration – his head is blessed and he is called 'separate' (Genesis 49: 26). And Samuel, the prophet who sanctified Saul's head with the oil of kingship, is again named as a member of this 'Sect of the Holy Head' in the Jewish apocryphal writings (Sir 46: 13).

The greatest Nazarite prohibition seems to have been reserved for the hair. Nazarites were strictly forbidden to cut either their head hair or (if men) their beard. And this taboo is, according to the law of the Nazarites given in Numbers, Chapter 6, very closely associated with the idea of the head as a holy object. Verse 9 states that, if any man dies suddenly next to a Nazarite, then the Nazarite 'hath defiled the head of his consecration; then he shall shave his head in the day of his cleansing, on the seventh day he shall shave it'. The Nazarite must then bring two pigeons to the priest: 'and the priest shall offer one for a sin offering and the other for a burnt offering, and make an atonement for him, that he sinned by the dead, and *shall hallow his head* that same day' (Numbers 6: 11). This makes it clear that it was the head that was considered holy, not the hair, for if the latter was important, it would have been the hair, not the head, that was blessed. For Nazarites then, the hair is simply the outward manifestation of the holy head, and it is taboo solely because of the sacred nature of the head.

Epiphanius, the bishop of Constantia in Cyprus, gives further details of the Nazarites, details which brought me up short and set my own hair prickling on the back of my neck.[5] The Nazarites were Jews and observed the laws of the Sabbath, circumcision, and feast days. This was to be expected, but it was in their *divergence* from the orthodox tradition that the clues came thick and fast. The Nazarites rejected the canonical Pentateuch (the first five books of the Old Testament, said to have been written by Moses), and claimed that the real law was different from the one revealed to the general populace. In addition, they had an especial reverence for the ancient patriarchs and sages of Israel, up to the time of Moses (who has now been identified as Akhenaten). This statement is very significant, but even more significant is the fact that the Nazarites *rejected all the prophets after Moses/Akhenaten.*[6]

Here, then, was clear evidence that Akhenaten was regarded by some Jews as having left with them a teaching of great value, a philosophy that was at variance with all the prophets that came after him. This teaching was a secret, hidden from the ordinary Jewish population. And these beliefs were held by a group that reverenced the head and refused to cut their hair. It seemed that I was on the right track.

There was more. Epiphanius tells us that a subsect of the Nazarites, the Sampsaei (Nazarites who especially reverenced the hero Samson) have their name from the word for the solar disc, which echoed Akhenaten's symbol for the Aten, and confirmed the 'Man of the Sun' derivation for Samson. But these were not merely followers of a solar hero. The good bishop of Constantia tells us that Sampsaei means Heliacaei or Solares (the Children or Worshippers of the Sun). This was very telling: Akhenaten from the beginning had styled himself as 'son (i.e. a child) of the Sun'.[7] And the Sampsaei, once again mirroring Akhenaten's own beliefs, were not simple sun worshippers, regarding the fiery object that sailed daily through the sky as a god. Their conception of the sun was identical to Akhenaten's, merely a symbol of the Great Power that filled the universe.[8]

So, these people who reverenced Akhenaten/Moses, also paid homage to the Aten, the sun disc of the heretic pharaoh, whose temples had faced the east towards the rising sun. It should also be remembered that Moses was said to have built a similar temple in Heliopolis (City of the Sun).

Epiphanius, the Bishop of Constantia and 'scourge of all "heresies"' reports in his *Heresies* that the name of the sect, Naziraei as he calls them, means 'Consecrated' or 'Sanctified' (*Haer.* xxix: 5). He also confirms that Samson was a Nazarite, as were many others, among them most interestingly, John the Baptist, the cousin of Jesus. John is described as being unshaven and long-haired and eschewing alcohol, an ascetic life very much in keeping with Nazarite philosophy. Even more telling, James the Just, the brother of Jesus, was also numbered among the Nazarites.

These details from Epiphanius provide useful information, as the

Gospels themselves have very little to say concerning the family of Jesus, and especially his four brothers (James, Joset, Simon and Jude) and an indeterminate number of sisters (like their Jewish contemporaries, the early Christians did not usually consider women worthy of being named individually!) It is almost as if the family are an embarrassment to the Gospel writers' view of the divinity of Jesus (or perhaps an embarrassment to the editors who followed and excised and added to the writings in order to advance their particular vision of the man who had been Jesus). However, much can be gleaned from the little that remains in the New Testament, and from the writings of the early Church fathers.

Eusebius (c. 260–340) was bishop of Caesarea. He is a champion of the orthodox view that had triumphed at the council of Nicaea in 325. He is also one of our best sources for information on the tales that the Jews told of Jesus in the decades after his death. Eusebius informs us that it was James the brother of Jesus, who, after the execution of Jesus, took on the role of leader in the tiny proto-Christian church.[9] Eusebius quotes from another source, Hegessipus' *Memoirs*, which, in a strange echo of the Samson story, says that Jesus' brother James

> ... was holy from his mother's womb; drank no wine or strong drink, nor ate animal food; no razor came upon his head; he neither oiled himself nor used the bath; he alone was permitted to use the holy places, for he never wore wool, but linen ... Indeed, on account of his exceeding great righteousness he was called 'the righteous' and 'Olbias', which means in Greek 'defence of the people' and 'righteousness'.[10]

Given this portrait, we are quite justified in regarding James as a Nazarite, and this is confirmed by a number of other ancient sources, as well as by modern biblical scholarship. These 'new' Nazarites are described by Epiphanius as mystics who traced their descent back to pre-Christian times and who had rejected the version of the Jewish Torah accepted by the temple priesthood of their day. They therefore conform to what we know of the Sampsaeans and Nazarites of earlier times, and we can be confident in asserting that they, like their forebears, also reverenced the patriarchs, rejected all prophets after Moses, and believed in a 'hidden' teaching. They were worshippers of the Aten and secretly carried within their sect Akhenaten's occult teachings and a cult of the head.

It is now widely acknowledged that the famous phrase 'Jesus of Nazareth' is in fact a mistranslation of the Greek 'Jesus the Nazarene' or 'Nazorean', which many authorities take as being cognate with Nazarite. Nor is this the only fact that suggests a Nazarite affiliation for Jesus. After his execution, it was his brother James the Just (who has been clearly identified as a Nazarite) who took over the leadership of the early 'Christians', who were known as Nazoraei. That a Nazarite led a group known as Nazoraei is surely suggestive that the two terms were identical. These new Nazarites were equally dedicated to the Jewish God Adonai. They regarded themselves as Jews, were circumcised, kept the dietary laws and religious feast days and worshipped in the temple. Later, the followers of James were also known as Ebionites, a name much misunderstood (Epiphanius regarded the teachings as originating with a certain Ebion) but which translates as 'The Poor'.[11] This may explain one of the 'dark sayings' of Jesus, comments that have withstood our understanding for nearly two millennia. In the Sermon on the Mount, the beatitudes include the phrase 'Blessed be ye poor, for yours is the kingdom of God' (Luke 6: 20). If 'the poor' are in reality 'The Poor', that is the group of Nazarites which included James the Just, then the saying at last makes sense, as what Jesus is really saying is that those who follow the way of the Nazarite/Ebionite will find salvation. For Jesus to say this and not be himself a Nazarite is highly unlikely and, given the weight of evidence in favour, we are quite justified in regarding Jesus as a member (if not the leader) of the Nazarite community. In passing, it should also be mentioned that when the Jews accused the recently converted Paul (St Paul) and brought their case before Felix, the Roman procurator (Acts 24: 5) Paul was an acknowledged 'ringleader of the sect of the Nazoraei'.

In the Nazarites we can see the true spiritual descendants of Akhenaten, reverencing the patriarchs and regarding all prophets after Moses/ Akhenaten as of no account; initiates of an occult teaching, holding to a secret doctrine kept hidden from the general population; worshipping the sun as a symbol of the Cosmocrator, the ultimate reality of the universe; forbidden to cut their hair; and regarding the head as sacred. And a group to which Joseph, Judah, Samuel, Samson, John the Baptist, Jesus and his brother James all belonged. This cult can be accurately described as the 'sect of the holy head'; and if my theory was correct, it took the heads of their most revered leaders, embalmed them and used them in its most secret rituals. And Jesus had been one of them, a high-ranking member of the Nazarites. I was not at all sure that I liked the direction in which my researches were leading.

6

The Heretic Tribe

The Nazarites did not belong to any single clan or tribe. According to their tradition, any member of the Children of Israel, if they would undertake the discipline, could vow themselves to Adonai in this way. The only requirement was that the Nazarite had to be a Jew. But my research had now revealed a much more specific blood-link – the tribe of Benjamin was more implicated in the ritual of head worship than any distinct kin-group among the Hebrews. And the tribe of Benjamin proved distinct in other extremely suggestive ways. During the time of the Descent of the Israelites into Egypt, their ancestor Benjamin had opportunities to become closely associated with the Egyptian court and its many deities. In fact, as we will see in Chapter 9, the Benjamite bloodline became linked directly to the lineage of the pharaohs of Egypt, and to one king in particular, to Akhenaten the 'heretic pharaoh'. And finally, it had been the tribe of Benjamin that, many years after the Exodus, had been forced out of Palestine by the rest of the Children of Israel and, after a long period of migration, had apparently finally settled in Europe.

The Benjamites

The people of the tribe of Benjamin were the descendants of Benjamin, brother to Joseph 'the Nazarite', who was sold into slavery in Egypt by his ten brothers. This statement is not entirely true, because Joseph's father, Jacob, had sired children on more than one wife. At the time of his abduction and sale, Joseph was the only child of Jacob by his wife Rachel. This would have set Joseph apart from his fellow 'brothers' from the time of his birth. Compounding the problem, Jacob seems to have favoured Rachel over his other wives. He made no secret that he regarded Joseph as his favourite son – 'the son of his old age' – and it was to Joseph that Jacob gave the famous 'coat of many colours'. As the Bible relates, this was one of the main sources of friction between Joseph and the rest of Jacob's sons and the reason for his being sold as a slave.

Far from suffering forever in the land of Egypt, Joseph, after being thrown into prison on the false charge of attempting to seduce his owner's wife, eventually prospered in his new home. Joseph is said to have correctly interpreted the pharaoh's famous dream of the seven full and empty ears of corn and the seven fat and thin cows, which Joseph stated was a warning of seven good harvests to be followed by seven years of famine. In gratitude, pharaoh raised him to the position of vizier, and set him over the land of Egypt. It was a position of immense power, second only to the king himself. The Bible has pharaoh say, 'Thou shalt be over my house, and according unto thy word shall all my people be ruled: only in the throne shall I be greater than thou' (Exodus 41: 40).

This bestowal of such an exalted rank upon Joseph always seemed to me out of all proportion to the service Joseph had performed. In fact, a little thought will show that, when pharaoh raised Joseph to this position, he could have had no idea if the 'slave's' interpretation of his dream was correct. Its veracity could only be fully vindicated after the passage of a further fourteen years. Had pharaoh bestowed the position of vizier on Joseph after these fourteen years (or even after eight years when, following the seven full years, the first of the seven lean years Joseph had predicted would have begun) then the story would hold together. But none of this applies; we are asked to believe that pharaoh raised Joseph to this, the highest of positions, simply because the *idea* of Joseph's interpretation appealed to him! This is so unlikely that we cannot seriously believe the biblical account here – there have to be other factors involved in Joseph's sudden promotion to so high a rank in the Egyptian hierarchy. As Chapter 9 discusses in more detail, there is much to suggest that the biblical version of events withholds some of the main factors in the story and that there was indeed another secret and (to the minds of the Jewish scribes) shameful reason for Joseph's elevation to such an exalted position.

Joseph had only one full brother, Benjamin (who gave rise to the Benjamites), both of them deriving from the union of Jacob and Rachel. Benjamin had been born only after Joseph was sent as a slave to Egypt and the two brothers had never set eyes on each other (in fact, Benjamin believed Joseph had been killed long before he was born). We know from the Bible that Benjamin had taken the place of Joseph in his father's affections: Jacob is loath to have the only remaining son of his favourite wife go down with the rest of his sons into Egypt during the time of famine. An indication of Joseph's feelings towards the brother he had never seen is when, in Egypt, Joseph confides to Benjamin alone the secret of his true identity, that the Egyptian name by which the Canaanites know him is not his true name, and that he is in reality, his 'long-dead' brother, Joseph.

Isis

As Joseph's only full brother, Benjamin would clearly have been closest of all in his affections (in addition, he had not been born at the time of Joseph's sale into slavery and, unlike Joseph's remaining half-brothers, did not share in any way the guilt over this episode in his brother's life). Given this, it is inconceivable that Joseph did not involve him closely with his life at court. It is here, I believe, that Benjamin, and through him his descendants, were exposed to far more than the seeds of Akhenaten's new religion. They also absorbed the secrets of the ancient gods of Egypt, in particular Isis, the Egyptian version of the Great Mother Goddess.

Isis was originally a deity of the Egyptian delta, but over time her cult gradually increased in popularity until ultimately she had absorbed almost all other Egyptian goddesses. She was the sister-consort of Osiris, god of the dead, and was renowned for her incantations and powers of magic. When her other brother, Seth, murdered Osiris and cut him into fourteen pieces, Isis patiently searched and gathered together the remains of her beloved husband. Then, for the first time in the history of mankind, she performed the rites of embalment which re-established her husband's immortality.[1] But most importantly, just prior to performing this resurrection, Isis had lain with the dead Osiris and conceived a son, Horus. However, as the only part of her dismembered husband that Isis had failed to find was his phallus, this insemination was a magical one, a motif that echoes other stories of gods and men born without recourse to physical intercourse. As Osiris was dead when Horus was conceived, Isis was actually a widow when she was magically impregnated. This made Horus the 'Son of the Widow' – a phrase that was to resurface much later in my investigation with a startlingly new interpretation.

Isis was often portrayed with the infant Horus in her arms, and such figures bear an uncanny resemblance to Christian statues of Mary and the infant Jesus. Indeed, many of the 'Black Virgins' found in medieval churches and cathedrals (often with Templar associations) have been identified as statues of the goddess. Pierre Plantard de Saint Clair, a grand master of the enigmatic Priory of Sion – a mysterious cabal who appear to be in possession of much information concerning the origins of the Knights Templar – is insistent that the Black Virgins be identified with Isis, and gives her the name Notre Dame de Lumière (Our Lady of Light). This implies that the very term 'Notre Dame' (the title of many Christian places of worship) should be interpreted as symbolising not the Virgin Mary, but Isis. Strangely enough, the epithet Queen of Heaven, used by the Catholic Church for the Virgin Mary, is likewise identical to one of the titles used for Isis.

Isis was often represented as a female carrying upon her head a throne (which is the ideogram for her name). Sometimes she has a headdress of cow's horns with a sun disc set between; less frequently she bears a cow's head on a human body. This has been interpreted as showing that, at the time such representations were made, Isis was identified with Hathor, the cow-goddess whom Egyptian mythology credited with creating the whole world, including the sun. However, the Roman historian Plutarch gives another intriguing explanation.[2] His story tells that Osiris' son Horus planned revenge on his uncle Seth, the murderer of his father. But Isis tried to intercede for Seth who, though a murderer, was still her brother. In righteous rage Horus turned on his mother, and cut off her head. Thoth, the god of wisdom, used his magic to save Isis, but the goddess's head was left in its severed state, and Isis was given the head of a cow instead. It is because of this celestial beheading that the cow is now sacred to Isis.

The cow, bull or calf turns up in many of the cultures linked with our investigations. It is noteworthy that, like the worship of Isis, the veneration of Belial in Palestine was allied with bulls, cows and calves, and that in Ireland, the animal was also sacred. The *Scotichronicon* records that, chief amongst the gods that the Scoti came to worship were Isis and the sacred bull of Apis. In addition, the backsliding of the Hebrews that Moses faced in the wilderness centred around their worship of a golden calf. It seems likely that the golden calf (symbol of Isis and Belial) was a specifically Benjamite idol, a supposition that is greatly strengthened by the biblical account of a war fought between Benjamin and the other eleven Jewish tribes.

The Outcast Tribe

The story of the tribe of Benjamin's conflict with the rest of the Children of Israel is told in Judges 19–21. It begins when a Levite (a man of the hereditary priestly caste) is returning to his home on Mount Ephraim with his concubine. Forced by the onset of night to seek shelter, he dismisses the chance of staying in Jerusalem, the Benjamite capital, and instead seeks lodgings in Gibeah, another Benjamite town. An old man of Gibeah offers them a place in his house and while they are enjoying his hospitality, 'certain sons of Belial' surround the house, demanding that the stranger be brought forth, and apparently intending to commit group sodomy upon him. In an unheard of display of hospitality, the host offers his virgin daughter as a substitute, but the sons of Belial refuse, only relenting when the Levite decides to give them his concubine. The unfortunate woman is raped repeatedly throughout the night and is found the next morning, dead on the threshold of the old man's house. The sons of Belial have apparently sought diversion elsewhere by this time, and the Levite is free to take his dead concubine's body back to his house on Mount Ephraim. Here, in a particularly gory episode, he proceeds to cut her body into twelve portions. He sends the dismembered pieces 'into all the coasts of Israel', presumably to all twelve tribes, with a message relating the crime that had been committed and asking for aid in punishing the miscreants.

Strangely, when the rest of the Children of Israel ask the Benjamites to give up the rapists so that they could be punished, the Benjamites side with the 'sons of Belial' and are prepared to fight their kinfolk rather than submit. The rest of the Hebrews are loth to war against their blood relatives but, having asked before the Ark of the Covenant if they should prosecute the war, they are commanded by God to proceed against them. After several setbacks, the eleven tribes emerge victorious, the Benjamites are overcome and their cities laid waste and burned. It must have been a particularly bitter and merciless campaign, as only six hundred Benjamite warriors are said to have remained alive in Israel at the end of the war. It appears that their women and children had all been put to the sword, for the rest of the Jews (who had sworn an oath not to give any of their womenfolk as wives for the Benjamites) took great pains in planning how to provide new mates for these last six hundred Benjamite males, so that the tribe should not become extinct in Israel.

The Benjamites may have been decimated in Israel, but other accounts (notably one of the *Secret Documents* of the Priory of Sion) tell that a number of the defeated tribe left Palestine, perhaps in company with their allies the sons of Belial, and took ship for Greece, landing in the region known as Arcadia.[3] Legends from Greece also tell a similar tale, of Danaus, son of King Belus, who brought his daughters to Greece. They apparently landed in Arcadia, as they are said to have brought with them the religion of the Great Mother, to whose worship the inhabitants of the area became almost obsessively dedicated. In his *Greek Myths*, Robert Graves 'decodes' this myth as indicating that 'colonists from Palestine' migrated to the Peloponnesian peninsula, and that King Belus is to be identified not as a physical king, but as the god Baal, or possibly Belial, one of the names for the Great Mother, who was known in Egypt as Isis.[4]

This seemed to imply that the Benjamites were 'Jewish heretics', worshipping a male Adonai, but also a feminine aspect of the deity in the form of Isis. By this time, it seems Akhenaten's concept of the Aten as an ineffable force that vivified the universe had come to be seen by most Jews in terms of a heavenly All-Father, a definitely masculine god. It may be that, in worshipping both masculine and feminine aspects of the deity, the Benjamites were actually remaining truer to Akhenaten's original concept of an all-encompassing deity than the paternalistic orthodox Judaism of their day. Whatever the truth of this, the Benjamite 'heresy', the worship of Isis (known in Palestine as Belial) could not be tolerated by the strict monotheistic Jews who comprised the majority at that time, and for whom worship of their version of Adonai (Aten) was the only permissible religion.

The loathsome behaviour of the sons of Belial may be the biblical editor's attempt to disguise the true reason for the conflict, while still indicating the (for him) guilty parties. If the Benjamites worshipped Belial then it may be that the sons of this goddess were not allies of the tribe of Benjamin as the Bible implies, but were, in fact, the Benjamites themselves. In short, the sons of Belial may be another name used by the biblical editors for the Benjamites themselves. And the apparently incomprehensible decision of a Jewish tribe to fight a hopeless war to defend the pagan sons of Belial against overwhelmingly superior numbers becomes considerably more understandable. The Benjamites were not fighting for a neighbouring tribe or allies, but for themselves and the survival of their religion.

It was time to take stock of what we had learned. Benjamin, as Joseph's favourite brother and closest kin, is likely to have been granted access to the Egyptian mysteries that were forbidden to Joseph's ten half-brothers who had sold him into slavery. Of all the Egyptian pantheon, Isis, the Great Mother, would have been perhaps the most attractive new deity to a stern, male-orientated society such as the Hebrews, and the Benjamites had become followers of the goddess. There had been a religious war fought between the Isis/Belial-worshipping Benjamites and the rest of the Jewish nation. The Benjamites lost the battle and, in the nature of religious wars, great slaughter had been made upon the vanquished. For them, the conflict ended in the decimation of their tribe and the emigration of most of its members to Arcadia at the southernmost tip of the Greek mainland. So, it appeared now that there had been a bifurcating of the secret tradition in Israel, with some followers of the sacred head rituals remaining in Israel, while the Benjamite initiates had for the most part fled to Greece.

Spartan Links

There was further evidence that Jewish immigrants had settled in the Arcadian region. In the Jewish apocryphal book, Maccabees 2, it is said that a company of Jews 'having embarked to go to the Lacedaemonians (Spartans), in hope of finding protection there because of their kinship', actually landed in Sparta (2 Maccabees 5: 9). In the first book of Maccabees, the ties of blood are spelt out even more clearly: 'It has been found in writing concerning the Spartans and the Jews that they are brethren and are of the family of Abraham' (1 Maccabees 12: 21).

The Spartans lived at the extreme south of the Peloponnese, the peninsula that forms the southern part of Greece. Their state was characterised by extreme militarism, with defective children being put to death at birth and boys entering military training at the tender age of seven. But what excited me was an unusual habit of these Jewish immigrants. Like the Nazarites, the Spartans regarded their hair as sacred and they, too, were forbidden to cut it. Like Samson and John the Baptist, like Jesus and his brother James, they accorded occult importance to the length of their hair; for them it 'denoted their physical vigour and became a sacred symbol'.[5]

The similarity with the Nazarite cult was striking. Again and again, over a time period that extended at least a thousand years, the taboo against cutting the hair, the sacredness of the hair, had been emphasised by apparently disparate groups. Yet all these groups ultimately traced their descent to the Exodus from Egypt, to the figure of Moses/Akhenaten. Was there, I wondered, something more to all this? The laws of the Nazarites had given me a vital clue and allowed a more acute perception of what was actually at the root of the prohibition on hair-cutting: throughout the centuries the hair had been revered not for itself, but as an extension and a symbol of the sacred head, the house of the soul and the seat of the divine. In the sacred hair of all these interlinked groups, I was looking at the outward symbol of the ancient religion of the head that had had its origin in Akhenaten's Egypt.

The more I researched, the more likely this became. In the history of the Spartans I traced a reference to King Cleomenes, who ruled jointly with a second king, in the Spartan manner. Cleomenes possessed a sacred head with occult powers, the head of Archonides, which he had preserved in honey. At times of crisis, Cleomenes removed the head of Archonides and used it in oracular rites, believing that the head could inform him of the future and maintain his good fortune.

This was a further link in the chain, and one that allowed me to discern another reason for the persistence of the worship of the severed head. If the head was the seat of the divine, then the deity could perhaps be persuaded to speak and reveal the future or in some other way bestow advice and good fortune upon the possessor of the head. Such concepts reminded me irresistibly of those powers attributed to the Templar sacred head, the Baphomet. The similarity of Cleomenes' beliefs to those held by the Templars towards their own sacred head is remarkable, and surely more than mere coincidence.

Could there be a connection?

Obviously, what was required was some link between these migrant Jews who had left their homeland and migrated to the Peloponnese, and the Templars of the tenth century AD. This was a gap of more than one thousand years. Could it be bridged? Was there anything to link these two apparently disparate groups, so widely separated in space and time?

Once again, the tortuous history of the Benjamites seemed to provide an answer. According to the *Secret Documents* of the Priory of Sion, having settled in Arcadia for several generations, the Benjamites took part in the general westward migration of peoples towards western Europe. They are said to have headed north at first, then followed the Danube west into Germany. This is a quite plausible scenario: many other groups were moving westwards at this time, impelled by the flow of peoples issuing out of the Asian steppelands. And the Danube, as the only major river system to run across Europe from west to east, has long been an artery for travel and migration. In the eleventh century the northern crusaders used the river as a route to Byzantium, and the Ottoman Turks travelled in the reverse direction when, in 1529, Suleiman the Magnificent led his forces westwards to the very gates of Vienna.[6]

The Benjamites would undoubtedly have come into conflict with other groups as they travelled, and may often have had to compete for scarce resources, or fight their way through settled areas. The harsh circumstances of migration would have forced them to enter into unions and alliances with other non-Jewish clans and tribes. They did apparently intermarry with other migratory peoples, and appeared as the Sicambrians in western

Europe in what is now Germany. The Sicambrians were a mixed Celtic/Teutonic tribe, a testament to the high degree of 'interbreeding' between the tribes (which, if the 'Priory Documents' are to be believed, included a large admixture of Judaic blood from the wandering Benjamites). The territory of the Sicambrian Franks was on the present-day borders of Germany and France, along the east side of the Rhine, and they settled here for several generations. Eventually, during the fifth century AD, they crossed the Rhine and conquered a huge part of the Gallic heartland under their monarchs, the mysterious line of priest-kings and magicians, the Merovingians.

It came perhaps as no surprise that this royal line held to an inviolable taboo, one which was followed above all other traditions. The Merovingians had a prohibition on the cutting of the hair, which was held to be sacred.

7

The Magician Kings

Apart from the *Secret Documents* of the Priory of Sion, there is a frustrating shortage of information on the origins of the Merovingian dynasty. Unlike Akhenaten, Moses, and the story of Gaythelos and Scota, we have no ancient writings, no chronicles that assert a Judaic origin for this group, no legend or fable which claims that they were descended ultimately from the Benjamites who are said to have left Israel. We have the word of the Priory of Sion (whoever this shadowy group may ultimately turn out to be) and nothing else. Except, that is, for two faint clues. There was, firstly, the Merovingians' own strange assertion that they were descended from the Trojans.[1] This places their hypothetical ancestors in the same geographical region as the exiled Benjamites. And, as ancient Greek writings claimed that Troy was founded by settlers from Greece, the concepts of Greek Benjamites and Trojan Merovingians may not be as far apart as they first appear. Then there was the link between the hair-cutting taboo of the other Judaic groups I had been studying, and the same taboo which existed among the Merovingian kings.[2] It was little enough to go on, but it did seem to constitute a slender thread which, if followed, might lead to additional discoveries and hopefully allow us to decide if we could put any trust in the idea that the Benjamites had survived the vicissitudes of their exile and finally emerged in France as one of the most enigmatic of all the European royal houses.

The Franks were a group of Germanic people who irrupted from Germany, crossed the Rhine and entered France, sometime in the fifth century AD. They had been in communication with Roman civilisation for more than one hundred years and as a result were not the wild, wood-dwelling barbarians that some authors have portrayed. At the same time, neither were they entirely civilised. Although secular literacy was encouraged, and Merovingian artisans produced beautiful trade goods, the twin martial 'virtues' of war and raiding were still regarded as legitimate ways of extending the group's territory or of filling the coffers of the king. The concept of the blood feud or vendetta was strong; kinship remained crucial and it was a man's duty to avenge his kin at all hazards, even though common sense and cold *realpolitik* would have cautioned otherwise. Such feuds often involved large numbers of people; they took in every stratum of society, including the king and his family, and they could last for generations.

One story, told by the principal chronicler of Merovingian times, Gregory of Tours, tells of two friends, Sichar and Austregisil, who are feasting with their family and friends when the servant of a local priest arrives unexpectedly and invites them to his house.[3] Presumably under the influence of too much drink, Austregisil takes exception to this generous invitation and kills the servant, thereby initiating a feud between Sichar and himself.

The next we hear, Sichar and his followers are lying in wait for Austregisil at the nearby church, but Sichar is bested in the ensuing fight and flees to his home, leaving behind four wounded servants and a quantity of goods. Austregisil kills all Sichar's wounded followers, before carrying away the goods as plunder.

A tribunal is called, and Austregisil is adjudged guilty of murder and theft. Reparations are agreed but before these are paid Sichar hears that Auno, a kinsman of Austregisil, is enjoying the use of the property Austregisil plundered. He renews the feud with a surprise onslaught at the dead of night in which Auno and Austregisil are killed. Sichar then retreats to his home, carrying with him the spoils of his victory. For this act of violence Sichar is required by a second tribunal to pay composition (reparations) to Chramnesid, the son of Auno. Chramnesid, however, refuses to accept either gold or goods in compensation for his dead father and instead destroys Sichar's house and rustles his cattle. Yet another tribunal judges that Sichar should pay only half the composition originally offered. This is now accepted and, honour apparently satisfied on both sides, the antagonists swear solemn vows that the feud is at an end. 'And,' says Gregory of Tours, with palpable relief, 'an end was made of the altercation.'

But the roots of the blood feud ran deep in Frankish veins. Several years after this, Chramnesid and Sichar are feasting together, their old enmity seemingly forgotten and apparently firm friends. Sichar jokes that Chramnesid should thank him for his good fortune, for if he had not killed his

relatives Chramnesid would not have received the handsome compensation that allows him to live so well. In reply, Chramnesid snuffs out
the candles and crushes Sichar's skull, striking him dead on the spot.
Then, as required by the traditions of feud (which demanded that acts of
vengeance should not be secret, but should be openly displayed) he hangs
Sichar's body from a fence before fleeing to King Childebert and throwing
himself upon his mercy. Despite the recent murder, Childebert rules in his
favour and, in an act which signifies the power and status of the Merovingian kings, 'by the voice of the king' the feud is finally brought to an end.

Childebert's decision seems enlightened and even lenient to our modern
ears, but Merovingian kings themselves were just as prone to vendetta and
blood feud as any other Germanic group, despite their possible Judaic
pedigree. Their feuds are the stuff of opera or sometimes of soap opera.
The most celebrated feud involved the entire royal house and continued
for three generations. It began when the king, Chilperic, allegedly suf-
focated his Visigothic wife Galswintha, apparently at the instigation of
one of his mistresses, Fredegundis. Chilperic wished to keep the death
quiet, in the hope of retaining Galswintha's sizable dowry. But Chilperic's
brothers discovered the deed and plotted to remove him from the throne
and (because Merovingian princes were as prone to self-interest as anyone
else) to seize the dowry and divide it between them. They were encouraged
by Brunechildis, the sister of the murdered woman, who hated Fredegundis
with a cold, undying fury, and seems to have kept the feud simmering
when everyone else would have let it quietly be forgotten. At the same
time the Visigothic king was also clamouring for vengeance against Fredegundis, but Chilperic refused to give up his mistress to certain death
and the feud rolled on towards its next round of killing, which included
Chilperic himself. At one point, a Merovingian participant, Guntramm,
the brother of Chilperic (who had just been murdered) swears to pursue
the kinfolk of one of his foes 'in nonam generationem' – to the ninth
degree of relationship. The unforgiving, wide-ranging and ruthless nature
of the vengeance extracted on both sides is appalling to twentieth-century
minds but is absolutely characteristic of the blood feud in Merovingian
times (and indeed beyond). Equally strange, to modern eyes, is that
Guntramm knew of his brother's crimes and that Chilperic undoubtedly
deserved his grisly fate, but this in no way relieved Guntramm of his duty
to follow the feud to the bitter end. There is a tragic inevitability about
the entire story. It was also debilitating and time consuming; as much as
anything else, it was the tradition of the blood feud that was to weaken
the Merovingian dynasty and contribute to its eventual downfall.

Fantastic Beginnings – Fabled Ancestors

The line of the Merovingians was royal long before the Sicambrian Franks crossed the Rhine and settled in Gaul. Like Athena's birth from the head of Zeus, the family seem to have emerged fully formed, their regal status generally acknowledged, and apparently with an exalted and altogether mysterious pedigree. This stemmed in part from the parents of Merovech (or Merovée), the king who gave his name to the dynasty. Tradition relates that, during a warm summer's day, Merovech's mother, the wife of King Clodio, went to bathe in the sea when she was already carrying the infant Merovech in her womb.[4] Here she was violated by a Quinotaur, an enigmatic sea-creature, which mystically inseminated her a second time so that, when her child was born, two separate bloodlines were united in the young prince. (That the beast is described as a Quinotaur may be important: like the minotaur, the bull-headed monster of legend, the 'taur' of Quinotaur also speaks of a bull connection. And, as we have seen, the bull or calf was sacred to the Benjamites. The mystical 'son' of the Qui-notaur is named Merovech and, intriguingly, at Heliopolis – that strong-hold of Aten worship – there was a sacred bull of Meroe.) The symbolic nature of this story is obvious, it is the interpretation of the symbols that is problematical: evidently, in Merovech was embodied two distinct and important bloodlines, one from his Frankish (and we may assume Benjamite) father, the other from some equally exalted family, somehow associated with, or perhaps coming from, the sea. But which family, and why should such importance be accorded it?

Of great importance in solving this enigma are other traditions that surrounded the Merovingian house. The descendants of Merovech claimed a further distinction of blood. Just as the high kings of Ireland claimed descent from the biblical King David through the marriage of Eochaid the Heremon to Tamar Tephi, daughter of King Zedekiah of Jerusalem, the descendants of the Merovingians believed that they were also descended from this august Hebrew king. If this is true, then the legend of Merovech's 'two fathers' is an allegory referring to the co-mingling of King Clodio's (Benjamite) bloodline with that of King David (the creature from the sea – or perhaps from across the sea – the Quinotaur).

Interestingly, a prior link between the two tribes can be shown. The first king over Israel was Saul, of the tribe of Benjamin. When Saul lost the favour of the king-maker, the prophet Samuel, David fought against Saul and eventually became king in his stead. But for a long time prior to this conflict, David was a favourite of Saul. He was allowed to enter the king's chamber, and would play the harp for Saul, to raise the king's spirit when he descended into one of his periodic depressive moods. After his victory over Goliath, David became inseparable from Saul's son, Jonathan. He lived and fought and even slept next to him. Though David was not a Benjamite, Saul treated him for a while almost as a foster son. It is at this time that David could well have been initiated into the Benjamite mysteries.[5]

But there was still the problem of how and when this co-mingling of the Benjamite bloodline with the House of David had been brought about. It was one thing to be descended from a 'lost' Jewish tribe but, if the hypothesis of the 'Merovingians as Benjamites' is true, then for around one thousand years the Benjamites were either in Greece, or struggling and fighting their migratory way across central Europe. Their chances of joining in a dynastic marriage with the House of David seem impossibly remote. Could there, I wondered, be other possible points of contact? Was there any time that the travels of a descendant of King David complied with the legendary origins of Merovech by 'crossing the sea'?

My first thought was the story of Tamar Tephi's escape to Ireland. She had been a descendant of the Davidic line, and may possibly have put in at a port in Greek Arcadia which, as we have seen, the Benjamites are said to have once made their temporary home, and which was also the land of the Spartans, who were 'linked by blood' with the Hebrew nation. Indeed, it speaks of a very strong link between the Irish and the Jews that Tamar Tephi did not also settle in Arcadia, in a land already peopled by a group related to her by blood, but instead chose to make the long and dangerous sea journey to the far northwest, presumably to a nation as, or more, closely related to her own. I reread the chronicles but, try as I might, I could find no reference to any landing by Tamar Tephi in mainland Europe. Besides, if she had put ashore, it would have been along the edge of the Mediterranean sea or on the coasts of Spain and France. Arcadia was the only chance she might have had of meeting with the Benjamites. And at the time of her travels the Benjamites (if the Priory of Sion is to be believed) would have already been deep in central Europe.

But the idea of a Davidic/Benjamite link may not be as far-fetched as it sounds. The resolution of the problem lies in the fate of the followers of Jesus after the crucifixion. There is a deafening silence in the Gospels concerning Jesus' friends and his immediate family after his death on the cross. This may be because the writers of the Gospels were more concerned with the message of Jesus than with his kinfolk. It may also be that they did not wish to acknowledge such a human dimension to Jesus' character, especially if, as some traditions insist, he was married and had sired children. However, if we are to believe in the idea of Jesus as a man living as other men then, married or not, his family and acquaintances were not simple abstractions, but real people. They did not disappear after Jesus' arrest. The ground did not simply swallow them up after the crucifixion. What happened to these folk? It is hardly likely that they stayed in Jerusalem in such traumatic times. Where did they go?

Mary Magdalene – A Second Exile?

Several ancient documents and legends record that Mary Magdalene, far from being the reformed harlot of Catholic tradition, was in fact the wife of Jesus. Others state that she was of high birth, perhaps even of royal blood herself.[6] Michael Baigent, Henry Lincoln and Richard Leigh have summarised the evidence that points to the truth of this tradition.[7] In essence, their argument is that the lack of information about Jesus' marital status in the New Testament argues for, rather than against, Jesus having been married. In the context of Jewish tradition at the time, had Jesus advocated and practised celibacy he would have drawn much attention upon himself and the authors of the Gospels could not have failed to commit this information to writing. Moreover, Jesus is named as 'Rabbi' or 'teacher' in many sections of the Gospels. This may have been an 'honorary title' given to a self-proclaimed orator and teacher of the people, but this is unlikely. The fact that the word translated as 'carpenter' in the Authorised Version of the Bible should more properly be rendered as 'scholar'[8] indicates that Jesus had received formal training and was a true rabbi (the normally hostile Jewish literature also supports this conclusion).[9] If so, Jesus must have been married: Mishnaic law demanded no less and made marriage a prerequisite for a rabbinical career: 'An unmarried man may not be a teacher.'[10] On this basis, and if Mary Magdalene was indeed Jesus' wife, it has been suggested that children could well have been born of that union, who would have carried on the bloodline of Jesus, and the royal line of David. As I was later to discover, there is a 'lost' reference to the children of Jesus in ancient Jewish writings, though its existence has never previously been acknowledged.

If the reality of Jesus' marriage and his having sired children is accepted, then following the crucifixion, the offspring of Jesus, as carriers of the bloodline, would have been of paramount importance. As the New Testament and other ancient texts record, Palestine at that time was a dangerous place for those associated with Jesus' teachings. Exile would be the safest option. And intriguingly enough, several ancient manuscripts record details of just such an exile, in a story that would place the Magdalene and Jesus' descendants in France, in the very location they 'ought' to be to make possible a union between the Merovingians and line of David.

In his book *The Coming of the Saints*, J. W. Taylor quotes from the Life of Rabanus, whose veracity the Latin Church accepted for over a millennium.[11] This tells that the Magdalene was set adrift in a boat off the coast of Israel by certain Jews. The tradition is quite detailed and records that thirteen other members of Jesus' entourage accompanied her: Lazarus, Joseph of Arimathea, Mary wife of Cleopas, Salome and her maid, Martha and her maid, and seven other men, Trophimus, Maximin, Cleon, Eutropius, Sidonius, Martial and Saturninus. These last were probably members of the 'seventy-two', the outer circle of disciples. Taylor also cites the Breviary of St Martha's Day (29 July), where a lection for the second nocturn describes how the Magdalene, with Lazarus, Martha and several others

... were seized by the Jews, placed in a boat without sails or oars, and [apparently with the aid of divine intervention] carried safely to the port of Marseilles. Moved by this remarkable fact, the people of the neighbouring lands were speedily converted to Christianity. Lazarus became bishop of Marseilles, Maximinus of Aix, Mary lived and died an anchoress on a high mountain of those parts.[12]

The conversion of the people of Marseilles to Christianity, recorded in this ancient text, is not quite as simple as it seems. As we will see later, the Christianity of Jesus was not yet the Christianity we know today, but simply a variant of orthodox Judaism. Both Jesus and his immediate followers regarded themselves as Jews, they were circumcised, worshipped in the temple and kept the Jewish feast days. The lection therefore records the conversion of many people in the south of France, not to orthodox Christianity, but to a form of Judaism. Intriguingly, it was in the south of France that, seven hundred years later, a Jewish kingdom was established under a king who was acknowledged in the same terms as Jesus, as a 'seed of the Royal House of David'.

In addition, Caesar Baronius, cardinal and historian, records in his *Ecclesiastical Annals* that, at about the same time that the Acts of the Apostles state that all of Jesus' followers, except the apostles, fled Judea (around AD 35):

Lazarus, Maria Magdalene, Martha, her handmaiden Marcella, Maximim a disciple, Joseph the Decurion of Arimathea, against all of whom the Jewish people had special reasons of enmity, were exposed to the sea in a vessel without sails or oars. The vessel drifted finally to Marseilles, and they were saved.[13]

So, the union of a Benjamite bloodline with one descended from the tribe of Judah and the House of David (more specifically, from the lineage of Jesus) was by no means impossible. In fact, given the testimony of the chronicles, it seemed to be a distinct possibility.

The Magician Kings

The linking of these two lines made Merovech, and the Merovingians who followed after him, in some way 'special'. Each one was said to possess a birthmark, a red cross, which was to be found either between the shoulders or over the heart, a sign which affirmed their sacred blood. The similarity of this mark to the red cross of the Templars has been commented on by several authors.

The Merovingians carried with them a reputation for occult powers: they were said to wear as a talisman a torque or necklace imbued with magical properties. Jean Hoyoux, a French scholar, believes that the words of St Remi when baptising Clovis as the first Christian Merovingian monarch – 'Mitis depone colla, Sicamber, adora quod incendisti, incende quod adorasti!' is in fact a request for the king to dispense with these magic necklaces which he had, until then, worn constantly.[14] Popular tradition endowed the Merovingians with a miraculous ability to dominate the natural world: they could communicate with animals and could change the weather. In an echo of Jesus and other holy men, they were said to possess healing powers and they could cure disease simply by the laying on of hands. Even the fringe of a Merovingian monarch's robes was considered a sure remedy for a variety of ailments. Gregory of Tours reports the story of a woman with a sick son who approached the king from behind and removed several tassels from the royal robe. She soaked them in water and gave the solution to her son to drink, and so cured him. Gregory, a bishop himself, is quite prepared to believe this story of magic (or miracle, depending on your point of view): he had on many occasions heard tales of demons being banished from the possessed by the simple expedient of invoking the monarch's name.[15]

If the healing powers of the Merovingians recalled the behaviour of Christian holy men, another aspect of their behaviour did quite the reverse. The Merovingian kings were addicted to the charms of the female of the species. Like the pharaohs and the biblical King David from whom they claimed descent, they practised polygamy on a sometimes lavish scale. Except for the occasional fulmination by a stern cleric (as when St Columbanus refused to tolerate Merovingian polygamy) the Church seems not to have dared to pursue this particular royal sin, even when they found time and energy roundly to condemn the practice among commoners and aristocracy alike. John Wallace-Haddrill, Fellow of Merton College, Oxford, commented on the curious tolerance of the Merovingian polygamous tradition in his book *The Long-Haired Kings*:

> Why was it tacitly approved by the Franks themselves? We may here be in the presence of ancient usage of polygamy in a royal family – a family of such rank that its blood could not be ennobled by any match, however advantageous, or degraded by the blood of slaves. The Merovingians saw no gain of prestige in their marriage alliances ... it was a matter of indifference whether a queen was taken from a royal dynasty, or from among courtesans or the unfree.[16]

But whose blood could command such great respect, could rise above the admixture of any other line, even the most royal? At first I was inclined to see the bloodline of Jesus, considered a god at the time of the Merovingians, as the reason for this exalted status. Later, I came to believe that Jesus and his descendants were important, but only as a link in a chain that (for those who were privy to the secret) stretched back to even more illustrious forebears. That it was, in short, the true ancestors of Jesus who were the wellspring of the mythic importance of the blood.

Judaic Links

Along with their legendary mystical powers and holy blood, the Merovingians also ascribed religious and occult importance to their hair. It symbolised the magic power of their royal race. Extant royal seals (of Theuderic III, Clovis III, Childebert III and Chilperic II) all without exception depict the monarch with flowing locks. This attribute above all others sets them apart from their contemporaries, and linked the long-haired kings to a Judaic origin, and to the cult of the severed head. Like Samson and other lesser-known Nazarites, like John the Baptist, Jesus and his brother James, and like the Spartans, the Merovingians never cut their hair. In a telling echo of the Nazarite cult, they believed that their hair contained their strength, their unique powers, and that to cut the hair was to desanctify the head from which it grew. The tragic story of two Merovingian princes symbolises this belief. When King Clodomir died, his two brothers, Clotaire and Clodil, coveting his lands, seized the dead king's two sons. Once the princes were safely in their power, the two 'wicked uncles' sent a messenger to the children's grandmother, Queen Clotilde, at her residence in Paris. The messenger carried with him a pair of scissors and a sword. He showed these symbols to Queen Clotilde, '... and bade her choose whether the children should be shorn and live or remain unshorn and die. The proud queen replied that if her grandchildren were not to come to the throne, she would rather see them dead than shorn.' The envoy returned and his message proved to be no empty threat. The two princes were murdered, and it was their merciless uncle Clotaire who himself did the deed.[17] That the choice was between a shorn head and death illustrates the powerful beliefs that lay behind the holy symbol of the Merovingian tresses: execution could be avoided by the simple expedient of cutting the hair. A king's death was not required to remove him from the throne, just a shorn head. This was shown when the last Merovingian king, Childeric III, was finally overthrown. The pope, a party to the usurpation, saw to it that the hair of Childeric III was cut from his head before immuring him in the monastery of Saint-Bertin.[18] In addition, perhaps to emphasise the loss of sanctity and power that was associated with the head of the Merovingian monarch, the head of the usurper, Pippin, was ritually baptised with the chrism of holy oil. This latter ceremony was a conscious emulation of the biblical anointing of Saul as king over Israel by the prophet Samuel.

A further clear Judaic link has been discovered deep in the complicated tracts that form Salic law, the tribal law that had governed the Franks from the earliest times, and that was finally codified in Merovingian times. Joseph Rabinowitz has shown that one section of this, Title 45, called De Migrantibus, is not derived from ancient Teutonic tribal law, as are most sections, but directly from the Talmud. That is, directly from the law, from the holy books, of the Jews.[19] How a group of Teutonic tribes had access to Talmudic teachings is a total mystery, in the face of which the Priory of Sion's tale of Benjamite migrants suddenly becomes far less incredible. Given the other evidence of a Judaic link presented above, the most likely explanation for the presence of De Migrantibus is that the Teutonic tribes had had access to Judaic writings, and more specifically the Talmud, at some time during the migratory period of the tribes. That an exiled Jewish tribe (the Benjamites) would be in possession of such texts is highly likely, and would provide an explanation for this otherwise unaccountable Judaic inclusion in the Salic law of the Franks.

Another find also spoke of the Judaic origins of the Merovingians, and again linked the dynasty with the Priory of Sion's records of a Benjamite connection. This was the discovery of the grave of an early Merovingian king, Childeric ɪ. Childeric ɪ stands between his legendary father Merovech, and his own son Clovis, a firmly historical character about whom much is known. His grave reflected this in a combination of the mystical and the pragmatic.[20] Unearthed in the tomb was a sword, helmet and other magnificent war gear, one hundred gold pieces and two hundred silver coins, a gold bracelet and buckles of fine workmanship, all firmly practical accoutrements of a normal Dark Age warrior king. But also interred with the body were objects of a decidedly more occult nature. A crystal ball was present, the traditional tool of the seer, allowing the initiated to scry the future. There was the severed head of a horse, beautifully caparisoned, and most telling of all the head of a golden calf or bull, an unmistakably Benjamite talisman.

Another unusual aspect of the grave goods has excited considerable scholarly comment: Childeric's cloak, which had been embroidered with three hundred winged insects, cast in pure gold. For some these are 'bees', for others 'cicadas'. They seem to have had some ritual significance: over twelve hundred years later, in 1804, Napoleon insisted on having the Merovingian 'bees' attached to his own coronation robe when, in another pointed reference to Merovingian times, he was crowned 'Emperor' not of France, but 'of the French' (or Franks). Most writers have accepted that the artifacts represent bees, though none has yet come up with a convincing reason why bees should have been of significance to the Merovingians. They are perhaps an oblique reference to Samson the Nazarite, whose riddle concerning the bees that made their home in the carcase of a lion he had killed ('out of the eater came forth meat, and out of the strong came forth sweetness' Judges 14: 14) is well known. But given the supposed history of the Merovingian/Benjamite line, cicadas may very well be the true identity of the gold figures. The lifecycle of cicadas involves a very long period of development underground. Some cicadas stay as long as seventeen years beneath the soil, slowly feeding and growing. Then they emerge from the earth and blossom into the beautiful, strident adult form.[21] It may be that the Benjamites and Merovingians saw in the cicada a symbol of their own existence. Banished from their homeland, their true worth unrecognised, they would, like the cicada, emerge one day, at just the right moment, to reveal to the world their true identity and to take back their rightful patrimony – Jerusalem and the land of the Jews.

Like David, the Hebrew king from whom they claimed descent, Merovingian kings were not merely earthly representatives of God's will; they were regarded by their contemporaries as priest-kings, as the living receptacle of God's spirit here on earth. Intriguingly (and ultimately of great significance to the trail we were following), the pharaohs of ancient Egypt enjoyed an equivalent status.[22] The Merovingian king might be a war leader, but he was also an almost godlike figure, whose responsibilities did not descend to the mundane ordering and running of government. This was left to the 'mayor of the palace', a position that corresponded closely to the vizier of Egyptian times. When the king was a strong and forceful character, the system seems to have worked well. But with the onset of a number of bloody feuds and internecine warfare between Merovingian states (brought about by the dynasty's tradition of sharing land equally among all the king's sons) the system suffered what was to prove to be terminal breakdown. Assassination and murder meant that a large number of Merovingian princes came to the throne at a very early age. They were easily controlled by unscrupulous mayors of the palace, who gradually subverted the governance of the country to their own advantage.[23] This is the time of the *rois faineant*, the 'do nothing kings', who were really no more than figureheads for the machinations of the palace mayors. Over time, more and more power accrued to the mayors of the palace. And, faced with weak and malleable kings, the mayors began to think the unthinkable, to wonder why they should be the effective rulers, and yet not be kings themselves. This was to lead, eventually, to the deposing of the Merovingians and their replacement by the Carolingians, the first of whom was Charlemagne, the grandson of a mayor of the palace who dared to act on his thoughts of greatness. But even before this, other attempts had been made to usurp the rightful place of the Merovingian kings.

Dagobert II

Dagobert II was one Merovingian who did not conform to the *rois faineant* mould. His father Sigebert died young and with little prestige, having been a spectacularly unsuccessful war leader. The succession to the throne was disputed by the mayor of the palace, Grimoald, and Dagobert was at first kidnapped, and then fled into exile.[24] His choice of refuge was significant – he is said to have fled to Ireland, to the Irish monastery of Slane,[25] one of the Christian monasteries and schools that had arisen directly from the druidic colleges of pagan Ireland. These colleges, just a century and a half before, had still been instructing devotees in the secret lore of the druids that, I believed, had descended in an unbroken chain from Akhenaten's teachings.[26] Dagobert is also said to have visited the high king of Ireland at his court in Tara, where the Stone of Destiny and the Bethel Stone had both been held before their transfer to Scotland. If he did not already know the stories of Gaythelos and Scota (and therefore the ultimate origins of both his own people and the Scoti in Egypt) it is inconceivable that Dagobert would not have learned the tale in Ireland. Subsequent events seem to indicate that (assuming he was not already privy to the secret), he also took something else away with him when he left Ireland – a knowledge of the cult of the head.

Dagobert was married twice, to Mathilde, a Celtic princess who gave him two daughters but died birthing their third, and to a Visigothic princess, Giselle of Razes, whom he married at Rennes le Château (a site to which the Priory of Sion attaches great importance). This alliance apparently provided him with the additional power and support he needed. In 674, Dagobert moved north out of Rennes le Château, revealed his lineage and took upon himself the title of his father, King of Austrasie. His reign was marked by an upsurge in the Merovingian fortunes. Giselle bore him two daughters and, finally, an heir to his throne, his son Sigisbert iv. The lineage, it seemed, was secure. And Dagobert proved himself an able leader; he did not shrink from confronting either the nobility or the clergy and within a very few years he had expanded his realm and built an efficient system of government. In doing so, he also made many powerful enemies who were determined to rid themselves of this strong king.

The chief conspirator was Peppin the Fat, Dagobert's mayor of the palace. On 23 December 679, Dagobert rode out to hunt in the forest of Woëvres. This ancient woodland had long been regarded as sacred and, given that the 'hunt' took place at the time of the winter solstice – the 'rebirth of the sun' – this may have been more than a pleasure trip and there may well have been some religious significance to the excursion. Peppin had earlier suborned one of Dagobert's servants, who crept up on the king as he rested, and lanced him through the eye with a spear, killing him instantly.[27] With the king dead, the conspirators then descended on the palace of Stenay, and butchered every member of Dagobert's family they could find, with the obvious intention of extinguishing the royal line completely.

Far from castigating what had been done, the Church upheld these hideous murders as exemplary deeds. Wilfrid of York, who had played a major role in engineering Dagobert's reinstatement, was sent a letter which attempts to excuse the murder on the grounds that Wilfrid had sent the Franks a king who:

> dissipator urbumconsilia seniorum despiciens, populos ut Roboam filius Salomonis tributo humilians, ecclesias Dei cum praesulibus contempnens
> (ruined cities, despised the counsel of the elders, like Rehoboam, son of Solomon had imposed taxes and treated the church of God with contempt)[28]

Reading between the lines it seems that Dagobert had set his face against a group of ecclesiastics and nobles (including Peppin the Fat) who effectively wished to rule his kingdom for him. When he proved not to be compliant, they had him removed. That the Church assisted in this is, however, remarkable. Many Dark Age bishops were no strangers to the realities of power, but to agree to regicide was almost unheard of. Was there something more behind this tale? Might there have been more than mere hyperbole, some hidden truth, in the Frankish prelate's claim that Dagobert 'treated the Church of God with contempt'? Might he have learned something during his stay in Ireland that (perhaps combined with information he already possessed) had led him to regard the Church with something approaching 'contempt'? Significantly, some time after his death, Dagobert's head was severed from his body and became the centre of a cult based around Stenay. The king's skull, ritually incised, survives, and is held in the convent of the Black Sisters at Mons.[29] Of great significance is the fact that the silver reliquary that holds Dagobert's skull has been formed in the shape of a chalice or grail – and the holy grail is later to form a central theme of our story.

Whatever the reason for the compliance of the Church in his assassination, and for the subsequent rise of his cult, with the murder of Dagobert his line disappears from history – and not just in terms of his lack of successors. In a strange echo of the story of Akhenaten, it appears that a concerted effort was made to remove him completely from the record of the Frankish kings; in effect to deny that Dagobert ever existed. His name was simply blotted out. Although other Merovingians were acknowledged, it was not until 1646 that Adrien de Valois was able to restore this lost king to history.

The Lost Kings

Although he became a non-person, the assassination and subsequent 'cover-up' may not have been the end of Dagobert's line. Once again, it is the Priory of Sion that takes up the story and provides the evidence. Their dossiers relate that not all of the royal house of Dagobert was murdered by the regicides. The king's young son, Sigisbert IV, was rescued by his sister and taken secretly to Razès, the home of his mother's family. There he seems to have been adopted by his uncle as, in or around 681, the documents record that he took upon himself the titles of Duke of Razes and Count of Rhedae, previously the titles of his uncle. Baigent, Leigh and Lincoln are inclined to believe the veracity of this account. They point out that the systematic attempt to remove Dagobert from history would have been unnecessary unless there had been an heir to his lineage: 'By denying his existence, any line of descent from him would have been invalidated'.[30] If there had no King Dagobert, then there could be no descendants of Dagobert to claim the throne. The parallels with ancient Egypt and the Priests of Amun's vengeance on Akhenaten are very strong and shed new light on the excision of Akhenaten from the Egyptian king lists. Apart from simple hatred and revenge, we may not be too far from the truth in ascribing similar motives, at least in part, to the attempts to eradicate the Amarna kings, and especially Akhenaten, from history. Put simply if Akhenaten never existed, he and his line could not have survived his downfall to linger on the sidelines of history as the rightful rulers of Egypt. This argues strongly for Akhenaten's survival after his disappearance from the historical annals.

Although there is a gap in other historical records, the Priory documents go on to claim that Sigisbert IV perpetuated his line and that his descendants married into a number of prominent families. They are especially at pains to mention Bernard de Plantavelu, in whom Sigisbert IV's line is said to have culminated towards the end of the ninth century. This is important, as Bernard de Plantavelu's immediate antecedents are known and they give great weight to the possibility that the Merovingian bloodline was, at least in part, Jewish. The first known ancestor of Bernard de Plantavelu was Theodoric, who is said to be of Merovingian descent, although none of his own antecedents have yet come to light. The link we are invited to make is that Theodoric was a direct lineal descendant of Sigisbert. This may well be the case; the circumstantial evidence is strong. Theodoric's son, Guillem de Gellone, was known as Count of Razes, a title very similar to that Sigisbert IV is said to have held after he fled south to escape the assassins of Peppin the Fat.

In 768 this same Theodoric became the ruler of Septimania, a Jewish principality in southern France that was created in a 'deal' between the Jews of Narbonne and Pepin, a descendant of Peppin the Fat who had been instrumental in the slaying of Dagobert. Pepin was another mayor of the palace and the *de facto* ruler of Merovingian lands. The Jews of Narbonne pledged Pepin their support against the Moors who were at that time threatening much of France, and received their own principality in return. When Theodoric died, his son Guillem de Gellone took his place. This scion of the Merovingian dynasty was accepted as being 'of the seed of the royal house of David' by Pepin, by at least one Muslim ruler (the Caliph of Baghdad) and, notwithstanding the embarrassment such acknowledgement must have caused, by the Roman Church itself.[31] If we accept that Theodoric was Merovingian (no real proof is yet extant as his ancestry is unknown) then in this Jewish king and his son Guillem is strong evidence that the Merovingians were regarded as Jewish, and of the royal House of Judah, by some very important contemporaries. The strength of this evidence is that these same contemporaries would, it is certain, gain no benefit from such an admission.

It appears that Guillem de Gellone's bloodline also intermarried with the Breton ducal house. This union gave rise in the fullness of time to one of the early Middle Ages' most intriguing figures – Godfroi de Bouillon, Duke of Lorraine. Several authors have now been able to confirm the Priory of Sion's account that Godfroi was instrumental in founding this enigmatic organisation, probably just before the launching of the first crusade.[32] In addition, it was the Order of Sion that (according to the *Secret Documents* of that group) was responsible for the inception of the Order of the Temple, that group of knights who appear to have been sent to Jerusalem with the express purpose of excavating for treasure of some sort beneath the Temple of Solomon. In addition, Godfroi's personal tutor was said to be Peter the Hermit, known for his charismatic preaching, and his insistence that it was the duty of all Christians to 'follow the cross' and to take back Jerusalem and the holy places from the 'infidel' Mohammedans. As Baigent, Leigh and Lincoln have noted, it seems that Peter the Hermit's 'preaching of a crusade might have been a manifestation not of rampant fanaticism, but of calculated policy'.[33] If so, the policy succeeded. The first crusade set out for Palestine, and within an almost miraculously short time, the Holy City had fallen to the Christian armies, Godfroi de Bouillon was the ruler of Jerusalem, and the Templars were beginning their work of excavating the tunnels below the Temple Mount.

In short, what has been promulgated in western history as a spontaneous upswelling of Christian zeal that swept along both commoner and noble alike, as an unpremeditated focusing of religious energies that resulted in the taking of Jerusalem, was in fact a carefully thought out conspiracy to return Jerusalem to its rightful owners, the Benjamite (and Davidic) bloodline that had culminated in Godfroi de Bouillon.

But there seems to have been more to it than the simple acquisition of land and titles. Godfroi de Bouillon had these already and yet, of all the crusaders leaving for the Holy Land, he alone gave up his right to his ancestral lands in Europe. But could the undoubted satisfaction felt in attempting to take back a long-lost patrimony possibly explain, or compensate for, the voluntary loss of all one's lands? Almost as soon as Jerusalem fell the Templars were formed, their sole *raison d'être* being to excavate beneath the Temple of Solomon. This spoke for the prior existence of a secret, perhaps known only to Godfroi de Bouillon and the members of a closed circle of initiates, perhaps the Priory of Sion, of something hidden centuries before below the Temple Mount. Given the ultimately Judaic connections of the Merovingians and their sacred hair, their association with magic and the cult of the head, I had a strong suspicion of what might have been hidden below the Temple. It was time to examine this enigmatic structure, first built almost two thousand years before the time of the Templars by the son of King David, Solomon, a man steeped in esoteric lore and renowned in history and legend as a magus of almost superhuman skill.

8

The Thrice Built Temple

The edifice that the Templars excavated early in the twelfth century was not the original Temple of Solomon. That building had been destroyed for over fifteen hundred years by the time the Christian crusader armies conquered Jerusalem. In all, there had been three Jewish 'temples', each built on the Temple Mount in Jerusalem: the Temple of Solomon, Zerubbabel's Temple and the Temple of Herod the Great. Each of them had been conceived with great piety, and designed with infinite care. Each was constructed at a terrible cost in human toil and labour, and built at immense expense, often plunging the king responsible heavily into debt. And each in turn had been conquered, looted or destroyed by successive invading armies.[1]

The Temple of Solomon

Solomon's temple was built in the middle of the tenth century BC (1 Kings 5–8). The Bible tells us that it was Solomon's father, King David, who first thought to build so magnificent an edifice in the city he had conquered from the Jebusites, the forerunners of the Benjamites. He wished to make it his capital city and had already brought the Ark of the Covenant to Jerusalem (2 Samuel 6: 16–17). Unfortunately, David's plans were thwarted when he was told by the prophet Nathan that, as a man who had shed the blood of others, it was not proper that he should build the House of God himself. The Lord required that the temple's construction be delayed – the honour of building it would be given to Solomon, David's son (2 Samuel 7: 13). David accepted this judgement, but we are told that it was he who held the plans for the temple, written in God's own hand, which he then passed on to his son and heir. (Moses is also said to have received instructions for the layout of the tabernacle – the tent where the Ark was kept during the Hebrews' time in the wilderness and the forerunner of the Jerusalem temple – from a plan shown to him by the Lord while he was on Mount Sinai.)

So the temple would be built. But who, or what, was to be worshipped here? The scriptural account tells us that it was Yahweh, but the story is not so clear as the Bible would have us believe. As ever in any religion, there were factions and sects among the Israelites. Some espoused the hard-line, puritanical teachings of Deuteronomy, which focussed on God alone, and accorded little importance to any royal line. They believed in God as an unseen, invisible presence, who made himself known by his voice alone. Others, followers of an equally (if not more) ancient tradition, believed otherwise. Their god could take human and physical form and appear to the elect of the human race. The 'Deuteronomists', inheritors of the puritanical view, were responsible for one of the two accounts given in the Bible of the temple and the monarchy, and they were not particularly charitable towards the king or his methods of worship. Indeed, certain aspects of the temple cult which did not find favour in their eyes, they simply omitted. As researcher Margaret Barker has pointed out, when reading the Deuteronomists' accounts (I & II Samuel and I & II Kings) 'we have always to bear their reforming zeal in mind ... Their view has come to be accepted as *the* view of what happened, and what they chose not to record is thought never to have existed. But there are other sources which give a significantly different view of Solomon's temple and its cult...'[2]

David's desire to build a temple to the Lord had been born of a vision he had on the eventual site of the temple, Mount Moriah. A destroying angel had appeared to him on the threshing floor of Ornan (or perhaps Araunah) the Jebusite, and it was here that the heavenly messenger commanded him that an altar must be built. This threshing floor was originally sacred to the god Tammuz, a harvest god who ritually died and was resurrected each year. Tammuz was another name for Adonis, whose name I was to discover was Syrian, and identical in meaning to the Jewish Adonai (My Lord). In other words, Adonis is the Syrian title of Aten.

There are two accounts of the construction of Solomon's Temple in the Bible, and they show marked differences in their treatment of the subject. This is in many ways fortunate, as it thereby gives us a little more information than a single account. The writer of Chronicles sees the temple as a glorious structure, and he spends two full chapters in a detailed description of the entire edifice, on the size of the building, how Solomon 'garnished the house with precious stones for beauty' and the huge quantities of gold that were lavished upon it, for even the nails that were used were made of gold 'and the weight of the nails was fifty shekels of gold'. The chronicler is obviously overawed by the splendour of the construction and he is also at pains to emphasise the wonderful music composed for it. By contrast, the Deuteronomist author of Kings is more concerned with the human cost of building the temple: eight thousand men toiled in the stone quarries; the labouring work was done by a further thirty thousand men pressed into the service of the king, and forced to work in Lebanon for one month in every three. And when it was all finished, twenty Galilean cities were forfeit to Hiram, the Phoenician king of Tyre, to cancel the debt incurred in the building of the temple (1 Kings 9: 11).

Whatever the cost of building, there is no doubt that the Temple of Solomon was an impressive structure, especially for the time it was built. It was constructed entirely of stone, and lined on the inside with the famous cedars of Lebanon, much of which was carved with cherubims and floral designs and all 'overlaid ... with fine gold'. There are no archaeological traces left of this temple, and scholarly opinion differs on its exact layout, but it is generally agreed that it conformed to the 'long house' type, twenty cubits wide and seventy long (1 cubit = 50.5cm). There were three divisions within this: the *ulam* or porch, which was ten cubits long, the *hekel* or temple, forty cubits in length, and the holy of holies, the *debir*, which was twenty cubits long. The *hekel* was thirty cubits tall, but the holy of holies was apparently raised above the level of the rest of the structure and stood over the sacred Great Rock. The *debir* formed a perfect cube, a symbol of perfection and a fitting place for the Ark of Covenant, the home of the god (1 Kings 6: 20). Here, in the inner sanctuary, were two cherubim, carved from olive wood and completely overlaid with gold. These cherubim were not the 'cherubic' cuddly infants beloved of Renaissance painters – they were 'power figures', guardians, composite creatures with men's faces, lions' bodies and eagles' wings. They were ten cubits high and their wingspan was also ten cubits so that, as they stood side by side they spanned the entire width of the *debir*, their outer wings touching the wall. The Ark was placed in the centre of the *debir*, beneath the protective cover of the outstretched inner wings of the cherubim. Significantly, these guardians of the god are of unmistakable Egyptian origin. In addition, we are told in Chronicles that King David told Solomon of his plans to build 'a golden chariot of the cherubim that spread their wings'. This chariot throne was actually built: in Isaiah, King Hezekiah speaks to the Lord as 'God of Israel, who art enthroned above the cherubim'

(Isaiah 37: 16). That the writer of Kings can omit this important part of the cult of Yahweh/Adonai indicates that he could quite easily have left out other details that did not fit his own preconceived ideas. As one prominent scholar has commented, the writer of Kings '... has omitted some significant details, and one wonders why'.

There was a single door to the temple and this, also significantly, faced east, towards the rising sun (echoing the sun temple raised by Moses/Akhenaten in Heliopolis). Before the door of the temple were two massive pillars, each said to be twenty cubits tall, and named Jachin ('to establish') and Boaz ('strength').

Zerubbabel's Temple

Solomon's Temple was destroyed by the Babylonian King Nebuchadnezzar in 586 BC when most of the Jews were taken into Babylonian exile. On their return, after a period of just under fifty years, King Zerubbabel commenced the rebuilding of the temple in 537 BC; this second temple was finally dedicated to the Lord in 515 BC (Ezra 6: 16–18). An ancient letter, written by Aristeas, a visitor to Palestine from Egypt, has left us a vivid description of the temple's appearance at the beginning of the second century BC:

> When we arrived in the land of the Jews we saw the city situated in the middle of the whole of Judea on the top of a mountain of considerable altitude. On the summit the temple had been built with all its splendour. It was surrounded by three walls more than seventy cubits (35.5 metres) high ... The temple faces east and its back is towards the west. The whole of the floor is paved with stones, and slopes down to the appointed places, that water may be conveyed to wash away the blood from sacrifices, for many thousands of beasts are sacrificed there on the feast days. And there is an inexhaustible supply of water, because an abundant natural spring gushes up from within the temple area.
>
> (Letter of Aristeas 83, 88–91)[3]

This imposing structure was overrun by the forces of the Syrian King Antiochus Epiphanes in 170 BC. An attempt to remove the temple treasure was made almost immediately by a representative of Antiochus, a certain Heliodorus, but celestial forces are said to have intervened to prevent this sacrilege: 'For there appeared to them a magnificently caparisoned horse, with a rider of frightful mien, and it rushed furiously at Heliodorus and struck at him with his front hooves' (2 Maccabees 3: 25).

Unfortunately, the heavenly rider seems to have been powerless in the face of the Syrian king himself. Antiochus visited Jerusalem in 169 BC and personally supervised the removal of the temple treasures. 'He arrogantly entered the sanctuary and took the golden altar, the lampstand for the light, and all its utensils. He took also ... the veil' (I Maccabees 1: 21). Not long afterwards, Antiochus rededicated the temple to Olympian Zeus. This sacrilege was halted three years later, in 164 BC, when the commander of the Israelite army, Judas Maccabeus, recaptured Jerusalem and ordered the temple's reconsecration to Yahweh/Adonai (I Maccabees 4: 36–59).

Just over a century later, in 63 BC the Roman legions under Pompey laid siege to Jerusalem. The Jews resisted bravely, but the city finally fell after three months of battle and privations. The temple itself was overwhelmed on the Day of Atonement, and the Romans gave no quarter. As the first-century historian Josephus has graphically described, even as the legionaries began to put the inmates of the temple to the sword, the priests continued their sacerdotal duties:

> Just as if the city had been wrapt in profound peace, the daily sacrifices, the expiations and all the ceremonies of worship were scrupulously performed to the honour of God. At the very hour when the temple was taken, when they were being massacred about the altar, they never desisted from the religious rites of the day.[4]

Pompey visited the temple almost immediately, and took the (to Jewish eyes) appallingly sacrilegious step of entering the sanctuary, something only the high priest was allowed to do, and then only on one day each year. What he saw must have impressed him deeply for, unlike Antiochus, he forbade any pillage of the temple and he commanded that it be purified, and that the sacred rites should recommence as soon as possible.

The Temple of Herod the Great

The third temple was essentially the second temple, expanded and rebuilt by Herod the Great in 20 BC. Josephus has left us an idealised account of its construction:

> He prepared a thousand wagons to carry the stones, selected ten thousand of the most skilled workmen, purchased priestly robes for a thousand priests and trained some as mason, others as carpenters ... he erected the temple which was a thousand cubits in length ... and twenty more in height, but in the

course of time this dropped as the foundations subsided ...

... the entrance doors, which with their lintels were equal in height to the temple itself, he adorned with multicoloured hangings with purple colours and with interwoven designs of pillars. Above these, under the cornice, spread a golden vine with grape clusters hanging from it, a marvel of size and artistry ... And he surrounded the temple with very large porticoes ... and he surpassed his predecessors in spending money so that it was thought that no one else had adorned the temple so splendidly ... And it is said that during the time when the temple was being built, no rain fell during the day but only at night, so that there was no interruption of the work.[5]

The outer courtyard of Herod's temple was a walled enclosure some 240 metres square. Within this first courtyard was the 'court of women', given this title because it was forbidden to women to enter any closer to the holy of holies. The court of women led to two areas of increasing holiness, the court of Israel and the court of the priests. These were, in essence, a single space, for the court of Israel was merely a slender area of land at the entrance of the court of the priests, and divided from it by a low balustrade and two steps. Above the court of the priests was the temple proper and the altar upon which burnt offerings were made. According to Josephus, the altar stood directly in front of the temple. It was 'fifteen cubits high and with a breadth and length extending alike to fifty cubits, in shape a square with horn-like projections at the corners ... No iron was used in its construction, nor did iron ever touch it'.[6]

This was the temple that still stood in Jerusalem in Jesus' time, and was only fully completed in AD 66. Four years later it was destroyed by the Roman legions under Titus.[7] It was the faint ruins of this third and last temple which, over one thousand years later, saw the arrival of the Templars and beneath whose foundations they began their enigmatic mining operations.

The Foundation Stone

On the threshing floor where the first temple was built there was a great rock. It was of great significance to the Jews, who knew it in later years as the *eben sh'tiyyah*, the Foundation Stone. They believed that all 'the waters under the earth' were brought together beneath the Temple Mount, and that it was essential that this great force be controlled: there had to be sufficient water to ensure the vitality of nature and the growth of crops, but not so much that a second flood might result. A story in the Babylonian

Talmud recounts how, in the time of King David, 'the Deep' began to increase and threaten a second flood. David asks if it is lawful to write the Name (of God) and to drop it into the waters. He is given permission to do so.

> David inscribed the Name upon a sherd, cast it into the Deep, and it subsided sixteen thousand cubits ... he said 'The nearer it is to the earth the better the earth can be kept watered' and he uttered the fifteen Song of Ascents and the Deep reascended fifteen thousand cubits and remained at one thousand cubits
>
> (b. *Sukkah* 53b)

There are several such stories illustrating the importance of the king in controlling this immense power, and other forces of nature that impinge upon the wellbeing of the people's crops and animals. They bring to mind the Frankish legends of Merovingian kings controlling the weather and speaking with animals. All these stories point to the ancient practice of viewing the king as a holy person, or as a god himself, an intermediary between man and the Most High. They serve to emphasise once again the identity of the monarch as both priest and king in early Israel, a status which mirrored that of the Egyptian pharaohs. This was something that the biblical editors, many of them Deuteronomists, were at pains to de-emphasise. In the light of what I was later to discover, there was good reason for this reticence.

One scholar of Christian origins has commented that the central ancient Israelite myth was a belief of God manifesting in human form, whose presence brought a rejuvenation of the land and its people, fertility and health (as the head of Bran in Celtic mythology was said to do, and as the Templars would later claim of the head they worshipped). 'The human figure was probably once the king who was also the high priest. He was able to enter the holiest place. In later times the high priest carried life-blood to the place of the throne ... One wonders what was done by the earlier kings who went up to occupy that throne.'[8]

It seemed likely that the veneration of the head was the secret that this scholar sought. If my theory is correct, the Temple of Solomon, conceived by King David, whose links with the head-worshipping Benjamites were well established, and built by his son Solomon, was the centre of this cult of the head. Jewish, Islamic and Christian legends all acknowledge Solomon as a man with strong occult leanings, as a magus extraordinaire, an *illuminatus* who could conjure and control spirits and demons to his will. Secret rites were integral to such systems of 'magic', which I believe descended from Egyptian rites. These had been taught to chosen initiates by the priests of that country (whom the Bible delights in calling 'magicians') and more especially by the Pharaoh Akhenaten, known to the Jews as Moses. This is admitted quite explicitly by the biblical book of the prophet Ezekiel. Here Ezekiel is taken by the Lord in a vision and shown various secret religious rites that are taking place in the temple itself, under the leadership of the elders:

> And there stood before them seventy men of the ancients of the house of Israel ... with every man a censer in his hand; and a thick cloud of incense went up. Then he said unto me, Son of Man hast thou seen what the ancients of the house of Israel do in the dark, every man in the chambers of his imagery?
>
> (Ezekiel 8: 11)

Later, Ezekiel sees further 'abominations'. At the north gate of the Temple: '... behold, there sat women weeping for Tammuz' (Ezekiel 8: 14).

Tammuz was, of course, another name for Adonis, whose name in the Syrian language is to be translated as Aten. Moreover:

> behold, at the door of the temple of the Lord, between the porch and the altar, were about five and twenty men, with their backs toward the temple of the Lord and their faces towards the east; and they worshipped the sun towards the east.
>
> (Ezekiel 8: 16)

From this it is abundantly clear that the secret rites practised in the temple were those of Akhenaten's god, the Aten, with the sun being worshipped as the symbol of the universal creator.[9] By the tenth century BC we can expect that some degree of syncretism would have taken place, with Canaanite practices having perhaps been incorporated into the rituals. But worship of the head as the seat of the divine would still have formed the central tenet of the cult. This thesis was strengthened immeasurably when I began researching the tales surrounding the temple and its legendary builder.

Solomon the Magus

Academic scholarship has long cherished the belief that the Jews were, are, and always will be, ardent monotheists. This is true for much of their history, but there have undoubtedly been long periods of time in which the idea of monotheism has been diluted, or even forgotten altogether.

This is difficult for many people to accept, for the Jews are, after all, the Chosen People – to many, such backsliding is uncomfortable to contemplate. However, as with established Christianity, orthodox Judaism is orthodox simply because, over time, its dogma prevailed against competing dogmas. The evidence for such 'non-Jewish' practices as the worship of different gods is, in fact, overwhelming and irrefutable.

By the time of Hezekiah (715–687 BC), there were pagan idols in the temple of Jerusalem in direct contravention of the interdict in the Commandments against graven images (Exodus 20: 4). Hezekiah set about reforming the temple and the country. He destroyed the high places, removed the pillars and, very tellingly, destroyed the Asherah, the symbol of a goddess (who was probably Isis worshipped under another name). It was Hezekiah, as we have seen, who destroyed the 'brazen serpent' of Moses, identified now as the pharaoh's royal sceptre, and to which prayers and incense had been offered. Although he was inflamed with religious zeal, there was undoubtedly a political element to Hezekiah's actions. Israel (Judah) was under Assyrian domination at that time and, by removing all foreign gods he was, in effect, declaring open revolt against his Assyrian overlords. Less than one hundred years later it was necessary for Josiah (640–609) again to cleanse the temple of pagan influences. Acting on a newly discovered 'book of the law' that was found in the temple, Josiah was determined to root out all 'uncleanness', and he did not shrink at executing any priests not faithful to Yahweh/Adonai. He ordered the high priest of the temple 'to bring forth out of the temple of the Lord all the vessels that were made for Baal ... and for all the host of heaven. And he burned them without Jerusalem ... And he put down the idolatrous priests whom the kings of Judah had ordained to burn incense in the high places ... them also that burned incense unto Baal, to the sun and to the moon, and to all the host of heaven' (2 Kings 23: 4–5). It is plain from this account that, at that time, the temple was not simply the house of the Lord, but a place of worship for many gods, and that the kings of Israel did, at times, follow gods other than Yahweh/Adonai.

The same was certainly true of the temple built by King Solomon. From the first it was invested with a pagan atmosphere: it was said that Solomon had conjured supernatural beings for the construction of the temple. His ability to control demonic beings is attested to in the Koran, and Muslim legend credits the demons with building at least part of the temple. Perhaps the most popular tale concerns the trick Solomon played on the demons when he realised his life was approaching its end. According to the account by the Islamic historian Tabari, several plants appeared mysteriously, one by one, within the temple. Solomon would pluck each plant and ask of it its attributes for healing, dye, etc., all of which he noted down. One day the plant he had picked replied that its purpose was 'the destruction of this temple', which the great magus took as a prediction of his imminent death, which would have freed the demons from the spells under which they were forced to labour on the holy edifice.

Solomon turned this warning to his own advantage by fashioning a staff out of this plant, which he used to support his body after he died. The body's erect posture fooled the demons into continuing their work, and they stopped only when termites had eaten through the staff and caused its collapse, so freeing them from the power of the spell. But by then the work on the temple had been completed.

Demons may safely be discounted as the builders of the temple, but 'foreign devils' were certainly there in abundance. Israel had no tradition of building in stone, and needed to import stone masons and other skilled men from abroad. Phoenician characters have been discovered on the temple's foundation stones.[10] King Hiram of Tyre is normally regarded as having provided the personnel to do this work, but it is not generally known that many of the men were not Phoenicians, but Egyptian in origin. This use of men who worshipped other gods seems odd, almost sacrilegious, if the temple was to be the sole home of the Jewish god, built by a king who acknowledged only this deity. In later times, around the time of Christ, there was a wall around even the second courtyard of the temple that Gentiles entered on pain of death. Josephus has described it as '... a stone balustrade three cubits (around 1.5 metres) high and of exquisite workmanship; in this, at regular intervals, stood slabs giving a warning, some in Greek, others in Latin characters, of the law of purification, to wit that no foreigner was permitted to enter the holy place, for so the second enclosure of the temple was called'.[11]

One of these stone warning signs has actually been discovered. It reads: 'No foreigner is allowed to enter within the balustrade and embankment around the sanctuary. Whoever is caught will have himself to blame for his death which follows.'[12] If such taboos were attached to the second enclosure, how much stricter must have been the laws relating to the temple itself. Ritual purification took up much of the temple priesthood's time. Even a call of nature demanded specific ablutions to repurify the individual concerned. Such strictures are in direct contrast to the great number of non-Jewish 'unbelievers' who were involved in the construction of the temple, men who revered Isis, Ashtoreth, Belial and Adonis. This last god presents some interesting correspondences. Adonis was a solar deity, whose myth is an allegorical retelling of the death and resurrection of the sun each year. Byblos was the Syrian coastal town sacred to Adonis. But this title is the Greek rendition of his name, the Syrian is Adoni which, like the Hebrew, means My Lord, the 'i' being a possessive pronoun. So, as with the Jews, once again we are left with the Semitic version of Aten. It may be that some of the men who worked on the temple were actually initiates, far advanced in the teachings of Akhenaten and the cult of the head. This seems extremely likely when the masonic legends concerning the Temple of Solomon are taken into account.

Hiram Abif and the Cult of the Head

The chief architect of the temple is known in masonic lore as Hiram Abif. He was a subject of his namesake, Hiram king of Tyre, whose cooperation was vital to the construction of the temple Solomon envisaged. The biblical chronicler calls this same man Huram, and he is said to have been 'skilful to work in gold, and in silver, in brass, in iron, in stone and in timber ...' He was the son of a Phoenician father and a woman of the Jewish tribe of Dan (II Chronicles 2: 13). He was therefore, in the eyes of the matrilineal Jews, himself a Jew. He is probably also the man known as Adoniram, that biblical character who is named in I Kings 5: 14 as being 'over the levy' of workers. Adoniram is a contraction of Adoni Hiram, strong evidence of the importance of Adon (the Aten) in the life of the man who bore this name. If true, this would imply that the true builder of King Solomon's Temple was an adherent of Aten, Akhenaten's god.[13]

But Hiram Abif is important for another reason. His story is absolutely central to the masonic brotherhood, whose antecedents, as we'll see, derive in large part from the teachings of the Knights Templar. The tale that is given to a third degree mason is that, just before the completion of the temple, fifteen 'foremen' masons, angry at not yet having received the full knowledge of a master mason, plotted to extract this secret lore, by fair means or foul, from the chief architect, Hiram Abif. All but three of the fifteen repented of their plot, but Jubelo, Jubela and Jubelum were determined to pursue their conspiracy to the end. The three hid themselves in the temple, one conspirator at each of the south, west and east gates, planning to confront Hiram Abif after he had completed his noonday devotions. The words of the masonic ceremony continue the tale:

His devotions being ended, he prepared to retire by the south gate, where he was accosted by the first of these ruffians, who, for want of a better weapon, had armed himself with a plumb rule, and in a threatening manner demanded of our master, Hiram Abif, the genuine secrets of a Master Mason, warning him that death would be the consequence of his refusal; but true to his obligation he replied that those secrets were known to but three in the world and without consent of the other two (by which is meant King Solomon and King Hiram of Tyre), he neither could, nor would divulge them ... as for himself, he would rather suffer death than betray the sacred trust reposed in him.[14]

The first conspirator's response to this reply was to strike the chief architect with a blow to the right temple. Wounded, Hiram Abif flees from his attacker to the west gate, where he refuses once again to divulge the secrets and is struck on the left by the second conspirator 'armed with a level', a blow which brings him to the ground on his right knee.

Finding all chances of escape in both these quarters cut off, our master staggered, faint and bleeding, to the east gate where the third ruffian was posted and who, on receiving a similar reply to his insolent demand, for our master remained true to his obligation even in this most trying moment, struck him a violent blow full in the centre of his forehead with a heavy stone maul, which laid him lifeless at his feet...

A horrific story, and one not easily forgotten. It comes as some surprise, therefore, to discover that both the Bible and the Koran are clear in stating that Hiram Abif was never murdered. On the contrary, he is said to have returned to Tyre and to have lived to a ripe old age.[15]

Apart from the obvious example of courage and fidelity that Hiram Abif sets to modern-day masons by his steadfast refusal to divulge the secrets of his craft, the fictitious story of his death seems to fulfil a second and more important function. It acts as a necessary preliminary to the next part of the tale, which, as far as I am aware, has never before been divulged outside masonic circles. Up until now this section of the tale has been a closely guarded secret and it proves to be of far more interest from the point of view of our story.

This part of the story was given to me under rather strange circumstances. I was told about it, surreptitiously, by an acquaintance who is, or perhaps was, a high-degree mason. I was first told the story, which excited me greatly, and was then given the chance to skim through the tale in a book that was reserved solely for members of the Brotherhood. This was followed by a promise that the book would be made available to me in a day or two so that I could take down this esoteric tale verbatim.

However, my informant did not contact me again and was markedly evasive when I called him to arrange a date to meet with him. Then suddenly, the offer to view the book was withdrawn, with an explanation that it had suddenly disappeared and 'could not be found anywhere'. Nor, it seemed, was there another copy of the book anywhere to be found. I did not press the point, but it was obvious that my informant was very concerned that he had spoken out of turn. Quite clearly, this story was a secret that should have remained the property of the Craft, and that should never have been betrayed to a general audience.

This secret tale recounts that, once Hiram Abif had been killed, the conspirators attempted to hide the murder by burying the body, and it is in the manner of his burial that obvious associations with the cult of the head become apparent. The grave they hurriedly dug for Hiram Abif was, it is said, made in the stone quarry and on such rocky ground that it proved impossible to dig it long or deep enough to conceal the master mason's body intact. The conspirators then took knives and cut the legs off at the top of the thighs and crossed them over their victim's trunk. This made the body shorter, but not short enough. So, they severed the head of Hiram Abif from his trunk, and placed it next to the crossed thighs. In this manner they were able to inter the strangely mutilated cadaver. But not on the horizontal; the secret masonic story is at pains to emphasise that Hiram Abif was buried at an angle.

As none of this happened to the real Hiram Abif, I was forced to the conclusion that the masonic story is acting as a 'vehicle', to carry a far more important piece of information. If the tale is without hidden content, why then the great secrecy, and the obvious fear of disclosure? This 'inner meaning' of the legend involves the ritual decapitation by a group of men (involved in some way with a religious building or secret system of knowledge) of an individual who is considered to possess superior occult, or spiritual knowledge, and the burial or storage of the head underground. Much later, as my quest drew to its conclusion, a carefully disguised Hiram Abif was to function as symbolic marker, pointing straight to the heart of the mystery.

The actual positioning of the body at an angle remains an unsolved problem. That it is emphasised is an indication of its symbolic importance, but as yet I have no adequate explanation for this particular aspect of the mythological burial.

One other facet of the story, however, opens up another symbolic area, one that is redolent in images of the head. Hiram Abif's head is laid over his crossed leg bones, which would, as the flesh rotted from the body, form the first skull and crossbones, a masonic motif that has an ancient pedigree.

Legend associated with the Templars echoes the same skull and crossbones motif (it was the battle flag of the order's fleet of galleys) but, in addition, adds a distinctly Egyptian provenance to the tale. Antonio Sicci de Vercelli was an Italian notary who, while not a Templar himself, had worked with the order in Palestine for around forty years. Called before a papal commission in 1311, he claimed that a Templar called Matthew de Sarmage, then Lord of Sidon, had fallen deeply in love with an Armenian lady:

> He had never known her carnally while she was alive, but at length he secretly had intercourse with her when she was dead in her tomb, on the night of the day on which she had been buried. When he had done this, he heard a certain voice, saying to him: 'Return when it is time for birth, because you will find a head, offspring to you.' And I have heard that, when the time was passed, this same knight returned to the tomb, and found a human head between the legs of the buried woman. Again he heard the voice saying to him: 'Guard this head, because all good things will come to you from it.'[16]

The head as the giver of all good things was a dominant feature of the Baphomet, the head the Templars were said to worship. I was later to find that an identical concept figured in the stories of the Holy Grail, which the Templars were said to guard, and also in Celtic legends.[17] A suspicion began to form in my mind as to the true nature of the Grail itself. Antonio Sicci also claimed that this same Templar, Matthew de Sarmage, was said to have made himself blood brother to the sultan of Egypt, which implies a strong heretical background, and perhaps links the land of the pharaohs to the story. A conclusive Egyptian connection is obvious in another variant of the tale which gives the name of the dead woman as Yse, a corrupt version of Isis, whose golden calf the Benjamites worshipped. Another rendering of the tale, by Roger de Howden, has the story being brought to mind as Philip II of France is returning from Outremer (Palestine), as the ship passes 'the Isles of Yse', another pointed reference to the Egyptian goddess.[18] In this version, the result of the necrophiliac liaison is not a head, but stillborn son. The voice commands the knight to sever the head and to keep it, as it had wondrous powers to destroy any enemy who gazed upon it. In yet another version, it is the head of the dead lady which is taken, as in the story given by a Templar knight, Hugues de Faure, from Limoges:

a certain noble had deeply loved a certain damsel of the castle of Maraclea in the county of Tripoli, and since he could not have her in her lifetime, when he heard that she was dead, he caused her to be exhumed, and had intercourse with her. Afterwards he cut off the head for himself, and a certain voice rang out that he should take good care of the said head, since whoever saw the head would be totally destroyed and routed.[19]

The earliest record of this motif has been traced to the writings of a twelfth century chronicler, Walter Map, but it is almost certainly based on earlier oral traditions.[20] In this version the necrophiliac lover is again told by a voice to return to the grave to find what offspring his illicit desire had produced. When he does so, the dead lady presents him with a human head, which he is enjoined to keep hidden, and only to expose when he wishes to harm the person that will look upon the head. Gervais of Tilbury, writing some twenty or thirty years later, tells a similar tale.[21]

These stories, taken together, point up a number of correspondences: whether it is a monstrous head, the head of the dead lady or the head of a stillborn son, in all the stories it is a severed head that forms the central theme. In all, the head is linked to a tomb or grave, whence it is retrieved by a knight, usually a Templar, who becomes the custodian of the head. Again, in all the tales the knight is commanded 'by a voice' to keep the severed head hidden from view as it is an object of occult power. The Templars, in some of the stories, are linked to the head and the crossed thigh bones, which brings to mind the skull and crossbones of both templar and masonic lore. An Egyptian link is also present, with Isis invoked in two of the tales, and the land of this Egyptian goddess is also mentioned. If the Hiram Abif legend is also considered as part of the same story group, a further list of characters can be added: the Jews, the Temple of Solomon, and (in Hiram Abif's alias, Adon-hiram), Akhenaten's god, the Aten. It is also worth noting that Hiram Abif's 'employer', King Solomon, is said in the Bible to have married the daughter of the pharaoh (1 Kings 3: 1).

So, we have a severed head of great power, the god Aten, the goddess Isis, the land of Egypt, the pharaoh's daughter, the Jews, the Temple of Solomon, Templars, and an underground tomb. Almost all of these I had come across already, but it was intriguing, to say the least, to find them all in the same cycle of stories. The only motif I had not yet considered was the underground burial chamber, and evidence for that was not long in coming.

Tunnels

If Solomon was building his temple above ground, it seems that he, and his father King David, were busy constructing below ground as well. The Babylonian Talmud briefly records such excavations close by the Great Rock on the Temple Mount: 'Rabbi Johanna said ..., When David dug the pits ...' (b. *Sukkah* 53,b). By the second century BC these excavations were of considerable scope and sophistication. Aristeas, the Egyptian traveller whose description and comments on the second temple we have already quoted, also notes that he saw 'wonderful and indescribable cisterns underground, as they pointed out to me, at a distance five furlongs all around the site of the temple, and each of them has countless pipes so that the different streams converge together. They led me more than four furlongs outside the city and bade me peer down toward a certain spot and listen to the noise that was made by the meeting of the waters, so that the great size of the reservoirs became manifest to me ...' (Letter of Aristeas, 83).[22]

These huge waterworks were necessary to provide the growing city of Jerusalem with water. But such expertise in underground excavation would have proved useful for resources other than water. Subterranean tunnels and vaults would have offered secure sanctuary for the most important temple treasures in times of siege and provided their entrances were well hidden, their contents could well have remained secure even if the temple was invaded and occupied. As we have seen, this happened to the different temples on several occasions. On most occasions, the Jews were able to reconquer Jerusalem and reoccupy the temple within a relatively short time. But this was not possible during the final destruction of Herod's Temple. On that occasion, the Jews were dispersed across the known world by the Roman legions, and it was not until close on two thousand years later that they were able to return and reclaim their land.

The Destruction of the Temple

Roman domination of Palestine at the beginning of the Christian era led to a series of small-scale insurrections that were put down with appalling ferocity. The continuing unrest led to a further full-scale uprising in AD 66, beginning when Jewish nationalists seized the temple and drove the Roman garrison from Jerusalem.[23] After initial successes the Jews were driven back onto the defensive by the Roman general Vespasian. Following the suicide of Nero, Vespasian left Judea for Rome to press his claim to the imperial purple, but he left the army, under the command of his son Titus, to suppress the revolt. Titus's campaign culminated in the siege of Jerusalem, which began in May AD 70 and lasted until the Roman legions overran the city on 28 August of the same year, pillaging and burning, and making their way grimly towards the Temple Mount.

Strange omens were said to presage the destruction of the holy place. A comet appeared in the sky and remained there for the best part of a year, and a star in the shape of a sword also hovered over the city. At midnight the great east gate of the temple's inner courtyard opened of its own accord and a light appeared around the altar during one night in April. A cow, about to be sacrificed in the temple precincts, gave birth to a lamb. And just before sunset on 8 June (at the beginning of the siege and eighty-one days before the city finally fell) 'throughout all parts of the country chariots were seen in the air and armed battalions hurtling through the clouds and encompassing the city'.[24] But perhaps the most morale-sapping portent became manifest on the feast of Pentecost, when the priests entered the inner courtyard to prepare for the ritual and became aware of an unaccustomed disturbance which rapidly increased until a voice, as of a host, was heard to declare, 'We are departing hence.' The supernal beings were, it seemed, abandoning the temple to its fate.

Josephus is our primary source for the fall of the temple. It should be remembered, however, that Josephus was a quisling, a Jewish rebel who turned his coat when captured by Vespasian, the Roman general who was soon to become emperor. He was with Vespasian during the subjugation of Galilee and Judea and, with Vespasian's son Titus, was an eye witness to the siege and fall of Jerusalem. Following this, Josephus took Vespasian's family name, Flavius, and spent his remaining days at Rome, under imperial patronage, writing various histories of the Jews.[25] So, he is pre-disposed to play down the horrors perpetrated by his Roman masters, and to demonstrate that the whole ghastly story was brought on the Jewish people by a few headstrong zealots. With the destruction of the temple, Josephus portrays Titus as a humane conqueror, at first attempting to save the temple from devastation. But eventually, he saw that this led only to the loss of his own troops and he ordered the silver-clad gates burned:

... the silver melting all around quickly admitted the flames to the woodwork, whence they spread in dense volumes and caught hold of the porticoes. The Jews, seeing the fire encircling them, were deprived of all energy of body and mind ... paralysed, they stood and looked on.[26]

At this moment, one of the soldiers ... moved by some supernatural impulse, snatched a brand from the burning timber and, hoisted up by one of his comrades, flung the fiery missile through a low golden door, which gave access on the north side to the chambers surrounding the sanctuary. As the flames shot up, a cry as poignant as the tragedy arose from the Jews ... On all sides was carnage and flight. Most of the slain were civilians, weak and unarmed people, each butchered where he was caught. Around the altar a pile of corpses was accumulating; down the steps of the sanctuary flowed a stream of blood and the bodies of the victims killed above went sliding to the bottom.[27]

Sometime before this, one of the priests of the temple appears to have come to an arrangement with the besieging Romans to give up the treasure of the temple in return for safe passage from the killing ground. Josephus again supplies the details:

... one of the priests named Jesus son of Thebuti ... came out and handed over the wall of the sanctuary two lampstands similar to those deposited in the sanctuary, along with tables, bowls and platters, all of solid gold and very massive; he further delivered up the veils, the high priests' vestments, including the precious stones, and many other articles used in public worship.[28]

It is these treasures that were taken as spoils to Rome and paraded through the streets in triumphal procession. But the Romans may well have missed the most important of the treasures. Given the fact that the veil of the temple was a vast piece of enormously thick woven cloth, shot through with gold, it could not possibly have been handled by a single man. Its dismantling and removal would have taken several days. Huge and massy gold tables would have required the strength of several strong men to lift, let alone to 'hand over the wall'. It appears therefore that Jesus, son of Thebuti, was the leader of a group of priests who tried to prevent the Romans from actually entering the temple by handing over the golden treasure of the temple intact, before the final assault took place. Note that the treasure was that 'used in public worship'. In other words, it was the treasure that was known to the general populace that was given up. This was an effective strategy on the part of the priests. It would be pointless to try to hide such a hoard, as the Romans, knowing of its existence, would certainly scour the temple until these particular pieces were found. It is probable that the plan was simply to delay the Roman assault until such time as the treasures not 'used in public worship', that is the treasure and relics that were worshipped *secretly*, could be safely hidden in their underground vaults.

It is telling that Josephus, in reporting the remaining temple treasure that the Romans were able to recover, mentions only relatively inconsequential objects:

> Furthermore, the treasurer of the temple, by name Phineas, being taken prisoner, disclosed the tunics and girdles worn by the priests, an abundance of purple and scarlet kept for necessary repair to the veil of the temple, along with a mass of cinnamon and cassia and a multitude of other spices, which they mixed and burnt daily as incense to God.[29]

This hardly amounts to treasure as we normally regard it, and it strengthens the idea that the outward treasure, the gold tables, utensils, the sacred lampstands and the veil of the temple, were all sacrificed as 'decoys' to preserve the true treasures of the Jewish priest-initiates, the temple records and the priceless relics of the holy place – the sacred heads.

The Hidden Treasure

That treasure was buried in and around Jerusalem at the time of the temple's destruction was confirmed in 1952 by the discovery of a copper scroll at Qumran near the Dead Sea (scroll 3Q15).[30] The scroll was badly degraded after almost two thousand years of storage but, when finally deciphered, it proved to be a treasure list, detailing sixty-four locations where gold, silver, spices and scrolls had been deposited in and around Jerusalem. The value of the treasure is quite incredible: *in toto*, the estimate is that sixty-five tons of silver and twenty-five tons of gold were hidden. Such vast sums have inclined some scholars to believe that the scroll is a work of fiction; most, however, are inclined to accept its veracity and believe it to be the greater part of the temple treasure (which would support the idea that only the publicly known treasure was sacrificed to the Romans).[31]

The idea of important relics or treasure being buried in Jerusalem is not new – on the destruction of the first temple and the disappearance of the Ark of the Covenant, stories arose of secret caverns beneath the temple where the Ark had been hidden.[32] The secret chamber is generally believed to be the work of King Solomon, or of one of the last of the kings of Judah, Josiah. Many ultra-orthodox Jews, who wish to see a new Jewish temple built on the Temple Mount, are convinced of this story. Unfortunately, although the area has been under Israeli authority since the Arab-Israeli Six Day War of 1967, the Supreme Moslem Council, the *wakf*, has been

granted control of the temple area. They have refused to allow any archaeological studies on the holy ground. This prohibition is due, in part, to
their reluctance to aid any excavation which might reveal evidence of
early Jewish occupancy and construction on the Temple Mount. Despite
this, according to researcher Gary Byers of Associates for Biblical Research,
in 1981 a number of highly placed rabbis began excavating in certain
rock-carved tunnels and chambers they found beneath the Temple Mount.
They worked in secret for a year and a half, and '... were convinced
another eighteen months would take them to the chamber with the
Ark. However, when their efforts became known, the Israeli government
discontinued their activities...'[33]

If, as seems likely, the priests of the Jewish temple hid their most secret
and revered treasure beneath the temple just before it was overrun by the
Romans in AD 70, then the treasure should still be there. Unless someone
has already dug it up. This information on the 'true treasure's' hidden
whereabouts seems to have been lost to all but a few Jewish families who
fled Israel to Europe and who, over one thousand years later, in AD 1100,
had formed new alliances and held power and lands in France. These
families were instrumental in the setting up of the Knights Templar, whose
function was said to be the protection of pilgrims but who, as I was later
to find, had in reality a very different agenda to follow – the recovery of
whatever constituted the true treasure of the temple of Jerusalem. This, I
believed, would have at its centre the sacred severed heads. But other
information seemed to show that, even before the Templars arrived, at
least one of the 'treasures' had been taken out of Israel, a treasure intimately
connected with Jesus and his bloodline.

9

The True Bloodline

Who Was Joseph?

We have seen in Chapter 5 that the selling of Joseph into slavery in Egypt was the catalyst that brought his only full brother, Benjamin, into close contact with the Egyptian mysteries and the cult of Isis. This began the schism in the Hebrew tribes which culminated in the 'civil war' between the Benjamites and the rest of the Children of Israel, which led to their expulsion and, after the passage of around one thousand years, to the establishment of the Merovingian dynasty in western Europe. But can we locate the time of Joseph's slavery and subsequent freedom in any episode in the known history of Egypt? In particular, is it possible to place Joseph in the reign of a specific pharaoh, and can we identify him as an accepted historical figure?

Many biblical scholars have been content to assign Joseph to that 'catch-all' of any record of Semitic people in Egypt, the time of the invasion by the Semitic Hyksos or Shepherd kings, around one hundred years before Akhenaten came to the throne.[1] At the same time, most traditional research has tried to fit Egyptian history into the Bible story, rather than (as common sense might suggest) taking the reverse approach. While the Bible was regarded as an unimpeachable 'authority', this *modus operandi* could be defended, but as most scholars have come to see the Old Testament as a tribal history of the Hebrews, the strategy has little to commend it. When the Bible is looked at in the light of Egyptian history, then many things become clearer. With the tale of Joseph, as Ahmed Osman has shown in his penetrating study of this Bible story, discussed below, a Hyksos identification for Joseph is quite untenable. However, where Joseph *does* seem to fit in the history of Egypt proves to be far more interesting and of great significance to our quest.[2]

The Story of Joseph

The scriptural story gives many clues which point to the date and identity of the man Joseph. When analysed, the Bible story of Joseph reveals numerous points indicating that the time of Joseph was not that of the Hyksos, but instead of the eighteenth dynasty, the same ruling house that included Akhenaten and the Amarna kings. The relevant sections in the story are italicised and discussed immediately after the story outline below.

Following his arrival as *a slave in Egypt*, the Bible describes Joseph as belonging to the House of Potiphar, whose wife, enraged when her advances were rebuffed by Joseph, accused him of trying to seduce her. Believing his wife, Potiphar had the young slave thrown into prison, where he successfully interprets the dreams of two fellow prisoners. Years later, one of these prisoners, now restored to his former high position in the pharaoh's entourage, remembers Joseph when the pharaoh himself has a dream which resists the analysis of Egypt's wisest men. Joseph is brought from his captivity and successfully interprets pharaoh's dream as a warning that seven years of plenty will be followed by seven of famine. Joseph is raised by the grateful king to the highest position in the realm: 'You shall be in charge of my household, and all my people are to submit to your orders. Only in respect of the throne shall I be greater than you.' Later, the Bible has pharaoh say to Joseph, 'See, I have set thee over *all the land of Egypt*' (Genesis 41: 41).

This astonishing reversal of fortunes placed Joseph, a foreigner, in an incredibly powerful position, and is certain to have bred resentment among the Egyptian nobles and priesthood. Joseph was given a signet ring of pharaoh's, a gold necklace and robes of the finest linen, and a wife was provided for him, '*Asenath, the daughter of Potipherah, Priest of On*' (Genesis 41: 45). Men were appointed to run before his chariot proclaiming, '*Bow the Knee!*' when he travelled around the country, preparing for the coming famine.

The famine duly arrived. It affected not only Egypt, but the land of Canaan also, and the ensuing hardships forced Joseph's father Jacob to send ten of his sons to Egypt in an attempt to buy grain, keeping with him his youngest son, Benjamin. They were brought before Joseph who, although he recognised his brothers, remained unknown to them. Joseph treated them harshly, accusing them of spying. Aghast at this turn of events, the brothers protested their innocence, explaining, 'Your servants were twelve brothers, the sons of one man who lives in the land of Canaan. The youngest is now with our father in Canaan, and one is no more.'

118

Joseph refused to be mollified, and demanded that they bring the younger brother with them from Canaan, and leave one of their number as hostage, swearing, *'By the life of Pharaoh* ye shall not go forth hence, unless your youngest brother come hither' (Genesis 42: 15). In the next verse, this same oath is used with Joseph saying that either their words will be proved '... or else *by the life of Pharaoh* surely ye are spies'. Later, at another meeting, we learn that Joseph is *using an interpreter* to speak to his brothers and to demand that Benjamin be brought down into Egypt. When the brothers finally return with Benjamin, the youngest, Joseph has a meal prepared: he ate alone, and the Egyptians ate apart from the visiting Canaanites as, the Bible tells us, *'the Egyptians could not eat with Hebrews, for that is detestable to Egyptians'* (Genesis 43: 32). This abhorrence of Canaanites is emphasised in Genesis 46: 33–4 when Joseph warns his brothers that *'every shepherd is an abomination unto the Egyptians'*.

Eventually, Joseph reveals his identity to his brothers, and tells them immediately not to fear his anger for their wrongdoing 'because it was God who sent me ahead of you to save lives ... So it was not you who sent me here, but God. He has made me *a father to Pharaoh*, lord over all his household and ruler of all Egypt. Now hurry back to my father and tell him: "This is what your son Joseph says: 'God has made me lord of all Egypt. Come down to me: don't delay. You shall live in the region of Goshen and be near me – you, your sons and grandsons, your flocks and herds, and all you have. I shall provide for you there, because five years of famine are still to come.'"'

The tribe of Israel (Joseph's father Jacob had been given the new name of Israel in the intervening years) settled in Goshen and prospered. Jacob had already been an old man at the time of the Descent into Egypt and when he eventually died, Joseph had his body *embalmed in the Egyptian fashion* and, true to a promise he had made his father, took his body back to Canaan. In the course of time Joseph also died. *He too was embalmed* and, according to the Bible, was taken to Canaan for burial. However, this latter part of the tale is believed by most biblical scholars to be a later interpolation (and it is more likely that the body of Joseph – who while alive had spent his entire adult life in Egypt – remained in his adopted country).

The Discrepancies

Slavery: in his book *Slavery in Pharaonic Egypt*, the scholar Abd el-Mohsen Bakir concluded that 'from the evidence before us, slavery, strictly speaking, existed between the Eighteenth and Twenty-second Dynasties, while before and after that period only various degrees of "bondage" can be demonstrated'.[3] So, if Joseph was sold into slavery in Egypt, the earliest time this event could have occurred was the eighteenth dynasty, after the time of the Hyksos.

All the land of Egypt: the Torah (the Pentateuch of the Christian Bible) has the word for Egypt, *misrim*, in the plural, signifying 'two Egypts'. According to A. S. Yahuda, in his book *The Language of the Pentateuch in its Relation to Egypt*, 'misrim is nothing else than a literal and grammatical adaptation of the Egyptian word *tzwy*, dual of *tz* (land) – that is, the Two Lands or the twin lands, these being as a matter of fact the designations given by the Egyptians to their country from time immemorial with reference to Upper and Lower Egypt'.[4] The style of writing therefore emphasises that Joseph was in control of the Two Lands, i.e., both Upper and Lower Egypt. However, during the Hyksos rule, the country was divided into three: the Hyksos ruled Lower Egypt as far south as Cursae; Upper Egypt remained under pharaonic rule; and Nubia was controlled by a native ruler. There was never a time that a vizier of the Hyksos had suzerainty over the 'Two Lands'.

Asenath, the daughter of Potipherah, Priest of On: the Hyksos repudiated all Egyptian gods except Seth, whom they were devoted to and whom they identified with the Canaanite Baal. The ancient Egyptian historian Manetho describes how the Hyksos destroyed the temples and sacred places of other gods. It is beyond belief that a Hyksos ruler would give his new vizier a wife who was a daughter of a Priest of On, where Ra (the sun god) was worshipped. This sounds much more like the behaviour of a native Egyptian pharaoh.

Bow the Knee: this phrase is *Abrek* in Hebrew, which is itself derived from an Egyptian command to bow before a superior. This word entered Egyptian as a 'loan word' only during the New Kingdom. Therefore it was only present in the Egyptian language after the period of Hyksos rule, from the time of the eighteenth dynasty.

By the life of Pharaoh: this form of oath is unheard of before the beginning of the New Kingdom. It is first seen in the eighteenth dynasty (the original phrasing had 'As Amun endures and the Pharaoh endures' and later became 'As Amun lives and the Pharaoh lives' – the biblical editor has excised the name of the god Amun). Once again, the use of such a phrase was unknown at the time of the Hyksos.

Using an interpreter: as Canaanite was the language of both the brothers of Joseph and the Hyksos, if this tableau had occurred in Hyksos times, the services of an interpreter would have been unnecessary. If an Egyptian pharaoh was on the throne, however, the story is far more credible.

The Egyptians could not eat with Hebrews, for that is detestable to Egyptians, and *every shepherd is an abomination unto the Egyptians:* the Hyksos or Shepherd kings were themselves nomads with flocks when they entered Egypt and subdued it. It was only after the Hyksos were expelled that Asiatic nomads became 'an abomination'.

A father to Pharaoh: this title is unknown from the Hyksos period. In fact, it occurs only once from the time of the Hyksos to the end of the New Kingdom, and then only in eighteenth dynasty.

embalmed in the Egyptian fashion and *he too was embalmed:* no Hyksos king or dignitary is known to have been embalmed in the Egyptian fashion. This information places Joseph and his family firmly in the time of an Egyptian monarch.

So, Joseph must have lived in a post-Hyksos period, and more specifically in the eighteenth dynasty. With the search narrowed to this period, there are numerous textual correspondences that link Joseph to one specific member of the pharaoh's entourage, so many correspondences that 'coincidence' seems hard put to account for them all. The person in question is the grand vizier of Amenhotep III, Yuya. And Yuya was the grandfather of Akhenaten.

Most telling of all these 'coincidences' is Joseph's description of himself as 'a father to Pharaoh'. This one phrase provided the key that allowed Ahmed Osman to unlock the secret of Joseph's Egyptian identity. From the time of the Hyksos until the end of the New Kingdom, this epithet was entirely unknown, except that, uniquely, it was bestowed on the vizier Yuya. The title is inscribed on an ushabti (the small tomb figurines of the deceased, dressed as a mummy but with head and neck unbandaged) found in Yuya's tomb and appears over twenty times in his Book of the Dead, also buried with him.

The burial itself revealed many other clues. Yuya was interred in the Valley of the Kings, between the tombs of Ramses XI and a prince of Ramses III. For anyone other than those of the royal line to be buried in the Valley of the Kings would be a unique honour – even leading courtiers were interred elsewhere, in the Valley of the Nobles. Why should Yuya be given such an exalted burial place? This singular distinction, conferred upon Yuya alone, raises the question of whether Joseph/Yuya was not after all related to the pharaonic line.

The tomb was found by Theodore M. Davis in the summer of 1905. With Arthur Weigall and the then Director General of Cairo Museum, he opened the tomb in early September. Davis describes the excitement of their first view of the treasures contained in the crypt in his book *The Tomb of Iouiya and Touiyou*:

> We held up our candles but they gave so little light and so dazzled our eyes that we could see nothing except the glitter of gold. In a moment or two, however, I made out a very large ... funeral sled, which was used to contain all the coffins of the dead person and his mummy, and to convey them to his tomb. It was about six feet high and eight long, made of wood covered with bitumen, which was as bright as the day it was put on. Around the upper part of the coffin was a stripe of gold foil, about six inches wide, covered with hieroglyphics. On calling Monsieur Maspero's attention to it, he immediately handed me his candle, which, together with my own, I held before my eyes, close to the inscriptions so that he could read them. In an instant he said 'Iouiya (Yuya)!'[5]

The mummified remains of Yuya gave fresh impetus to the belief that, despite his unique burial alongside the tombs of the Egyptian kings, Yuya was a foreigner.

Egyptian mummies usually have their ears pierced – Yuya did not. Even more significant is the fact that Egyptian dead are almost always embalmed with their hands crossed over the chest, palms flat against the ribs and shoulder, in a position mimicking that of Osiris, god of the dead. In contrast to this tradition, Yuya's body had been embalmed with the hands held in a very different attitude, with the fingertips under the chin, and the palms against the neck; almost in a praying position. This is the *first and only* occasion on which an Egyptian mummy has been found arranged in such an attitude. At very least, it implies a rejection of Osiris, and perhaps the whole Egyptian pantheon as well.

Although human variation precludes a definitive identification of Yuya's racial origins, his facial features are quite definitely not those of an average Egyptian. The body is well preserved, and the face of the dead man striking in appearance. One of its discoverers described Yuya as 'a person of commanding presence, whose powerful character showed itself in his face. One must picture him now as a tall man, with a fine shock of white hair; a great hooked nose like that of a Syrian; full, strong lips and a prominent, determined jaw ...'[6] The foreign nature of the features has been commented on by more than one researcher: Henri Naville stated, 'His very aquiline face might be Semitic', which would fit very well with the hypothesis that Yuya was the biblical Joseph, a Semite whose origins lay in the land of Canaan.[7]

Although the tomb had received the attentions of tomb-robbers some-time in the distant past, much of interest remained. The name Yuya, inscribed on several objects and the coffins themselves, is not an Egyptian name; it had never been recorded before this time. It seemed also that the Egyptians themselves had had trouble transcribing the name: there are no less than eleven different versions of Yuya in the tomb, as if each artisan or scribe had attempted his own interpretation of this (to them) odd-sounding, foreign name. Henri Naville, in his *Funerary Payrus of Iouiya*, concurred: 'the numerous transcriptions of his name seem to show that, for the Egyptians, it was a foreign sound which they reproduced in writing as they heard it, just as in our time two Egyptians will not spell alike a German, French or English name'.[8] The name Yuya was odd for another reason: it contained no god-name, the usual practice for Egyptians of this time. It seems therefore that Yuya, whoever he was, was not under the patronage of an Egyptian god. This, of course, begs the question as to which god's protection he was under. It may well have been the god which, by the time of Yuya's grandson, Akhenaten, was known by the name of Aten. Many scholars believe that the sudden appearance of the Aten cult in Akhenaten's time was not entirely without antecedents, and that Yuya is implicated in the introduction of the concept of an unseen, all-powerful creator to the Egyptian pantheon. Arthur Weigall, co-dis-coverer of Yuya, commented that 'One feels, on looking at his well pre-served features, that there may be found the originator of the great religious movement which his daughter and grandson carried to completion.'[9]

If the identification of Yuya with Joseph is accepted, then the four Amarna kings, Akhenaten, Semekhare, Tutankhamun and Aye, were all of mixed Egyptian-Israelite descent (because Tiye, the daughter of Yuya/Joseph, was Akhenaten's mother). This makes the 'adoption' of the Hebrews by Akhenaten/Moses a far more probable scenario than it first appears, because Akhenaten/Moses and the Hebrews would be related by blood via Yuya and Tiye. It also does much to explain the boundless animosity of the Egyptian religious establishment towards the four Amarna kings and especially to Akhenaten. His grandfather Yuya had brought the seeds of the new Aten religion with him from Canaan, a religion of one god that for a time looked as though it would sweep away the old gods of Egypt. To the Priests of Amun and their supporters, Yuya was the root from which all the other 'evil' flourished, a religious revolutionary and a foreigner.

But was Yuya a foreigner?

This question takes us back to the as yet unanswered question of why the pharaoh favoured Joseph. The Bible asks us to believe that pharaoh took an unknown, apparently worthless slave, and a prisoner to boot, and raised him to the highest position in the realm for a breathtakingly trivial reason – the interpretation of a dream that could not possibly be fully verified for a further fourteen years. To put all Egypt under the control of such a man, whose worth and ability were utterly untested, would quite rightly be regarded by most Egyptians as an act of complete irresponsibility, even of madness. Was there perhaps another reason for raising Joseph to his exalted position?

Abraham and the Pharaoh

The answer appears to lie in the equally strange tale of a still earlier pharaoh, and of the patriarch Abraham and Sarah, his wife. According to biblical sources, Sarah must be accounted a bigamist, in that, at one time, she was married to both Abraham and the Egyptian pharaoh.

The story of Abraham is itself very strange. He is born in Ur of the Chaldees, under the name Abram. He was of the line of Shem, one of the three sons of Noah. For some reason not given in the Bible, Abram leaves the city of his birth, in the company of his father Terah, his wife Sarai, and his nephew Lot. In the generally accepted version, after his father dies Abram wanders through the desert with his wife and nephew and a few sheep and goats, living in a rude tent, and eventually fetching up in Canaan, where he builds an altar to the Lord. Following a widespread famine in Canaan, Abram is forced to flee south to Egypt. At this point there is a very strange passage: Abram tells his wife Sarai that, because she is so beautiful, he is afraid that he will be killed by the Egyptians so that they can possess her. So, he begs his wife to pass herself off as his sister, 'and my soul shall live because of thee'. Abram's prediction is proved true, for the Egyptian princes do find Sarai fair, and word of her beauty even reaches the ears of the pharaoh. How the Egyptian nobles are able to look upon Sarai is not explained, but it does seem that Abram had made their acquaintance socially, for the nobility of Egypt were not in the habit of mixing with the hoi-polloi. This would mean that, far from being a ragged nomad, Abram must have been a man of some importance in his own country, and not without wealth. He would certainly not travel alone, but with an impressive entourage. And as a native of Ur (known to have been a large, prosperous city with a cultured ruling class)[10] he would almost certainly have been a match socially and intellectually for the sophisticated Egyptians.

Whatever the truth of this, the Egyptian king was not slow to appreciate

Sarai's beauty, 'and the woman was taken into Pharaoh's house'. That is, she was married to pharaoh. Abram is paid well for giving up his 'sister', the pharaoh 'entreated Abram well for her sake: and he had sheep, and oxen and he asses and men-servants, and maidservants, and she asses and camels' (Genesis 12: 16). It seems, therefore, that Sarai spent quite a long time in the house of pharaoh and, although the Bible does not state the fact specifically, it is highly unlikely that the Egyptian king did not make love to his bride. This seems certain when we read that Abram's god took exception to this bigamous marriage and 'the Lord plagued Pharaoh and his house with great plagues'. When the truth finally became known, pharaoh handed Sarai back to Abram and sent them out of Egypt. But it appears he let Abram keep the bride-price, for we are told in the next verse that '... Abram was very rich in cattle, in silver and in gold'.

Isaac

Sarai, we are told, was barren and could not give Abram a son. She therefore gave her handmaid Hagar to Abram and he fathered by her his first son Ishmael. (He also had six other sons by a later wife, Ketaurah, and another, Eliezar, by a slave woman, so Abraham can hardly be considered a man without a son and heir.) It is not until Sarai is ninety years old that she gives birth to her own son, Isaac. This is, of course, quite incredible. It has led a number of scholars to theorise that the large number of events and long time span that are interpolated between Abram and Sarai's expulsion from Egypt and the birth of Isaac is in fact a smoke-screen, a way of separating events that were once accepted as occurring close together in time, but which had since become too embarrassing to acknowledge. Ahmed Osman has been prominent in the championing of this view. In this scenario, when Tutmosis married Sarai and consummated the marriage, the fruit of their union was a son, the boy known in the Bible as Isaac, and born after the return to Canaan. Abram then was Isaac's stepfather, Tutmosis his real father, and the blood of the pharaohs ran in Isaac's veins.

Such a royal link might at one time have been a proud boast, but by the time the old traditions of the Hebrews were written down, the accepted lore of the tribe characterised the Egyptians as their evil oppressors, and such a link between the godless Egyptians and the founders of the Jewish nation was far too embarrassing to commit to writing. However, a number of clues have slipped past the biblical editors and point to the true father of Isaac. At the very time that God tells Abram that Sarai will bear a son, he insists that both of them change their names, to the familiar Abraham and Sarah respectively. The meaning of Sarai's name-change is significant: Sarah means queen, which is an apt name for one who has been the wife of the Egyptian king and is about to give birth to a prince, but makes very little sense otherwise.

Strangely, although Ishmael and the six other sons of Abraham are older than Isaac, it is to Isaac alone that God makes a number of promises: Abraham is told that Isaac's descendants will rule 'from the river of Egypt unto the great river, the river Euphrates' (Genesis 15: 18). This was precisely the extent of the realm over which Tutmosis III ruled during Abraham's time. The patriarch's seven other sons are also excluded from a promise that Isaac's descendants alone will return to Egypt (Genesis 15: 13).[11]

But the Bible is not the only witness to the 'otherness' of Isaac. The Jewish Talmud preserves the belief that most people at the time derided Abraham for pretending that Isaac was his son, saying the boy was a foundling. In the Koran, too, the same truth is expressed, albeit obliquely. A brief passage on genealogy (Sura XIX: 58) has both Abraham and Jacob (Isaac's son) named as the ancestors of Ishmael, Moses and Aaron.

Common sense alone suggests that, if Isaac was truly Abraham's natural son, then Jacob (Isaac's son) should have been numbered with Abraham's other descendants, Ishmael, Moses and Aaron. This strongly suggests that two bloodlines are being indicated in this passage, one descended from Abraham, the other from Isaac. This explanation may also reveal the true motive for Abraham's attempt to sacrifice Isaac, as a burnt offering to the Lord. Abraham relented at the last moment, and seems thereafter to have accepted his role as foster father. However, if Isaac were not genetically related to Abraham, and if he had been conceived 'in sin', then the attempted immolation, while still horrific in modern eyes, is perhaps a little more understandable from Abraham's point of view.

If this reading of the events behind the scriptural story is accepted, then the question we posed earlier in this chapter, 'Why was Joseph raised to such an exalted position, as second only to Pharaoh?' can be answered. Isaac sired Jacob (later called Israel), and Jacob was the father of Joseph. If Tutmosis III was Isaac's true father, then Joseph was the pharaoh's great-grandson. So, when Joseph was sold as a slave and taken to Egypt, if he was able to prove that his grandfather Isaac was a son of the pharaoh (this may have been common knowledge in the royal inner circle), he would have been acknowledged as kin by the pharaoh of his own day, and treated accordingly (i.e., given a position of rank at the Egyptian court). This is a far more likely explanation for the wholly improbable 'promotion' of a Hebrew slave to the highest position in the realm after pharaoh. Joseph was raised to this elevated rank because he was the great-grandson of Pharaoh Tutmosis III, who had 'married' Sarah, Abraham's wife.

But it is possible that the story of Semitic links can be taken back even further than this. Tutmosis III is regarded as the sixth pharaoh of the eighteenth dynasty. However, he came to the throne in a very different way from his illustrious forebears. He was the son of a concubine, not the heiress, and as such should not have inherited the throne. But it was said that the Ark of Amun became so heavy as it passed him that the priests carrying the god were forced to stop. This was taken as a sign that the god Amun had chosen Tutmosis as his new 'son', in other words, as pharaoh. Portraits of Tutmosis reveal that he had a particularly hooked nose and it is just possible that Tutmosis also had the blood of Shem in his veins, perhaps from his concubine mother.[12] Abram's journey to Egypt may then have been more than the unexpected arrival of a stranger. This can only be speculation, but Tutmosis III and Abraham may just conceivably have been distantly related. But there can be no certainty here.

What is sure is that the identification of Tutmosis III as the father of Isaac, essentially usurping the place of Abraham as the great ancestor figure of the Children of Israel, explains a number of puzzling features about another scriptural hero figure, King David. And it casts fresh light upon the ancestry of Jesus, and the prominence given to all the descendants of the 'House of David'.

The Two Davids

Careful scrutiny of the biblical story of David reveals two conflicting sides to the persona of this charismatic leader. On the one hand we have the guerrilla leader who killed Goliath with a slung stone, who fled from his king, Saul, to hide in the mountains of Palestine and who, on achieving the throne of the Children of Israel, was engaged in numerous 'bush-fire' wars, mainly with the Philistines, along the border of his small kingdom. By contrast, the other David is of inestimably greater stature. A true conqueror, he fights major battles across the length and breadth of the Near East, and holds dominion over the lands that lie between the Euphrates and the Nile. In other words, by a strange coincidence, this great biblical warrior 'King David' ruled an empire that is identical with that over which another great empire builder, the Pharaoh Tutmosis III, held sway.

The King David who ruled the Israelites and fought Goliath is known to have lived in or around the tenth century BC. Unfortunately, there is not the slightest scrap of archaeological evidence that this 'tribal' David ever controlled the vast territory that the Bible attributes to him. Quite simply, at that time, there was no such empire and, after the days of Tutmosis III, these lands were not brought under common rule until the 'King of Kings', Cyrus of Persia, conquered the region in the sixth century BC. This non-existent empire has proved rather embarrassing to biblical scholars. To circumvent the awkward fact of its presence in the Bible, but not in reality, they have fallen back on the rather lame excuse that the Old Testament scribes simply 'made up the whole thing', in an attempt to bolster the image of the tribal king. And yet the empire described remains identical to that of Tutmosis III.

There is another explanation. Rather than simply inventing the empire of the tribal David, could the biblical scribes have merged the stories of the Israelite king with that of the Egyptian pharaoh? Might we be dealing here with two separate individuals, both called David?

Ahmed Osman believes this to be true. He has shown that David, in Hebrew *dwd*, becomes *twt* when transliterated into Egyptian. And *Twt* is the first segment of the name Tutmosis. The mythology of all cultures gives many examples of the merging of gods and heroes, so there is no *a priori* reason why the Bible stories should not refer to two men, both royal, but one of infinitely greater reputation and stature, whose personalities, over the centuries, have been merged into a single biblical individual.

The pattern was finally becoming clearer. If Tutmosis III was the natural father of Isaac, and the original 'King David' of the great empire that stretched from the Euphrates to the Nile, then three important points followed. First, it was a royal pharaoh of Egypt, not Abraham the Shemite, who was to be regarded as the great ancestor of the Hebrew nation. Second, all the major players in the early history of the Hebrews (from Isaac to Moses/Akhenaten) had been members of the royal house of the eighteenth dynasty of Egypt. This would mean that their later descendants would also carry the blood royal of the pharaohs. And finally, these conclusions gave a whole new perspective on one of the most renowned phrases in the Bible, the 'House of David'. This meant, not a descendant of an obscure tribal king, but instead a descendant of a great royal line, the bloodline of the pharaoh.

Jesus was a descendant of the House of David. We knew now that he was a Nazarite, and this linkage helped to explain yet another puzzling aspect of Nazarite philosophy. As well as revering the sacredness of the head, following the teachings of Akhenaten/Moses, and worshipping the sun as a manifestation of the power of the creator, the Nazarites honoured only the Hebrew patriarchs up to and including Moses, Abraham, Isaac,

Jacob and Joseph. That is, they venerated the descendants of Tutmosis and the royal line of Egypt. The Nazarites were very clear about this; they specifically rejected all prophets after Moses.

That Jesus had been a member of the Nazarite sect was now proven. And he was also acknowledged as a descendant of the House of David. Was there, I wondered, any other evidence that Jesus was related to the royal line of Egypt?

10

Jesus, Son of Ra

In recent years it has become almost a commonplace to regard Jesus as a revolutionary, a true descendant of the tribal House of David, a man of strong views who, far from being a gentle saviour, was in fact a political figure, intent on the overthrow of Roman rule.[1] The proponents of this view cite in support of their thesis several perplexing verses in the New Testament, including Jesus' statement that he came not to bring peace, but a sword, and his command, towards the end of his ministry, that his disciples procure swords. This 'Jesus the Revolutionary' view, shocking to many orthodox Christians, has emerged relatively recently from a modern, critical reading of the four Gospels, Matthew, Mark, Luke and John, and from equally analytical studies of Acts and the various epistles that follow the Gospels in the New Testament. In all these analyses it is the New Testament that is used as the essential source. Different commentators might disagree on their conclusions, but they are all drawing on the same set of texts.

It comes as some surprise, therefore, to discover that there is a completely different collection of writings which stand against the Christian accounts, and give an altogether different view of Jesus. These are the Jewish texts, the Talmud, and the Toldoths, some of which can claim at least as old a pedigree as the New Testament Gospels.[2] The Talmud is made up of a vast number of Midrashim (explanations and amplifications of biblical topics) and consists of the generally older Mishna and later additions known as the Gemara. They are dated from around AD 100–500 but often reflect even earlier, oral traditions. The picture these Jewish texts paint of Jesus is far from flattering: he is variously described as the bastard son of a hairdresser or adulterer, a thief, a worker of magic who seduced the people of Israel away from the worship of the Judaic god, and, for this latter crime, was stoned to death. Such comments can outrage orthodox Christians even to this day, and in the past these Jewish texts were subject to proscription, papal bulls and mass burnings, as was the race that held them as part of its heritage.[3] Some of the more outrageous of the accusations against Jesus can be seen as reactions against this persecution, but others are cogent arguments and statements put forward to counter the Christian view of Jesus, and these are worthy of our consideration.

Bringing 'Magic' Out of Egypt

One of the most persistent accusations levelled by the Jewish writers against Jesus is that he had studied magic in Egypt. To this was added the tale that Jesus had managed to smuggle certain texts out of Egypt, either by writing the hieroglyphs on his skin, or by concealing the writing in an incision so that later, in a place of safety, the parchment could be slid out of his body and read! To modern-day minds, this accusation of 'working magic' conjures up images of sorcerers and warlocks communing with the devil and practising fiendish rites in churchyards at the dead of midnight. However, the Jewish definition of magic was somewhat different. If we remember that the 'magicians' of the biblical Moses stories are simply Egyptian priests dedicated to a god other than Yahweh/Adonai, then, stripped of all rhetoric, the accusation against Jesus is seen to be far less heinous. It seems that he was a follower of a deity other than the god of mainstream Judaism, and that he was apparently a high initiate in the mysteries of this god. In the Talmud Balaam Jesus stories (Balaam means corrupter or destroyer and would seem to refer to the charges levelled against Jesus), a gloss is given for the phrase 'neither shall any plague come nigh thy tent' in the following terms: 'that thou shalt not have a son or disciple who burns his food publicly, like Jeschu ha Notsri (Jesus)' (Bab.Sanhedrin 103a). The biblical researcher George Mead concluded that what this strange phrase 'burns his food publicly' actually means is revealing secret teachings publicly, to ordinary people, to the poor, the peasantry and to manual workers such as carpenters and stone masons. As Mead makes clear, for the Jewish religious elite, 'These ignorant and unclean livers were *Amme ha aretz* (men of the earth) and the Torah (the books of Moses) were not for them. If it was that no *Am ha aretz* was admitted to the schoolhouse, much more strictly were guarded the approaches to those more select communities where the mysteries ... were studied. To some such community of this kind we believe Jeschu (Jesus) originally belonged; and from it he was expelled because he "burnt his food publicly", that is to say, taught the wisdom to the unpurified people and so violated the ancient rule of the order.' Although Mead was talking about the 'theosophists' of Judaism, it is quite clear that the 'community' to which Jesus belonged was the Nazarites, who, as I had discovered, reverenced the head as sacred, and followed the ancient teachings of Akhenaten.

In this connection it should also be noted that the Bible states (and the Talmud agrees) that Jesus spent his boyhood in Egypt. Several authors have suggested that King Herod's 'slaughter of the innocents' in an attempt to remove the threat of a 'new king' is simply a pretext to explain Jesus' sojourn in Egypt, where, as the source of the ancient sacred head religion, he could have been initiated into further mysteries.[4] Certainly the slaughter of the innocents would appear to be a fiction. There is simply no historical evidence of the wholesale destruction of Jewish children. It is not mentioned by Josephus, who is not averse to cataloguing Herod's many other crimes. Nor does the Talmud record any such holocaust, and yet the rabbis who composed the text hated Herod with a vengeance. The New Testament pretext for the infant Jesus' 'escape' to Egypt does seem to be a cover story for other, more recondite, motives. In this context, and remembering the story of Gaythelos' and Scota's emigration from Egypt, it is perhaps interesting that the only other place that tradition has Jesus visit is the British Isles.[5]

Jesus a True King

The Christian tradition delights in portraying Jesus as a simple child of humble parents, standing quietly by, watching his father working with hammer, plane and adze in his carpentry shop. However, there is very little solid evidence that Joseph was ever a worker in wood, and much to suggest that the family into which Jesus was born was far more high born than tradition allows.

The humble appellation 'carpenter', which has followed both Joseph and Jesus for nearly two thousand years, is almost certainly a misnomer, brought about by a mistranslation of the original text. Matthew's Gospel recounts that when Jesus first began teaching before his neighbours in the synagogue at Nazareth, the onlookers were astonished and asked, 'Is not this the carpenter?' (Mark 6: 3), or 'Is not this the carpenter's son?' (Matthew 13: 55). The Jewish original uses a word that can have both a literal or a metaphorical meaning. In Aramaic, the language used by the Jewish population at the time of Jesus, the word is *naggar*, which can mean either a craftsman or, metaphorically, a learned man or scholar. The question in the synagogue should more properly be rendered, 'Isn't this the scholar?' or 'Isn't this the scholar's son?', which alters Jesus' social status quite dramatically.[6]

The Gospel of Luke gives us a genealogy, starting with Joseph and stretching all the way back to Adam, which indicates that Jesus was of the House of David and it is, at first sight, difficult to reconcile a scion of this renowned royal house with a simple carpenter. In Matthew, and in the Book of James, it is Mary, Jesus' mother, who is said to be of the line of King David. The concept of Jesus as a humble workman becomes less and less tenable in the light of this information: either via his mother or his father (or perhaps via both), Jesus was of royal blood. The high-born nature of his ancestry is also borne out by the Jewish writings on the subject. While normally hostile to Jeschu (Jesus), they still admit to his importance as a member of the elite of Jewish society:

> But there is a tradition: On the Sabbath of the Passover festival Jeschu was hung. But the herald went forth before him for the space of forty days, while he cried: 'Jeschu goes forth to be executed because he has practised sorcery and seduced Israel and estranged them from God. Let any one who can bring forward any justifying plea for him come and give information concerning it.' But no justifying plea was found for him, and so he was hung on the Sabbath of the Passover festival. Ulla has said, but dost thou think that he belongs to those for whom a justifying plea is sought? He was a very seducer, and the All-merciful has said: 'Thou shalt not spare him or conceal him' (Deuteronomy 8: 8). However, in Jeschu's case it was somewhat different, for his place was near those in power.
>
> (Bab.Sanhedrin 43a)

As George Mead has noted: 'The real reason for all those precautions was that Jeschu was a person of great distinction and importance, and "near those in power" at the time, that is to say presumably, connected by blood with the Jewish rulers – a trait preserved in the Toldoth Jeschu.'[7] That the kingship devolved from an Egyptian royal line can be shown from another Toldoth story, which deals with the conception of Jesus.

Conception

The Toldoth Jeschu gives details of Jesus' conception which are in complete opposition to the Gospel story of the Virgin Birth, and make Jesus out to be a man born of a woman like other men. It was the Jewish custom at that time for a woman before her marriage to separate herself from her betrothed. It was also quite common for the man to visit his fiancée during the night at this time, and children were often conceived in this period. The Jews actually had separate terms for a child born out of wedlock (*mamzer* = bastard) and a child conceived during this time of separation by the betrothed couple (*ben ha-niddah* = son of a woman in her separation).

The Toldoth relates that Miriam (the Hebrew name for Mary) was betrothed to Rabbi Jochanan, who was of the royal House of David (other stories have Miriam herself as a member of this august bloodline). During her separation, at night, a man entered her room whom she took to be her betrothed Jochanan, but was in fact another man, who is named as Ben Pandira. Despite her protestations that she was in her separation and should not be touched, she allowed 'her betrothed' to make love to her in the darkness. A short while after, Rabbi Jochanan chose to make his own secret visit to Miriam and she protested with even more vehemence:

> 'What meaneth this? Never hath it been thy custom, since thou wast betrothed to me, twice in a night to come to me.'
>
> He answered her and said: 'It is but once I come to thee this night.'
>
> She said to him: 'Thou camest to me, and I said to thee I was in my separation, yet heeded'st thou not, but did'st thy will and wentest forth.'
>
> When he heard this, forthwith he perceived that Joseph ben Pandira had cast an eye upon her and done the deed ...[8]

In the Toldoth story, Jesus' bastardy finally became known, and also the name of his natural father. From then on he was known as Jesus ben Pandira, Jesus son of Pandira (ben is a patronymic in Hebrew, like Mac in Scottish Gaelic, meaning 'son of').

There is something very strange about this story. The name of Jesus' 'true father', Pandira, is not a Jewish name. Several explanations arose in tradition to account for the name, and it was even claimed that Pandira was the name of a Roman legionary who had had an illicit affair with Miriam, and the child Jesus was a result. But by far the most cogent argument that has been put forward to explain this enigmatic title gives the name an Egyptian origin, and relates it directly to the sun god of the Egyptians, Ra.[9] According to this theory, in Hebrew the word breaks down as Pa-ndi-ra, which in Egyptian is transliterated as Pa-ntr-ra, or (with additional vowels added) Pa neter ra. This is an ancient title of the sun god Ra, as the deity was worshipped in ancient Egypt. So, if Jesus is named as 'Jesus ben Pandira', then he is actually being identified with the Egyptian god Ra, as 'Jesus, son of Ra'. But this is not simply the name given to all followers of this particular god. The title 'Son of Ra' was an essential epithet for every pharaoh all the way back to the fourth dynasty, some 2,700 years before the birth of Christ. What we have here is the identification of Jesus with the ancient line of the pharaohs. This is exactly what we might expect if the Tutmosis-sired-Isaac theory described in Chapter 9 is correct, but it is extremely difficult to explain otherwise.

It does appear that the Ben Pandira information is very important, as it has been excised from a number of texts by hands unknown. For example, in Origen's *Contra Celsum*, the church father rails against a Jew called Celsus, and quotes him as saying that the lover of the mother of Jesus was named Panthera (an obvious corruption of Pandira), an accusation that Celsus repeats later in the text.[10] In the oldest Vatican manuscript of this work, the name Panthera has been excised from the text in both sections.[11] It is hard to believe that this happened by chance, or that the name alone offended. The story of Jesus' bastardy must have been far more offensive to Catholic ears than the apparently arbitrary name of the father. Why, then, was the tale left intact and just the name deleted? The answer can only be that the name Pandira does indeed carry hidden information and that certain persons or vested interests knew of the connection of Jesus to the Egyptian royal house, and preferred that this information remain hidden.

What is especially telling is the fact that the teachers of the Talmud retained the name without really knowing what it meant. This is in itself strong proof of its authenticity. As many anthropological studies have shown, it is quite possible for information to be transmitted down the generations without any transmitter necessarily knowing the meaning of what is transmitted. Indeed, in order for the 'data' to remain intact over long periods, it is often better that the tellers be unclear as to the meaning of the message. That way they are less likely to tamper with it. This is further evidence of the antiquity of the information contained in this altogether anomalous name. But why Ben Pandira, 'Son of Ra'? If this theory is correct, if it is true that Jesus is descended from Tutmosis III, whose great-great-grandson was Akhenaten, the champion of the universal god, the Aten, why then, was Jesus not named as 'Son of Aten'? This, rather than 'Son of Ra', would seem to be the most logical and succinct way of indicating his ancestry. The answer seems to be that it was Jesus' connection with the Egyptian royal line of David (Tutmosis III) that was being emphasised in this story, and the Pharaoh Tutmosis was regarded as a Son of Ra. In fact, it would have been extremely difficult, not to say dangerous, for a Jewish chronicler to name Jesus a 'Son of Aten'. As we have seen, Aten in Hebrew is Adonai; to have called Jesus son of Adonai would have been to identify him as 'Jesus, Son of God', a title obviously acceptable to Christians, but rank heresy to any Jew!

In their book *The Hiram Key*, Christopher Knight and Robert Lomas unconsciously confirm this thesis of Jesus' connection to the royal Egyptian house. Up until the time of the fourth dynasty, the pharaoh identified himself not as the human offspring of the god Ra, but instead with Horus, the falcon-headed god of the Egyptian pantheon, and son of Osiris and his sister Isis. As we have seen, in the Osiris myth, the jealous brother Seth kills Osiris, and cuts him into fourteen pieces, which he scatters. But Isis collects all the scattered remnants (except Osiris' phallus), wraps them in linen, and lies with the body. As a result she miraculously conceives Horus, before Osiris is resurrected. So Horus was, paradoxically, the son of a woman whose husband was dead before he was conceived. Horus was, therefore, the son of a widow. As Knight and Lomas comment: 'It seems logical therefore that all those who thereafter became Horus, i.e., the kings of Egypt, would also describe themselves as "Son of the Widow".'[12] This was confirmation indeed of my belief that Jesus was a descendant of the royal line of Egypt. Astonishingly, in many heretical Christian sects, this term is used to indicate Jesus. Moreover, in masonic lore, which claims an ancestry from ancient Egypt, both Hiram Abif and Jesus himself are known as 'Son of the Widow'.

The Wife and Sons of Jesus

Although the Talmud accuses Jesus of crimes against orthodox Judaism, it is also quite clear that he was a learned man.[13] On this, if on few other points, the Gospels agree with the Talmudic portrayal of a learned Jesus – he is called Rabbi, or teacher, in numerous passages in the New Testament. But if this is so, then Jesus must have been married, for Mishnaic law is categoric: 'an unmarried man may not be a teacher'. In fact, there is a deafening silence on Jesus' marital status in the Gospels. If Jesus were celibate or had advocated celibacy, it is inconceivable that this would not have been mentioned – in the context of the times, celibacy would have set Jesus apart and made him special, something the Gospel writers were at pains to emphasise and would not have overlooked. Theological researcher Charles Davis was not overstating the case when he concluded: '... any practice or advocacy of voluntary celibacy would ... have been so unusual as to have attracted much attention and comment'.[14]

Several researchers have drawn attention to anomalous passages in the Gospel that seem to point to the fact that Jesus was indeed married. Michael Baigent, Henry Lincoln and Richard Leigh have put forward strong arguments for believing that three of the primary female characters in the New Testament – Mary of Bethany, the woman who anointed Jesus' feet with oil, and Mary Magdalene – are in fact the same individual, the wife of Jesus.[15] Several ancient legends are clear on this fact, that Jesus and the Magdalene were indeed married, and the same 'truth' was held as a 'great secret' by the Cathar heretics.[16] If Mary Magdalene was the wife of Jesus, it would explain her inclusion as a principal character in a number of later legends. In addition, several legends specifically state that the Magdalene was of the tribe of Benjamin, and this both opens up an intriguing possibility and makes the likelihood of a marriage more likely. The tribal King David (who was descended from the House of Judah) had usurped the throne from the Benjamite Saul, and had added insult to injury by taking over the Benjamite city of Jerusalem as his capital. It would have been natural, given the emphasis on lineage in ancient Jewish society, if these events had been points of friction between the House of Judah and the House of Benjamin. Both slights could have been remedied if Jesus (of the tribe of Judah) had joined in a dynastic marriage with a Benjamite of high rank. And as well as being of Benjamite descent, Mary Magdalene was herself reputedly of royal blood.[17]

If such a marriage had taken place, then one would expect that Jesus would have fathered children by his wife. Indeed, the only real purpose of such a union would have been the creation of a bloodline that reconciled the competing claims of the tribes of Judah and Benjamin. If there were children, it would accord with the hypothesis that Jesus' line was continued outside Israel, in the south of France, whither, as we have seen, the Magdalene is said to have fled. Until now, there has seemed to be no documentary evidence of any offspring of Jesus, and the argument has had to be supported by logical deductions, historical correspondences and later legendary accounts, and by noting intriguing gaps in the story of Christ. It seems to have passed the notice of every other researcher that, astonishingly, a reference to the children of Jesus actually exists in the literature.

I found it in the Jewish writings, in the Toldoth. Here, we find a passage that confirms the gospel account that, just before the feast of Passover,

Jesus entered the city of Jerusalem riding on an ass. But there is one telling addition to the story:

> Now in that year Passover fell on a Sabbath, and he **and his sons** came to Jerusalem, on the rest-day of Passover, that is on a Friday, he riding on an ass and saying to his disciples: 'Of me it was said: Rejoice greatly, Daughters of Zion' . . .[18]

The phrase 'and his sons' is included so simply, without comment, that it is easy to miss. The text is telling us that Jesus had at least two sons (and probably an unspecified number of daughters, females rarely being considered as worthy of note in Jewish writings). If the Talmudic scholars had added this fact maliciously, they are likely to have made far greater play of the children's existence. But they do not choose to make political or religious capital out of the fact. The passage simply states that the sons of Jesus accompanied their father to Jerusalem, and is not mentioned further. The fact that the existence of Jesus' children is treated so lightly, that they are not emphasised or commented upon, is further proof of the antiquity of this passage and its likely veracity.

Trial and Execution

The Jewish writings make no mention of any Roman involvement in the death of Jesus. Pontius Pilate is not mentioned, nor the crucifixion. Several students of Judaism have denied that crucifixion was ever practised by the Jews. A condemned person, they say, might be put to death by beheading, the garrotte, hanging or stoning. But the cross was quite unknown as a method of capital punishment. In general this seems to be true, although there have certainly been occasions in Jewish history where crucifixion was used. Perhaps the most horrible episode of all occurred during the time of Jannai, a king of the Maccabaean dynasty who ruled over Palestine 104–78 BC (i.e., just eighty years or so before the birth of Jesus). Jannai deprived the Pharisees of most of their privileges. In addition, what particularly irked these holy men was the sight of Jannai sacrificing in the temple, for this warrior king had arrogated the role of high priest to himself. After many years of dissension, the Pharisees led a rebellion against Jannai, which was put down with unbelievable ferocity. No fewer than fifty thousand Jews are said to have died in the revolt, with the leaders of the rebellion taking refuge in the bastion of Bethome, which Jannai besieged and eventually took.[19] Eight hundred Pharisee prisoners were dragged back to Jerusalem, where they were forced to watch the slaughter of their wives and children. Then they were all crucified as Jannai and his wives and concubines looked on and made mock of their sufferings. While crucifixion on this scale was exceptional, it is clear that the punishment was used at least occasionally, so we cannot be completely certain that the cross was not an option for someone like Jesus, whose crimes were considered particularly heinous.

As we have seen, the main charge that the Jewish rabbis brought against Jesus was that he practised magic. The formal charge is given as Jesus 'having practised sorcery and seduced Israel and estranged them from God'. So, remembering that the Jewish concept of 'magic' and 'sorcery' included the practice of almost every other religion, it does seem that Jesus was attempting to introduce new patterns of worship to the mass of the Hebrew nation, perhaps (as the 'burning his food in public' text suggests) revealing teachings that others believed should be vouchsafed to only a chosen few. For the orthodox believers this was grievous heresy for which the only possible punishment was death. According to the Jewish accounts, two witnesses were hidden in a house that Jesus was to visit, apparently in an attempt to bring its owner within his new teachings. This was standard procedure against those who tried to seduce Jews into following other gods. The Mishna details the procedure followed:

> ... witnesses are placed in concealment behind the wall, and he says himself to the seducer 'now tell me once again what thou wast saying to me, for we are alone'. If he now repeats it, the other says to him: 'How should we forsake our Heavenly Father and go and worship wood and stone?' If then the enticer is converted, well and good; but if he replies: 'This is our duty; it is for our good', then those who are standing behind the wall bring him before the court of justice, and he is stoned.
>
> (Pal. Sandhedrin 25c)

To this passage the Palestinian Gemara adds that particular care is taken to obtain an unambiguous identification of the enticer, by lighting a lamp over the place where he is to stand. It continues: 'Thus, for instance they managed with Ben Sot'da (a pseudonym for Jesus) ... and he was brought before the court of justice and stoned.' The Babylonian Gemara confirms the stoning and adds, 'and they hanged him on the day before Passover'. This apparently refers to the Jewish custom that the bodies of those subject to death by stoning were hung upon a post as a warning to others.[20] As in Christian tradition, where the word hung is still occasionally used as a synonym for crucifixion, it is possible that the stoning and hanging was, over time, transposed to the more horrific death of crucifixion as the new religion's teachings and history were carried to the Romanised world where death on the cross was a more commonplace and familiar form of punishment.

Burial

The Gospels claim that after his death, Jesus lay dead in his tomb for only three days before his resurrection which, according to Christian dogma, was a literal return to life in the body which had hung on the cross. Mary Magdalene, on visiting the garden tomb of Joseph of Arimathea, found that the body had disappeared, and an 'angel' told the distraught woman of Jesus' resurrection, after which she spread the joyful news to the rest of the disciples. In contrast, the Jewish chronicles have a far more prosaic explanation for the disappearance of the body. The disciples, they say, stole the corpse of Jesus from the sepulchre. The Toldoth recension preserved in the Strassburg MS has a slightly different version. It states that, after his execution, the body of Jesus was left to hang until the time of afternoon prayer, when it was 'taken down from the tree ... They buried him ... on Sunday and the apostates wept over his grave.' Some young men came to look at his grave and to their surprise, and the surprise of Jesus' followers, the grave was empty. The disciples (or 'foolish ones' according to the Toldoth) jump to the conclusion that Jesus has been resurrected, and call on the Queen of Israel, named as Helene, to witness that their master has ascended into heaven. She is inclined to believe them, for the wise men of Israel are apparently at a loss to explain the strange disappearance of the body. The queen gives them a certain time in which to find the body and '... all Israel remained lamenting in fasting and prayer, and the apostates (the disciples) found occasion to say: Ye have slain God's anointed'.

The body remains elusive until the very end of the time allotted by the queen for its discovery. A rabbi, wandering and lamenting in the fields, tells his troubles to a gardener, who then admits that he has stolen away the body 'because of the apostates, so that they should not take him and have the opportunity for all time' (that is, presumably, the opportunity to claim that their master had risen from the dead).

Whether we believe in the gardener's tale or not (and it does seem, on balance, to be rather too convenient a story), the fact remains that the Jewish tradition was adamant that the body of Jesus was stolen by his followers. I was inclined to believe this part of the tale, but it seemed to me that the body could well have been removed by Jesus' Nazarite brethren, and for ritual purposes. Given the facts that I had uncovered concerning the links between Akhenaten, the apparent fount of head worship, and the Nazarites, who followed his teachings faithfully and whose reverence of the head was undoubted, there seemed to be only one conclusion to be drawn, though it was a conclusion which left me feeling distinctly uncomfortable. Would, I wondered, the head of Jesus have been taken from the body, and embalmed as a holy relic? Given the status of Jesus, a true king of the line of Tutmosis III and Akhenaten, and an admitted adept of 'Magic', it seemed to me inconceivable that the ritual would not have been performed.

This was, to say the least, a disturbing conclusion, but one to which all the evidence pointed.

To sum up the essentials of this chapter, there is much evidence to show that Jesus was regarded by his contemporaries as a priest-king, an embodiment of the divine, as the pharaohs, the Israelite kings and, later, the Merovingians were. He was of royal blood and a descendant of the true House of David (i.e., of Tutmosis III of Egypt). He was an initiate of Akhenaten's mysteries, and he was condemned to death for trying to bring at least some of these teachings into wider currency, which was anathema to the orthodox Judaic authorities of his time. He was quite certainly a Nazarite, and as such he would have reverenced the sun as a manifestation of the one creator. Like his Nazarite contemporaries, Jesus would have held the early patriarchs (who we now know were also of Tutmosis' royal line) in high esteem, and he would have considered Moses/Akhenaten as the source of the true religion, which was held as a secret doctrine. And finally, as a Nazarite he would have regarded the head as holy, and followed that prohibition on cutting the hair which had figured so strongly in my investigation and which I now felt sure was the overt manifestation of the sacred head cult. He was executed, probably by the Jewish authorities, for in their view, 'attempting to seduce the children of Israel and lead them after other gods'. With his death the body disappeared. Given his position as a true king and adept of the hidden religion, his sacred head would certainly have been removed and kept as a holy relic.

It seems likely that Jesus was not the wild revolutionary beloved of so many 'revisionist' books. The purpose of his mission was less political than religious, and his antagonism towards Roman authority was more incidental than a main 'plank' in his strategy. He embarked on a carefully planned religious revolution to restore the worship of the Aten, with himself in the role of Akhenaten, priest-king of the 'new' religion, and a direct descendant of the House of David, i.e., of the Egyptian royal line that began with Tutmosis III and culminated in the Amarna kings, most notably Akhenaten/Moses. All sources agree that the attempt failed and he was taken prisoner. Thereafter, he was either stoned to death or crucified.

Tradition states that, after the failure of their hopes, the Magdalene (who, as we have seen, is likely to have been Jesus' wife) and Joseph of Arimathea sought exile in France, along with a number of others, including Lazarus, whom Jesus had 'raised from the dead'. The Magdalene is said to have brought the Holy Grail with her into exile. Of great interest is the story of one of Mary's fellow-travellers on this journey, Veronica.[21] She is said to have taken pity on Jesus as he made his way with his cross to Calvary. She offered the condemned man a cloth which she had on her arm. In return, she was rewarded with the impress of his holy face upon the cloth, which she kept as a relic, and which became known as the Veronica. The Veronica was therefore the head of Christ, apparently impressed on a cloth. Could it, I wondered, be an allegorical version of a real event, something which had to remain secret from the world at large? Was the story of the Veronica's shipment across the Mediterranean a way of recounting the carrying of the holy head into France? As I was later to discover, other texts also alluded to just this possibility.

While Mary is said to have brought the Grail to France, other stories tell that Joseph of Arimathea carried the Holy Grail to England (to Glastonbury). The Cathars were also said to possess the Grail, and other legends place the Grail elsewhere, in Scotland for example. As we will see in Chapter 12, the Templars discovered something beneath the Temple of Solomon and they too, almost simultaneously, became known as 'guardians of the Grail'. It was obvious that a single Grail could not be in all these geographical locations at the same time; unless one subscribed to a supernatural origin for the object it could not be everywhere at once. If even only two of these several stories were true, I was forced to conclude that there must have been more than one Grail, perhaps a series of holy objects which, through the vagaries of history, had been dispersed across the ancient world. And I began to have an inkling as to exactly what the Grail, or grails, might be. The similarity between the attributes of the Grail and those of the embalmed head that the Templars had worshipped was extremely suggestive. Could it be that the Grail was a 'cover name'? Could the grails of legend be the sacred relics of the Judaic cult of the head? In short, was the Holy Grail the holy head?

11

The Holy Grail

The origins of the Holy Grail stories are generally agreed to lie in the intertwined strands of two cultures – the Jewish tradition and Celtic (and more specifically Irish) culture. This in itself is intriguing, as the cultural foundation of the legends therefore mirrors the dissemination of the mysteries of Akhenaten and the cult of the head into Israel and Ireland. As we have seen, the teachings of the Aten (represented initially as a sun disc) and the mysteries of the cult of the head, were carried to Israel by Moses/Akhenaten and also, by Akhenaten's daughter, to Ireland, before the coming of the Celts. And there is a second correspondence: most scholars recognise that the ultimate origin of the Grail mythology lies in solar worship.[1] In one version of the Grail cycle, the hero Lohengrin is given the title Helios, or Sun, calling to mind Samson, Man of the Sun, and the alternative name of the Nazarites, the Heliaci (Children of the Sun).[2] Given these correspondences in geography and the religious grounding of the stories in sun worship, was it possible, I wondered, to find specific evidence of sacred or severed heads in the stories of the Grail cycle? And could these be related to any of the pieces of the complex puzzle I had been attempting to piece together. For this it was necessary to study the convoluted, confusing and often contradictory Grail legends one by one. Gradually the long hours of research bore fruit and a fairly complete picture began to emerge.

Despite the complexity of the Grail stories themselves, the disembodied head motif was not difficult to find. A severed head was in the first legend I studied, the Old Welsh *Peredur*, and in the next, the *Perlesvaus*, and the next, and the next.[3] To my surprise, it turned out to be hard to avoid references to severed and sacred heads – they were scattered through the Grail legends in great abundance. Although its significance has been

143

downplayed by orthodox scholars, I discovered that the sacred severed head is one of the primary motifs in the tales that comprise the Grail cycle. Quite simply, there were heads everywhere.

Miraculous talking heads are, of course, widespread in folklore, but the heads in the Grail stories do not fall into this category. They do not speak, nor are they particularly miraculous in themselves. Many of them are mentioned specifically as being embalmed, sealed in lead or silver. Moreover, several of the heads are linked to a lineage, a 'holy' and expressly Jewish lineage. And close study of those sections containing references to severed heads revealed hitherto unsuspected data, information that pointed unmistakably in only one direction. It linked not only the lineage of Jesus, but Jesus himself, to the cult of the head.

To me, this correspondence revealed once again the links that existed between the 'heretic' philosophy unearthed by the Templars in Jerusalem and the Celtic (or more correctly pre-Celtic) religion of Ireland. In both, the sacred head was of paramount importance.

The Grail Quests

Although there is great variation in the details of the stories that comprise the Grail cycle, the notion essential to them all is that of the quest. The hero is searching for an object of great virtue, power and sanctity and he is faced with a series of trials, sometimes of martial prowess, sometimes of piety and occasionally of guile; succeeding in these tests takes him deeper and deeper into the secrets of the Grail. Such a motif is as old as history; one of the first stories we have from ancient Babylon, the *Epic of Gilgamesh*, takes the form of just such a quest, where the hero strives through many ordeals and hardships in his search for the plant of eternal life, only to lose his prize at the moment of victory.[4] In Celtic literature the quest is also a central theme, as in the class of tales known as the 'Journey to Fairyland', or the cycle of stories known as the *Tochmarca*, or 'Wooings'.[5] The famous hero Cú Chulainn is the subject of one of these stories, where he is forced to undertake long journeys and great trials in order to possess the hand of the fair Emer. Similarly, the three sons of Turenn are carried across the sea by the magical coracle of Manannan, the Irish sea god, to face various adventures in a long series of quests.[6]

The Celtic Connection

The Celtic stories contain other strong resonances with the Grail cycle, similarities which betray the Celtic origin of much of the Grail's symbolism. One of the least of the Grail's attributes was its ability to provide any number of people with an unlimited quantity of food and drink. This magical quality is mirrored in a much earlier Irish tale, that of the *Cauldron of Dagda*, said to have been brought to Ireland by a godlike race of men.[7] Dagda was one of the major gods of the Irish pantheon, the 'Lord of Life and Death', and his cauldron was full of the choicest meats and drink, which could never be depleted and which satisfied all who ate from it. In just the same way some Grail texts (such as the *Continuation of the Conte du Graal* by Gautier de Doulens) state that the relic serves the Grail company with a wonderful array of seven dishes, and that none who partook of this miraculous repast left the table unfilled. The costliest meats are described as issuing from the Grail, often, though not always, accompanied by the finest wines. Robert de Borron's romance *Joseph*, or *Roman de l'Estoire dou Saint Graal*, tells of a famine that afflicted the companions of the Grail's first keeper, Joseph of Arimathea. This famine was, the narrator tells us, due to the sin of luxury into which some of Joseph's followers had fallen. Joseph prayed to Christ before the Grail and was told to expose the relic openly on a table. He was then to invite all the members of the company to sit before it, warning that only those that had not fallen from Christ's teachings should attempt this. Those that do are, as in the Celtic cauldron legends, fed with anything that their hearts desire. But when one of those so blessed, Petrus, addresses the sinners, the author of the romance makes him ask them if they do not feel any of the good which suffuses those that sit before the Grail. But the sinners admit that they feel nothing. Here, de Borron seems to be at pains to point out the spiritual side of the Grail symbolism, that the 'food' that the Grail provides is at least as much spiritual sustenance as it is material nourishment.[8]

Attributes of another cauldron, that of Bendigeid Vran, have also been subsumed to the Grail's powers. This cauldron, mentioned in the Old Welsh *Mabinogion*, had the property of resurrection, in that any dead man deposited therein would, on the morrow, be as well as he had ever been in his life, except that he would be struck dumb.[9] In this he is like Perceval, the hero of several Grail romances, who was under a spell of silence when he stood in the presence of the Grail. This cauldron seems to carry vestiges of the old druidic religion. As one Grail researcher has put it: '... the druidic Mysteries are like other initiations: the candidate is passed through the experience of a mystical death and is brought back, as for example, by the Cauldron of Ceridwen, to a new term of existence; but although in this sense the dead are raised, they are not ... restored with the gift of tongues – life, but no word of life. In other words, the silence of the Great Pledges is henceforth imposed upon them.'[10] With illumination of the Secret comes an absolute obligation to secrecy.

Another hero of myth, Bran the Blessed, possessed a similar cauldron of rebirth, which he gave to King Matholwch of Ireland. Bran also owned a salver which, like the cauldron of Dagda and the Grail, would instantly supply 'whatever food one wished ...' But more important from our point of view are other aspects of the tale of Bran, which is suffused with Grail symbolism and which also centres around a wondrous severed head, that of Bran himself.[11]

The *Mabinogion* relates that Bran was a king of Britain, 'exalted with the crown of London'. During an overseas expedition he was wounded in battle with his adversary Caswallawn, struck on the heel by a poisoned lance. Immediately, the islands of both Britain and Ireland are said to have been rendered desolate and infertile. Realising his impending death and also, apparently, the ruin that was visited upon his kingdom because of his mortal wound, Bran ordered his followers to cut off his head, which, magically, remained alive after decapitation. Bran's head was carried by his seven trusted companions to Harlech, where they spent seven years in a palace with three doors. Thereafter obeying the orders of Bran's still-living head, the company moved to Grassholm, 'an island where was music and good fellowship'. Here, it seems, Bran's companions regaled themselves with food and drink for a further eighty years, growing no older with the passage of time, a period known in myth as the 'Hospitality of the Wondrous Head'. Eventually, Bran's head was buried in the White Hill of London, facing towards the continent. It was still possessed of occult powers, including the ability to defend the people and the land against invaders, and to ensure the fertility of crops and beasts throughout the British Isles. Significantly, the Grail too was said to maintain the fertility of the land, protect from enemies, and gave food and drink in abundance to all who needed it.

It was just these characteristics, mirrored in the Grail romances, that were attributed to the head that the Templars were accused of worshipping. The Inquisition's 'Articles of Accusation' claim that the order believed that the head could save them from enemies, that it gave them all the riches of the order, and that it made the trees flower and the land germinate.[12]

Holy Grail and Templar 'idol', both sharing identical occult powers. I was convinced that this had to be more than mere coincidence; something else was involved. If the powers the Grail and the idol shared were identical, could the two objects themselves be identical, physically identical? Could the 'Grail' and the 'idol' be equivalent terms, two names describing the same object? In short, was the Grail a 'cover name' for a sacred severed head? This was a plausible hypothesis, but I would have to put together a lot more evidence in order to be sure that it was correct. It was time to go back to the Grail romances and see if these correspondences between Grail and severed head were simply serendipitous, or whether there really was some substance in my conjectures. I began with the first of the Grail romances, Chretien de Troyes' masterpiece *Le Conte du Graal*, and almost immediately, I 'struck gold'.

Chretien de Troyes and The Perceval

At some time in the twelfth century several of these Celtic tales were fused, remodelled, and given a specifically Christian slant in the form of the Grail legends. But, it was Christianity of a decidedly heterodox or heretical nature, and the reconfigured legend was used not only as a vehicle for heretical philosophy, but also as a cloak in which to hide it from the uninitiated. It was also a form of self-preservation, which allowed the writers to intimate heretical beliefs and yet still escape the murderous attentions of the Church, and later the Inquisition, who were zealous in their self-imposed task of rooting out God's enemies and the 'evil' of heresy.

A 'quest' story such as the Grail legends is ideal for anyone wishing to wrap a secret within an apparently ordinary tale. The episodic structure and dream-like quality of the narrative allows the author to introduce elements or themes, individuals or locations almost *ad libitum*, weaving a dense, imaginative and highly complex web of events, characters, supernatural beings and dream-locations that defies all but the most careful and thorough analysis, and then only if the researcher is equipped with the correct key. Using this strategy, those elements that matter, and can be 'read' by the *illuminati*, are effectively camouflaged, hidden behind a smoke-screen of relatively unimportant symbols and characters. Those who know and possess the key can look beyond, or through, the non-essential elements, and read in the symbols the true message of the book, while those not privy to the secret enjoy the tale simply for its adventure and romance, understanding only the surface of the legend and not its deeper meaning.

Chretien de Troyes is credited with the first telling of this new Christian version of the tale, *Le Conte du Graal*.[13] Chretien was a twelfth-century cleric and poet, and he seems to have worked at Troyes under the patronage of Marie, Countess of Champagne. At all events, many of his works are dedicated to this lady, who was a guiding star to the courtly nobles of northern France. It may be at Troyes that he met Philip of Alsace, Count of Flanders, who sued unsuccessfully for Marie's hand when her husband Count Henri died. Chretien's Grail romance is dedicated, in a rather fawning manner, to Philip of Alsace who, says Chretien, has asked him to undertake the work. He declares that it is the finest tale ever told in royal court and was taken from an older book which Philip gave him to read.

As the Grail scholar Alfred Brown has shown, Chretien's early romances, such as *Lancelot* and *Erec*, all include motifs that are to be found in far earlier Irish stories depicting a 'Journey to Fairyland'.[14] To take just two correspondences, the Dolorous Tower and Castle of the Maidens are central themes of the Irish stories and they are to be found in every one of Chretien's early works. Many such motifs also appear in Chretien's *Perceval*, and the Celtic origins of the story are therefore undoubted. Severed heads also appear in the early stories: in *Lancelot*, the eponymous hero has just vanquished a knight when a lady rides up and demands his head. Lancelot gives the knight his sword again, reconquers him and takes his head.[15] He gives the head to the lady, who then rides off. Again, in *Erec*, we read of a row of spikes with heads upon them and at the end of the row, an ominously vacant spike.[16] However, these heads are simply 'props' to the main story, and they are certainly imbued with no great numinous significance, unlike the heads of the later Grail stories.

Chretien's *Le Conte du Graal* is set in the time of King Arthur. We first meet the hero, Perceval, as a young untutored boy whose father has been killed in battle. He is therefore named, intriguingly, as the 'Son of the Widow Lady', a title we have met before when considering the bloodline of Jesus. This calls for an explanation, but we do not get one. Chretien takes this link no further, although later Grail authors have much to say in this regard.

By chance, Perceval meets several of Arthur's knights. Impressed by their bearing, he decides to follow the profession of arms himself and sets out in search of 'the king who made knights', leaving his mother swooning with grief. At Arthur's court and elsewhere Perceval's social graces are shown to be sadly lacking on a number of occasions, until he is finally taken under the wing of Lord Gornemant, who gives him training in arms and who, eventually, knights the gauche youth. Gornemant also advises him against being too loquacious, guidance which is destined to bring disaster upon the head of the newly dubbed knight.

Having achieved his ambition, Perceval sets off back home. On the way he finds his path barred by a deep river, with no ford or bridge or ferry to allow him to pass. He asks for directions from two men fishing in a boat and is told that one of them will give him lodgings for the night. The lodgings turn out to be a fine castle and Perceval is treated royally, given fresh clothes, his horse cared for, and a sumptuous banquet prepared. His host, who is known as the Fisher King (Roi Pescheor) fails to rise when the knight enters, because of a javelin wound through the thighs which has rendered him lame. The Fisher King makes Perceval a gift of a fine sword, and seats him by his side for the feast. But before the banquet commences, Perceval witnesses a strange procession passing between the fire and the couch on which he sits. A squire enters bearing a spear or lance from which there drips blood. Two youths follow, with candelabra, accompanying a damsel bearing between her two hands the Grail, containing – in most versions – a mass wafer. A second damsel, carrying a carving dish of silver, completes the procession. 'The Grail which preceded her was of refined gold. And it was set with precious stones of many kinds, the richest and costliest that exist in the sea or in the earth. Like the lance, these damsels passed before the couch and entered another chamber.' Through all this Perceval sits silent; and although he longs to ask concerning these marvels, he remembers the words of his tutor Gornemant and holds his peace. As each course is served, the Grail procession is repeated but Perceval, although consumed with curiosity, fails to ask a single question about the mystical pageant he has just witnessed. Still perplexed, he retires to bed and next morning wakes to find the castle deserted.

Forced to his travels once more, he encounters a maiden, weeping bitterly. She is sitting beside a headless corpse. The maiden, who is Perceval's cousin, reproaches him for not asking about the Grail; this question, it appears, would have cured the Fisher King of his wound and led to great good fortune. But failure to ask the question has foredoomed Perceval and others to much misery and woe. This is because he has sinned against his mother by leaving her; since his journey to Arthur's court she has died of grief. Perceval is stricken by this news, but offers to help his cousin and to escort her safely on her journey. He returns to King Arthur, and is at court when a Loathly Damsel (the Kundry of Wagner's opera *Parsifal*) arrives: '... never was there a creature so loathly save those in hell ... Her eyes were two holes, as small as those of a rat; her nose was like that of a monkey or a cat ... her teeth resembled in colour those of an egg; she had a beard like a goat ... Her figure was perfect for leading a dance!' This hideous creature berates Perceval in the same manner as his cousin, deriding his silence in the presence of the lance and especially of the Grail. Apparently, he should have asked 'whom one serves with it'. This is a deliberately ambiguous question, which can be understood as asking for whom does the Grail provide food and drink, or alternatively, what master does one follow by serving the Grail.

The Loathly Damsel then tells of the 566 knights of Castle Orgulous, where any knight seeking to perform feats of chivalry should go. And of a damsel besieged below Montesclaire, whose salvation would bring great honour to the rescuer. Hearing her words, Sir Gawain vows to lift the maiden's siege, and the other knights, more than fifty, make various heroic pledges. Perceval, however, remains obsessed by the events that had occurred in the hall of the Fisher King, and by the mystery of the Grail itself. He '... vowed that henceforth he would not lie two nights in the same lodging, or avoid any strange passage of which he might hear, nor fail to engage in combat with any knight who claimed to be superior to any other, or even two other knights, until he could learn whom one served with the Grail ...' This he never does, for Chretien's epic is, sadly, unfinished. The last we hear of Perceval is when, having renounced belief in God for more than five years, he meets his hermit uncle, rediscovers his faith and is given sound Catholic advice by his relative on how to conduct himself in a Christian manner. And there the tale abruptly stops, with every indication that it has been left unfinished by its author, who died around 1188. From a narrative point of view, this is far from satisfying. Having 'set up' the questions of 'what is the Grail?' and 'whom does one serve with it?' earlier in the story, Chretien fails to give even a sniff of the answers. Perhaps, had he lived to complete the tale, we would have them. Fortunately for our investigations, other authors are more forthcoming.

The Peredur and The Body of Christ

Although the first official 'release' of the Grail theme is usually ascribed to Chretien de Troyes, many scholars believe that a Welsh tale, *Peredur*, is at least contemporary with Chretien's story, and that they both derive ultimately from some common source, now lost.[17] It is in the *Peredur* that we meet the first of the sacred severed heads. As in Chretien's romance, Peredur (the Welsh equivalent of Perceval) is given a banquet in his uncle's

A skull carved in oak with great anatomical precision and attesting to the importance of the head in Templar ritual. It rests on an inlaid silver stand. Knights Templar regalia, probably eighteenth century.
© R. Bryden

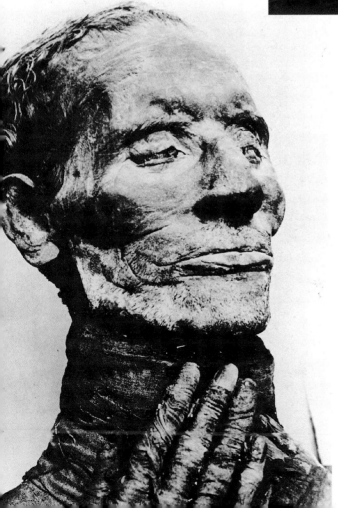

The mummified head of Yuya, the biblical Joseph. The mummy's Semitic features, commented upon by several authors, are astonishingly well-preserved.
© Cairo Museum

The Amarna style, inaugurated by Akhenaten, was a radical departure from earlier ritualised portrayals of the pharaoh and his entourage. Here Akhenaten's god, the Aten, shown as a solar disc, sheds his life-giving force over the royal family. © Hulton Getty Images

Ahmoses
    Amenhotep I
        Tutmoses I
            Tutmoses II
                Hatshepsut
                    Tutmoses III
                        Amenhotep II
                          Tutmoses IV
                          Amenhotep III
                            Amenhotep IV
                            (Akhenaten)
                              Semenkhare
                                Tutankhamun
                                  Aye
                                    Horemheb

Pharaohs of the eighteenth dynasty (approximately 1575–1308 BC)

Pharaohs in bold = Amarna kings

Medieval portrayal of the emigration of Gaythelos and Scota from Egypt to Ireland (*Scotichronicon*). © Corpus Christi College Cambridge

The Stone of Destiny or the Bethel Stone or Jacob's Pillar. This 65cm-long block of calcareous limestone (fitted with two iron rings to take a carrying pole) links the history of the Hebrews with that of Ireland. © Longmore House, Edinburgh

Delilah cutting Samson's hair. Samson belonged to the Nazarite sect, a group that esteemed both the head and the hair as holy, and whose teachings link them to the secrets of Akhenaten. © British Library, London/ Bridgeman Art Library, London/NY

The pharaonic lotus was probably transmuted into the Judaic 'lily', shown in this coin of Antiochus VII, minted in the century just prior to the birth of Christ. The affinity of this image to both the Egyptian lotus and the fleur-de-lis are striking.

Coin depicting King Childeric I. Like Samson, the Merovingian kings were forbidden to cut their hair.

The sacred lotus, symbol of pharaonic Egypt, as inscribed on a column in the temple of Amon, at Karnak. The lotus bears a close resemblance to the Judaic 'lily' and the French fleur-de-lis.
© Bridgeman Art Library, London/NY

The belief in the divine origin of the fleur-de-lis symbol is attested to in the fifteenth century *Legend of the Fleur-de-Lys*, where it is given by God to the Merovingian monarch, Clovis I. © British Library, London/Bridgeman Art Library, London/NY

Arrest of the Templars, from the Chronicle of France or of St Denis (fourteenth century). © British Library, London/Bridgeman Art Library, London/NY

Jacques de Molay, last known Grand Master of Knights Templar, is burn at the stake for heresy, fr the Chronicle of France of St Denis (fourteenth century). © British Libra London/Bridgeman Art Library, London/NY

his eighteenth *century* woodcut of *the* Tomb [*sic*] of *Jacques* de Molay' *reveals* in symbolic *form* the central secret *of* the Templars.

below The tomb of *William* Sinclair in *Rosslyn* Chapel. The *stone* is far shorter *than* the height of an *adult* man, indicating *a* Templar burial. *Note,* too, the Lombard *lettering:* the surname *has* been changed to *'r',* and these last *two* letters have been *placed* at right angles *to* the preceding letters, *giving* it two alternate *meanings:* William *Sinclair* 'and his *remains'* or *et reliquae,* *'the* relics'. *©* Liz Laidler

Rosslyn Chapel, Sir William Sinclair's 'Grail Chapel', seen from the air.
© Commission Air, Peterborough

Right The barrelled roof of Rosslyn Chapel, with its multitude of carvings.
© Antonia Reeve/Rosslyn Chapel Trust

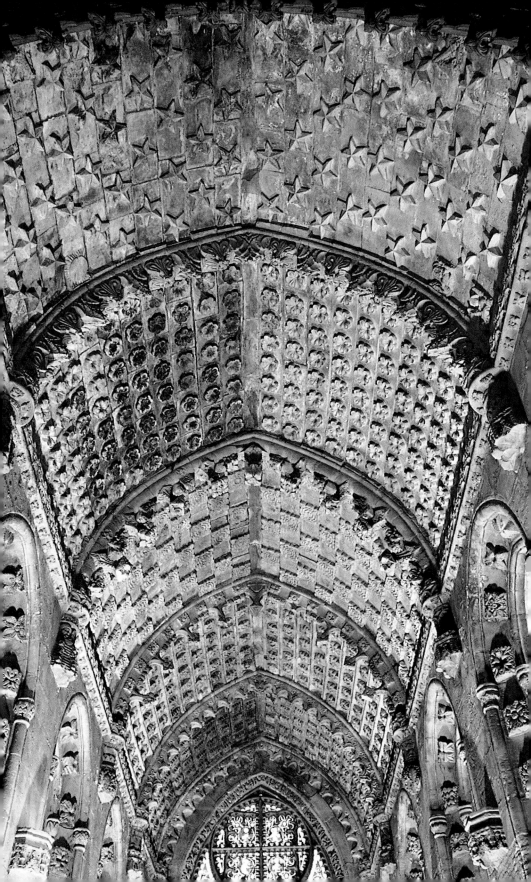

A head of the 'Green Man', festooned with leaves, a symbol of the fecundity of Nature (and much else besides). This is one of scores of 'green men' to be found all over Rosslyn Chapel
© Antonia Reeve/Rosslyn Chapel Trust

The Rosslyn Crucifixion scene. Note the tau cross, the position of the feet, and the arms bound (not nailed) to the Cross.
© Antonia Reeve/Rosslyn Chapel Trust

The 'Veronica' or perhaps a representation of a sacred head. The identity of the person holding the object has been destroyed 'for a reason', according to one authority. © Liz Laidler

The head of the Apprentice. Once again, deliberate damage has occurred, this time to the lower portion of the face, but careful examination reveals the remains of a moustache and beard. The Apprentice is, in fact, 'The Master'. © Antonia Reeve/Rosslyn Chapel Trust

The Apprentice Pillar: its spirals of leaves and other carvings testify to its identification as (amongst other things) the Tree of Life, a synonym for Jesus, and the Yggdrassil, the World Ash of Norse mythology.
© Antonia Reeve/Rosslyn Chapel Trust

The top of the Apprentice Pillar showing Isaac and the ram, an allusion to the Old Testament story of Abraham's near-sacrifice of Isaac. © Liz Laidler

Detail showing the damage (thought to be deliberate) done to the figure of 'Abraham' standing between the ram and Isaac.
© Liz Laidler

The Nidhogg serpent winds itself around the base of the World Ash. The serpent traditionally fed on the roots of the Ash but it was another object hidden beneath the roots of this mythical tree that proved a vital clue to the identity of the Temple treasure. © Liz Laidler

Apollo's head on the cross. Apollo is, of course, the sun god. In one sense it is the Greek equivalent of the Aten. Templar regalia of the higher degrees. © Robert Bryden

The sun's 'head' on the Cross: Templar regalia of the higher degrees. The parallels between this cross and the others on this page are striking. © Robert Bryden

The Head of God crucifix, Rosslyn Chapel. This image of Christ's head on the Cross appears to be unique in the history of Christian iconography. That it is to be found only in the Rosslyn 'Grail' Chapel makes it doubly significant. © Liz Laidler

The head of Sarah, Abraham's wife. This carving in jet stone was acquired in Galatia and resides with the Scottish Templars. It begs the question why Sarah is of such importance to the Templars. © Robert Bryden

Below The Templars worshipped an actual head, or, when this was lacking, a representation of the head. This Templar head painting, found at Templeton in 1951, bears an impressive resemblance to images of Jesus. © Bridgeman Art Library, London/NY

castle, and a mystical procession is enacted before his eyes. However, although a spear streaming with blood substitutes for the lance, in place of the mass wafer there is, grotesquely, a severed head, swimming in blood on the platter and a yellow-haired youth, not a maiden, is named as the 'Grail bearer'. This, of course, invites the question of whether the Grail is the platter on which the head is carried, or the head itself. As if to emphasise this point, the same motif of a severed head on a platter is also found in several later Grail romances. This riddle is given no solution in the *Peredur* text but, as my research continued, the extraordinary answer became abundantly clear.

This discrepancy between severed head and mass wafer has forced several scholars to try to determine which story retains the original symbolism, to answer the question: which of the two processions mirrors most clearly the common source of the tales? Most believe the Welsh *Peredur* holds most closely to the original. As Glenys Goetinck has noted 'the talismans [in *Peredur*] ... are very different from those in the castle of the Roi Pescheor and less refined. The spear is huge, it does not drip but streams with blood, there is not merely a mass wafer on the Grail, but a severed head, surrounded by blood in the dish, and the household breaks into wails of anguish as it passes by, instead of observing its passage in silence.'[18] Now, given the fact that both *Peredur* and Chretien's Perceval are derived from an older source, and that Chretien was writing for the French nobility, in an atmosphere of genteel *courtoisie* and high culture, it is legitimate and logical to deduce from this that the severed head swimming in blood is the original image of the story, and that Chretien introduced the mass wafer so as to make the tale more palatable to his devout and sophisticated readers.

But this scholarly research had not, I realised, commented upon the most important aspect of these substitutions. Why exchange a mass wafer for a severed head? What was Chretien de Troyes attempting to convey by this change? Chretien did not simply pick the idea of the mass wafer out of thin air – the symbol was important to him, and he must have chosen it for a specific purpose. And what is the mass wafer but the corpus Christi, which, according to the dogma of the Church in Chretien's time (and of the Roman Church today), was quite literally the body of Christ. When I first understood the import of this identification, the shock I felt was physical. There could be only one reason why this symbol was chosen. By making this substitution, by choosing the mass wafer, Chretien was specifically and deliberately linking the severed head with the body of Christ.

This much was obvious. But there was another connection which supported my suspicion that the Grail was a cover name for a sacred embalmed head. I had not yet been able to determine if the Grail was the platter itself, or the object which was carried upon it. But now the conclusion was clear. There was nothing to connect the platter with Jesus. But Chretien had linked the severed head with the body of Christ (by substituting the host); and the Grail was also linked to the body of Christ (as the receptacle holding Christ's blood). It seemed logical to deduce that it was the object on the platter, and not the platter itself, that was the Grail the 'Grail bearer' carried. If this was so, then the head, the host and the Grail were all names for the same object. And, as the severed head is the original object of the oldest story, it followed that the head was in fact the object that the other two names were covertly referring to. That is, the host was the head, and the Grail was also the head.

A Surfeit of Heads

The *Perlesvaus* is a slightly later, anonymous, romance that is thought by many to have been written by a Templar.[19] And it is brimming over with heads. In this romance one character, the Haughty Maiden, shows Sir Gawain three tombs and expresses her intent to behead him, Lancelot, and Perceval. 'Thus will I cut off their heads when they go to worship the relics . . .' At a banquet in the Castle of Beards, Lancelot watches a strange procession of maimed knights which ends when 'with the fifth course came noble and handsome knights, each carrying a naked sword in his hand, and they presented their heads to the lady', who cuts off each in turn and 'Lancelot sat there and watched what happened to these knights, and deplored the service they paid.' Again, at the Waste City, Lancelot makes an utterly incomprehensible agreement with another knight, who asks Lancelot if he will swear that, after he has cut off the knight's head, Lancelot will '. . . return here a year from this day, at the hour at which you kill me, or before, and offer your head freely, without defence, as I shall in a moment offer mine'. Lancelot swears, the knight kneels and stretches out his neck and Lancelot 'raised the axe and smote off the Knight's head with such a terrible blow that he sent it flying seven feet from the body'. He mounts and rides off quickly but, looking back, sees that both the body and the head have been spirited away. Towards the end of the romance, as King Arthur sits with his knights, a maiden of great beauty enters the hall carrying a coffer of pure gold, richly adorned with gems, and within which lies a severed head.

Why such an abundance of head symbolism? We can be sure that they have not been included in the story in such numbers by chance, or simply to titillate the audience, and the most likely explanation is that this is a deliberate intention on the part of the author to draw our attention to the concept of the severed head. Thus, we have examples of beheading in connection with both worship and a tomb or tombs (the Haughty Maiden), of ritual beheading (at the Castle of Beards), ritual beheading and the disappearance of both head and body (Lancelot's promise), and the keeping of a severed head in something that sounds suspiciously like a reliquary (the Head in the Coffer).

Again, in the *Perlesvaus*, we read that when the Loathly Damsel arrives at the Cardeuil, where King Arthur has his court, '... in her hands she held the head of a king, sealed with silver and crowned with gold'. A second damsel brings the head of a queen, sealed in lead and crowned with copper, and a shield emblazoned with a red cross (the sign of the Templars), which we learn is the shield of Joseph of Arimathea. The Loathly Damsel tells the king that outside in a rich cart, draped in black samite and pulled by three white stags, there are the heads of one hundred and fifty knights, some sealed in gold, some in silver and the others in lead. The gloss that is put on this later in the story is that the heads sealed in gold are Christians, those in silver Jews, and those sealed in lead belong to Saracens (i.e., Muslims). Bizarrely, the king's head is said to be the head of Adam, the queen's that of Eve. This is obviously the 'external' meaning of the tale, a surface story designed for the uninitiated. The subtext appears to be the admission that there is indeed a line of preserved heads, which include members of all three peoples of the book (i.e., Christians, Jews and Muslims) and that the heads are in some way connected to royalty. A further link to royalty has been noted by Glenys Goetinck who, in discussing the *Peredur*, ties the severed head and the platter swimming in blood to earlier Welsh motifs symbolising the loss of sovereignty.[20] Could this loss of kingship be referring to Akhenaten, to Jesus and to the Merovingians, all of whom forfeited their royal pretensions? It would seem likely. Thus the head serves two purposes for the author in this part of the tale: indicating one of the root mysteries of the secret religion (the cult of the head), and symbolising the loss of secular power of the bloodline.

Again, in the *Perlesvaus*, Lancelot is made to visit the Grail castle. He comes upon three grey-haired knights in a boat, one of whom is fishing with a rod of gold. With them is a damsel, holding a severed head. Three other maidens have previously been introduced, each carrying a similar gruesome object, and three more are to follow later. Their reason for accompanying the three aged knights, indeed their very presence in the narrative, is never overtly explained. They are simply there, like spectres hovering at the edge of the story, grasping their gruesome trophies as if to ensure that the severed head is always held in the reader's thoughts. Robert Loomis, in his book *The Grail* is one of the few scholars to address this problem of the surfeit of heads. But he can find no reason for the recurring motif, exclaiming in exasperation, 'Is this macabre obsession another symptom of an abnormal mentality?'[21] This seems to be as far as modern orthodox scholarship has got in explaining the mystery of the severed head in the Grail romances: that the heads are there because the writers of the Grail stories had a 'macabre obsession' or that they were mentally unstable. It is only now, possessed of what we know concerning the cult of the head and its provenance, that we can begin to make sense of this recurring motif and see it for what it really is, a covert description of the occult teachings of a line of 'adepts' stretching back into history.

But was there any other evidence that could corroborate this explanation of the presence of the heads in the Grail romances, and connect with the trail I had been following from Joseph/Yuya through Moses/Akhenaten, the Benjamites, and the Temple of Solomon, Jesus and the Merovingians?

The Parzival

The answer came in yet another Grail romance, the *Parzival*, written almost one hundred years after Chretien de Troyes' initial unveiling of the Grail theme to the world.[22] Such a length of time could mean that the work is derivative, that the writer of *Parzival* used Chretien's work and all the many versions and variations that derived from it, and assembled his own version, with perhaps a few literary devices of his own invention thrown in for good measure. But the author of *Parzival*, Wolfram von Eschenbach, specifically denies any connection with Chretien's poem. In fact, he is adamant that Chretien's Perceval is far less authoritative than his own work, which contains the true secret of the Grail. It is the source of Wolfram's knowledge that is so interesting and important to our own quest. He himself tells us that he had the story from a man whom he names as Kyot de Provence. Several researchers have since identified Kyot very plausibly as Guiot de Provins. Guiot was a monk and troubadour whose songs included stories of love, denunciations of the Roman Church and verses supporting the Templars and their mission. Indeed, the Templars form one of the main themes of Guiot's work.

Wolfram von Eschenbach's *Parzival* is similarly at pains to praise the

Templars, who are made guardians of the Grail, and of the Grail family, in whose charge the Holy Grail is held. In this Wolfram is echoing the *Perlesvaus* which, while it does not name the Templars directly, speaks of a group of initiate knights whose dress and demeanour can only refer to The Order of the Poor Knights of the Temple of Solomon. This is strange, as the *Perlesvaus* is constantly alluding to Josephus as an authority for the events that occur in the romance. As Josephus was writing in the first century AD, the author is obviously indicating that the events described in the story also occurred at, or before, this time. The medieval Order of the Temple is out of place here. It may be that we are to understand that the events described as occurring in the first century still had relevance at the time that the author was writing, and that, in the twelfth and thirteenth centuries, it was the Templars who were the guardians of the secret of the Grail. This would seem to be confirmed in another section of the *Perlesvaus*, where a high initiate of the Grail is unusually candid concerning the sacred heads. He tells the hero Perceval: 'There are heads sealed in silver and there are heads sealed in lead, and the bodies whereunto these heads belonged.' This initiate is clad in white garments with a red cross on the breast, the uniform of the Templars. According to the *Perlesvaus* then, the Templars were in possession of preserved heads, though whose heads these were is never revealed. As we've seen, the heads worshipped by the Templars were said to be able to 'save them ... make riches ... made the trees flower ... made the land germinate'[23] (see Appendix I). These are powers indistinguishable from both Bran's severed head *and* the Holy Grail.

Guiot de Provins's troubadour connection is equally interesting, and quite as revealing. Troubadours were poet-musicians of southern France whose work was usually composed in their native tongue (usually the *langue d'oc*) rather than in the more literary and generally used Latin. Their themes were the ideals of courtly love and the glorification of womanhood. This, at least, was the external content of the poetry. However, it is generally and convincingly argued that the greater part of the troubadours' love poetry does not exalt carnal or physical love (as appears at first reading) but is in fact a species of religious allegory which expounds a heretical view of Christianity.[24] The parallels with the Grail legend are obvious. It is also widely acknowledged that many troubadours found patrons in the great houses of the Cathar nobility in France, and the 'heretic' Cathars were later to figure in my research as reputed possessors of the Grail. Intriguingly, the music and verse of the troubadours disappeared after the Albigensian Crusade had destroyed the power of the

Cathar lords in the south of France, which again suggests strong links between these hermetic poets and the 'heresy' of the Cathars.

The Learned Jew

Guiot de Provins, the reputed mentor of Wolfram von Eschenbach, is known to have visited Germany in 1184, when Frederick Barbarossa dubbed his sons and raised them to the knighthood in the Cathedral of the German town of Mayence. Wolfram von Eschenbach was himself a knight owing fealty to Barbarossa, the Holy Roman Emperor, and would have been duty bound to be present at such an important ceremony. It is therefore certainly plausible that the two men met, and that Wolfram could have learned the story of the Grail, as he said, from Guiot. This adds credence to other details Wolfram gives concerning the provenance of the Grail story. According to Wolfram, Kyot (Guiot) had the tale from a learned man, a Jew named Flegetanis. This in itself is strange – what is a Jew doing with secrets pertaining to so Christian an object as the Grail? Or perhaps, not so strange, given our new insights into the true history of the individuals that comprised the House of David. Wolfram gives additional details concerning this learned Jew which indeed indicate that the 'Grail' story known to Wolfram was originally a tale held in secret by Jewish initiates. And these *adepti* seem to have been members of two specific Jewish tribes, each of which had already figured prominently in the course of our quest:

> A heathen, Flegetanis, had achieved high renown for his learning. This scholar of nature was descended from Solomon and born of a family which had long been Israelite until baptism became our shield against the fire of hell. He wrote the adventure of the Grail. On his father's side, Flegetanis was a heathen, who worshipped a calf...

The correspondences in this short paragraph were startling. Once again, the themes of King Solomon and the House of David, and of the calf-worshipping Benjamites, had resurfaced. And of Jesus, who was also descended from Solomon and the Davidic line, and to whom the Grail is specifically linked in all the legends. And all this in the context of a poet with Templar affiliations.

To recap: the Templars are identified as the guardians of the Grail, whose attributes are tellingly identical to the severed head of Bran and to the heads the Templars worshipped. Chretien de Troyes had specifically linked the Grail and the severed head, and intimated that the head was syn-onymous with the mass wafer, the 'body of Christ'. My initial conclusion, that the Grail was a 'cover name' for a sacred severed head, seemed vindicated. The romances also pointed to the Order of the Temple's pos-session of this sacred object or objects. In addition, this head (or heads) was related to Judaism and specifically to Solomon and the calf-worshipping Benjamites.

But why would a group of Jewish initiates be concerned with a story in which Jesus was the main protagonist? As we saw in Chapter 10, the Jewish tradition, where it mentioned Jesus at all, did so in unflattering terms, as a seducer of the Children of Israel, a worker of magic, whose end, stoned to death and hung on a post, was less than noble. It seems likely that with Flegetanis and his Jewish adepts we are in the presence of esoteric Judaism, of heretical Judaism, which I have identified as those Jews who followed a radically different conception of God from the orthodox Yahweh, one linked to the original teachings of Akhenaten. And for such an esoteric group Jesus and his lineage were important, as they represented the living continuation of that most sacred bloodline, the bloodline of the pharaohs.

Jesus and the Grail Family

Although it is said to be a specifically Christian legend, the fact remains that the majority of the central characters in the Grail story are Jewish, or descended from Jewish stock. The same, of course, is true of the pro-tagonists in the New Testament. In most Grail legends, the hero, Perceval, is named as the Son of the Widow, a title which, as we have seen, could apply both to the Egyptian pharaoh and, as a descendant of that bloodline, to Jesus. This indicates that Perceval, as a Son of the Widow, is also of the same lineage as Jesus. Moreover, Perceval is described as a close relative of Joseph of Arimathea and/or that enigmatic personage, the Fisher King, an identification that was to make the link between Jesus and Perceval all but indisputable.

There is much evidence to indicate that these two Grail characters, Joseph of Arimathea and the Fisher King, are in fact, one and the same individual. In the vast majority of medieval Grail legends, it is Joseph of Arimathea that carries the Grail to the West, to France and then to Britain. However, in Robert de Borron's work, *Roman de l'Estoire dou Saint Graal*, the Grail comes into the possession of Joseph of Arimathea, who appar-ently hands the Grail on to Brons, the Fisher King. And it is he, not Joseph, who carries it to the West. What appears to have happened here (given the fact that most Grail romances disagree with Robert de Borron) is that he has interpolated an extra character, Brons, into the narrative. It seems safe, therefore, to assume that the Fisher King and Joseph are one and the same. That being so, all the Grail legends are therefore pointing up the fact that Perceval is quite certainly of Judaic origin and that he and Joseph of Arimathea share the same bloodline.

Knowing this, it is possible to try to discern the exact relationship between Joseph/Fisher King and Perceval. In all the works we have been considering (except the romance of de Borron), that is, in Chretien's *Le Conte du Graal*, in the *Peredur*, in the *Perlesvaus*, and in the *Parzival* of Wolfram von Eschenbach, Perceval is the nephew of either Joseph or the Fisher King. If the Fisher King and Joseph are identical, as appears to be the case, then on this analysis it does seem that Joseph of Arimathea is to be regarded as Perceval's uncle. This identification proved to be vital to unlocking some key sections of the Grail story, and the identity of the sacred head.

The Head of the Cousin

In the Welsh *Peredur*, Perceval is told later in the narrative that the head which he had seen borne through the hall of the Fisher King was, in fact, that of his cousin. This is the head which had been carried in the Grail – or which was, more probably, the Grail itself. Again, in Chretien's *Le Conte du Graal* we are given a scene in which Perceval meets a lady sitting under a tree and holding the head of a man in a vessel of ivory. The lady tells Perceval that the head is that of his cousin. The same scenario is repeated in the *Perlesvaus*, where it is again emphasised that the head in the box of ivory is that of Perceval's cousin.

Why is our attention being drawn to this head? And why is the head named as Perceval's 'cousin'? Obviously, lineage is again important, for the head is not identified by name, only by relation to Perceval's family. Who, then, was Perceval's cousin? The Grail romances are all extremely coy on this subject, and strangely so. Although almost every other character is given a title of one sort or another, we are never told the name of the head in the ivory box. Or at least not directly. It is almost as if we are being invited to divine the name ourselves, to answer a puzzle or a riddle. However, the solution does not appear to be contained in the Grail stories. Its solution requires a brief 'holiday' from the intricacies of the Grail romances, and the study of an individual who is at the same time both a central character in the Grail cycle and one of the most enigmatic of New Testament figures – Joseph of Arimathea.

Joseph of Arimathea

Although he figures largely in the romances, the Grail authors tell us very little of Joseph of Arimathea. For the most part, he is simply a 'given' in the plot. He is the guardian of the Grail and the uncle of Perceval. His shield (in the *Perlesvaus*) is a red cross, the Templar symbol *par excellence* (or perhaps it was the Templars who took the red cross from Joseph's 'coat of arms'). One Grail legend states that Joseph was 'a soldier of Pilate for seven years' and at least one romance, Robert de Borron's *Roman de l'Estoire dou Saint Graal*, places the events of the Grail story in the time of Joseph of Arimathea.[25] In similar vein, the *Perlesvaus* makes continual reference to Josephus Flavius, the first-century historian, as an authority, which, while obviously spurious, again indicates that the author wishes us to understand that the events in the romance occurred in the time of Joseph of Arimathea (i.e., at, or just after, the time of Christ).

The Bible is even less forthcoming about Joseph. He is described as a rich man, a member of the Sanhedrin, a group of influential men who governed Jerusalem, though they themselves remained under Roman rule. Joseph is the man who begs Pilate for Christ's body, and who eventually takes possession of the corpse and lays him in the tomb that Joseph had kept for his own use. He then disappears from the Bible story. This is odd, not least for two important reasons.

Firstly, not anyone could take possession of the body of an executed man. According to Jewish tradition, this could only be done by the closest, and most senior, surviving male relative. As Jesus' own father, Joseph, was by all accounts dead, and Jesus had no elder brothers, this duty would presumably have been undertaken by the next most senior relative. This would logically (given the large families produced at that time) have been one of the brothers of Jesus' father Joseph, or of his mother Mary. That is, the person requesting the body would be Jesus' uncle. Thus, Joseph of Arimathea is, by this line of reasoning, the maternal or paternal uncle of Jesus. This is made all the more likely in view of the statement in the *Perlesvaus* concerning the 'holy lineage of Joseph of Arimathea'. Why should Joseph's line be considered holy, unless it was closely connected with that of Jesus and the House of David? The argument is strengthened by a second line of evidence, taken from the Bible and from several ancient manuscripts, and relating both to Mary's and to Joseph of Arimathea's activities after the crucifixion.

In a poignant episode from John's Gospel, we are told that, as Jesus hung on the cross, he tried to arrange that his mother be cared for after his death. 'When Jesus saw therefore his mother, and the disciple (John) standing by ... he saith unto his mother, Woman, behold thy son! Then saith he to the disciple, Behold thy mother! And from that hour that disciple took her unto his own *home*' (John 19: 26–7). Whether the word home is included or not, the import is the same – John became the guardian of Mary. John's status as guardian or *paranymphos* is confirmed in two ancient chronicles, the *Magna Glastoniensis Tabula*, and the Cotton MS Titus. However, both these manuscripts relate that a second guardian was appointed, and this guardian is given as Joseph of Arimathea. Jesus had named John guardian on the cross and the request of a dying man is seldom refused. But, traditionally, the guardian was the closest living adult male, and it seems Joseph was appointed to fulfil the obligations of this very custom. Certain traditions speak of Joseph as the cousin of Mary, but this would mean that she lacked both a surviving father and any living male brothers which, while possible, must be considered unlikely given the typical large family size and the fact that Mary's own mother, Anne, is said to have married three separate husbands. The evidence of tradition therefore points, once again, to Joseph as being the brother of Mary. These factors, Joseph's relationship to Jesus, and his relationship to Mary, reinforce each other, and together turn the balance of probabilities in favour of Joseph of Arimathea being a sibling of Mary, and an uncle to Jesus.

If this is accepted, then we can collate this conclusion with the information we have drawn from the Grail romances, and the identity of the severed head in the ivory coffer, the head of the cousin, can at last be established.

Joseph of Arimathea, according to the Grail legends, is the uncle of Perceval and also, on the evidence of the Bible and other sources, the uncle of Jesus. This means that Jesus and Perceval can only be cousins. Now, the mysterious, unnamed head in the ivory box is said to be Perceval's cousin. Are the Grail romances telling us, covertly, that the head is that of Jesus? Other explanations are of course possible. There could be a hypothetical 'third cousin' related to both Jesus and Perceval, whose head was taken and preserved.[26] But knowing that Jesus was a Nazarite to whom the head was sacred; knowing that the Nazarites preserved the traditions of Akhenaten's secret teachings and the cult of the head; and knowing Jesus to be a descendant of the pharaonic line, then there is a high degree of probability that we are, in truth, being informed by the Grail authors that the head is that of Jesus. Even if we wish to follow the Grail romance of Robert de Borron, which insists that Perceval was the grandson of Joseph of Arimathea, Perceval and Jesus are still second cousins, which, given the fact that the degree of relatedness is not mentioned in the romances, means that the conclusion that the head in the ivory box is that of Jesus, is still valid.

The Head of God

This was, of course, a difficult conclusion to accept but, after the revelations of the previous months, it was not entirely unexpected. Nevertheless, I was not prepared to accept these findings completely. Not until there was further corroborating evidence that connected Joseph to the head of Jesus. It was only when another piece of the puzzle fell into place that I was able finally to accept the true identity of the head.

I found it in a rereading of the *Continuation* of the Old French *Perceval*, in the section relating to events that took place after the crucifixion of Jesus,[27] and which in turn draws heavily on the *Evangelicum Nicodemi*, one of the New Testament Apocrypha. This follows the Gospels in stating that, after the crucifixion, Joseph of Arimathea took the body of Jesus and placed it in his tomb. The *Evangelium Nicodemi* continues the story by informing us that, shortly thereafter, Joseph was imprisoned by certain Jews, but when, on Easter Day, the door to his gaol was opened, he was found to have miraculously escaped his captors, by virtue of the risen Christ's appearance, and to be living at his home in Arimathea. The *Continuation* of Chretien's poem then tells us that 'the Jews':

... held a council in order to banish Joseph and expel him from the land, and they informed him at once that he must depart because of his crime, he and all his friends, and also Nicodemus, who was a marvellously wise man, and a sister of his. Nicodemus had carved and fashioned a head in the likeness of the Lord on the day that he had seen Him on the cross. But of this I am sure, that the Lord God set His hand to the shaping of it, as they say: for no man ever saw one like it nor could it be made by human hands...

When Nicodemus knew that he must depart and leave the land, he took the head secretly, without the knowledge of anyone, and carried it without delay to Jaffa, put it in the sea and commended it to the Lord God, in whose likeness he had shaped it...

161

This Nicodemus was a man of high standing in the Jewish community, like Joseph of Arimathea a member of the Sanhedrin. As John's Gospel relates, he was the only person, other than Joseph, who was present at the laying out of Jesus and who performed whatever ceremony and ritual took place around the body in the sepulchre: 'And there came also Nicodemus, which at the first came to Jesus by night, and brought a mixture of myrrh and aloes, about an hundred pound weight' (John 19: 39). The herbs mentioned, and the weight (close on thirty kilograms, a formidable amount of material), are extremely suggestive. Aloe and myrrh were often used in embalming.

Let us see what we have here: Nicodemus was one of the only two persons present at the 'anointing' of Jesus' body; he brought with him an enormous quantity of embalming spices and, according to the author of the *Continuation*, Nicodemus just happens to have in his possession a head of Jesus, not a simple portrait, but one from 'the day he had seen him on the cross', a head that 'could not be made by human hands', and 'that the Lord God himself set his hand to the shaping of it'. No mention here of why the head was 'carved', nor to what purpose. Embalming spices, a secret 'laying out', and afterwards the body vanishes and Nicodemus is left in possession of a lifelike head of Jesus, which he is at pains to keep secret. What are we to think?

We should also remember, when reading this, the dangerous milieu in which it was written, and the risks any author took in committing 'heresy' to paper or parchment. Far lesser heresies, such as denying that the eucharist was the body of Christ, could bring down the vengeful wrath of Holy Mother Church on the miscreant, and lead to terrible punishment. If we accept the 'unthinkable' for a moment, and consider the possibility that Jesus' embalmed head was taken from his body by Nicodemus, how could a medieval initiate of this secret convey the information to those he wished to reach? To state the fact baldly would be to deny the resurrection in the body (rather than, as most gnostic Christians believed, resurrection in the spirit), a proposition which was a central tenet of Church dogma. Given the power of the Church, a full exposition of the facts was, quite simply, impossible. Anyone advancing such a view would risk arrest, imprisonment, torture and the flames of the *auto da fe*.[28] The document itself would have been anathematised and all copies consigned to the flames. The closest one could come to committing the truth to writing would be to construct a tale in which the person who was present in the tomb immediately after the crucifixion and who 'anointed' Christ's body was brought into close association with *a* head of Christ. And this is exactly what we do find in the *Continuation* with Nicodemus as the craftsman who carved the head of Christ (that a highly placed, wealthy member of the Jewish elite is portrayed as a man possessed of superhuman skill in a manual craft by itself reveals the improbability of the 'carved head' story). But the author of the Nicodemus story goes much further: we are told that the head is precious and that it was secretly removed from Jerusalem. And we are informed that this 'carved' head was so lifelike it was impossible for mortal man to have made it, '... *nor could it be made by human hands.*' The author of the *Continuation* could not have been more plain without risking a hideous death: '*the Lord God Himself set His hand to the shaping of it*', i.e., God made it.

In other words, the head was real. It was, quite literally, the head of God.

12

The Templars and the Sacred Head

If the Holy Grail was in fact the head of Jesus, what had become of it? Had it been carried abroad, as the *Continuation* implies? Or was it returned to Jerusalem as a sacred relic, and perhaps hidden beneath the temple of Jerusalem, along with more ancient sacred heads that I believed lay buried there? The answer seemed to lie with the Knights Templar and whatever they had found beneath the Temple Mount. It was time to examine the history of The Order of the Poor Knights of the Temple of Solomon in more detail. Knowing what had been discovered so far, I was optimistic that a close study of the order would shed more light on the true motives behind their 'heretical beliefs', their strange burial rites, passion for secrecy and reverence for embalmed heads. And it would also, I hoped, answer the question that continued to haunt me – what had been the ultimate fate of the sacred heads, and more especially, the head of God? Was it possible that this unique, priceless relic still existed? Could it be traced from the time of Christ, across two thousand years of history, perhaps even to the present day?

The Advent of the Warrior Monk

The origin of the Christian military orders, the Templars, the Hospitallers, the Knights of Lazarus, the Teutonic Order, and a host of other, smaller groups, has long been debated by historians. That secretive Muslim sect, the Assassins, has been suggested as a model for the structure underlying the organisation of at least the Order of the Temple.[1] Other scholars, while agreeing on an origin in the Holy Land, believe that the idea of the military order was borrowed, by cultural diffusion, from the Islamic *ribat*, a fortified convent where the members followed a regime of religious discipline but were also sworn to fight against the enemies of the prophet.[2] Still others see the beginnings of military orders rooted in a change in Christian perceptions of the role of the warrior, and this does seem to be the most reasonable explanation for these extraordinary soldier-monks. In the eighth and ninth centuries, the distinction between the *miles seculi* (secular soldiers) and the *miles Christi* (soldiers of Christ, as monks were then known) was clear. The Abbot of Saint-Mihiel, Smaragdus, writing in the ninth century, was in no doubt who held the moral high ground:

> ... secular soldiers bear feeble and perilous arms, while those of the soldiers of Christ are most powerful and excellent; the former fight against their enemies in such a way that they lead both themselves and those they kill to everlasting punishment; the latter fight against evil so that after death they may gain the reward of eternal life; the former fight in such a way that they descend to Hell, the latter fight so that they may achieve glory; the former fight in such a way that after death they serve with devils in Hell, the latter so that they may possess the Kingdom of heaven in eternity with the angels.[3]

In essence, the view was pacifist. The soldiers of Christ fought with prayer, incense and chant against the devil and all his minions. Acts of violence, even against evil-doers, were in themselves reprehensible and condemned the perpetrator to eternal damnation.

By the time of the Gregorian reform movement, churchmen had softened their views. Now, warriors were expected to embody Christian values, even in war and amidst the horrors of the battlefield. This attitude was summed up by Bonizo de Sutri, writing towards the close of the eleventh century:

> It is their duty to obey their Lords, not to covet booty, not to spare their own lives in protecting those of their lords, to fight to death for the welfare of the state, to make war on schismatics and heretics, to defend the poor, widows and orphans, not to violate their sworn fidelity and in no way to forswear their lords.[4]

With the advent of the crusades in 1095 this linkage between the warrior class and their ability, indeed duty, to fight and slay for the Christian God was emphasised to an even greater extent. Combat came to be seen as another route to salvation, and crusaders were promised absolution if they fell fighting to recapture the holy city of Jerusalem from the infidel Muslim.

Guibert de Nogent spoke for many churchmen when he commented on the salvific powers of the crusade:

> In our time God has instituted holy wars, so that the equestrian order and the erring people, who like the ancient pagans were commonly engaged in mutual slaughter, might find a new way of meriting salvation. They are no longer obliged, as used to be the case, to leave the world and to choose the monastic life and a religious rule; they can gain God's grace to no mean extent by pursuing their own profession, unconfined and in secular garb.[5]

Pope Urban II, whose speech at Clermont-Ferrand on 27 November 1095 had formally instituted the First Crusade, stated that the crusaders were doing Christ's bidding and 'have exposed their possessions and their persons for the love of God and their neighbour'.[6] With the Church thus embracing the profession of arms as a route to heaven (as long as the violence was inflicted upon the infidel) the way was now open for an amalgamation of the secular and the religious, for an order of warrior-monks who combined the ecclesiastic's religious discipline and devotion with the ferocity and martial ardour of the professional fighting man. The first of these military orders was The Order of the Poor Knights of the Temple of Solomon.

The Knights Templar

According to the orthodox accounts of the Templars' inception, Hugues de Payens, Lord of the Burgundian castle of Martigny, appeared unannounced before the King of Jerusalem, Baldwin II, along with eight other knights. The chronicler, William, Archbishop of Tyre, claims that this occurred in 1119. These knights:

> ... devoted to God, religious and God-fearing, professed the wish to live in chastity, obedience and without property in perpetuity, binding themselves in the hands of the lord patriarch to the service of Christ in the manner of regular canons ... Since they did not have a church, nor a settled place to live, the king conceded a temporary dwelling to them in his palace ... The canons of the Temple of the Lord, under certain conditions, conceded a courtyard which they had near the same place, to be used for the functions of the Order. Moreover, the lord king with his nobles, as well as the lord patriarch with his prelates, gave to them certain benefices ... from which they could be fed and

clothed. The first element of their profession ... was 'that they should protect the roads and routes to the utmost of their ability against the ambushes of thieves and attackers, especially in regard to the safety of pilgrims.[7]

The nine knights moved into their new quarters, the al-Aqsa mosque which lay on the southern edge of the Haram al-Sharif or Temple platform. This building was said to lie above the foundations of the ancient Temple of Solomon, and it is from this that the Order of the Temple derived its name. They were also given a square near the mosque where they could worship. For nine years they stayed there, receiving no more members in their brotherhood and, as we will see, apparently doing very little to aid or protect pilgrims. It was not until 1128, at the Council of Troyes, that the order began to show its true ambitions. Here the Templars were granted official recognition, and Bernard of Clairvaux (later St Bernard) drafted and wrote their Rule (a species of constitution by which the order would be governed), basing it in part on the clerical order of which he was a member, the Cistercians. The Rule was composed of seventy-two articles, which created, initially, two classes of Templar: knights and sergeants (or serving brothers, as they were also known).[8] Later, a separate class of priests, all members of the order, was also created. There was a total rejection of the female sex in the articles of the Rule, symbolised by the wearing of distinctive white vestments. Only knights were allowed to wear white, the sergeants, as befitted their inferior status, wore brown or black mantles. And whereas other orders occasionally had convents of nuns attached to them, this was expressly forbidden by the Templar Rule. No married man was allowed to join the brotherhood, as all members had 'promised chastity to God', although some were allowed affiliate status with the order.

St Bernard articulated the creed of these warrior monks in his *De Laude Novae Militiae* (*In Praise of the New Knighthood*), written in support of the Templar philosophy sometime in the early 1130s.[9] Armed with the authorised approval of the Council of Troyes, and with the approbation of St Bernard, the Templars underwent an extraordinary change of status, strategy and fortune. Instead of remaining an exclusive band of nine brothers, they enlisted numerous new members, garnered from recruiting campaigns that scoured every nation in western Europe, from Portugal and Italy to Scotland and the Eastern Marches of Germany. Almost without exception, the knights first joining the order were landed nobles, each possessed of considerable revenue. And without exception, each was required to donate all his patrimony to the order upon admission. At the same time, the Templars began to amass wealth on a scale hitherto undreamed of, from donations and gifts by wealthy nobles who, while not prepared to undergo the rigorous disciplines of the order themselves, nevertheless supported their aims. Within a few years the 'Poor Knights' had received cash gifts, lands and manors that made them among the wealthiest of all holy orders. Gifts, acts of true piety, came from all classes of people, from donations of small change collected at churches (the Templars were given rights to open churches that had been closed by the Church authorities), to food, armour and horses. But it was from the nobility that the important wealth-producing donations derived, as the charters make clear. Even as early as 1127 the Templars had been granted a house, grange and meadow by Theobald, Count of Blois. Another high noble, William Clito, gave to the Templars the rights to feudal reliefs in his land. William de St Omer and his sons donated income from several churches in Flanders. That the donations were made to further the Christian cause in the Holy Land is obvious from the wording of many of these charters. The Count of Flanders, when listing his donations, spoke of 'the Knights of the Temple perpetually fighting for God by strongly defending the Oriental Church from the filth of the pagans'. King Louis VII outdid his nobles and gave the Templars the entire town of Savigny.[10] In just over ten years, the order owned land in at least nine European countries, much of it substantial estates.

With this great wealth came influence and power. Throughout Christendom the Temple was treated with respect and honour. They were the valued counsellors of Kings, involved in decisions of great moment and used almost as ambassadors in negotiations between the monarchs of western Europe. Templars on occasions formed the bodyguard of the Pope. When King Louis IX of France's son, Peter, Count of Alençon was born it was in the Templar castle of Atlit, and the Grand Master Reginald of Vichiers, acted as godfather.[11] And in the final years of Latin Syria, it was the Master of the Temple William de Beaujeu, who undertook the perilous negotiations with the Mamluk sultan.[12]

At the same time, thanks to the generosity of several popes, the order was effectively placed outside both secular and canon law. Pope Innocent III began the process with three definitive bulls of privilege, *Omne datum optimum*, *Milites Templi* and *Militia Dei*, and by the end of the twelfth century the Templars had been granted a stunning list of privileges, including the right of sanctuary in their churches, exemption from all tithes and taxes, exemption from interdict and complete independence from episcopal rule.[13] Later popes extended and confirmed these privileges and immunities. Excommunication was the fate of any who wounded or even struck a Templar, and it was made an offence even to annoy members of the order. According to the papal bulls, the Templars were to obey only the pope himself, they were to recognise no other authority save the Supreme Pontiff of the Catholic Church. Regardless of the crime, the Templars could not legally be tried by either church or temporal courts; only the pope had the right to judge them. And as, within a short time, their allegiance to the pope proved to be purely nominal, by the end of the thirteenth century the Templars had become wholly independent of all authority. They were a unique institution, an autonomous military grouping spread across the whole of Christendom. They were, in effect, a sovereign power.

The Freedom to Think

Such autonomy brought with it another commodity in very short supply in medieval Europe – freedom of thought. Unlike its contemporaries, the order was prepared to take information and learning from any and every source, from Christian, Arab or Jew. The Templars' open-mindedness was effectively unique in European society for another 150 years, until the beginnings of the Renaissance in the mid-1300s. The Templar freethinking *Umwelt* separated the order from most of medieval Christendom, whose thought patterns were dominated by the rigid teachings of the Roman Church. Their minds were no longer shackled to tradition, nor bound to one 'correct view' of anything, and it was this intellectual freedom that, more than anything else, allowed the Templars to flourish. In Outremer, as they called Palestine, they adopted many habits from their erstwhile enemies. Some leading Templars spoke fluent Arabic (often learned during periods of captivity) and many employed Arab secretaries. As a result, they were exposed to the learning of this alien culture, whose knowledge in many fields was far in advance of their Christian opponents.[14] Arab centres of learning were at that time the repository of much wisdom, and their libraries contained many ancient Greek and Egyptian manuscripts that had been lost to the West: medical authorities such as the *Corpus* of Galen, the *Aphorisms* of Hippocrates and books dealing with astronomy, physics and mathematics. These treasures had perished in Christendom during the Church's fanatical destruction of 'heretical' books. The Templars' growing power and *de facto* autonomy allowed them to investigate these new sources of learning without the ever-constant fear of ecclesiastical interference and the threat of the stake.

Such willingness to accept new ideas and new concepts brought great advantages. The Templars were instrumental in bringing to the West advanced techniques in surveying, medicine, architecture and masonry. But perhaps the most lasting legacy that the Templars gave to the world was financial: almost single-handedly, the order changed the Christian view of money. They were the first true bankers – at first the castles of the Templars were used simply as 'safe deposits', a place where money could be stored in a secure location under the protection of professional warriors.[15] But the order soon expanded their 'services'. Although in the early days money deposited in one country was physically moved to another by the Templars, it soon became possible to make this a purely 'paper' transaction. When, in 1235, the Count of La Marche was granted a pension of eight hundred livres a year by Henry III of England, it was the temple in London who received the money from the king and the temple in Paris who made payment to the count, without any of the cash actually crossing the Channel.[16] Similarly, in 1270 there is a record of a knight of Catalonia depositing funds with the Templars in the Holy Land, and obtaining payment from Palau in Spain.

The order could also deal in three-way exchanges of funds. When Louis IX urgently needed to send four thousand *livres tournois* to his representatives in Outremer (Palestine), he turned at once to the temple. The loan was obtained by the Templars from the merchants of Acre (one of the chief negotiators for the king being the grand master of the temple) and they were reimbursed with a similar amount in France. Thanks to the Templars, money was becoming an international commodity. It was even possible to hold a current account with the order. Just like a modern bank, the temple would regularly receive the account holder's income and disburse payments to creditors.[17] A number of French princes and nobles made regular use of this facility.

The temple also acted as the treasury for French kings from the reign of Philip Augustus to that of Philip IV. The order lent money, vast sums on occasion, to a number of European kings, a policy which tied the monarchs to the temple and helped speed the order's fortunes and long-term goals. Louis VII borrowed from them to help finance the Second Crusade, and during the thirteenth century the Templars regularly provided loans for the kings of Aragon. Their rates were reasonable (ten per cent per annum, as against the normal twenty per cent charged by Jewish moneylenders), trade was brisk and the profits huge.[18] When the Saracens captured King Louis IX of France and demanded 800,000 bezants for his release, it was the Templars who forwarded almost the entire amount to ransom the sovereign from the hands of the infidel.[19] In short, the Templars were the medieval equivalent of today's international bankers and, like them, they were, in modern parlance, 'into money' in a big way.

But riches alone could not defend the order and the rest of Latin Syria from the harsh realities of Levantine *realpolitik*. The Latin kingdom was a coastal strip of land, never extending more than five hundred kilometres north to south, and with an average of just one hundred kilometres between Arab lands and the Mediterranean Sea. Its length and narrow width made it extremely vulnerable to attack, a vulnerability partially offset by the crusader strategy of building massive formidable castles such as Gaston and Crac des Chevaliers, from which a relatively few Latin soldiers could dominate the surrounding area. But it was a policy fraught with risk. While the Muslims remained divided, the Europeans were comparatively safe, playing one side off against the other. But the rise in power of Mamluk Egypt placed the Latin state within the jaws of a huge pincer, all but surrounded by hostile neighbours, and with the sea at its back. The prospects for Christian Palestine looked bleak, but the appearance in 1260 of the Mongol army of Hulagu, Ilkhan of Persia, gave some respite. The Muslims agreed to truces with the Christians, in order to fight off the invading Mongols, who had already destroyed Baghdad. But in many respects this simply replaced one threat by another, for the Mongols (known also as Tartars) were no friends of the Christians and in time threatened the Latin kingdom quite as much as had the Mamluks. The writer of the St Albans Chronicle *Flores Historiarum* graphically describes the terrified reaction when news of the Mongol invasion was brought to England by a Templar messenger:

This man covered so great a distance with such speed that, compelled by intolerable necessity, he took thirteen weeks from the day he left the Holy Land to the day he entered London ... However, when they had read these letters, both the king and the Templars, as well as the others who heard them, gave way to lamentation and sadness, on a scale no one had ever seen before. For the news was that the Tartars advancing with an innumerable force, had already occupied and devastated the Holy Land almost up to Acre. And what was astonishing to hear, they intended to occupy all of that land with their army ... and more widely extend their destruction. And the same messenger added that they exposed all foreigners fleeing to them or captured by them in the first line of battle, and when fighting, men and women shot arrows as well behind them as they did in front. Nor will Christendom be able to resist them, unless supported by the powerful hand of God. Also, they have already killed almost all the Templars and Hospitallers there, unless help is quickly brought, God forbid, a horrible annihilation will swiftly be visited upon the world.[20]

Despite this terrible threat to Christendom very little was done, and it was left to the Muslim armies to stem the Mongol advance. In July 1260, the Mamluk Kutuiz asked the rulers of the Latin kingdom for safe passage for himself and his army through their lands, and for an alliance in order to defeat this common threat. While granting the first request, the Christians refused the second. On 3 September of that same year, at 'Ain Jalut, just to the south of Nazareth, the Muslim armies crushed the Mongol forces. It was a great victory, and enormously increased Mamluk morale and confidence. Within a generation, it was this same power that would oversee the collapse of the entire Latin kingdom.

The decline was gradual, with the castles and territories furthest from the coast falling one after another to Muslim forces. There were times of respite, such as Prince Edward of England's truce of 1271, and those of 1281 and 1282.[21] But this last agreement, in which Templar Master William of Beaujeu and the Mamluk commander Kavalun agreed to a peace of ten years and ten months, was broken by the Muslims in 1285. Shortly thereafter, one by one, the coastal castles went the way of the inland fortifications. Latakia fell in that same year, as did al-Marqab, a castle of the Knights Hospitaller. Four years later Kavalun sent his army against Tripoli. It is said that the Templars had advance knowledge of the attack through spies, but that, because of their known connections with the Arabs, their warning was ignored until it was too late,[22] and Tripoli was taken in April of that year. It was obvious that Acre, the nerve centre of crusader power, would be next to feel the might of the victorious Mamluk forces.

Western Christendom bestirred itself at this time of crisis, and in 1290 a score of ships with reinforcements and supplies arrived at Acre. But the inexperienced newcomers, initially hailed as saviours, proved to be the undoing of the great city. They instigated a riot, and murdered many Muslims. According to the anonymous chronicler, 'The Templar of Tyre', those killed were not fighting men but simple peasants who were accustomed to bring their produce to the city for sale.[23] It was all the pretext Kavalun needed. He sent messengers demanding expiation of the crime and threatened the destruction of the city if his demands were not met. The Templar master, a veteran of Levantine diplomacy, proposed that all European prisoners presently under sentence of death should be given over to the Muslims and named as the perpetrators of the massacre. They were going to die anyway; if they could turn away the wrath of the Mamluks by doing so, so much the better. His counsel was rejected. And the fate of Acre was sealed.

Kavalun died before the attack on Acre began, but his son was just as zealous in prolonging the war and in April 1291 the Mamluk army marched on the city. Although all men capable of bearing arms had been mustered for the defence, it took the Mamluk forces only forty-three days to breach the city's defences, breaking in at the 'Accursed Tower' and, despite a ferocious defence by the military orders, gradually taking over the whole city.[24] The entire complement of the Knights of Lazarus and the Knights of St Thomas died in the defence, as did all members of the Teutonic Order except for one survivor, the Hochmeister. However, one Templar did do rather well out of the disaster: Brother Rutger von Blum commandeered a galley and forced exorbitant fees from the fleeing refugees for safe passage to Cyprus.[25] A few Templars apostatised when captured, and were spared to end their days as slaves in Egypt. Most, however, died fighting, including the Master William de Beaujeu, who was struck with a crossbow quarrel while leading a small mixed band of Templars, Hospitallers and Italians in a forlorn attempt to retake the 'Accursed Tower'.

The survivors fell back on the only defensible structure still under Christian control, the Templar fortress that lay in the southwest corner of the city, and close to the last possible escape route, the sea. Their numbers were swelled by a multitude of refugees who had so far escaped the Muslim massacre but had failed to find a berth on the escaping galleys. For all the tales of Templar cupidity, the Marshal, Pierre de Sevrey, saw to it that the women and children were put aboard the few remaining Templar galleys as they prepared to leave. Not one of the Templar garrison left with the ships, even the wounded elected to stay behind. According to an eyewitness report: 'when they set sail everyone of the Temple who remained raised a great cheer, and thus they departed'.[26] Only a single boat remained in reserve, and this had a special mission.

One week after the fall of the city, al-Ashraf Kalil proposed the surrender of the fortress on what seemed excellent terms, including safe conduct for the refugees and all its defenders. Pierre de Sevrey agreed, and Mamluk soldiery was allowed to enter to run up the Crescent flag. However, once inside, the Mamluks began raping both women and young boys; the enraged Templars closed the gates and killed them to a man. The piebald flag of the Templars, 'Beau Séant' was once more run aloft, to flutter defiantly atop the fortress. There was no hope of safety now. All within knew that their fate was sealed, they could expect no quarter from the Saracen outside the walls. Only then did the last boat set sail, under cover of night. Under the command of the Templar commander, Theobald Gaudin, the boat carried with it the treasure of the order, and 'the holy relics'. Whatever these relics were, the Templars were obviously loath to see them leave the Holy Land. Only when all was clearly lost were they evacuated.

Surprisingly, the following morning, al-Ashraf Kalil again offered terms, saying that his men had acted wrongly and had been worthy of death. The Marshal, Pierre de Sevrey, agreed to parley and left the fortress to discuss terms. No sooner had he reached the Mamluk lines than he was seized and summarily beheaded. The message was clear: there would be no surrender; the defenders could expect no quarter from their foes. All within the Templar castle knew that they faced the final martyrdom. They held out for a further three days, while Mamluk sappers mined beneath the fortress, working in relays until all that held up the Templar ramparts were the timber props of their enemy. When these were fired, on 28 May, a section of the wall fell and two thousand Mamluk warriors poured into the breach. They were met by the last remnants of the Templar force who, true to their oath, fought to the end, the walls of the fortress collapsing inwards as the battle raged, burying Christian and Muslim beneath a sepulchre of broken stone and flame.

With Acre lost, the position of the remaining Christian forces was hopeless. Only the castles of Sidon, Tortosa and 'Atlit remained. Sidon was abandoned in July, Tortosa and 'Atlit a month later. But of all the Latins, it was the Templars who refused to give up hope of returning to the Holy Land. They masterminded the invasion of one small corner of the Levant, the tiny waterless island of Ruad, from which they hoped to launch a counter-attack against the Mamluks. Ruad finally fell in 1303.[27] The survivors of the garrison were taken in shackles to Cairo, where they met their deaths before a festive multitude, riddled with the arrows of Mamluk bowmen. With them died the dream of a Christian Holy Land, and the *raison d'être* of the Templar Order.

The Occult Order

This standard version of the history of the Knights Templar is, for the most part, undisputed. Their influence on Christendom, their breadth of interest and learning, financial innovations, and the important role the order played in the politics of their time are all beyond debate. Nor is there any doubt that the knights fought and died for the Latin kingdom of Jerusalem, that they gave their lives on countless occasions for the cause of Christ. However, there are other facets of the Templars, and their beliefs, that have aroused bitter dispute. Many professional historians would prefer for these unorthodox aspects of the order to be quietly forgotten. To my surprise, a number of academic works on the Templars that I consulted made no mention of the heads the Templars were accused of worshipping. For the authors, it seemed that if the problem was not mentioned, it did not exist. But the evidence for this and other unorthodox practices continues to mount, to such a degree that it is now impossible to accept the orthodox account as a full and fair description of the Order of the Temple. Something more was going on within the closed confines of this secretive order of warrior-monks. Credible explanations must be found for the Templars' obsessive secrecy, their excavations below the Temple of Solomon, their extraordinary burial rites, and the worship of severed heads, especially the veneration accorded the 'idol' Baphomet. Such facts are a recorded part of Templar history, and they cannot simply be ignored because they are 'inconvenient'.

The very inception of the Order of the Temple is shrouded in mystery. Just after Hugues de Payens and his eight knightly comrades presented themselves before King Baldwin in Jerusalem and requested the right to defend the Christian pilgrims, the chronicler William of Tyre tells us something quite odd. These knights, pledged to protect the hundreds and thousands of pilgrims that flocked to the Holy City, refused to accept any new members to their fledgling order for nine years.[28] William does not dwell upon this, but states the fact simply: for all but a decade The Order of the Poor Knights of Christ and the Temple of Solomon went into a self-imposed 'suspended animation'. Why? It can hardly have been that their services were not required. The pilgrim Saewulf, who visited Jerusalem a few years after its conquest by the crusaders, makes plain how perilous the journey was:

We travelled from Joppa to the city of Jerusalem, two days journey, by a mountainous route that is very difficult and dangerous, as the Saracens are always seeking to ambush the Christians: they lie concealed in the caverns of the mountains and the caves of the rocks, on the lookout night and day for anyone they can easily attack, either pilgrims travelling in small bands or exhausted stragglers separated from their companions.[29]

Things were no better in 1118 which, according to orthodox historians, was the year of the establishment of the Templars. In that year a company of seven hundred pilgrims were surprised in the mountains between Jerusalem and the River Jordan. More than half were either killed or taken captive by the Saracens.[30] A year later conditions were even worse. In a letter to the Archbishop of Compostella, the Prior of the Holy Sepulchre, Gerard, and the Patriarch Warmund, both beg for aid and succour. Saracens were everywhere, raiding and pillaging and, without an escort of armed troops, it was impossible to travel. The enemy was so confident that they rode even to the gates of the Holy City itself.[31] If pilgrim travel was so perilous at the time of their inception, why did the Templars insist on remaining quiescent, and avoid taking on additional recruits for a further nine years? What was so important that they could not find the time to fulfil their vows and protect pilgrims by keeping an adequate force of knights on the pilgrim roads leading to and from Jerusalem?

As if this were not suspicious enough, there is evidence that the Order of the Temple was in fact in existence several years before 1118, the official date of their inception given by William of Tyre. As several authors have pointed out, if William of Tyre is correct, then no new Templars should have been accepted until 1127. However, there is documentary evidence that at least two new knights were recruited within six years of the order's supposed inception, and a further two had joined by 1126.[32] And again, a letter to the Count of Champagne from the Bishop of Chartres reveals that the count had pledged to join 'la milice du Christ', in other words, the Templars. The date of this letter is 1114, which is, according to orthodox historians, four years before the Order of the Temple was founded.[33] What is happening here? Why is the 'orthodox' date of the founding of the Templars false? Why did the Templars abrogate their vow and fail to protect the pilgrim routes? And what were the nine original members doing during their nine years of self-imposed isolation on the Temple Mount?

The answer would seem to lie not in what the Templars did on the Temple Mount, but what they did beneath it. Beneath and to the east of the al-Aqsa mosque which formed their headquarters were the Stables of Solomon, a huge underground complex which bore witness to the architectural abilities of the Jews who had built them over a thousand years before. The German pilgrim Theoderich, visiting the area some fifty years after the Templars had taken up residence, has left the most detailed description of the stables. Below the Templar headquarters, he tells us:

... they have the stables once erected by King Solomon. They are next to the

Palace, and their structure is remarkably complex. They are erected with vaults, arches, and roofs of many varieties, and according to our estimation we should bear witness that they will hold ten thousand horses with their grooms. A single shot from a crossbow would hardly reach from one end of this building to the other, either in length or breadth.[34]

The Templars' apparent lack of activity in their formative years seems to have been due to some form of covert project beneath the Temple Mount. The nine knights were engaged on excavations either in the Stables of Solomon or nearby, an operation that could not be revealed to any but a few high-ranking nobles. Given the stories of 'treasure' secreted under the temple, stories confirmed by the Qumran treasure scroll (which listed sixty-four separate treasure hoards buried beneath the temple and elsewhere in Jerusalem), it seems very likely that the nine knights had come to the Holy Land not in a fit of self-denying martial zeal, but to embark on a 'treasure hunt' of immense importance, and that the tale that they had arrived in Jerusalem to protect pilgrims was simply a smokescreen to deflect any interest or idle curiosity from their true task. Their possession of the temple area and the Stables of Solomon makes this scenario all the more likely. Indeed, they were probably the only group with the ability to undertake such excavations, while their nine years' 'exile' on the Temple Mount gave them the ideal opportunity, and the time, to carry out extensive mining operations.

There is no doubt that there are tunnels and caves, hewn from the solid rock, beneath the temple. We saw in Chapter 8 that ancient manuscripts describe these tunnels, and that highly placed rabbis have in recent years undertaken extensive excavations within these underground passageways. Nor is this the only report of such hidden vaults. An Israeli archaeologist, Meir Ben-Dov, has written of his excavations in Jerusalem. He investigated a tunnel with an entrance outside the Temple Mount which then passed under Solomon's Stables, and beneath the temple compound. 'The tunnel leads inward for a distance of about thirty metres from the southern wall before being blocked by pieces of stone debris. We know that it continues further, but we had made it a hard-and-fast rule not to excavate within the bounds of the Temple Mount ... the tunnel was indeed built by the Crusaders ...' Ben Dov concluded, by the Poor Knights of the Temple of Solomon, as 'The Temple Mount served as a military headquarters for the Templars.'[35]

Further evidence comes from an earlier source. Captain Charles Wilson, of the Royal Engineers, led a party which began survey work beneath

Jerusalem during the 1860s and excavated tunnels and cisterns below the Temple Mount.[36] The group discovered many artifacts, including a number that were of definite Templar origin. These remains are currently held in Scotland by a relative of Captain Wilson, Robert Bryden. I spoke with Mr Bryden at length about the finds, and he confirmed that the remains do exist. They have been dated to the twelfth century and comprise a spearhead, spurs, a sword hilt and, most telling of all, a leaden cross pattee, the symbol of the Templars.[37]

Three vital facts are now incontestable. First, there is definite, documentary evidence that treasure of some kind was hidden beneath the temple. Second, there are ancient, man-made tunnels and vaults carved from the rock under the Temple Mount. And finally, the Templars spent much time and energy excavating at least some of these tunnels, as evidenced by the Templar artifacts discovered in passageways under the Temple Mount. Taken together, this makes the argument that the Templars found a treasure of some sort during the early years of their formation, extremely persuasive. And there is one other piece of evidence that not only strengthens the argument outlined above, but also makes plain an early Templar connection to the worship of sacred heads – the startling and gruesome change that occurred in the burial habits of the Templar initiates.

Templar Burial

It is quite certain that some profound change occurred in the beliefs of the Templar knighthood in the years following the excavation beneath the Temple Mount. While much of what occurred remains veiled in mystery and lost to history, there is one solid piece of evidence that no one has, as yet, explained: the riddle of the Templar burial ceremony.

At some time following the inception of the order, certain Templars took to burying their dead in a most unchristian manner. The normal mode of interment across Christendom was burial of the intact body. The method of burial, of course, depended upon rank and wealth, as did everything else in the medieval world. For the common folk there was a rough shroud and a trench long enough to take the remains and deep enough to deter the attentions of wild animals. Nobles and kings were buried with much greater pomp, often in leaden coffins which on occasions halted the process of putrefaction. Some of them were deliberately embalmed.[38] But for all, commoner and king alike, the body was left intact. This, of course, was to allow for the easiest possible awakening at the Last Trump, when the departed souls were to be restored to their revivified bodies. Such a belief was central to Christian dogma.[39] All human souls would be resurrected in the bodies in which the soul had had residence during their earthly existence. (The similarity here with Egyptian beliefs is quite striking, though rarely commented on – although they differed in the mechanics of the process, both religions believed in the resurrection of the body.) So, we find a uniformity of burial procedure in respect to the body itself – it was not to be mutilated or defiled in any way.[40]

By contrast, the bodies of certain high-ranking Templars were subject to what most Christians of their day (and of our day for that matter) would have regarded as the grossest mutilation. A clue to the 'disfigurement' enacted on the Templar corpses is evident in the obvious, but little-noted, size of their tombs; these are quite tiny, hardly capable of taking a child let alone a grown warrior. The external dimensions of the stone tomb of Sir William Sinclair, the Scottish Templar, are 100 × 28 centimetres and, as the tomb is carved from solid stone, the internal measurements are correspondingly even smaller. The grotesque reason for this small coffin size is that the body was not all in one piece.

The bodies of the Templar dead were partially dismembered and ritually beheaded. From any orthodox perspective this is a deliberate defilement of the dead, nothing short of butchery. The Templars' view was clearly different. It is important to note that the cadavers were only partially dismembered. The arms were left intact. It was only the lower limbs that were disarticulated and laid cross-wise over the trunk. The severed head was likewise placed on the trunk, just above the crossed lower limbs. This is, of course, the classic skull and crossbones, still to be seen on both Templar and masonic gravestones, and it is strongly reminiscent of the stories of the lady of Maraclea and the miraculous severed head that would be to its owner a protector and the giver of all good things, attributes identical to those of the Grail and the severed head of Bran. But, probably of more importance, this burial rite directly mimics the manner in which, in masonic lore, the body of Hiram Abif, the builder of the Temple of Solomon, was consigned to the ground. I had already discovered evidence (discussed in Chapter 8) that associated Hiram Abif with the Aten, the god of Akhenaten, and with the secret cult of the severed head that had been practised at the temple of Jerusalem. Now the manner of Hiram Abif's burial had proved to be the model of the Templar burials, providing a solid link between the Templars and the ancient religion of Akhenaten.

The Templars had conducted excavations beneath the Temple Mount.

It was in this very place that we have evidence that many of the holy relics and records of the Jews – which I believed included those of Akhenaten's secret teachings – had been hidden. And no sooner had the Templar initiates completed their excavations than they began burying their dead with their heads removed, in the self-same way that, in myth, the Aten-worshipping builder of the temple, Hiram Abif, was interred. We have already seen that the Hiram Abif tale was an allegory, designed to convey occult information to those initiated into the mysteries of Akhenaten's religion. It follows then that, by embracing this manner of burial, the Templars were also privy to the secret teachings. They had found something beneath the temple that had fundamentally altered their beliefs, something that persuaded them to allow their heads to be removed after death, just as I believed had happened to Jesus after he had been executed. And, as we have seen, one of the central charges later laid against the order was the worship of a severed head, or heads, more especially the head named Baphomet.

The Baphomet

Within a short time of the Templars achieving prominence in medieval western society, the order reverted to conducting its ceremonies in conditions of the greatest secrecy. Their receptions and chapters were held at night under tight security, with armed sentries at the entrance and a guard high above on the roof. Spurred on by their clandestine rituals, and perhaps also by jealousy of their wealth and privileges, dark tales concerning the Templars began to circulate, rumours of necromancy and strange practices. At the trial of Aragonese Templars, held at Lerida, a Dominican prior, Pedro Olivonis, testified that he had heard from the King of Aragon's vicar Ferrario de Bigletto, that it was rumoured that the Templars worshipped heads. The uncle of Ferrario, who was a Templar priest, had often worn a cord outside his shirt, from which hung a silver head with a beard. He had therefore assumed that the rumour of head worship among the Templars was true.[41]

There is no doubt that a preserved, severed head was involved in Templar ritual, and that it was regarded with great veneration and awe. After their arrest, Templar after Templar admitted to this reverence of the head, often while rejecting the wilder flights of fancy of the Dominican inquisitors, such as satanic worship of a cat. Several Templars, including Jean de Tour, the treasurer of the Paris temple, admitted 'adoring' a painted head in the form of a picture. Others confessed to seeing and being required to worship a 'representation' of a bearded head. One of the brothers, Jean Taillefer, said at his reception that 'an idol representing a human face' was set before him, on the altar. It was 'about the natural size of a man's head, with a very fierce-looking face and beard'. Hugues de Bure testified that a head of a man with a long beard and apparently wrought in silver or gold was taken from the aumbry in the chapel. Bartholomew Bochier had also seen a head with a long beard, but whether it was made of wood, metal, bone, or was human, he could not tell.[42] Descriptions of the head varied from one which 'seemed to be white with a beard' to 'a foul and black idol'. Clearly, along with various representations, several actual heads were involved.

However, one relic stood pre-eminent – the long-haired, bearded head that was seen almost exclusively at the Paris temple. Many tales centred around the worship of this severed embalmed head, a head whose name, as many Templars admitted after their arrest, was *Baphomet*. The derivation of this name has been the cause of some dispute, but it now seems clear that it is derived from the argot of the Spanish Moors, *bufihimat*, which is itself a corruption of an Arabic word *abufihamet*.[43] The translation of this word is Father of Wisdom, a title that meant little to me at the time, but which was to recur in the most dramatic circumstances towards the end of my investigation.

That the Baphomet was the object of the greatest veneration, and was not normally seen by the 'rank and file' of the order, was confirmed by another Templar, Guilliame d'Arbley, a relative of Hugues de Bure. Guilliame stated that, while copies of the 'idol' were fairly widely seen, the true object of veneration 'was exhibited at general chapters', implying that it was only shown to senior members of the order on special occasions. A leading researcher into the Turin Shroud, Ian Wilson, came to a similar conclusion about the Templar heads while studying the apparent burial cloth of Christ: 'Other descriptions, clearly referring to copies, included mention of gold and silver cases, wooden panels, and the like. But the Paris head is different. One gets the distinct impression that this was the holy of holies, accorded ceremonial strikingly reminiscent of that used by the Byzantines (to honour the embalmed heads of St Peter and St Paul).'[44]

The contemporary descriptions of the 'Paris head', the Baphomet, all make plain that the head was not a copy or carving or any sort of 'graven image'. It was a real embalmed severed head. Brother Raoul de Gizy's testimony is typical:

Inquisitor: Now tell us about the Head.

> *Fra Raoul:* Well, the Head. I've seen it at seven chapters held by Brother Hugues
> de Piraud and others.
> *Inquisitor:* What did one do to worship it?
> *Fra Raoul:* Well, it was like this. It was presented, and everyone threw himself
> on the ground, pushed back his cowl, and worshipped it.
> *Inquisitor:* What was its face like?
> *Fra Raoul:* Terrible. It seemed to me that it was the face of a demon, of a maufé
> (an evil spirit). Every time I saw it I was filled with such terror I
> could scarcely look, trembling in all my members.[45]

Under further questioning, Raoul de Gizy stated that he had seen the idol
on seven separate occasions, several of which had been held by Hugues
de Piraud, who was Visitor of France, a post which made him the virtual
overlord of all the Templar houses, at least in Europe. Piraud was outranked
only by the Grand Master, Jacques de Molay. This made him a very big
fish indeed, and he was soon brought to the question. His testimony was
dynamite: Piraud acknowledged the existence of the head and, questioned
by the Dominican inquisitor Nicolas d'Ennezat, agreed that he had

> seen, held and stroked it at Montpellier, in a certain chapter and that he and
> other brothers present had adored it with the mouth ... and not with the
> heart; however, he did not know if other brothers had worshipped it with the
> heart. Asked where it was he said he sent it to Pierre Alemandin, Preceptor of
> Montpellier, but did not know if the King's people had found it.[46]

Etienne de Troyes' testimony corroborated that of Raoul de Gizy, and
again implicated the second in command of the order, Hugues de Piraud.
Within a year of being received into the order, he attended a ritual in
Paris:

> ... and they began to hold the first vigil of the night, and they continued until
> prime (6.00 a.m.), and at the prime of the night they brought a head, a priest
> carrying it, preceded by two brothers with two large wax candles upon a silver
> candelabra, and he (the priest) put it upon the altar upon two cushions on a
> certain tapestry of silk, and the head was, as it seemed to him, flesh from the
> crown to the shape of the neck with the hairs of a dog without any gold or
> silver covering, indeed a face of flesh, and it seemed to him very bluish in
> colour and stained, with a beard having a mixture of white and black hairs
> similar to the beards of some Templars. And then the Visitor (Hugues de Piraud)
> stood up, saying to all: 'We must proceed, adore it and make homage to it,

which helps us and does not abandon us', and then all went with great reverence and made homage to it and adored that head.[47]

This deposition was the same testimony that I had read at the beginning of my researches and that had set me on the trail of the Baphomet, and the secret religion it represented. Seen in isolation, Etienne de Troyes' statement had been dramatic enough, but considered together with the many other depositions concerning the head, it had now an even more profound effect upon me. Of equal interest was the obvious mystery school nature of the Templars. Many occult matters, including the denial of Christ and the cross, were apparently part of the inception process but the existence of the head was known as a secret only by the higher grades of Templar initiation, and the younger brothers were not permitted to view it. Etienne de Troyes seems to have been an exception to this rule (he had been inducted into the order less than a year before); however, he was told that the head was that of Hugues de Payens, which is obviously an explanation given to those in the lower grades of initiation, to satisfy them until the true nature of the head was revealed when, and if, the recruit had proved himself worthy of entering the inner mysteries of the order.

The depositions of the Templar witnesses can be seen to divide into three separate types. There are those who saw only a representation of a head, those who saw other embalmed heads, and those who were privy to the holy of holies, the mysterious severed head known as Baphomet.

We must remember here that we are in the presence of a mystery religion, with a hierarchical system of grades or degrees. Initiates were gradually immersed in the secrets or mysteries; these were deemed so powerful that they were not to be divulged to the ordinary masses, or even to those of a lower grade within the brotherhood. It is very likely that the order comprised an inner circle of *illuminati*, privy in various degrees to the Secret, while most of the sergeants and many of the knights were held at a distance, and according to their worth and temperament were either kept in ignorance throughout their lives, or allowed to enter only the lowest grades of the hidden order. This was acknowledged by Philip le Bel in the instructions given to his seneschals at the time of the suppression of the order. The idol was:

a man's head with a large beard, which head they kiss and worship at all their provincial chapters, *but this not all the brothers know, save only the Grand master and the old ones.*

The lower grades saw only representations of the head, copies and paintings, such as the long-haired, bearded face painted on a board that can still be viewed at Templecombe in Gloucestershire. Those who had progressed further, or who showed natural aptitude, were allowed to participate in rituals that included severed heads other than Baphomet, whilst it seems that this most holy relic was normally reserved for the highest grades of initiation.

It is of great interest that almost all the brothers confirm a description of the head as having both a long beard and long hair. As Noel Currer-Briggs has pointed out, '... the Templars, like the majority of their contemporaries, regarded long hair as effeminate, so the length of the 'idol's' hair was remarkable for this, if for no other reason'.[48] This speaks for the head being a true, and ancient, relic. Had it been a contemporary fake, one might reasonably expect it to embody the Templars' own perceptions and values, and long hair would definitely not have been among the required attributes. Indeed, its 'womanly' connotations would have been strenuously avoided by an order that eschewed all contact with the female sex. The fact that the 'idol' is long haired reveals that it was not made by the Templars, but came into their possession by some unknown route. That such a discovery or gift was not rejected as 'unworthy' by the Templars, despite the effeminate length of its locks, points very strongly to it having been important to the Templars before it came into their possession. And given their position as warrior monks of Christ, it is reasonable to suppose that this importance must have been primarily connected with Jesus.

Once again, the long hair supplies the clue: one is immediately reminded of the Sampsaei and the Nazoraei, whose locks were never touched by razor, for whom the hair was sacred and untouchable, and who revered and followed the ancient teachings of Akhenaten/Moses. And as we have seen, Jesus was most certainly a member of this cult. He was very probably its leader at the time of his death when, as the *Continuation* records, a head of Jesus was in the hands of one of the two men who had been with the body in its tomb, and that it was said of this head that *'the Lord God set His hand to the shaping of it'*, and *'... nor could it be made by human hands'*. This head, the head of Christ, would have been that of a man with long hair and long beard, exactly as the Baphomet is described.

This was a stunning and, to be honest, an uncomfortable subject to contemplate, but the conclusion was inescapable. It seemed likely that the mysterious head of Christ that Nicodemus possessed had indeed survived the centuries since its 'creation', just after the death of Jesus.

The evidence suggested that the Templars' most holy relic, known as Baphomet, the Father of Wisdom, was none other than the embalmed head of Jesus, the head of God. The most likely scenario for its discovery is that it was recovered during the excavation of the Poor Knights beneath the Temple of Solomon. There is little doubt that a head, or heads of some kind, was found by the Templars at this time, as witness their acceptance of extraordinary burial rites. But it is also possible that this most sacred of relics was sent abroad, as the *Evangelicum Nicodemi* seems to imply, and that it came to the Templars by another, altogether more circuitous, route. It may well have been bequeathed to them by the 'heresy' that constituted the major threat to the Roman Church in the early Middle Ages, by the followers of Gnosticism, the Cathars.

13

The Cathar Connection

The Cathar Connection

The Cathars were a heretical Christian sect active in the south of France and northern Italy for almost one hundred years, between 1142 and their suppression around 1250. They were known by a variety of other names: Texerants, Patarenes, Piphli and Albigens. This latter name originated in a stronghold of dualist belief, the town of Albi in southern France, from which derives the infamous war of slaughter against the Cathar believers known as the Albigensian Crusade. Although the name Cathar encompasses several variations in belief, they can all be regarded as Gnostic dualists, united in their conviction that it was possible to achieve Gnosis, the direct experience of the godhead.[1] This experience, while requiring the guidance of *perfecti* (perfected ones) who had already achieved this union with the cosmic, was ultimately dependent upon the individual's own actions rather than the intercession of priests or of sacrifices. This, of course, set the Cathars directly at odds with the Roman Church, whose hierarchy of prelates and priests would have been all but redundant had Catharism gained the ascendancy in the minds of the ordinary people, which it threatened to do on several occasions.

For the Cathars, the material world was evil, brought into existence not by the Good God but by the Demiurge. This lesser and evil god was sometimes regarded as the elder son of the Good God who had rebelled against the dominion of his father. In this cosmology, the evil 'son' was, therefore, ultimately subordinate to the Good God. Later, this monarchial dualism was largely superseded by an absolute dualism, the belief that there were two co-eternal principles of equal power, one evil, one good, and that they waged an incessant and everlasting battle across the cosmos.[2]

It was the evil god who had seduced or captured a proportion of the angelic beings and entrapped them in the material world, to form the first men. For the Cathars, humanity was composed of intrinsically good angelic beings, imprisoned in bodies that were composed, like the rest of the world, of evil, corrupting matter.[3] Their conception of Christ reflected this world-view. Jesus had been sent into the world in order to redeem these lost angelic souls from the confines of matter, and to return them to their 'natural' abode with the Good God. But, unlike the Roman Church, while most Cathars greatly revered Jesus, they still regarded him as distinctly human. A man filled with the spirit of the Good God, but a man nevertheless. In some cases, this was conceived as a heavenly Christ within the earthly Jesus, who had been begotten normally as other men. Accordingly, the Cathars repudiated the dogma of the virgin birth. They also discounted the crucifixion and the cross.[4] The resurrection in the body was ridiculed; the Cathars preferred (as in many mystery religions) to regard 'resurrection' as a rebirth that came about during life, as a result of union with God. The apocryphal Gospel of Philip casts scorn on the 'bodily resurrectionists' and states the Gnostic position clearly: 'Those who say they will die first and then rise are in error. If they do not receive the resurrection while they live, when they die they will receive nothing.'[5] Many of these beliefs echo the accusations brought against the Templars when they were accused of heresy, and may indicate a close connection between the doctrines of the two groups.

In order to escape from this 'hell on earth' it was necessary to eschew the pleasures of the material world. In this the ordinary Cathar believers were shown the way by the Cathar 'priests', the *perfecti* or perfected ones, who had received the *consolamentum*, a ritual that apparently allowed the communicant direct access to the godhead. The *perfecti* had been initiated into the inner mysteries of the religion and had renounced sexual relations, even with their spouses (Cathar *perfecti* could be of either sex, and many were married).[6] These priests were at the top of a hierarchical 'pyramid' of three levels. At the bottom were the listeners, who were apparently just starting out on the path of Catharism. Above these were the 'believers' who had been initiated into some of the secrets of the sect, but had not yet received the *consolamentum*, which conferred upon the individual the title of *perfectus*. The *perfecti* travelled in pairs and, symbolising their simplicity and contrasting their beliefs with that of the ostentatious Catholic Church, they held their services in barns or ordinary houses, or in the open air. The *perfecti* were instantly recognisable, for they wore long vestments from neck to ankle, rather like an orthodox priest except that their robes were invariably black or, after the persecutions began, dark blue.[7] These vestments were fastened at the waist by a girdle, and a hooded cloak, also black, was sometimes worn in inclement weather. Several authorities have claimed that the *perfecti* wore a cord under these garments, tied around the waist next to the skin. A similar cord is said to have been worn by the Templars.[8] And in a telling echo of the Merovingians, Nazarites and the other groups prominent in our story, the *perfecti* were forbidden to cut their hair, which they always wore long.

The centre of Cathar worship was the Languedoc, a region in the south of France that is fringed by the Mediterranean and is bordered to the west by the Pyrenees, and by Provence and Italy to the east. Learning flourished in this region during the early Middle Ages; secular literacy was encouraged and Greek, Hebrew and Arabic were all studied. The Languedoc is, of course, the region of the old Jewish principality of Septimania, and there is much evidence to suggest that the Cathars were at the very least influenced by the Jewish traditions of the region.[9] Religious tolerance was the norm in the Languedoc. Jews were not persecuted; indeed the counts of Toulouse were often taken to task by the clergy for appointing Jews to public office.[10] Schools of the Jewish Qabbala at Narbonne and Lunel practised openly, and several strands of Cathar thought seem to reflect aspects of this esoteric Judaism. During the twelfth century, as the Cathars emerged, the Jews of Provence also underwent their own spiritual renaissance and were responsible for production of the occult *Sepher Bahir*, a classic of medieval Qabbala literature.[11]

Apart from this possible Jewish influence, the origins of Cathar thought appear to lie with the eastern heresies, especially with a group called the Bogomils, although even here there is persuasive evidence that Judaic influences were at work.

The Bogomils

The Bogomils were a sect which apparently arose in the Balkans, although even this is in such doubt that one scholar despairingly entitled a chapter on the subject 'The Riddle of Bogomil Beginnings'.[12] They were founded by the 'greatest heresiarch of the middle ages', the priest Bogomil, a man whose energy and charisma were responsible both for the initial establishment and the survival of the sect. Their beliefs prefigured that of the Cathars, in that the Bogomils were dualists, believing in a good spiritual god and a 'fallen angel' or lesser god that had created the material world. In addition, orthodox tracts anathematised the priest Bogomil for spreading the Docetic belief that Christ's passion and resurrection were illusory, and for rejecting the veneration of the cross (accusations later made against both the Cathars and the Templars).[13] Moreover, the Bogomil organisation was identical to that of the Cathars, which it predated, with an 'elite of Bogomil' who had received a spiritual baptism analogous (if not identical) to the Cathar *consolamentum*, and below this the grade of 'believer', with a third and less-defined grade of 'listeners' making up the base of the hierarchical pyramid.[14]

The Bogomil teachings were carried from the Balkans into the West sometime around the end of the first millennium. There is a hint of such teachings as early as 991 when, at his consecration as Archbishop of Rheims, Gerbert de Aurillac was required to swear that he believed in both the Old and New Testaments, in marriage, eating meat, and in the presence of the devil as willed by God and not existing independently of the creator. All these items directly contradict Bogomil (and later Cathar) teachings. It is believed that Gerbert had come under suspicion of 'infection' by the heresy and had made a public profession of his faith in order to deflect any misgivings by the orthodox establishment of Rome. The heretical suspicions of his superiors may have been well founded: in his youth Gerbert had studied at the Arab universities of Spain, where the Qabbala was highly regarded, and he was later to be accused of organising a school of magic during his time in Rome. Gerbert later became the first French pope, taking the name Sylvester II. Intriguingly, he was also rumoured to possess an 'oracular' severed head, which gave advice and helped to secure his succession to the papal throne.[15]

Bogomil missionaries are known to have visited the West on several occasions, using the Byzantine colonies that existed in Sicily and southern Italy as bridgeheads, jumping-off points from which to carry their teachings into northern Italy and southern France and as far north as Flanders (where they were called Piphli).[16] There are documented accounts of Bogomil missionaries in Palermo from at least 1082. In addition, the inquisitor Anselm of Alessandria reports in his *Tractatus de hereticis* that crusaders 'who went to Constantinople to conquer the land' were converted to Bogomilism. They established their own branch of the dualist religion in Byzantium, and even had their own bishop.[17] These men would have carried the teachings back with them when they returned to western Europe. However, it may be that the traffic in heretical thought was not all one way, and that a transfer of beliefs from west to east also occurred. In an orthodox index of forbidden books there is a record of two shadowy westerners who brought heterodox teachings to the Bogomils. The two men, Sydor Fryazin and Jacob Tsentsal, who is also named as a 'fryazin' (a Frank) are said to have introduced certain heretical books to Bulgaria.[18] The time of their visit is not specified but, as one historian has concluded, there remains 'the intriguing possibility of an early intercourse between eastern and western heretics prior to the first serious outbreaks of heresy in western Christendom'.[19] It is also of great interest that the men are described as Franks, for the possibility also exists that Merovingian 'ambassadors' had travelled to the East in order to make contact with a group that shared at least some of their beliefs, and perhaps even their own bloodline.

While it is known that the Bogomils had a great influence on the rise of the Cathars, their own roots remain shrouded in mystery. The origin and development of the eastern dualist 'heresies' is badly under-researched, and is fraught with problems of poor documentation. What documentation does exist is often a one-sided diatribe against the 'heresies' by Roman inquisitors and therefore unreliable, though in their zeal the inquisitors do often let slip valuable information. Syncretism, the union of concepts from different religions and cults, was widespread in the East, and it seems that almost every teacher and leader added or absorbed influences from other sects. The huge number of cults that arose in the vast swathe of lands that lay between the Balkans and Anatolia, and the almost inconceivably large number of complex belief systems that these sects espoused, makes a straightforward analysis impossible, and the subject is a minefield for scholars. Nevertheless, certain facts are commonly accepted. It was these facts, allied to the knowledge I had already gleaned in other areas, that forced me to the conclusion that the foundations of Bogomil philosophy were, at least in part, derived from heretical Judaism.

The Aaronids

Balkan political history is almost as complex as its religious history, but there is one section of this labyrinthine saga remarkable for its apparently Jewish connections. The Bulgarian empire, the home and stronghold of Bogomilism was thrown into chaos in the tenth century by a Russian invasion. Byzantium, on the southeastern borders of Bulgaria, viewed the Russian incursion as a threat to its own security and invaded in its turn, eventually repulsing the northern invaders and forcing the tsar of the Bulgarian empire, Boris II, to abdicate. The Byzantine emperor John Tzimisces moved to annexe the Bulgarian lands, and was strongly resisted by a group of four brothers, all sons of a Bulgarian count. These four siblings were known as the Cometopuli, as their rise to prominence apparently coincided with the arrival in the skies of an enormous comet. The names of these brothers generated a number of tantalising questions. The Cometopuli were styled David, Moses, Aaron and Samuel, patently Jewish names that speak of a Jewish ancestry. Bulgaria has as its northern border the Danube, the river along which the Benjamite exiles are said to have begun their long march to Sicambria and the West. I began to wonder if there could be a connection between the Jewish Cometopuli and the heretic tribe whose migration could easily have taken them through Bulgarian territory. Further research revealed that the Bulgarian Apocryphal Chronicle referred to the four men as the royal 'sons of the widow-prophetess',[20] suggesting an Egyptian/dualist link, and a title almost identical to that given Jesus, Hiram Abif, and the hero of the Grail romances, Perceval.

The youngest of the Cometopuli, Samuel, eventually conquered most of Albania and Greece, restoring the Bulgarian empire and was crowned tsar in 997. But Byzantium still harboured territorial ambitions against the Bulgars and the beginning of the second millennium saw the two empires locked in combat along their borders, with neither side able to gain the advantage. However, the balance of power was illusory. Byzantium was by far the stronger of the two, but was at that time fighting on two fronts, with the Bulgars in the west, and with the Fatimid Caliph al-Hakim in the east. In 1001, the new Byzantine Emperor Basil agreed a ten-year truce with al-Hakim, and he was then able to turn the full might of his extensive empire upon the Bulgars, gradually overrunning Tsar Samuel's domains in a series of pitched battles. A Byzantine victory of 1014 proved decisive; having captured thousands of Bulgarian warriors during the battle, the ruthless Basil had every one of the Bulgar prisoners blinded before sending them back to their homeland. Tsar Samuel went to meet them, and collapsed on seeing the hideous spectacle of his eyeless army groping their way towards him. He never recovered, and died within a few days. This was the beginning of the end. After four further years of resistance, the Bulgarian empire finally fell to Basil's conquering army in 1018.

However, this was by no means the end of the Cometopuli family. An Arab chronicle records that they intermarried with Byzantine nobility and eventually gave rise to the Aaronids, another obviously Jewish line. The Aaronids prospered, and by the end of the twelfth century two Aaronid women had married Byzantine emperors. Much later, two female descendants of one of these royal wives, Irene Ducaina, married into the Frankish royal House of Jerusalem, one marrying Baldwin III and the other Almaric I.[21]

This raises a number of interesting questions. As we have seen, the line of Godfroi de Bouillon, the conqueror of Jerusalem was, through his Merovingian ancestors, of Jewish and Benjamite descent. Were the Cometopuli brothers, David, Moses, Aaron and Samuel, and the Aaronids who were descended from them, also descendants of the 'heretic tribe'? Such obviously Jewish names marked the family as Judaic, and begged the question of where this family had originally come from. Could they have been of Benjamite stock? The possibility exists that the Cometopuli and the Aaronids were the remnants of a group of Benjamites that chose not to undertake the arduous migration to the West, and instead moved only a little way to the north. Macedonia is just 450 kilometres from the Peloponnese where the heretic tribe was said to have landed after leaving Israel, and the Danube (along which the remaining Benjamites are likely to have travelled westwards) forms the modern border between Bulgaria and Romania. These 'eastern Benjamites' may well have been the source of the eastern heresies, just as the 'western Benjamites', the Merovingians and their descendants, seem to have been at least partially responsible for the instigation of the Cathar heresy in the Languedoc. It may be that the two branches of the heretic tribe coalesced once more, when the Aaronid females married into the royal line of Jerusalem, descendants of those Benjamites who had travelled westwards into Europe. The Benjamites were the original Jewish owners of the city of Jerusalem. By marrying the Frankish kings of Jerusalem, were the Aaronid females, like the Merovingian line of Godfroi de Bouillon, also attempting to recover their long-lost patrimony?

The Crusade against Gnosticism

As we have seen, just as the Languedoc, with its Judaic/Benjamite connections, became the seat of heretical agitation in the West, Bulgaria (ruled by a descendant of the Judaic Cometopuli) was a hotbed of heretical teachings in the East. As heresy erupted around them on all sides, the prelates of the Roman Church did not stand idly by. The counterattack can be dated from the elevation of Pope Innocent III. In his first year as pontiff, Innocent declared heresy *lèse-majesté* against God and later he sent a commission, headed by a papal legate, to Bosnia, to investigate religious affairs there and to bring those 'in error' back to the fold.[22] Just prior to this, Innocent had sent a similar mission, led by Cistercian monks, to the Languedoc, both to prevent the further spread of Catharism, and to reform the Roman Church of Languedoc, whose venality and corruption were legendary. The Languedoc nobility pledged to drive the Cathars from their territories, but it seems that the promises were made simply as a means of persuading the Cistercians to leave, as in both 1204 and 1205 Innocent was calling on Philip Augustus, the King of France, to intervene militarily in the area to rid the land of the 'foul corruption of heresy'. Philip resisted these calls, and the papal legate Peter of Castelnau was forced to fight with the only other weapon at his disposal. He excommunicated the principal protector of the Cathars, Raymond vi, the Count of Toulouse, in 1207. Peter of Castelnau was murdered two years later, and the pope used this as a pretext to accuse Raymond vi of his murder, and to call for a crusade against the Languedoc and the hated Albigensians. The pope sweetened his call to arms with a promise of indulgences (remission of sins) for all who took part, and the granting of any land that might be taken to the conquerors. Greed, rather than piety, was the chief motivator, and in the early summer of 1209 a large army of northern barons and prelates mustered at Lyons, before pressing on into the Cathar heartland. The infamous Albigensian Crusade had begun.

While much of the northern nobility took part in the crusade, the military orders were conspicuous by their absence. The Templars in particular refused any active military role in the despoliation of the Languedoc.[23] Given the similarity of the order's hidden philosophy to that of the Cathars, this is not surprising. Many of the southern nobility were known both to protect the Cathar *perfecti* and to be patrons of the Order of the Temple. In addition, they also supported the troubadours and their mystical poetry.[24]

The 'crusade' rapidly became a war of conquest. The cities of Carcassonne and Béziers fell and the crusaders murdered Catholic and Cathar alike, 'showing mercy neither to order nor to age or sex' according to a central figure in the crusade, Arnold Aimery.[25] Simon de Montfort (who was a claimant to the earldom of Leicester in England) was declared leader of the crusaders at this time and pressed on with the conquest. The war raged across the Languedoc with increasing ferocity. When Simon de Montfort conquered the dominions of Trencavel and occupied the town of Minerve, 140 Cathar *perfecti* were consigned to the stake. In a particularly brutal episode, de Montfort condemned a widow, Geralda of Lavaur Castle, as a heretic; on his orders she was thrown into a well and then buried under a hail of stones.

The Cathar supporters fought back desperately and the fortunes of war rocked back and forth between 'heretic' and 'crusader', with first one side then the other gaining the upper hand. When all seemed lost for the Cathars, their most vociferous opponent, Pope Innocent III, died. Shortly thereafter, the feared and hated Simon de Montfort was killed in the siege of Toulouse, struck down by a rock cast from a mangonel and, as one contemporary song had it, dying 'bloodied and pallid'.[26] In the contemporary 'Song of the Cathar Wars', the account of the Cathar victory at Baziege reveals the depth to which both sides had sunk, with quarter neither asked nor given. When the French knights had left the field, the Cathar foot soldiers scoured the battleground, killing all the enemy wounded and any knight who had been unhorsed and could not flee:

> Now all together sergeants entered the battle to kill the fallen. Steel flashed on steel, on overthrown and beaten men; knights and sergeants struggled, and they slashed, slew and finished them. Eyes, brain-matter, hands, arms, scalps and jawbones, bits of limbs, livers and guts sliced up and tossed about, blood, flesh and carrion lay everywhere...[27]

Cathar resistance was stiffening once more and the crusaders were again on the defensive, with the new pope, Honorius, exhorting the French monarchy to come to the aid of the hard-pressed 'defenders of Christ'.

This call was belatedly answered by a new French king, Louis VIII, who overran most of the Languedoc in 1226, before dying that same year. Louis IX continued the pressure, and the principal Cathar nobles, in the person of Raymond VII of Toulouse, were forced to sign the Peace of Paris in 1229, by which much of their land was ceded to the French crown, and onerous religious restrictions were imposed. That same year, the Council of Toulouse attempted to consolidate the power of the Catholic priesthood by banning any copies of the Bible that had been translated into Provençal French, rather than Latin. The people of Languedoc were also required to take an oath every six months, reaffirming their orthodox beliefs. In reality, these strictures did little to suppress the Cathar religion, and many Languedoc noble houses continued to act as safe havens for the *perfecti* and their rites. It was not until another pope, Gregory IX, founded the effective and implacable Holy Inquisition, that the scales of fortune weighed once more in favour of Catholic dogma. Although they suffered many setbacks, the Dominican friars of the Inquisition (known as 'Hounds of the Lord') worked diligently, ruthlessly rooting out heresy wherever it was found.

Initially, when they entered any town the Dominicans instituted an amnesty of one month's duration, during which time anyone who confessed their heresy would be granted pardon. These repentant heretics were, however, required to name other heretics, or those who sheltered them. After this the entire weight of canon law fell upon the miscreants, who were hauled before secret trials, where the names of their accusers were also kept secret. Those found guilty were given severe penances or, if their heresy was considered too deep rooted to be cured, they might be turned over to the secular authorities to be 'purified by fire'. So fanatical were the friars that even the bodies of long-dead heretics were disinterred and paraded through town or village before being cast into the purifying flames.[28]

These over-zealous and turbulent priests stirred up much resentment and hatred in the Languedoc, and it was only a matter of time before the populace took revenge. Matters came to a head in May of 1242, when two well-known inquisitors, Guilliame Arnaud and Pierre Seila, together with nine of their followers, arrived in Avignonet and were welcomed by Roger VII's factotum, Raymond d'Alfar. While he offered them hospitality, one of his men was already speeding towards the Cathar citadel of Montségur, to alert the garrison. A large number of men gathered, each eager to take revenge on the inquisitors. Twelve were chosen and, armed with axes, they descended upon the house of Raymond d'Alfar and were speedily admitted. They immediately fell upon the inquisitors and their entourage as they took their ease, slaughtering them to a man.[29]

The Cathars were ecstatic at this 'victory'. It is recorded that when the garrison commander of Montségur, Pierre-Roger de Mirepoix, saw the executioners he asked, 'Where then is the cup of Arnaud?' by which he meant Guilliame Arnaud's skull, which he had intended to use as a drinking vessel. Told that it was broken, he asked why the pieces had not been brought to him, as he would have 'bound them together with a circlet of gold and drunk wine from this cup all my life'.[30] Do we have, in this strange vignette, perhaps a grotesque echo of Cathar knowledge of the sacred head cult, or is this simply the victor exalting over his vanquished foe? If the motive was jubilation, it was destined to be short lived. As with the murder of Peter of Castelnau thirty-four years earlier, the papacy used the assassination of two of its inquisitors as an ideal pretext for launching the final phase of the destruction of the Cathars. Helped by the French king, the crusading armies moved against the final stronghold of Catharism in the Languedoc, Montségur.

Montségur

Situated on an abrupt 1207-metre peak in the northern foothills of the Pyrenees, Montségur towers over the surrounding land. The castle was considered all but impregnable (Montségur means 'Mount Safe') and it had offered a safe haven for Cathar refugees and for *faidits*, rebel southern nobility, for decades. The castle was owned by the Count of Foix, whom the Bishop of Toulouse accused of cherishing and supporting the heretics. The bishop also claimed that the count's 'whole country is crammed and seething with heresy, that the peak of Montségur was deliberately fortified so that he could protect them, and he has made them welcome there'.[31] In addition, mercenaries had been hired to strengthen the garrison. But Montségur was not simply a fortress, and it was said to hold far more than heretics and hired warriors. It was also reputedly the refuge of the semi-mythical 'Cathar Treasure', rumours of which had been abroad from at least the beginning of the crusade against the Languedoc. The stories were vague, but they imbued the treasure with a religious and deeply mystical dimension. Whatever it was, the Cathar treasure was believed to be much more than simply gold or precious stones. And it lay at Montségur, which was now about to face its severest test. Despite rumours of help from additional mercenary forces and aid from the Count of Toulouse, both failed to materialise.[32] Montségur stood alone, defiant, before the power of King Louis of France, who was determined to crush the 'heresy of the south' once and for all.

In 1243 Montségur was besieged by an army of ten thousand men led by the king's seneschal of Carcassonne. The defenders fought off attack after attack, refusing to surrender and inflicting heavy casualties on the besieging forces. Because of the nature of the terrain, and the Cathars' intimate knowledge of the locality, it was impossible completely to cut off the defenders of Montségur from the outside world. At one stage a message arrived from the Cathar Bishop of Cremona, offering one of the defenders, Bertrand Marty, Bishop of Toulouse, safe haven in Lombardy. Six months into the siege, two Cathar *perfecti* managed to slip through the line of investing troops. They reportedly carried the Cathar treasure, or at least the material wealth of the sect. This part of the treasure was never seen again.

Three months into the siege, with no hope of succour, the position of the defenders was fast becoming desperate. Pierre Roger, the commander, opened negotiations with the besiegers. Given the barbarous nature of the crusade, and the huge cost in men and materiel that investing Montségur had imposed upon the besiegers, the terms granted the Cathars were generous in the extreme: the *faidits* and mercenaries were to be pardoned and allowed to leave with all their possessions, including their arms. The *perfecti* had only to recant their heretical ways, confess to the Church authorities, and they too, after penance, would be free to go. But should the *perfecti* refuse to recant, no quarter was to be given – they would be burnt to death.[33] A two-week truce was agreed to allow the defenders to consider the offer, but this lengthy period seems to have been requested by the defenders in order to gain time so that a ceremony of great importance to the Cathar faith could take place on its due date. One day before the termination of this truce, on the vernal equinox, 14 March 1244, the ritual was held within the castle of Montségur. No one is sure what happened there, or what was revealed, but whatever occurred it produced such an effect on the defenders that some of the mercenaries (who were to receive their freedom the following day) voluntarily converted to the Cathar faith and received the *consolamentum*, choosing 'baptism by fire' and effectively condemning themselves to death. The next day, the attackers seized all the *perfecti* they could find in the castle, more than two hundred men and women, and led them down to the foot of the mountain. Not one *perfectus* abjured the Cathar faith and they were all consigned to the flames on a plain still known to local tradition as 'The Field of the Cremated'.[34]

Although the attacking troops had seized all the Cathar *perfecti* they could find, three or perhaps four had remained hidden among the castle garrison. The following night, 16 March, they attempted an audacious escape under cover of darkness, climbing down the sheer rock face on the western side of the castle. According to legend, they carried with them the rest of the fabulous Cathar treasure. Luck was with the escapees; they passed undetected through the 'crusader' lines and, like their two compatriots who had escaped three months earlier, they, and their 'treasure', simply disappear from the pages of history.[35]

But what was this treasure of the Cathars? How much gold and silver could three *perfecti* carry? It could not have been monetary; the amount of gold carried by a trio of desperate men who had to travel quickly and silently could hardly be dignified by the name 'treasure'. It had to be something else, something that had been held in Montségur until the very last moment, something that had been essential for the ritual that took place on the vernal equinox, the day before the castle capitulated. This 'treasure', whatever it was, had persuaded men to change their faith and voluntarily to accept death by burning the following day. Gold alone could never have done this. Nor could holy books, sacred texts, or any other 'secondary relic' the Cathars may have possessed. Only a relic of great worth and sanctity might have changed these men's minds, and persuaded them to forgo life and freedom and accept instead a martyr's death at the stake. Could the Cathar treasure possibly have been the Baphomet, the embalmed head of Jesus, the head of God? And if this was the case, by what accident of history could the holy relic have come into the possession of the Cathar *perfecti* trapped in the castle of Montségur?

There is a plausible route for this seemingly astonishing suggestion. The legend of Mary Magdalene's escape from the Jews, of her drifting in a boat with Lazarus and other biblical characters, has already been described in Chapter 7. It is very telling that the port the group fetched up in was Marseilles, in the south of France, the very area that saw the rise of the Jewish principality of Septimania, linked by blood to the Merovingians, and heartland of the Cathar heresy. The Magdalene is said to have brought with her to France the Holy Grail. I had already identified this title as a 'cover name', a cypher used to hide the object's true identity as a severed, embalmed head. If Mary Magdalene was Jesus' wife, it is very likely that she would carry 'the Grail', the head, with her into exile. And the 'carved' head in Nicodemus' possession, of whom it was said '*no man ever saw one like it nor could it be made by human hands*', was taken to Jaffa by Nicodemus who '*put it in the sea*'. In the time of Jesus, Jaffa was the main entrepôt for Jerusalem. If elements in the Jewish establishment did force the flight of the Magdalene and many other of Jesus' followers, it is almost certain that they would have been taken to Jaffa for a ship to begin their exile. So it is at least possible that the head of God had been carried into France. And that it had made its way into the possession of the Cathars, perhaps via the Qabbalistic Jews of Septimania and their Merovingian rulers, whose links with heretical Judaism have been well established, and who shared several points of belief with the Christian dualists.

But, if we accept that the Cathars may have held the head as part of their mystical treasure, what became of it after the fall of Montségur? Where did the three escaping *perfecti* escape to? More to the point, where *could* they go? Although certain diehards among the *faidits* held out against the French authorities until 1255, when their last stronghold, the château of Queribus, fell, the Cathar cause was effectively lost in France with the destruction of Montségur. It was, as Lawrence Durrell has said, 'the Thermopylae of the Gnostic Soul',[36] a final stand by the adherents of dualism against the overwhelming power of orthodoxy. Faced with such a disaster, where could the Cathar escapees go, on the run with their books and relics, to avoid capture? There was only one place in France that was beyond the reach of the king, an organisation that was to all intents autonomous and which shared essentially the same Gnostic world-view as the Cathars: the Order of the Temple.

The Templars had pointedly refused to participate in the crusade against the Cathars and the two groups were close, with many southern nobles supporting the Cathar heresy and acting also as patrons to the Templar Order. That the higher echelons of the temple held secretly to Gnostic doctrines is now widely believed; even their piebald battle flag Beau Séant, half-black and half-white, symbolising the division of the universe into good and evil, pointed to the dualist beliefs of the order.[37] And it is known that during the Albigensian Crusade, many Cathars were accepted into the ranks of the order to escape the clutches of the Inquisition.[38] It is highly likely, then, that the Cathars should have brought their 'mystical treasure' to the temple for protection. And this treasure could well have included the sacred head of Jesus, held in the south of France from the time of Mary Magdalene.

Whatever the provenance of the head of God, from the Cathars or from beneath the Temple of Solomon, it seems certain that by the end of the thirteenth century the holy head was in the possession of the Order of the Temple. That it was no ordinary religious object can be proved by one aspect of the Templars' treatment of the relic when it came into their possession – their obsessive desire for secrecy. Why was the sacred head worshipped in such deep seclusion, away from prying eyes? Although to most modern-day minds the reverencing of a severed, embalmed head is grotesque, with even a whiff of necromancy attached to the practice, the Templars' worship of a holy head was, in fact, not at all unusual for the time in which they lived. As I was to discover, they were simply conforming to a general trend, evident throughout the Middle Ages, of honouring the remains of dead saints and other holy men and women. This custom is well documented and is known to historians as the cult of relics. It is a story full of surprises and grotesque ritual, and it was to provide me with compelling evidence that again linked the identity of the Baphomet with that of Jesus.

14

The Forbidden Relic

The cult of relics has its origin in what seems to be a basic human need to honour the dead, especially those regarded as having lived an heroic life or one steeped in sanctity. In Africa the bodies of dead Ghanaian kings were allowed to decay at the grotesquely named 'Place of the Drippings', and the skeletons afterwards reassembled with golden wires.[1] The Buddhists of Asia, thought by many to be free from the taint of any such 'superstitition', still revere the relics of Gautama Buddha, reverencing his teeth, collar bones, hair and nail pairings. Long before Gautama's time, the body of an earlier buddha, Kasyapa, was said to have been preserved entire in a tall tower.[2] Even the followers of Mohammed have occasionally succumbed to the seductive potency of holy relics: his footprint, on Mount Sinai, was visited by Muslim pilgrims, and hairs said to be from the prophet's beard were carried by Sultan Ibrahim II to Bijiapur in India.[3] No culture, religion or ethnic group seems immune to this desire for holy remains. But for all its worldwide prevalence, it was in medieval, Christian Europe that the cult of relics reached its apogee.

The veneration of certain relics began very early in the Christian era. In AD 238 St Ursula, and over eleven thousand virgins who accompanied her, were slaughtered by the Huns as she returned from a meeting with the pope in Rome to the city of Cologne. A church was built over the burial site and became a site of pilgrimage. Around sixty-five years later, in Italy, Januarius, the Bishop of Benevento, was beheaded during the persecution of Christians by the Emperor Diocletian. His martyred body and head were venerated at various churches and monasteries (the monks being forced to move the body continually during the Norman invasion of Italy). Many holy remains were accorded the same honours. For example the body of St Cuthbert, which was carried from Lindisfarne and wandered the north of England until the body of the saint itself (by miraculously becoming too heavy to be carried) indicated its final resting place on a hill above the city of Durham, where now stands one of the most imposing and beautiful of the medieval Gothic cathedrals.

Despite such occasional veneration, it remains true that, until medieval times, the relics of most saints and holy men were not regarded with the great esteem that was soon to be accorded to even the meanest of them. The Middle Ages saw a great burgeoning in the cult of relics.[4] The cult of St Ursula and her eleven thousand virgins was one of the first to benefit. In the twelfth century a superb new church, in the Gothic style, was built for her remains. Inside was the famous Golden Chamber, a chapel built four-square and housing scores of saintly skulls wrapped in red cloth. There are busts on shelves, some with a removable top of the head, so that the faithful may observe the holy skull within. St Ursula's skull is set in the place of honour, on the altar of the Golden Chamber.

In a similar way, it was not until 1497 that the holy remains of St Januarius found their final resting place in the newly built cathedral of Naples. Even then, the body remained in two parts, as it does to this day; the trunk lies in a sumptuous crypt (designed by the Renaissance master Tommaso Malvito) beneath the cathedral. The head is displayed in a bust behind the main altar of a side chapel, flanked by two phials of the saint's blood. On three days each year (19 September, 16 December and the Saturday before the first Sunday of May) the head is removed and displayed on the altar. The phials of blood are brought close to the holy object and, almost invariably, the congealed blood returns to its pristine state.

The head of St Januarius is by no means the only example. Skulls and heads have always been important in Christian relic worship. A by no means exhaustive list includes the skull or head of Saints Ursula, Januarius, Fursey, Blaise, Lazarus, Basil the Great, Julian of Brioude, Winifred, Magnus, Edmund (King of England), Maxim, Lucian, and the head of the child martyr St Pancras. Moreover, in ancient Byzantium, the heads of St Peter and St Paul were worshipped with great pomp, reminiscent of the Templar ceremonies in honour of their mysterious sacred head. The heads of the two saints were later removed to Rome. The chronicler records that in 1191 the French king, Philip Augustus, visited Pope Celestine III as he returned from the Third Crusade. As a mark of respect, the holy father showed the King of France and his men the heads of the apostles Peter and Paul. The basilica of St John Lateran still holds the holy heads of these two most important of the Christian apostles.[5]

Although the skull itself may be looked upon as a grisly, perhaps even hideous relic, this is to ignore the perception that the faithful – medieval or modern – have of such relics and the miracles with which they are surrounded. St Januarius' head, for example, has the power miraculously to renew his congealed blood. As James Bentley has perceptively put it '... the liquefying blood points towards a proper understanding of the relic as something far more than a gruesomely preserved corpse. In the eyes of the faithful, Januarius' blood liquefies as a sign that the martyr is not dead, but alive in Heaven'.[6] These remains are not *memento mori*, but symbols of hope in the afterlife. The hallowed dead point the way to eternal bliss.

The Power of Holy Bones

That powerful emotions could be evoked in the faithful made such relics symbols of great potency. It has been argued persuasively that it was the pope's possession of important relics, especially that of St Peter (who, according to orthodox Christian teaching, was the rock upon whom Christ's church was founded), that was the underlying reason why his authority was accepted, '... the Pope, whatever theoretical claims were made for him, in practice owed most of his authority to the fact that he was the guardian of the body of St Peter. This brought men to Rome and made them listen to the voice of St Peter mediated through his representative here on earth.'[7]

The power of relics was shown in Merovingian times when Chilperic I had the temerity to appropriate certain treasures from the church of Sainte-Colombe. St Eloi of Paris took exception to this and, instead of confronting the king directly, placed a prohibition on worship at the shrine of St Colombe, in effect suppressing the cult of the saint completely. The citizens of Paris were incensed by the loss to themselves and to their city of the saint's protection, and they were quick to blame the king for this disaster. Insurrection threatened, and Chilperic quickly relented, restoring the treasures and thereby assuaging the wrath of the populace. The Count of Anjou, Fulk Nerra, faced a similar withdrawal of saintly aid when he strode, in full martial splendour, into the church of St Martin. Such sacrilegious violation of God's House was not to be tolerated. The churchmen removed the remains of St Martin of Tours from their place of honour and, laying them beside the cross, heaped thorns over the holy bones. Following this symbolic act, the doors of the church were barred to all members of the laity. Denied the comfort of the saint's protection, Fulk's peasants began to murmur their discontent and his liegemen to reconsider their vows of fealty. Fearful of the consequences, Fulk Nerra, the powerful and all-conquering Count of Anjou, came barefoot to the saint's remains, prostrated himself before them and, in front of a company of churchmen and common folk, begged forgiveness for his act of impiety. Honour satisfied, Fulk was shriven of his sin and the cult of the saint reinstated.[8]

Powerful cities demanded powerful relics and, in its time, Byzantium was the most powerful of all.[9] It became, in the words of one scholar, 'one enormous reliquary'. The robe of the Virgin Mary was deposited in one of the city's many churches, as was a sample of her breast milk. Here could be found the heads of Saints Peter and Paul, the head of John the Baptist, the bodies of Saints Stephen and Andrew, the teeth of St Christopher, the arms of Saints Clement and Barnabas, the finger of St Michael, the knee of St Simeon and the foot of St Comas. There was the sponge and the reed of the crucifixion, and a piece of the true cross, together with, as Archbishop Antony of Novgorod reported after his visit in 1200, 'the hammer, the gimlet and the saw with which the cross was made'. Nor were Old Testament figures ignored. Constantinople boasted the axe used by Noah to build the Ark, the trumpet blown by Joshua outside the walls of Jericho, Elijah's belt and headdress, and a sample of the 'manna from heaven' which had sustained the Israelites during their forty years of wandering in the wilderness of Sinai. The power of the great city had even drawn to itself the Ark of the Covenant, and the Tablets of the Law, given to Moses by God, and written with the finger of God.

Great power was vested in these relics, political and financial. Such marvels were worth seeing; they brought in a steady stream of visitors and pilgrims, who had to be housed and fed, all at a tidy profit. Then, as now, the pilgrims wished to take back with them some memento of their visit, tangible proof that they had seen and perhaps even touched the saintly remains. And they were prepared to pay for the privilege. The abbeys, churches and cathedrals that owned the most sought-after relics received thousands of visitors each year, and could become fabulously rich on the proceeds of this trade. In some areas of Europe sinners requiring absolution were required to deposit at least their own weight in wheat or barley before the holy remains.[10] Count Robert of Namur did this when he visited the relics of St Gengulphe. Persons of great status might leave their weight in silver or gold. Even lesser individuals, carrying meaner gifts, could still swell the coffers of the saint's keepers, if they came in large enough numbers. In 1174, just one year after the canonisation of St Thomas à Becket, over 100,000 pilgrims came to visit his bones in Canterbury cathedral. By 1221 the monks of Canterbury had learned to take great advantage of the more gruesome aspects of Becket's death, creating 'points of sale', or rather points where offerings could be made, at no less than four sites within the cathedral. The pious pilgrim was led to these holy locations, to the very place Becket had been martyred, to his old tomb, to a shrine where the top of his skull had been cut clean off by one of his assassins, and to the magnificent new shrine that had recently been erected to house his bones. The offerings for that year alone came to £565 14s 10d, a fabulous revenue for the early thirteenth century.[11]

The Trade in Relics

Given the money to be made, there was naturally a tremendous demand for relics, any relics. To make commercial transactions easier, the 'merchandise' was categorised. First in rank, and normally commanding the best prices, were the primary relics. These included the bodies, limbs, shoulder blades, feet, hands, fingers or foreskins of the holy ones themselves. Heads and skulls were highly sought after, and were second only to the 'whole body' in terms of cost, although the 'status' of the saint was also taken into account, with small parts of major saints bearing a higher price tag then a whole cadaver of a local holy man of no international importance. The secondary relics were objects and clothing which the saint had owned, worn, or in some cases had been executed with. The Bishop of Constantinople, St John Chrysostom, rationalised this attitude to what were, essentially, material objects: 'The virtue of saints is so great,' he reasoned, 'that Christians venerate not only their words and bodies but also their garments.'

Relics became big business, with middlemen scouring Europe and beyond for saleable remains of the sainted. One trader, Deusdona, started what may be the first recorded account of Christian 'relic rivalry' when he obtained permission from Pope Eugene II to take the remains of St Sebastian to Soissons in France. Here he sold the saint, apparently for a good profit. The churchmen of the nearby town of Mulinheim found the saint's arrival disconcerting – fearing a decline in their own revenues if the body of St Sebastian drew the pilgrim trade to Soissons. So they counterattacked, employing the services of one Ratleicus, another trader in relics. After some delay, Ratleicus topped Deusdona's efforts and was able to bring them the remains of two saints, Marcellinus and Peter, both killed during the Emperor Diocletian's persecutions. But Mulinheim's ploy did not work; in this case, two saints were not better than one. St Sebastian's status far exceeded that of the two lesser divines and, despite all their efforts, Mulinheim's reputation remained eclipsed by the sainted glories of Soissons.

Income from relics was taken so seriously that even clerics stooped to robbery to obtain a coveted set of bones. A monastery at Agen was guardian of the remains of St Foy, and they became a source of considerable revenue to the Agen monks. But the monks of nearby Conques found their own revenue and prestige slipping, so they planned a robbery. One of their clerics, Arinisdus, joined the monks of Agen and spent ten years as a secular priest, working patiently and rising through the hierarchy until he was finally promoted to the position of guardian of the treasury. As soon as his post was confirmed he waited until nightfall, then seized the saint's bones and made haste to return to Conques where the holy relics were put on display.[12] Other clerics (later canonised themselves) took even more grotesque measures. St Hugh of Lincoln, when visiting the reputed body of St Mary Magdalene at Fécamp in Normandy, bowed over the sainted remains as if to kiss them. Instead, to the horror of the onlookers, St Hugh bit two pieces of bone from the arm of the holy body. Nothing abashed, the robber-saint used sophistry to excuse this sacrilege: he argued that as he took Jesus' body and blood into his mouth during the service of the eucharist, why should he not do the same with the bones of a saint? But the wily saint had his comeuppance. When he in his turn died, his body was divided into two pieces in order to increase its value and attraction to the faithful.[13]

Such was the demand for holy bones, the trade rapidly became a seller's market. But if the true relics of saints were in short supply, they could always be forged. This was especially easy in the Middle Ages, with its lack of communications, credulity, petty rivalries and absence of any real authority to authenticate or repudiate the claims of rival relics. So, we find the bodies of the three wise men being miraculously discovered in the same location (despite the fact they hailed from different regions and had presumably returned there) and carried with great pomp to Cologne cathedral. And we see no less a person than Charlemagne solemnly presenting to the monks of the Benedictine chapel of Brantôme the preserved body of an infant, supposedly one of the children murdered in Herod's Massacre of the Innocents. With demand high, saints' bodies proliferated like mushrooms: there were two bodies of St Thomas (one in the cathedral of St Thomé in India, the other at Ortona in Italy) and, as the scholarly research of Nicole Herman-Mansard has shown, were every relic of St Mary Magdalene genuine, she would have possessed no fewer than six separate bodies![14] Similarly, St Gregory the Great can lay claim to no fewer than four bodies and two heads. St Teilo of Wales had three bodies, but this was explained by his followers as a holy miracle to prevent arguments between the different communities that claimed his remains. St Teilo, it seems, '... miraculously provided three bodies of himself by a singular, and perhaps unique, act of celestial diplomacy'.[15]

It is easy, from this great distance in time, to ridicule the cupidity and credulity of the medieval mind. But this search for physical remains of holy men, this longing after sainted relics and sanctified remains, attests to the presence of a much deeper religious attitude than that found today, and a profound need to believe. It also reveals just how acceptable relic worship was to the medieval mind, and emphasises the most puzzling question with regard to the Templar relics: why did the order need to worship their particular holy head in the deepest secrecy?

Relics of Christ

Of all sainted remains, those of Jesus himself were the most sought after by the faithful. However, this desire for physical relics of Christ posed an almost insurmountable theological problem. Jesus had been translated, in the body, directly to heaven. It followed, therefore, that no bodily remains of the Saviour could possibly exist. To claim possession of such a relic was to deny the literal truth of the teachings, at least as interpreted by the Roman Church, whose word was law and which, at least in theory, had the power of life and death over the whole of Christendom. Primary relics (i.e., bodily remains) of Christ were therefore strictly taboo. However, secondary relics, such as the clothes that Jesus wore, were not proscribed. And they duly turned up, in the from of the seamless robe,[16] the Veronica (the face of Christ upon a cloth), and the famous Turin Shroud, with its remarkable full-length negative image of the crucified Jesus.[17] The true cross we have already seen at its shrine in Constantinople, but many, many smaller pieces of this relic were scattered all over Europe and the Levant. Like the purported body of St Teilo, the true cross seemed to be able to multiply in order to provide for the needs of its followers. The same was also true of the crown of thorns, or at least of thorns said to have been taken from the crown that the Roman soldiers had made for Jesus when they mocked his claim to be King of the Jews. Almost every important city and church had at least one holy thorn, and even Eton College boasted one. The crown itself (by this time totally devoid of any thorns) was sold by Baldwin II of Jerusalem to Louis IX of France. As trafficking in holy relics was, at that time, considered a sin, the sale was masked beneath a convenient fiction, Baldwin 'freely giving' the crown of thorns to Louis who, just as 'freely', gave Baldwin a 'gift' of 13,134 *perperi*.[18]

Quite as valuable as the crown of thorns were the nails that had attached Jesus to the cross; and these too were seemingly able to multiply themselves at will. They were proudly shown in many places of worship, including Aachen, Cracow, Florence, Naples, Paris and Vienna. Twenty-nine cities in Europe laid claim to possession of a 'true' nail or nails (Venice alone owned three, which, notwithstanding the legend that St Helena had had the four spikes made into twelve smaller nails, rather reduces the number of true nails the other cities might possess). The pincers that removed the nails did not escape the notice of the relic-hunters; there were at least two pairs extant during the early fourteenth century. The lance that pierced Christ's side was found by crusaders in Antioch, at the height of a debilitating siege, and spurred the weary defenders on to ultimate victory.[19] Unfortunately for this particular holy weapon, according to many believers the true lance had already been discovered. It had been brought from Jerusalem to Constantinople in 614, to escape the depredations of Chosroes, King of Persia, and by the twelfth century it was hanging in the chapel of the Virgin of Pharos. The discoverer of the Antioch lance, Peter Bartholomew of Provence, was so sure of his facts that he agreed to undergo ordeal by fire in order to prove its authenticity. Sadly, Peter Bartholomew died in the attempt. But, despite the enormous number and variety of these 'relics of Jesus', none was actually a part of the holy body, and did not violate the cardinal dogma that Christ had ascended bodily to heaven.

However, it was not long before the inventive medieval mind was able to find a way round even this apparently insurmountable taboo, when it was realised that certain parts of the anatomy, especially during the childhood of Jesus, would have been lost naturally and could quite easily have been preserved. And so we find the monks of Saint-Médard-de-Soissons proudly displaying a 'milk tooth' of Jesus as a holy relic. A Benedictine scholar, Guibert de Nogent, took exception to this, commenting sarcastically that if this were true, then there must be other teeth, not to mention hair, that would have fallen naturally from the Saviour as he went about his mission in Galilee and beyond. Guibert should, perhaps, have bitten his tongue. Before long, the town of Namur was claiming to possess the holy hair of Jesus, while Clermont Ferrand averred that it held not only hair cut by Mary from his head, but beard hair too, together with five parings from the nails of his left hand, and two from his right. Christ's blood, shed at the crucifixion, was contained in several phials spread across the length and breadth of Christendom, including one at Hailes in Gloucestershire, England, as celebrated in Chaucer's *Canterbury Tales:*

> By God's precious heart, and by his nails,
> And by the Blood of Christ that is in Hailes.[20]

In France, there was a cult of the tears of Christ in at least eight centres of worship, including Marseilles cathedral and the church of St Pierre-le-Puellier at Orléans. There was an even more incredible relic at Lucques in the Auvergne – Christ's 'holy navel'. And not just here; other 'holy navels' were also revered at Rome and at Chalons-sur-Marne in France. Presumably, these relics were of the birth-cord or umbilicus, yet another 'part' of Jesus that Church dogma did not require to have been taken up with the Saviour into heaven.

But the most celebrated and contentious relic of all supposedly derived from that quintessentially Jewish ceremony – circumcision. This rite would have removed a piece of the Saviour's very flesh. And, indeed, the Apocryphal Gospels do record that the *prepuce* of Jesus was preserved, at least until the beginning of his ministry.[21] So, the way was open for such a relic, and it was duly found. Or, rather, *they* were duly found: no less than thirteen holy foreskins turned up at one time or other during the Middle Ages. And each was accorded great reverence by its followers. One of the first to be obtained was given by Charlemagne to monks in the diocese of Poitiers. This particular holy foreskin gave its name to Charroux Abbey in which it was kept, Charroux being a corruption of *chair rouge*, red flesh.

Despite the reverence in which each relic was held, the possession of an actual piece of the Saviour's flesh came perilously near to overstepping the theological line. Several churchmen argued that, if Jesus had been raised to heaven in perfect form, surely his foreskin could not have been missing? Such arguments were part of a wave of theological thinking that was at pains to diminish the Jewishness of Jesus who, as a Jew, would have been required by holy law to have been circumcised. This was a great stumbling block but, fortunately for the faithful, the Jesuit Francisco de Suarez eventually advanced an argument that neatly circumvented the problem. As the Son of God, said de Suarez, the risen Christ could have easily regrown any missing part of his anatomy, including his foreskin. So, Jesus' foreskin could be in heaven, and here on earth, both at the same time! With the acceptance of this somewhat magical explanation, the holy foreskins passed once more within the pale of Catholic respectability. The story does, however, serve to emphasise that inherent in Roman dogma was the absolute requirement to believe that Jesus ascended to heaven in the body, and in a perfect, unblemished body. Apart from milk teeth, navels, foreskins and other minor relics, to claim ownership of any physical remains of Christ would have been regarded as the grossest heresy, and would have called down upon the claimant the most severe punishments the church could devise.

The Forbidden Relic?

The cult of relics is a fascinating study in itself, but enough has been said to illustrate the main points of our story. To sum up, the veneration of relics was accepted, even encouraged, by the church. Public veneration was likewise an accepted mode of worship. There was absolutely no need for secrecy. In fact, leaving aside the intrinsic holiness of the remains, secrecy would have robbed the relics of their other two main attractions: the power to influence secular events and the ability to raise considerable revenues for their possessors.

As we have seen, the Templars were consummate diplomats and could not have been unaware of the power that an especially venerated relic would possess. It could have been used to further Templar interests, to force concessions from allies and protect the order from its enemies. Yet the Templar hierarchy chose to keep the Baphomet head a closely guarded secret, and to show it only in closed chapters to the most senior members of the order. Why this insistence on the absolute seclusion of the head?

Again, as we have seen, choice relics could generate fabulous amounts of revenue for their possessors. And the Templars, as the founders of modern capitalism, would not have been blind to the possibilities of increasing the size of their treasury. Their reputation for avarice was unmatched. And yet they made no use of what was, for them, an extremely valuable 'asset': a sacred relic, an embalmed head. As the foregoing section has shown, sainted heads were common in the Middle Ages, and highly valued. Even if the Templar head was that of John the Baptist, as some researchers have suggested, why should it be kept hidden? There were already at least two heads extant in Europe at the time, each supposedly of the Baptist, one from Constantinople and a second 'discovered' in 1010 in France, at Saint-Jean-d'Angély. Any other order, or churchman, would have trumpeted the possession of such a relic to the rooftops. On the face of it, the Templars had nothing to fear and everything to gain in publicising the existence of this relic. Why, then, the deafening silence, the secrecy, the *hidden* worship of this head?

There can be only one reasonable explanation. Exposure of the relic to the public notice would have brought down upon the Templars the very doom which eventually overtook them – the accusation of heresy. And given the licence which the church accorded to the display of every conceivable type of bodily part from just about any biblical character one can imagine, there remains but a single relic whose exhibition was absolutely forbidden – the bodily remains of Jesus. Possession of such an object would have proved that Jesus did not ascend to heaven in his physical body and would have directly contradicted the Roman Church's teachings. One of the main planks in its interpretation of the life of Christ, that Jesus had been translated to Heaven in the body, a teaching which even then had been promulgated for almost a thousand years, would be set at naught. Proof that the bodily resurrection did not take place would have brought the whole complex, powerful edifice of Roman domination crashing down about the ears of the incumbent pope. Even if such a relic was found, its existence would have to be suppressed and denied. This was theological and political dynamite.

The Painted Heads

Additional support for this argument comes from the paintings of a long-haired, bearded head found in Templar preceptories and houses. Several authors have pointed out the similarity of these paintings to the head of Christ on the Turin Shroud, which is supposedly the linen cloth in which Jesus' body was wrapped after he was taken down from the cross. Indeed, many researchers have considered that the paintings, which they agree were used in Templar head-worship ceremonies, are simply copies of the head on the shroud.[22] But the high initiates of the order did not worship a shroud or a painting: according to testimony an actual preserved head was the focus of their ritual. The conclusion is obvious and inescapable – if the painted heads were copies of the Templar embalmed head and at the same time copies of the image on the Turin Shroud, then the embalmed head was that of Jesus. His sacred head had been removed and embalmed as a member of the race of Jewish priest-kings who were themselves part of a line of sacred kings stretching back to the time of Moses/Akhenaten and beyond.

I had come full circle. Starting with the question of the identity of the Templar head known as the Baphomet, I had returned to the starting point with an answer. It was a shocking and provocative answer, which I knew might offend many people, striking as it did at the very foundations of their belief. But the conclusion I had reached did make sense of the whole confusing mass of information that had lain before me at the beginning of my researches. What was even more convincing, and to some extent surprising even to myself, was that other information I had uncovered during the course of writing this book slotted neatly into the framework of the original hypothesis. This scenario offered a coherent picture that at last allowed an explanation of many aspects of the puzzle which had eluded other workers in this field: why a Christian organisation should be linked with overtly Egyptian symbolism; why the appellation Son of David meant so much more than the descendant of a tribal chieftain; why Isis should be linked to the worship of Christ; what the appellation Son of the Widow really meant when applied to Jesus; why the masonic hero Hiram Abif was beheaded; why the Templars mimicked this myth in their burials; and why the true identity of Baphomet, the head the Templars worshipped, could never be revealed. These, and many other seemingly insoluble connections became an intricate and elegant web of interconnected events and beliefs once two pieces of evidence were accepted. That a royal bloodline connected Tutmosis III, Joseph, Akhenaten and Jesus. And that the Nazarites (of which Jesus was a prominent member) had kept Akhenaten's teachings of the holy head alive, to be rediscovered by the Templars via the exiled tribe of Benjamites.

But the more I considered it, the more it became apparent that the Templars were not the end, but the pivot, of the narrative. The puzzle of the sacred heads and the name of Baphomet had been solved, but the Templars' possession of these relics begged the question: what had become of them and, more especially, what happened to the head of God after the Templars themselves were suppressed?

The head of Jesus had apparently survived the vicissitudes of a thousand years and had been in the possession of the Templars not seven hundred years ago. Was it possible, I wondered, that the head had survived even longer? Could it still be extant, hidden, its location known to only a few modern-day initiates? Given its survival for over a millennium, there was no *a priori* reason why this should not be so. The implications of this were enormous and very troubling. My quest was no longer purely historical. It had taken on a new, very real dimension. I was now searching for the head of God.

15

The Templars Suppressed

By the beginning of the fourteenth century the Templars were at the height of their fame, wealth and power. Despite the loss of their lands in Outremer, the Templar Order owned a vast monastic network of manors, farms and estates, as well as the hoarded plunder from a hundred battles. Before the fall of the Holy Land to the Saracen, these resources had been necessary to keep the Templar knighthood in the field. A knight was an enormously costly piece of 'fighting equipment'; by the mid-1200s it took the production of around 150 manses (around 3,750 acres or 1,500 hectares) to equip and maintain an armoured horseman for one year.[1] The Templars often had three hundred combat knights in Palestine, not counting sergeants and esquires and, despite their huge land holdings, were often hard put to pay for the upkeep of this enormously costly standing army. However, with the loss of Outremer in 1291, the financial balance changed in the temple's favour. Outgoings were much reduced while the income from their properties remained much the same. This allowed the Poor Knights rapidly to accumulate wealth on a grand scale. By the close of the thirteenth century the Order of the Temple had never been richer or more powerful.

But the order faced a formidable foe in the form of Philip IV of France, better known to his contemporaries as Philip le Bel ('the fair'). Philip was the eleventh direct male descendant of the founder of the Capetian dynasty, Hugh Capet, who was crowned in 987. Although the kingdom Hugh ruled had originally been of no great extent, after a series of wars and dynastic alliances it had increased in size, so that, by the time of Philip II (1080–1123), Anjou, Normandy, Maine and Touraine were subject to the Capetian monarchy. The Albigensian Crusade brought the county of Toulouse within the royal demesne, although full control was not ceded until 1271, well after the crusade against the heretic Cathars had ended.

From the first, Hugh Capet had tried to legitimise and strengthen his claim to the throne of France by fabricating a connection to the Merovingian dynasty. In a conscious echo of the long-haired kings, the coronation ceremony of the Capetian dynasty was designed to underline the sacred nature of the monarch. When Philip le Bel was crowned, he was anointed (as all his predecessors had been before him) with holy oil. This divine unguent was said to have been brought to earth by a heavenly dove for the baptism of the Merovingian monarch Clovis, and never to decrease however many times it was used. The concept of kingship as divinely ordained (which the Capetian monarchs worked hard to foster) met strenuous opposition from the French barons. It ran counter to ancient feudal traditions which, in theory, called for rule by consent – for the nobility at least. Logic dictated that if a Capetian monarch ruled by divine right, the consent of his subjects, noble or base, was irrelevant.

The idea of a ruler ordained by God alone seems to have been Philip le Bel's perception of himself, and many of his courtiers were happy to pander to this conceit, flattering him shamelessly. According to one fawning account: 'The king has always in his marriage, both before and after, been chaste, humble, modest of face and in speech, never angry, hating no one, envying no one, loving all. Full of grace, charity, piety and mercy, always following truth and justice, never a detraction in his mouth, fervent in faith, religious in his life, building basilicas and engaging in works of piety, handsome of face and graceful in manner, graceful even to all his enemies when they are in his presence, through his hands, God affords clear miracles to the sick.'[2]

This picture of a paragon of Christian piety is, unfortunately, completely at odds with what we know of Philip the Fair. Although his good looks were legendary, so too was his ruthlessness and guile. Philip was a courageous warrior and a consummate politician but he could be utterly unscrupulous when his policy was thwarted. The Bishop of Pamiers, Bernard Saisset, famously compared the king to an owl, which according to ancient legend the other birds had chosen as king because of its beauty. Like the owl, Philip was an empty shell, declared the bishop, 'more handsome than any man in the world, and who knew nothing at all except to stare at men'.[3] But this was to underestimate the French king (and the good bishop was later to suffer for his presumptuous remarks). Another contemporary and altogether more cautious writer – he prudently chose to remain anonymous – came closer to the mark when he complained that the king had surrounded himself with corrupt and evil men, to whom Philip left most of the running of his country. As a result, justice had fled the land and would not return until these men were purged from the body politic. But Philip did nothing to reform his administration and, indeed, he himself is now seen as being the prime mover in most of the reprehensible undertakings of the French court.

By the beginning of the fourteenth century Philip and his government were in serious financial difficulties. The French administration, in common with other European governments, had not yet developed a regular system of yearly taxation, so that guaranteed income was not available to the state budget. Taxation tended to be on an *ad hoc* basis, with tithes, fiftieths and hundredths levied on the populace as and when needed, or if some unexpected emergency loomed. Long and costly wars with Gascony and Flanders had depleted the public purse and Philip and his officers were casting around wildly for other sources of funds to stave off bankruptcy. With his finances in such dire straits Philip turned to another expedient: the merciless persecution and despoliation of small and vulnerable sections of the population. Two groups were targeted at first: the Jews (who as moneylenders – one of the few trades allowed to them by law – were comprehensively despised) and the Lombards, merchants of northern Italy who also ran a number of banking establishments. Despite lending Philip enormous sums of money, from 1291 the Lombards were subjected to arbitrary arrest, fines, seizure of property and expulsion.[4] The Jews fared no better. In midsummer of 1306, a little more than a year before the Templars were suppressed, every Jew in the country was arrested and their goods and property made forfeit to the state. Left penniless, they were unceremoniously expelled from the realm.[5]

Despite the enormous funds that Philip garnered from these crimes, his income still did not keep pace with expenditure. At around the same time as the Jews were plundered of their wealth, in June 1306, Philip tried another, altogether riskier ploy: he devalued the French currency by a massive two-thirds of its current value. The kingdom erupted in anger and there were riots in Paris. Etienne Barbete, the man believed by the rioting crowds to have urged the depreciation on the king, was dragged from his house and lynched. Philip, in fear of his life, was forced to take refuge from the mob in the Templars' Paris headquarters.[6] The reality of the wealth of the temple was all around him during his enforced stay and, ironically, it may be at this time of peril, when the Poor Knights offered the only place of safety, that the king first turned avaricious eyes upon the Templar treasures and decided to acquire this wealth for himself. Although greed for gold was undoubtedly a spur to Philip's subsequent move against the order, it is possible his actions were in part motivated by the death of his beloved wife Jeanne de Navarre, in April 1305. Her passing seems to have affected Philip deeply and turned his mind towards more religious concerns. It is just possible that, until the time of his queen's demise, Philip was willing to turn a blind eye towards the wrongdoings of the Templars, but that after this event his desire to reform himself and his realm led him to mount an attack on the order.

Antipathy and Alienation

Whatever the reasons for Philip's onslaught, the Templars were decidedly vulnerable. Despite their undoubted power, they were relatively small in number and they shared with the Jews and Lombards one important disadvantage – they were actively disliked and mistrusted by the general population.

In many regions there was good reason for such suspicion. Almost two hundred years of unfettered autonomy had undoubtedly taken their toll on Templar morals; unbridled power had certainly corrupted many of the local commanderies, and their reputation for pride and avarice was well founded. Richard I of England, on being rebuked that he had three daughters that cost him dear, Pride, Luxury and Avarice, replied that he would marry the first off to the Templars, 'who are as proud as Lucifer himself'. In a famous tale of the order's cupidity, the Scottish Templars are said to have evicted a widow from a house they claimed. The unfortunate woman clung to the door casement in her despair, wailing and refusing to leave. Exasperated by this delay, one of the Templars drew his dagger and hacked off her fingers, so obliging her to release her grip. One contemporary, Jacques de Vitry, summed up the general view of the order when he wrote, 'You profess to have no individual property, but in common you wish to have everything.'[8]

Compounding these vices was the part played by the Templar Order in the loss of the Holy Land. The shock felt by the whole of Christendom at this defeat resulted in a colossal collapse of morale. The original occupation of Jerusalem by the infidel 'Turk' had been seen by most Christians in strictly feudal terms: the Saracens had usurped God's sacred kingdom and it was up to all Christians to redress this wrong. The 'Song of the Second Crusade' graphically illustrates this view:

God has brought before you his suit against the Turks and saracens who have

215

done him great despite. They have seized his fiefs, where god was first served and recognised as lord.

God has ordained a tournament between heaven and hell, and sends to all his friends who wish to defend him, that they fail him not.[9]

So, the crusades had been perceived as a species of 'trial by combat', an ordeal beloved of the medieval knight, a contest which pitted good against evil, and in which God sat in judgement to hand out victory to the righteous. As Christians were 'good' and God was on the side of good, then to the medieval Christian mind, the battle for the Holy Land was never really in doubt. Palestine was the *Terre Sancte*, the land where the Saviour had walked and preached and healed others and died, a kingdom sacred to God himself. There might be setbacks for the warriors of Christ, even terrible defeats, but God would never allow evil to triumph over good. *Ergo*, ultimately, Christendom would emerge from the fray victorious.

It had come as a supreme shock when Christendom was finally and definitively defeated by the Mamluk sultans, and the 'infidel' took possession of the entire Holy Land. The collapse of Christian power shook the faith of even the strongest believer. A poem written just before the final collapse, by a troubadour, Ricaut Benomel, who was probably also a Templar, shows the depths to which Christian morale had sunk:

Pain and wrath invade my heart so that I almost think of suicide, or of laying down the cross I once assumed in honour of he who was laid upon the cross; for neither the cross nor his name protect us against the accursed Turks. Indeed, it seems clear enough that God is supporting them in our despite.[10]

God had failed Christendom, and its fighting men had proved inadequate to the task of defending the Holy Land. To compensate for this colossal spiritual and material disaster, there had been a desperate attempt to apportion blame, a search for someone responsible for the débâcle, a scapegoat. It was in a sense natural that suspicion and opprobrium fell upon that small class of men who embodied both clerical and martial duties, the military orders and especially the Templars. In this climate of recrimination, men remembered the tales that had been told of Templar complicity with the Arab enemy. The St Albans chronicler records a speech made by the Count d'Artois against the Templars, while the Latins still held part of Palestine. The count accused the order (along with the Hospitallers) of plotting and scheming to prevent the Christian armies gaining complete victory over their foes. If this happened, said the count, the military orders would be redundant. Without an external enemy, it would be impossible for them to justify their existence and the rank and privilege they enjoyed. Whether, as some believe, this speech is pure literary invention, it nevertheless reveals the misgivings that many had concerning the ambiguous position of the military orders in Christian society.

With the loss of the Holy Land, the criticism changed to one of outright treason, of selling out to the Arabs. Even where this was not believed, the existence of these privileged warrior-monks was greatly resented by the mass of ordinary people. Despite the Templars' failure to secure victory against the Turk, despite the loss of their defining role as warriors in defence of the Holy Land, in western Europe they still possessed all their vast holdings in land and property, and their rights, immunities and privileges likewise remained intact. Unlike the common run of men, they were exempt from tithes and taxes, and from both church and secular law. No wonder they were subject to increasingly bitter criticism, as in the poem, written around the beginning of the fourteenth century, by Berenguier de Marseilles:

Since many Templars now disport themselves on this side of the sea, riding their grey horses or taking their ease in the shade and admiring their own fair locks; since they so often set a bad example to the world; since they are so outrageously proud that one can hardly look them in the face: tell me, Bâtard, why the Pope continues to tolerate them; tell me why he permits them to misuse the riches which are offered them for God's service on dishonourable and even criminal ends.

... since they and the Hospital have for so long allowed the false Turk to remain in possession of Jerusalem and Acre; since they flee faster than the holy hawk: it is a pity, in my view, that we don't rid ourselves of them for good.[11]

Some of this criticism was of course unfair: the Templars, and their rival military order, the Hospitallers, could hardly be blamed for the loss of the Holy Land, which had come about as a result of a constellation of unfavourable factors, including the lack of support and resources from the very people in Europe who now bemoaned the loss of the sacred places. Nor could the Templars and Hospitallers alone be expected to mount a crusade to rescue the Holy Land from the Saracen. That was a huge financial and logistical operation, requiring the cooperation of most of Christendom (in fact, several plans were mooted for just such an undertaking, right up until the time of the Templar arrests). However, while some criticism was unmerited, many complaints could be substantiated: the Templars especially seem to have been completely insensitive to public opinion, and to have been intent on jealously guarding every one of their ancient exemptions and immunities, despite the ill will such privileges engendered in the population.

The Order of the Temple was therefore already vulnerable, but not much more so than the Hospitallers, who were also blamed for the loss of the Holy Land and for vigilantly preserving their own wealth and privilege. However, the Temple suffered from further weaknesses which rendered it a far easier target for the plotting of Philip IV. The Knights Hospitaller had taken the island of Rhodes from the Greeks soon after their retreat from Palestine. Rhodes was the Hospitallers' own mini-kingdom, a region where they exercised sovereign rule, an inviolable bastion well fortified and supplied with men, from which they could be expelled only with the greatest difficulty and at huge expense. By contrast, the Templars still dreamed of a return to Jerusalem and had made no effort to carve out an independent base for themselves. They were spread all over the face of western Christendom, from Cyprus, where they had their headquarters, across France, England, Aragon and a dozen other realms and principalities, each of whom could, if it chose, turn on the order. For the Templars, there was no safe haven.

Moreover, the order had laid itself open to attack by its renowned penchant for secrecy. Receptions and chapters that were held at the dead of night, the doors locked and guarded, were sure to arouse suspicion, and rumours of the order's heretical leanings, of necromancy, conjuration of devils and the worship of idols, of rituals involving secret embalmed heads, were rife and continued to grow.

Despite these disadvantages, Philip knew that the Templars would be a tougher nut to crack than either the Jews or the Lombards; they might be a relatively small group, but with their impressive fighting skills the order could make any move against them the excuse for combat, using their sole allegiance to the pope as an excuse to resist. However, King Philip believed that he now had a means for the suppression of the order, and a legal rationale, in the form of the Holy Inquisition. The Inquisition had been instituted in 1231 by Pope Gregory IX for the express purpose of seeking out and suppressing heresies of all kinds.[12] For Philip, the Inquisition was the key. It was ostensibly an arm of the papacy, to whom the Templars owed allegiance and whose authority they were duty bound to acknowledge. But in France, senior prelates of the Inquisition had been brought under the influence of the French crown. While nominally under papal governance, the French arm of the Holy Inquisition was in fact wholly controlled by the monarchy. Small wonder, then, that Philip le Bel considered an attack on the order a strategically sound option.

The Attack on the Templars

Philip and his lieutenants prepared the ground thoroughly. The king had meetings with the pope at Lyons and at Poitiers in May 1307, five months before the arrest of the Templars. On both occasions the rumours inimical to the Templar Order had been discussed. One of the king's main informants was Esquin de Floyran, who had previously taken his accusations to the King of Aragon but, finding this monarch sceptical, had carried the tales to the King of France, where he found a more ready ear. Floyran was not slow to claim the credit for the Templar exposé, and quickly wrote to King James II of Aragon, seeking the reward he had apparently been promised:

> ... I am the man who has shown the deeds of the Templars to the Lord King of France, and know, my lord, that you were the first prince in the whole world to whom, at Lerida, in the presence of Brother Maryin Detecha, your confessor, I previously revealed their activities. For which you, my lord, did not wish to give full credence to my words at that time, which is why I have resorted to the Lord King of France, who has investigated the activity and found [it] clear as the sun, certainly in his kingdom, so that the pope has been fully convinced of the affair ... My lord, remember what you have promised to me when I left your chamber at Lerida, that if the deeds of the Templars were found to be evident, you would give to me 1000 livres in rents and 3000 livres in money from their goods. And now that it is verified and when there is a place, think fit to remember.[13]

Although this attempt to gain monetarily from the Templar's misfortune is hardly praiseworthy, it does reveal that the stories concerning the Templars were not simply fabrications of the French king, but that the 'wrongdoings' of the order had previously been reported to other notables. Despite Philip le Bel's predisposition to think ill of the order, there is strong evidence that Clement v was also concerned by the scandalous and heretical nature of the rumours that were now current throughout most of Europe. On 24 August 1307 he wrote to King Philip concerning their discussions at Lyons and Poitiers, saying that when he first heard the accusations he could not bring himself to believe them. However, since that time he had 'heard many strange and unheard-of things'. He had spoken at length with his cardinals and, though it upset him deeply, he had decided that it was necessary to set up an enquiry into the Templar Order. At the same time and in the same letter Pope Clement made it clear that he did not believe such an enquiry was urgent. He was not well and would not be able to receive emissaries until around 14 October.[14]

While news of the pope's decision to institute an enquiry must have been welcome to Philip (it did, after all, support his apparent belief that there was something amiss in the Order of the Temple), the pontiff's lack of haste did not fit in with his own plans for the destruction of the Templars. For the King of France, immediate action was necessary: rumours of Templar wrongdoing abounded, the pope had agreed to an enquiry and, most importantly, the Templar Grand Master Jacques de Molay and other officers of high rank were resident in France (though for how long, no one knew – they might slip away to their headquarters in Cyprus at any time). If the leaders of the Poor Knights escaped abroad, Philip's crackdown on the order would have had minimal effect and would not deliver the death-blow he intended. For Philip, it was now or never.

The French king took pains to ensure that his onslaught on the temple was made under the strictest security. A reconnaissance of the order's property was ordered, under the smoke-screen of a general inventory of all religious houses, the story being that the king was about to levy a tithe. Sealed orders, dated 14 September, a full month before the arrests, were sent to the king's seneschals and *baillis* throughout the realm. They were to be opened on 13 October and their contents acted on immediately.[15] Despite immense logistical and security problems, the plan went ahead without a hitch (helped no doubt by the experience gained in Philip's attacks on both the Lombards and the Jews). At dawn, on Friday the 13th – a day forever since regarded as unlucky – the king's men broke into the Templar houses and preceptories and arrested every Templar they could find. The Grand Master, Jacques de Molay, was surprised with sixty brethren at the headquarters in Paris and quickly taken captive. It was a scene repeated throughout France. There was, by all accounts, no resistance, primarily because most of those arrested were middle-aged non-combatants, and they were hurriedly taken to prearranged collection points and imprisoned in the name of the Holy Inquisition.

The Trial

The arrests had been made on the orders of the French king. This made the action illegal, as the Templars were under the sole authority of the pope. An attempt was made to hide the questionable manner of the arrests under a cloak of legal respectability by claiming that the request for the arrests had come originally from Guilliame de Paris, the Chief Inquisitor of France, and an acknowledged deputy of the pope. Although Guilliame was a Dominican, he was also deeply involved with the king and was, indeed, his confessor. Moreover, as Malcolm Barber has stated, '... the Inquisition was becoming, through its leader in France, another arm of state power'. Though it was in theory the pope (through his deputy) who had instigated the attack on the Order of the Temple, in reality it was the King of France who was in command.

A list of accusations comprising more than 120 'Items' had been compiled before the arrests began and it was this list that was used as a template to extract confessions from the brethren. Amongst a comprehensive list of wrongdoings (see Appendix 1), the Templars were accused of holding their receptions in secret and at night; of the denial of Christ as god; of spitting, trampling and urinating on the cross; of kissing brethren on the belly and anus; of sodomy; and of the worship of idols, especially a sacred head or heads. This latter accusation is worth considering in detail:

Item, that in each province they had idols, namely heads, of which some had three faces, and some one, and others had a human skull.

Item, that they adored these idols, or that idol, and especially in their great chapters and assemblies.

Item, that they venerated [them].

Item, that [they venerated them] as God.

Item, that [they venerated them] as their Saviour.

Item, that some of them [did].

Item, that the majority of those who were in the chapters [did].

Item, that they said that the heads could save them.

Item, that [it could] make riches.

Item, that it gave them all the riches of the Order.

Item, that it made the trees flower.

Item, that [it made] the land germinate.

Item, that they surrounded or touched each head of the aforesaid idols with small cords, which they wore around themselves next to the shirt or the flesh.

Item, that in his reception, the aforesaid small cords or some lengths of them were given to each of the brothers.

Item, that they did this in veneration of an idol.

Item, that it was enjoined on them that they should wear the small cords ... continually ... even by night.[16]

The detail and number of these items shows the importance that the king, and the inquisitors, attached to the Templars' worship of the head. As the investigation was, in theory, being held under the auspices of the Holy Inquisition, the use of torture was permitted; in fact the orders specifically state that the investigators were to 'spare no known means of torture',[17] and they do not appear to have held back in any way. The list of methods used to inflict suffering on the Templars makes harrowing reading. Many brethren had their nails ripped out by the roots, or had wedges hammered beneath them. Some had their teeth drawn with pliers, one tooth at a time, the inquisitor intoning his questions as each tooth was pulled. Metal spikes were inserted into the bleeding sockets if the answer did not match the inquisitor's required response. Red-hot irons, held just inches from the body, seared the flesh while the questions were asked, and were applied directly to the blackened skin if the answer failed to satisfy.

Some members of the order suffered the strappado, the victim having his hands tied behind his back, and a rope, thrown over a beam, fastened to the wrists. The unfortunate Templar was then pulled off the ground to dangle in the air in excruciating agony. Weights were sometimes attached to the genitals to increase the torment. The rack was used on some brothers, tearing ligaments and dislocating their limbs, but perhaps the most horrifying instrument of all was the innocent-sounding 'iron bed', to which many of the brethren were strapped so that their feet and calves protruded from the end of the apparatus. The feet were then carefully oiled, and a brazier of burning charcoal slid beneath them. The questioning began as the living flesh of the victim's feet was slowly roasted. The pain was excruciating and is said to have sent several of the brothers mad. 'A number had their feet totally burned off, and at a later enquiry a footless Templar was carried to the council clutching a bag containing the blackened bones that had dropped out of his feet as they were slowly burned off. His inquisitors had allowed him to keep the bones as a souvenir of his memorable experience.'[18]

In the face of such tortures, or threats of torture, most Templars confessed, including the Grand Master Jacques de Molay, and Hugues de Piraud, the Visitor of France. The confessions by these 'great men' of the order enormously strengthened the French king's hand. With such evidence at the crown's disposal, the crimes of the Templars were preached throughout France by Franciscan friars to huge and incredulous crowds. It seemed impossible to the common people that the proud Templars had at last been brought to book.

A papal commission was convened to investigate the order in November 1309. At first it appeared that the Templars would submit meekly to their fate but, led by two of their priests, Pierre de Bologna and Renaud de Provins, the brethren began to fight back, repudiating their confessions one by one until, by May 1310, nearly six hundred Templars had revoked their confessions and had committed themselves to defending the order. In the face of this threat to his plans, Philip IV reacted ruthlessly. A creature of the king, the Archbishop of Sens, immediately reopened an enquiry against Templar prisoners in his jurisdiction. He quickly found that fifty-four brethren were relapsed heretics, and passed them over to the king's men for punishment. All fifty-four were burned alive on 12 May.[19] The immolations had a decisive effect on the prisoners' morale. The Templar defence wavered, then collapsed, as most of the brethren admitted the validity of their original confessions.

By October 1311, at the Council of Vienne, the pope himself was demanding the suppression of the order, almost certainly spurred on by the presence of Philip IV, who arrived at Vienne with a small army at his back. There was much disagreement, and the pope took the exceptional step of threatening excommunication on any member of the council who voiced an objection to any of his pronouncements, an action which effectively muzzled all opposition and set the seal on the Templars' destruction. Five months later, the papal bull *Vox in excelso* suppressed (but did not condemn) the Order of the Temple, and two months after that a second bull, *Ad providam*, gave the Templar assets to their great rivals the Knights Hospitaller. After much wrangling, Philip IV extorted a huge sum, 200,000 *livres tournois*, as compensation. In addition a further 60,000 *livres tournois* were granted to pay for his expenses in carrying out the 'pope's' command to arrest the heretic brethren, followed by another 50,000 *livres tournois* paid by the Hospitallers as a final quittance of all money owed.[20] All things considered, the French crown did very well out of the destruction of the Poor Knights.

Verdict on the Templars

Many authors have sought to excuse the Templars of all the accusations set before them, on the basis that the confessions were obtained under torture and that while in torment a man will say anything that his persecutors require of him. The Templars themselves, in their defence, used this argument, saying that:

> ... beyond the Kingdom of France no brother of the Temple in all the lands of the world will be found who says or who will speak these lies, on account of which it is clear enough why they have been spoken in the Kingdom of France, because those who have spoken, have testified when corrupted by fear [of torture] prayers or money.[21]

This at first sight seems a plausible defence, but there are a number of points about the confessions, and the later confessions from other Templar areas, that made me feel that this argument was less strong than it first appears. The first concerns the charge of homosexuality made against the Templars. This accusation was certainly no more heinous than that of denying Christ or spitting upon the crucifix or worshipping an idol in the form of a severed head. And yet the proportion of Templars confessing to sodomy as opposed to the other crimes is extremely small. Of the 138 Templars who were put to the torture in Paris only four confessed to an act of sodomy with other brethren, while a massive 123 confessed to spitting on the cross (with many confessing to additional 'heretical' crimes).[22] Why should this be? If torture was forcing a victim to confess because of pain alone, why should over ninety-seven per cent of the captives resist that pain when it came to a question of admitting to being a sodomite? Why should only three per cent of Templars 'crack' under torture and admit homosexual liaisons, when the same torments were apparently able to force eighty-nine per cent of these same brothers to confess to spitting on the cross? Could it be, I wondered, that the brethren were made of sterner stuff than most authors have given them credit for? That they were able heroically to resist those accusations they personally found distasteful and shameful (i.e., sodomy), but were less inclined to suffer for something that they had actually done?

This theory gains much strength when we look at the response of English Templars to the same investigative methods. All the evidence accumulated thus far points to France as the seat of the sacred head religion within the Templar Order. France was the home of the Merovingians, the Jewish principality of Septimania, the place where the Magdalene and the 'Grail' landed, and the country that had given birth to the Albigensian heresy. It was the Paris headquarters of the temple that held the holy of holies, the relic I have called the head of God. By contrast, except for the Templecombe painted head, very little evidence has been found to indicate that the English temple was ever involved in the secret worship of the sacred heads.

This being so, if the theory that the French Templars had confessed more easily to those actions they had actually committed is true, then we should see fewer English Templars admitting to activities associated with the denial of orthodox church dogma, such as spitting on the cross.

Although the English authorities were slow to act after Philip's assault on the Templars, they did eventually comply with Pope Clement's orders and 228 Templars were arrested. The pope generously provided ten professional torturers to 'question' the Templars, and when these men had arrived, they began their gruesome work almost immediately.[23] Yet, strangely, although they presumably plied their trade in agony with as much enthusiasm as their colleagues had done in France, the number and content of Templar confessions was startlingly different. From over two hundred English Templars subjected to agonising torture, the number admitting to spitting on the cross was miniscule – only four of them confessed to this crime. It is worth reviewing these figures: in France ninety-seven per cent of the Paris Templars confessed to spitting on the crucifix; in England the figure was less than two per cent. It is impossible that such a huge discrepancy occurred by chance or that the English Templars were more able to withstand the agonies inflicted upon them by the Inquisition's dealers in torment. The only plausible explanation for this astonishing discrepancy in numbers is that the French Templars were indeed guilty of at least some of the 'heretical' accusations levelled against them.

The Inner Circle

This is not to say that all French Templars were party to the 'heresy'. The truth is seldom straightforward, and in this case it seems clear that there was an inner circle of initiates centred around the Paris headquarters, who were privy to some, or all, of the mysteries associated with the ancient worship of the sacred head.

It is often cited in the Templars' defence that the brothers of the order had fought for Christ and died for Christ in their thousands for almost two hundred years. They possessed an impressive reputation for reckless courage and, if captured by the 'Turk', most went to their deaths rather than renounce their faith. To give just one example among many: when the castle of Safed in the Holy Land fell to the Saracens, eighty Templars were among those taken prisoner. They were offered their lives if they would agree to deny Christ. To a man, the Templars refused to recant their faith to save their lives, and all eighty brethren were beheaded that same day. Surely, therefore, the argument goes, it is quite impossible to believe that the Templars were heretics, that their apparent belief in Christ was a sham, a front for a cult that spat on the cross and vehemently denied the very God they were apparently so ready to die for.[24]

Such an argument is simplistic. It ignores the fact that words are simply 'handles' for objects or concepts, and that a single word can mean very different things to different people. It is quite possible for a large organisation to be fighting for a cause, but for that cause to mean two separate things to different parts of the group. In the Second World War the soldiers of both the SS and the Wehrmacht (regular army) were fighting for 'Germany'. But the concept of Germany held by the SS (or at least its ruling elite) was very different from the Germany for which the ordinary Wehrmacht soldier was prepared to give his life. For the Wehrmacht, the 1939–45 conflict was like any other war, a battle for geopolitical influence in the world, as von Clausewitz so succinctly put it: 'nothing but a continuation of politics'.[25] The SS elite saw the battle in very different terms, as a fight for racial purity, as a battle of 'Fire against Ice'.[26] The Wehrmacht infantryman was scarcely aware of the esoteric theories of the SS; he was fighting for his own version of Germany. And yet, had Germany proved victorious in the conflict, it would have been just these 'heretical' SS theories that would have formed the new orthodoxy of a Nazi Europe. Despite this, even today we rarely point out the distinction between these two groups when discussing the conflict in general terms. How much easier would it be for the historian one thousand years hence to lump these two disparate segments of German society together and make the bland statement that both groups fought for 'Germany'.

We risk the same mistake with the Templars if we ignore the fact that the structure of the Order of the Temple was rigidly hierarchical. Enough has been said in the preceding pages to show that the elite of the order were privy to certain mysteries that were forbidden to the ordinary rank and file. It is therefore possible that the two segments of the Templar Order, while both were fighting for Christ, were in reality fighting for completely different *concepts* of Christ. It is highly likely that many of the lower ranking knights and sergeants of the order were orthodox Christians, believing in the prevailing church dogma of the time and willing to die, as other crusading warriors were, for a Christ who had been born of a virgin, who had been crucified and had risen from the dead and ascended bodily into heaven. The same would also be true of the many non-combatant Templar members, those who spent their lives as shepherds, husbandmen, and in other agricultural pursuits, and who formed the majority of those arrested in other parts of France, outside the city of Paris. This would then account for the many depositions made before the Inquisition that, in their outraged denial of any wrongdoing, have the unmistakable ring of truth about them. At this level of the Templar organisation, the rank and file were completely orthodox and the accusation of heresy utterly unjustified.

But while the ordinary Templar warrior may have been unversed in the secret mysteries of the order, it is very doubtful that the elite were in any way attached to the central dogmas of the Roman Church. By all accounts they held the theory of the virgin birth in contempt, and utterly rejected the idea that Christ had either died and been raised from the dead on the third day, or that he had ascended, in the body, to heaven. At this level, among the 'great men' of the order, the verdict must be that some, and probably most, were guilty of heresy, as it was construed in the Middle Ages.

But we must beware of being sucked into the medieval orthodoxy. To deny these dogmas should not, and does not, immediately place anyone beyond the pale of Christian fellowship. The Templar elite simply followed a 'Christian' tradition that, to the ecclesiastics of their day, was most certainly a 'vile heresy', but which was not necessarily inimical to Jesus. They seem to have viewed Christ (as did several other Gnostic sects) as a chosen individual, filled to overflowing with the spirit of God, and giving voice to teachings that were indeed the very word of God. Rather than the 'risen Christ' of the medieval Church, Jesus can, in Gnostic terms, be conceived as the son of the Good God, sent to bring the Good News and to release the spirit of man from the earthly prison of the material body.[27] Jesus was, to such people, the living embodiment of the godhead. Many groups who believed just this also believed that, when Jesus died, the spirit of God that had filled his body departed to join the Father, leaving just the husk, the earthly remains of the holy teacher. These remains were, I believe, venerated and given the traditional rites accorded to such receptacles of God's spirit here on earth, as prescribed in the ancient mysteries of the Akhenaten cult – the head was ritually removed and embalmed as a sacred relic.

So, the elite of the Order of the Temple were definitely 'heretics' according to the lights of the medieval church, but were they Christians? While certainly not orthodox Christians, men holding to this belief in a 'Gnostic Christ' would, nevertheless, be just as likely to fight for Christ as their orthodox brethren. They would, quite rightly, regard themselves as 'Christians', men who revered Christ as a receptacle of God's spirit and teachings. That the body of Jesus remained on earth at the time of his death was immaterial to the teachings. Its importance was solely as a relic for the rituals of the ancient religion.

In brief then, the Order of the Temple did fight and die for Christ, but it was made up of two quite separate groups, one essentially orthodox in its beliefs. The other, composed mainly of French Templars, held to a much more heterodox and Gnostic view of Jesus as a holy priest-king, and followed the ancient traditions of Akhenaten and the Nazarites in their reverence of the head.

The Death of Jacques de Molay

This view gained much credence when I looked at the story of Jacques de Molay, the last grand master of the Order of the Temple. Although the order was formally suppressed by the pope in 1312, it was not until the early spring of 1314 that the grand master and three other high-ranking members of the Templar Order, the Visitor, Hugues de Piraud, Geoffroi de Gonneville, Preceptor of Aquitaine and Poitou, and the Preceptor of Normandy, Geoffroi de Charnay, were brought forth from their prison and set before a special council of prelates and doctors of theology. As far as the authorities were concerned, the prisoners were simply there to confirm the accusations brought against the order and to hear final sentence pronounced against them. However, as a contemporary chronicler records, matters went awry almost from the start:

> Since these four, without any exception, had publicly and openly confessed the crimes which had been imputed to them and had persisted in these confessions ... they were adjudged to be thrust into harsh and perpetual imprisonment. But lo, when the cardinals believed that they had imposed an

end to the affair, immediately and unexpectedly two of them, namely the Grand Master and the Master of Normandy, defending themselves against the cardinal who had preached the sermon and against the Archbishop of Sens, returned to the denial both of the confession as well as everything they had confessed.[28]

This was high drama indeed; by retracting their confessions the two men were condemning themselves to death as relapsed heretics. That they were well aware of their fate can be seen from Jacques de Molay's defiant speech, his final testimony:

> I think it only right that at so solemn a moment when my life has so little time to run I should reveal the deception which has been practised and speak up for the truth. Before heaven and earth and with all of you here as my witnesses, I admit that I am guilty of the grossest iniquity. But the iniquity is that I have lied in admitting the disgusting charges laid against the Order. I declare, and I must declare, that the Order is innocent. Its purity and saintliness is beyond question. I have indeed confessed that the Order is guilty, but I have done so only to save myself from terrible tortures by saying what my enemies wished me to say. Other knights who have retracted their confessions have been led to the stake; yet the thought of dying is not so awful that I shall confess to foul crimes which have never been committed. Life is offered to me but at the price of infamy. At such a price, life is not worth having. I do not grieve that I must die if life can be bought only by piling one lie upon another.[29]

Hugues de Piraud and Geoffroi de Gonneville stood grim and silent, but the Preceptor of Normandy was equally defiant. Standing shoulder to shoulder with the grand master and endorsing his words, Geoffroi de Charnay effectively spoke his own death sentence. While Piraud and de Gonneville were taken away to 'harsh and perpetual imprisonment', de Molay and de Charnay were held awaiting 'fuller deliberation' by the assembled cardinals the following day. But Philip IV, incensed by their defiance, was not prepared to wait. Acting with unseemly haste, he ordered their immediate execution:

> ... as soon as this news came to the ears of the King, who was then in the royal palace, he having communicated with the prudent men of his council, although not upon the clergy in the same manner, around the hour of vespers on the same day, on a certain small island in the Seine ... ordered both to be burned to death.[30]

It was no small irony that the two Templar notables were to die facing the cathedral of Notre Dame, 'Our Lady', whom the order esteemed so much and who many have linked to the worship of the Egyptian goddess, Isis, under her name of Notre Dame de Lumière, Our Lady of Light.[31]

Jacques de Molay and Geoffroi de Charnay were rowed across to the Ile-des-Javiaux, where the kindling and charcoal for the execution were already being made ready. The chronicler reports that:

> They were seen to be so prepared to sustain the fire with easy mind and will that they brought from all those who saw them much admiration and surprise for the constancy of their death and final denial.[32]

That same evening, Monday 18 March, the two Templar brothers were brought out, bound, and roasted slowly to death before a charcoal fire. Some said that as their flesh seared in the flames, de Molay called Pope Clement and Philip IV to account for their crimes before the tribunal of God within the next twelve months. Whether this is true or no, Clement was dead in just over a month (he had been ill for several years) and Philip IV died just nine months later, on 29 November, the result of a riding accident while hunting, a sport to which the king was addicted. Their sudden deaths added to the mystique and occult aura that was attaching itself ever more strongly to the Knights of the Temple.

Many saw the two Templars as martyrs, burned by an avaricious king with the complicity of an evil and corrupt pontiff. This martyrdom, in the medieval mind, made their remains a potent source of religious power. According to the *Cronica* of Villani, once the fire had burned itself out 'their ashes and bones were collected as sacred relics by the friars and other religious persons, and carried away to holy places'.[33]

The Head of Jacques de Molay?

So, the bodies of Jacques de Molay and Geoffroi de Charnay had been comprehensively destroyed by their execution, the flames reducing their bodies to ashes and a few bone fragments. Even if a Templar Order had been extant at that time, it would have proved impossible for either of these two brethren to have been accorded any of the rites of the sacred head religion that I believe the Templars in France had followed in such great secrecy. Nor, for that matter, could the bodies of the two men have been accorded any burial rites whatsoever, save those for their ashes.

Why, then, does an eighteenth-century book show a woodcut revealing Jacques de Molay's body as a headless trunk?[34]

When I first saw this woodcut I could scarcely believe my eyes. The body of de Molay is resting in what can only be described as a cave or sepulchre. He is lying on a stone slab that is covered with a shroud. The parallels with the Gospel stories of the laying out of Jesus in the sepulchre of Joseph of Arimathea are too obvious to labour. But what is even more shockingly apparent in this picture is that de Molay's corpse lacks a head. There has been no attempt to hide this fact; the artist who conceived the work wished to emphasise the amputation, and the wound at the neck is shown in graphic detail. That this action was deliberate, and that the head has been cut off inside the tomb, is evident from the figure walking towards the entrance of the sepulchre – in his right hand he is holding a thick lock of hair, from which swings a severed head.

What is happening here? What is the artist trying to convey in this bizarre picture? De Molay's body is in a sepulchre, lying on a slab with a shroud – it seemed to me quite obvious that the artist is placing de Molay's body in the setting of Jesus' burial in order to indicate a link between the Order of the Temple and Jesus. And further study of the woodcut reveals additional confirmation of this thesis. Intriguingly, the figure holding the severed head has in his left hand a spearhead. This is not the sort of instrument needed to remove a head (in fact a short sword, ideal for decapitation, hangs from a strap around his shoulder), and the spearhead seems to be yet another visual reference to Jesus, the spear of Longinus that pierced Christ's body as it hung on the cross. The figure holding the spear and the severed head is looking towards a second warrior, who is advancing towards the sepulchre. Both men are dressed oddly, in a strange amalgam of styles. One has a Roman-style helmet upon his head; the other is bare headed, but sports a filet or headband that is typically Roman. However, both figures are far from classical in the rest of their dress; they are wearing plate armour unknown in that period. Once again the artist appears to be trying to link the time of Jesus (in the form of Roman war gear) with that of the Middle Ages (or perhaps with his own time, when plate armour was still occasionally worn).

But why the severed head? There is absolutely no reason why the artist should have included this macabre motif in the scene. Had he wished to link the Templars with Christ, then de Molay's body lying in the sepulchre and the oddly dressed figures would have been sufficient. The head is superfluous, indeed its shocking presence tends to detract from the message, *unless it is the message itself*. Seen in the context of the cult of the severed head, the message is clear: the body on the slab is that of Jesus, who had been decapitated in the sepulchre; and the Templars were in possession of the head which had come down to them from Roman times. Moreover, the very fact that the woodcut was commissioned reveals that this secret information was known to a number of individuals as late as 1796, when it is believed the image was first published.

If the Templars held the head of God, they could not have been believers in the bodily assumption of Jesus, and this lends credence to the claims that they regarded him as a man, not a god. There is additional evidence for this from the inscription to the right of the woodcut. The inscription reads: 'JBM, and below A. 1314'. This is obviously the initials of the Grand Master Jacques B. de Molay, but it is the treatment of the date that is most significant. That year, of course, commemorates the date that de Molay was executed, but note that the date is rendered A. 1314, *Anno 1314*, not the usual *Anno Domini* 1314, abbreviated as AD 1314. Anno *Domini* is 'The year of our Lord (or God)', but the artist has omitted *Domini*, leaving a translation of 'the year 1314', and indicating that for him, and also for the Templars, Jesus was not regarded as God, but as a receptacle of God's spirit, whose body remained on earth at the time of his death.

It is also interesting to note that the inscription lies beneath a structure dominated by two pillars, atop each of which is a severed head. It was not until this book had almost been completed that I discovered that central to modern-day Templar ritual is a head or skull set atop a small pillar. Moreover, behind the two figures is an image of the disc of the sun and, as we have seen, the sun disc was the symbol of the Aten, the god of Akhenaten, the apparent originator of the cult of the severed head.

With the dissolution of the order, and the death of de Molay and his companion, it seemed that the last chapter of these mystical warrior-monks had finally been written, that the secret of the cult of the sacred head, and especially the head of God, had been lost for ever. However, as with most aspects of the Order of the Temple, appearances proved deceptive. I was to discover that this was, in fact, far from being the end of the Poor Knights of the Temple of Solomon.

The Escape

What, then, had happened to the sacred relic; what had become of the head of God? Search as they might, the king's men had been unable to find the records of the Order of the Temple or (save for the enigmatic Caput fifty-eight M) the strange 'idols' the Templars had worshipped.

There was no apparent answer to this mystery, and I was left echoing the words of a medieval poet:

> The brethren, the Masters of the Temple,
> Who were well-stocked and ample,
> With gold and silver and riches,
> Where are they? How have they done?

Hitherto, there has always been a tendency to portray the Templars as passive victims, unsuspecting 'innocents', ensnared in the web of guile and deceit cast over them by the wicked King of France. This is, to say the least, a naive view. The Templars were consummate politicians, skilled in diplomacy and *realpolitik*. They can hardly have been unaware of the French king's assaults upon the Lombards and the Jews, or of Philip's unscrupulous and ruthless nature. The order had spent its life on the knife edge that was Levantine politics, and its political instincts had been honed during two hundred tempestuous years. They were involved in a running battle for supremacy with their main rivals among the military orders, the Hospitallers, much of which was fought in a covert, clandestine way. They had dealt with Saladin, the Mamluk sultans and the notoriously cunning Assassins. And they had wrestled successfully with the complex web of double-dealing and deceit that had made up the unstable Christian alliances in Outremer.[35] It is therefore absolutely inconceivable that the Order of the Temple did not have spies set among the members of Philip's entourage, or that word of the possibility of arrest and suppression of the order had not been brought to the attention of the organisation's leading members.

The record shows that some, at least, of the brethren were privy to the danger that faced the order. A few weeks before Philip IV ordered his assault on the temple, the Grand Master, Jacques de Molay, recalled a number of copies of the Temple Rule, along with other manuscripts, and ordered them all consigned to the flames.[36] One Templar had fled as much as fifteen days before the arrests began. Another knight had been informed that his intention to withdraw from the temple was wise as danger was fast approaching.

So there is strong evidence that the high initiates of the order were given advance warning of the king's plans and that they could have had an escape plan in place long before the king's seneschals broke into the first temple preceptory. For the Templar *illuminati*, land, buildings and those brothers not initiated into the secrets of the order would have seemed of little consequence compared to the inestimable value of the head of God, the remaining relics, and the secret teachings. It appears that they were all regarded as expendable, and were sacrificed to protect the real treasure of the order. And it is true that, although the Templar soldiery was arrested *en masse* and the order's property seized, the records of the temple and its treasure (which I believe included the head of Jesus), all escaped the king's clutches. How, then, was the escape arranged? And where was the Templar treasure, both sacred and secular, now? To what safe haven had it been carried?

Under repeated 'questioning' from the Inquisition, Jean de Châlons de Poitiers revealed a number of facts which, together, do seem to point to a prearranged escape planned by those brethren close to the treasurer of the order, Hugues de Piraud. According to Jean de Châlons, the Preceptor of France, Gerard de Villiers, had been given prior knowledge of the arrests and had fled Paris with fifty Templar knights, whom he later ordered to La Rochelle, where they put to sea in the Templar fleet of eighteen galleys. This informant also said that another Templar knight, who hailed from the same area, Hugues de Châlons, had loaded three carts '*cum toto thesauro fratris Hugonis de Peraudo*' (with all of brother Hugues de Piraud's treasure), i.e., with the treasure of the order, and fled the city under cover of darkness. These facts had not been disclosed, said Jean de Châlons, because any Templar who had any knowledge of the escapes believed he would be killed if he spoke of it.[37]

Both Hugues de Châlons and Gerard de Villiers were later captured, but Gerard's fifty knights, and whatever Hugues de Châlons had taken with him in the three 'treasure carts' had long since escaped the kingdom of France and the clutches of Philip le Bel's men. The treasure, like the fifty knights, had made its way to the Templar naval base of La Rochelle and had been placed upon the Templars' fleet of eighteen galleys by the fugitive brethren. They sailed out into the wintry darkness that same night, and disappeared.

16

To the Extremity of the World

Murder in the Sanctuary

Robert the Bruce, Earl of Carrick, waited impatiently on the steps of Greyfriars church, Dumfries, Scotland, for the arrival of his greatest rival, John 'the Red' Comyn. The year was 1306. The Comyn family were masters of vast tracts of land beyond the Tay, while the Bruces held Annandale and Carrick, lands in the southwest of Scotland, on the border with England. For years they had vied with each other for the prize both desired above all else – the crown of Scotland. The year before, in 1305, the two rivals had come to an arrangement, an agreement born out of the sickness of the English king. Edward i, 'Edward Longshanks' to his contemporaries, had spent most of his life trying to subdue his northern neighbours. But now the Hammer of the Scots was an old man and was likely to die from the illness which afflicted him. Compared to Longshanks, Edward i's heir was a weakling and this future relaxation of English dominance offered Scotland the first real chance in decades of regaining its independence. Bruce had spoken with Comyn and offered him terms designed to submerge their differences and to join the two powerful nobles in a united front against the English. 'Give me your lands,' Bruce had told Comyn, 'and you shall have the Crown. Or take my lands and I shall be King.'[1] The Red Comyn had apparently preferred lands to a royal title and sealed documents agreeing these terms were exchanged between the two parties.

Unfortunately for the Scottish plotters, against all expectations, Edward i recovered from his malaise and set about Scottish affairs with his usual vigour and a mind full of suspicion. For some reason, probably fear of discovery by Edward's efficient network of spies, John Comyn's courage failed him and he secretly disclosed to the English king the substance of his agreement with Bruce. King Edward, suspicious to the last, wished to see documentary evidence of Comyn's claims and, until these arrived, he treated Bruce, who was at the English court in January 1306, with warmth and good humour, hiding his true intentions. However, during one particularly convivial banquet, the king let slip that he was inclined to arrest Robert Bruce the next morning on a charge of treason. Luckily for Bruce, at the banquet was the Earl of Gloucester, whose family had been friends of the Bruces for generations. He sent a cryptic warning to the Scotsman: the gift of a pair of spurs.[2] Taking the hint, Bruce fled on horseback for Scotland that same night.

In another stroke of good fortune, as the fugitive approached the Scottish border, he encountered a lone Scots traveller on the road, making his way in the opposite direction, into England. As mid-winter was an unusual time to be making a journey, Bruce had the traveller stopped and searched, and discovered a letter from Comyn to the English king, and with it the proof Edward had requested, the bond with Bruce's signature and seal upon it.

This was the reason Bruce fretted and fumed outside Greyfriars church on 10 February 1306, while he awaited the arrival of his one-time conspirator, the Red Comyn. When Comyn arrived with his uncle, Sir Robert Comyn, he and Bruce went immediately into the church, repairing to the high altar where they could speak without fear of being overheard. There, Bruce pulled out the secret bond and revealed his knowledge of Comyn's treachery. Comyn, who had a reputation for hot-headedness, replied angrily to Bruce's charge, the argument rapidly escalated, and both men reached for their daggers. They came to grips, Bruce's stroke went home and John Comyn fell bleeding before the high altar. Sir Robert Comyn rushed forward and struck at Bruce with his sword, but his armour turned the blow and Christopher Seton, who had accompanied Bruce into the church, struck the second Comyn down. As they left, it is said that Christopher Seton asked Bruce if he was sure Red Comyn was dead. Bruce stopped and in an infamous comment declared that he would 'mak siccar' (make sure), before returning to the high altar to administer the *coup de grâce* to the wounded man[3] The die was now cast for Bruce. There was no turning back. He raised the banner of revolt against the English and declared himself King of Scotland.

This murder, in a place of Christian worship, before the high altar, and Bruce's callous return to finish off his victim, sent shockwaves across Europe. Far more than the insurrection itself, Bruce's murder of Comyn outraged even the ruthless King Edward of England. The crime could not be left unpunished. For the moment, Bruce was safe from military reprisals in his Scottish fastnesses, but there was one sanction that could be taken against him, a religious penalty that would follow him anywhere, that would pursue him throughout all the lands of Christendom. On the instigation of Edward I, for his sin in slaying his rival in a place of sanctuary and 'for damnably persevering in iniquity', Pope Clement v declared Robert the Bruce excommunicate.[4]

By a strange quirk of fate, it was this supreme act of papal power, initiated by the very pope who had ordered the Templars' destruction, that was to provide the Order of the Temple with a place of safety, and that was to save their most precious relic, the head of God.

The Knights of Christ

The Templar fleet, which had left La Rochelle with the order's records and treasure, did not simply flee in panic. They seem to have acted on a prearranged plan, and are known to have split up almost as soon as they left harbour, one smaller group heading south, while the rest of the galleys sailed north.

The movements of the southerly flotilla are fairly well documented. They made for Portugal and landed near the coastal town of Nazaré.[5] The Templar headquarters was not far away in Tomar, and there the fugitive Templars finally found refuge. Why the southern Templar fleet chose Portugal is not known – although it was an independent kingdom far removed from French influence, it still lay within papal jurisdiction. Whatever the reason, it was here that the Templars encountered their first piece of good fortune since the horrors of the suppression. Despite the urgings of both the pope and the French king, the ruler of Portugal, King Dinis, was not at all inclined to destroy the order; or rather, he would not act unless he benefited directly from its dissolution. King Dinis was concerned that the destruction of the Order of the Temple might enable the remaining major military order in Portugal, the Knights Hospitaller, to grow over-powerful within his own kingdom. They might even pose a threat to his own rule. He therefore petitioned the pope to allow the crown to acquire all the Portuguese holdings of the Templars. The pope refused. King Dinis responded by apparently acceding to the pope's command for the dissolution of the Templar Order. But he complied with the letter, rather than the spirit, of the pope's instructions. The Portuguese king simply deleted the title of the order, and gave the Templars a new name, 'The Order of the Knights of Christ'. With this title they were allowed to keep almost all their holdings in Portugal.

For their part, the renamed Poor Knights relinquished their Templar pretensions as crusaders for the Holy Land, and instead turned their attention towards unknown lands beyond the sea. Within a short period, galleys of the order had begun voyages of exploration. And the Knights of Christ, like their Templar forebears, were enterprising and imaginative, constantly seeking out whatever technology proved most useful, no matter what its provenance. Foremost among these maritime innovators was Prince Henry the Navigator, a grand master of the Knights of Christ, who used Christian, Jewish and Arab experts in his search for ever-more precise techniques of map-making and navigation. The knights' inquisitive, open-minded world-view made them Europe's foremost seaborne adventurers. Their journeys took them to Madeira, to the Canary Islands, and thence down the west coast of Africa. These expeditions culminated, in the person of Vasco da Gama (himself a Knight of Christ), in a seminal voyage around the Cape of Good Hope and on to the riches of India, paving the way for the expansion of European trade and culture across the globe. And while da Gama sailed east, Christopher Columbus (whose father-in-law had been a member of the Knights of Christ) journeyed westward. When Columbus' three ships crossed the Atlantic to discover Hispaniola and the West Indies, they sailed, like all vessels of the Knights of Christ, under the red cross pattée of the Templars.[6]

The Templars in Scotland

A very different, far more covert route awaited the main section of the Templar fleet that sped north. Their destination was Robert Bruce's newly independent kingdom of Scotland. These northbound ships seem to have split again, into a larger and a smaller flotilla. The smaller group emulated the Jewish princess Tamar Tephi and sailed – 'to the extremity of the world at the sun's going' – to Ireland, the Land of Hiber, son of Gaythelos and Scota, and the region in which the druidic cult of the head had survived longest. By all accounts, the fugitive knights did not tarry in Ireland, but stayed just long enough to strip the Irish Templar estates of all their moveable assets. Certainly, when the pope's orders were finally obeyed in Ireland, and the Templar lands seized, the preceptories were found to have been plundered of all valuables.[7] Laden with these spoils, the Templars set sail for Scotland. They followed much the same route that the descendants of Scota had taken almost a thousand years before, crossing the narrow North Channel between northeast Ireland and Scotland's west coast. Here some settled on the lands surrounding Loch

Awe. In Kilmartin church, near Loch Awe, and in several other graveyards in this region, there are numerous Templar graves attesting to the fact of settlement by fugitive members of the order at around this time. Just as important, for what was to follow, was the discovery hard by of gravestones covered with masonic motifs, some carrying the skull and crossbones, the sign of Hiram Abif and the sacred head cult, and the maritime battle-flag of the Templars. One or two graves showed other combinations of Templar and masonic figures on the same grave slab, hinting at the manner in which the Order of the Temple was eventually to evolve.

The remaining galleys of the northern flotilla, numbering some nine boats, sped up the east coast of the British Isles, making for Edinburgh and the central lowlands of Scotland. As this was the largest contingent of the original fleet of eighteen ships that had fled the port of La Rochelle, it is reasonable to assume that it was these boats that carried with them the most valuable of the Templar possessions, the worldly treasure and the sacred relics, including the head of God. An old French masonic tradition states that, just after the suppression of the order in France, nine Templar vessels landed on the Isle of May in the mouth of the Firth of Forth.[8] And the same account also asserts that it was this fleet that carried with them the records and treasure of The Order of the Poor Knights of the Temple of Solomon.

This tradition makes very good sense indeed. There were a number of reasons, several unique to Scotland, that made this northern kingdom the country that posed the least risk for the outlawed order. These factors gave me every reason to believe that it was to this safe haven on the east coast of Scotland (and not to Portugal) that the fugitive galleys had brought their priceless relic: the head of God.

Scotland possessed the geographical advantage of being part of a sea-girt island, making pursuit that much more difficult. The Templars had been established in Scotland almost since the order's inception, and the Templars had strong links with Edinburgh (the Isle of May lay just forty-eight kilometres to the northeast), and especially with one region just to the south of Scotland's capital city. One of the two founder members of the Poor Knights, Hugues de Payens (whose coat of arms consisted of three severed heads) had owned land here, obtained when he married Catherine de Saint-Claire.[9] And, the Holy Land excepted, the very first Templar preceptory to be built by the order was constructed on land owned by the Saint-Claires, at Balantrodoch, just south of Edinburgh.[10] Even today, this settlement has strong connections with the order and is known simply as

'Temple'. Close by is a small forest, planted in the shape of a cross pattée, and known as Templar Wood.

Scotland had a further unique advantage. It was the physical and spiritual home of the Scoti, the descendants of Akhenaten's daughter who had fled from Egypt many hundreds of years before. Akhenaten's daughter had carried with her the throne of her father the pharaoh, the 'marble chayre' that became known as the Stone of Destiny, whose hidden resting place in Scotland is still a closely guarded secret. The Egyptian immigrants also carried with them Akhenaten's religion of the Aten, and the secret reverence for the holy head. The Scoti had flourished in Ireland, helping to establish the druidic religion and the cult of the head on the *Insula Sacra*, before they migrated en masse to Argyll, and eventually colonised most of the Scottish mainland. The Scoti had brought with them on their travels both the Stone of Destiny and the Bethel Stone of Tamar Tephi. It was logical to assume that they had also brought with them the cult of the head, and indeed there were several strands of evidence that pointed to this conclusion. With the predominance of the Roman Church during the Middle Ages, the cult of the head had been forced to go underground, but its ancient echoes still reverberated amongst the Caledonian hills and glens. So, when they arrived in Scotland, the Templars were in a sense coming home. It was a country peopled by descendants of Akhenaten himself, a land in which reverence for the sacred head was already an ancient tradition.

The Excommunicated King

But there was yet another, utterly vital, reason for choosing Scotland. It was, at that time, the realm most insulated from the power of the Roman Church, whose ecclesiastical tentacles wound across Europe and held almost all of Christendom in thrall. The incumbent pope, Clement v, was a creature of Philip le Bel, indebted to the French king for his election, and on most occasions the pope was prepared to bend his will to that of the French crown. As the Council of Vienne had shown, Clement was unable to withstand the French king's demands, especially when backed up with the threat of force. Philip was quite happy to use violence when all else failed: his agents had already engineered the kidnapping of one pope, Boniface, for which Philip le Bel was briefly excommunicated.[11] If the French king wished for the destruction of the Templars across Europe, there was a very good chance that he would get his way. Despite the obvious pressure and manipulation of successive popes by the French court, most of Europe regarded a papal bull as the word of God, spoken by the Vicar of Christ. The pontiff's words still had the power and force of holy writ throughout the length and breadth of Christendom, including Portugal, and they were not to be ignored except under threat of excommunication. Scotland, however, was quite another matter.

The murder of John Comyn had given Robert the Bruce the strongest claim to the Scottish crown, but it had also left him a religious and political pariah, excommunicated by the pope and shunned by most of the Christian powers. This was most unsatisfactory for Bruce, though he must have known that in time the situation could be remedied by a sufficiently public repentance and support for the pontiff in his continuing struggle against secular powers. But if his excommunication was a stumbling block for Robert the Bruce, it was an absolute blessing for the outlawed Templars. Because of it, King Robert was the only monarch in the whole of Christendom against whom the pope could not threaten the ultimate sanction of excommunication. For this brief period in history Robert the Bruce could do exactly as he wished, without regard to the pope's demands, because that 'great and puissant pontiff' had already shot his last sacerdotal bolt. King Robert was damned already in the eyes of the church.

So, not only was Scotland geographically isolated from most of Europe, with an ancient tradition of head worship and an enduring Templar presence, it also had the unparalleled advantage of being ruled by a king who was excommunicate and therefore unlikely to heed any papal proclamations. Here was a country that could act as a refuge for the beleaguered knights, and as a repository for their secrets.

Bruce seems to have received the fugitives with open arms. His own position in 1307 was quite as grim as that of the Templars. The Scottish king was fighting an increasingly forlorn battle against Edward I's vastly superior forces. He was desperate for trained men and equipment and when a body of the foremost warriors in Christendom fetched up on the shores of his realm as outlaws, seeking sanctuary, he must have believed that fortune had at last begun to smile on him. Until mid-1307 and the arrival of the Templars, Bruce had been facing ruin. Bruce had been crowned upon the true Stone of Scone on 25 March 1306, but only four earls had been present at the coronation, and since that time no more than one hundred knights had rallied to his banner. King Edward had asked for Bruce's excommunication, and this had been granted by the pope (though the Scottish clergy refused to acknowledge it). This news was followed by a disastrous defeat outside the walls of Perth castle, when

Bruce's only coherent force had been treacherously attacked and many of his most stalwart supporters captured. Edward I exacted a terrible revenge on the rebels, having most of the nobles hung, drawn and quartered and the rest beheaded.

Soon after, Bruce's wife, twelve-year-old daughter, his sister and other ladies of his household had been captured by the Earl of Ross and the women were now in English hands. So fierce had been the English king's hatred that he ordered heralds to proclaim throughout the country that the wives of his Scottish enemies were outlawed also. They had no protection, anyone could rape or murder these women without fear of retribution. Once captured, Edward had spared the women's lives, but devised a particularly humiliating fate for two of them. Bruce's sister Mary, and the Countess of Buchanan (who was reputed to be the Scottish king's mistress), were dealt with in an especially barbaric manner. Taken from the main group of prisoners, they were exhibited separately in wooden cages on the walls of Roxburgh and Berwick castles, where they languished, at the mercy of the elements, for four years.[12] Queen Elizabeth, wife of Robert the Bruce, would no doubt have suffered a similar or perhaps worse fate, but for the fact that she was the daughter of the Earl of Ulster, a noble whose friendship was politically vital to Edward. He contented himself with keeping her at Burstwick-in-Holderness, under house arrest. Bruce's daughter was banished to a nunnery at Walton. The fate of the men captured with them was far less kindly and notable for its grisly humour.[13]

But fate again took a hand when things looked bleakest. Edward I, the Hammer of the Scots, died on 11 July 1307 at Burgh-on-Sands, near Carlisle, as he marched northwards on yet another campaign to subdue his northern neighbours.[14] Edward II, his successor, did not have his father's implacable and ruthless nature, and most of his time was given over to pleasure and hunting. He lavished money and lands on court favourites, ignored his barons, and tried very hard to ignore Scotland as well. Bruce took his chance and, from his base in the mountains of Carrick, began a series of guerrilla actions that harried the English ceaselessly and gradually brought many more men to his side. Soon, most of Scotland was under his control. Eventually, only Stirling castle in the central lowlands of Scotland remained in English hands. The Scots laid siege to the fortress, and this threat to the last English possession in Scotland finally roused Edward II from his life of indolence. He led an army north to raise the siege, though many of his disaffected barons refused to join the muster. As the English moved along the old Roman road towards the castle, the Scots drew up their forces across their path, positioning themselves on the

242

opposite side of a small burn, the Bannock, that was to become famous in Scottish history and legend. The scene was set for the Battle of Bannockburn, where Scotland won its independence and the Templars amply repaid the Scottish king for his kindness in giving them sanctuary.

Bannockburn

The Roman road to Stirling ran approximately north-south, dipping down into the valley of the Bannock, where there was a shallow ford. To the west lay the dense Torwood and New Park forests, all but impenetrable to mailed knights and their huge war horses. On the east side of the road, the land was slightly more accessible, but soon ran down into boggy marshland that stretched away into the mudbanks of the Firth of Forth. For the English army there was no path to Stirling except through the Scots, who stood at arms, in their schiltrons (hollow squares or circles of pikemen) awaiting the onslaught. At one point King Robert, on a grey palfrey, rode out alone to inspect the Scottish lines. It was, perhaps, a foolhardy thing to do, and a young English knight, Sir Henry de Bohun, seeing Bruce alone and unguarded, spurred his horse towards him. The prudent course for Bruce was to retreat behind his men rather than risk the dangers of single combat; if he was killed, the battle would be lost before the armies joined. But equally, for the king to retire without facing this challenge would be disastrous for Scots' morale. Moreover, there was probably a personal facet to this combat. When Bruce's 'insurrection' began, Edward I, and later Edward II, had turned over Bruce lands in both Scotland and England to the de Bohuns, acts which must have angered the Scottish king and have given him a personal impetus for vengeance. Whatever his reasons, Bruce did not seek refuge with his army; he cantered forward on his little pony towards the approaching foeman. It was a contest of the palfrey's agility against the furious, bull-like charge of the war horse. And like a matador facing a bull, Bruce used his palfrey neatly to side-step the lance of the thundering juggernaut. Rising in his stirrups, he brought his axe down two-handed upon the head of his foe as he careered past, crushing his skull.[15]

The Scots were euphoric at the outcome of this single combat but, strategically, it changed very little. As an army they were still outnumbered three to one, with a horrific disadvantage in mounted knights. The English vanguard attacked and was beaten off, as was a flanking movement by six hundred mailed knights, the schiltrons moving forward in disciplined ranks to overthrow the heavy horse. The Scots scented victory but by this time the day was far spent, and both sides bivouacked for the night, intending to renew the conflict at first light on the next day.

The following morning, to the astonishment of the English commanders, the Scots advanced on their positions. This was unheard of; the English had expected the Scots to melt away at the sight of their heavy cavalry, or at very least to stand fast and await their charge. Armoured knights were to medieval warfare what tank divisions are today: all but unstoppable except by a similarly equipped foe. So strong was this belief that, when Edward II saw the Scots stop briefly and kneel in prayer, he is said to have cried out jubilantly, 'They kneel for mercy.' Sir Ingram de Umfraville, who had much experience in the Scottish wars, answered, 'For mercy yes, but not from you: from God for their sins. These men will win all or die.' The king, somewhat chastened, replied, 'So be it'; the trumpets were sounded, and the main body of both armies advanced on one another.[16]

The battle lasted most of the day. At one stage, the English managed to get their Welsh archers into position on the left flank of the Scots and they began to pour their frighteningly effective arrow-storm into Bruce's schiltrons. The Scots king engaged his reserve of mounted men-at-arms and successfully destroyed the archer formations. With all warriors fully committed on both sides, the outcome of the battle swayed from one side to the other. The Scots were the more disciplined, but the English were better equipped and more numerous.[17] None could see how the battle would end.

It is at this crucial point that a fresh cavalry contingent is said to have appeared on the Scots' side, and to have born down upon the English. One version of the battle claims that it was an attack by the 'small folk', ill-armed camp followers of the Scots army. This is hard to believe. It is inconceivable that such a pitiful force could have made the proud English army turn and flee for their lives. A much more probable tradition records that it was a force of Knights Templar, carrying their piebald battle banner Beau Séant that appeared so unexpectedly.[18] This is clearly a more likely scenario. The English were already hard pressed. Had they looked up and seen the Beau Séant bearing down on them, and beneath it a company of knights whose foolhardy bravery was legendary, they could well have lost heart and fled. Edward II, with a band of five hundred knights, was one of the first to leave the field, which says much for the quality of the newcomers – such a force would hardly have fled in the face of an attack by grooms and camp followers. But the Templars were another matter altogether. Modern-day Templars in Scotland still commemorate the anniversary of Bannockburn, which was fought on St John's day, 24 June 1314, as a tribute to the Templar knights who fought and died in the cause of Scottish independence.

The Templar oath of fealty, said to have been taken in 1317, three years after the battle of Bannockburn, formally claims that the Templars were succoured by the Scottish nation. Part of the oath, rendered into contemporary speech, asserts:

> Inasmuch as the ancient realm of Scotland did succour and receive the brethren of the most ancient and noble Order of the Temple of Jerusalem, when many distraints were being perpetrated upon their properties, and many heinous evils upon their persons, the Chevaliers of the Order do here bear witness.
>
> Chevaliers of the Order do undertake to preserve and defend the rights, freedoms and privileges of the ancient sovereign realm of Scotland. Further they affirm that they will maintain, at peril of their bodies, the Royal House of the realm of Scotland, by God appointed.[19]

The Sinclairs

Also fighting with Robert the Bruce at Bannockburn were three members of the Sinclair family, the Bishop of Dunkeld, the Lord of Rosslyn, and a knight, Sir William Sinclair. Some sources claim that the leader of the Templar charge was Sir William Sinclair, as grand master of the Order of the Temple in Scotland, and this is highly plausible. The Sinclairs at Bannockburn were all direct blood descendants of a line that stretched back to Catherine de Saint-Claire, wife of the Templar founder Hugues de Payens. And Catherine de Saint-Claire was a distant ancestor of the present-day Scottish laird, Jamie Sinclair, whom I had met with during my research into the fate of Akhenaten's throne, the true Stone of Destiny, and who apparently knows the true location of this ancient artefact. There is no doubt that the Sinclairs are intimately connected with the secret hiding place of this ancient symbol of Scottish royalty.

Nor was this to be the last time I encountered the Sinclairs. With the arrival of the Templars in Scotland, the Sinclair name suddenly becomes hard to avoid. Again and again in the course of my quest for the head of God this noble and enigmatic family appeared. Although I did not realise it at the time, from this point on the family would begin to figure even more prominently in my research. It turned out to be no coincidence that they had intermarried with the family of one of the founders of the Order of the Temple, that the first preceptory outside Palestine had been built on Sinclair land, or that the Sinclair estates in southern Scotland adjoined those of the Templars. They were also strongly linked to the beginnings of the masonic order in Scotland. It seemed reasonable to assume that they might also be connected to the mystery I was pursuing, the whereabouts of the head of God. However, I could not, at that time, imagine just how crucial their participation in the story was to be. It was one long-dead member of the Sinclairs who proved to be an essential posthumous 'guide' to my research, leaving esoteric symbols carved in stone, mute messages that were eventually to lead me to the end of my quest, to the hidden resting place of the most sacred of holy relics.

17

Guardians of the Sacred Light

The St Clair family that held estates in Scotland had won their English lands by conquest. Nine warriors of that name had fought with Duke William Bastard, later the Conqueror, on Senlac field in 1066. The Norman victory at the Battle of Hastings eventually gained the Sinclairs estates in England and Scotland to add to the land the family already possessed in Normandy. They were close allies with the Bruces, future kings of Scotland, who also held land in Scotland, England and France. Like all Normans, the Sinclairs were originally Vikings (the name Norman derives from 'Northman'). They were the descendants of Rognvald 'The Mighty' (born AD 835, Jarl (Earl) of Orkney and of Møre and Romsdahal in Norway, and had been known by the Norse name Møre before their arrival in France.[1] The family had migrated south with the warband of Rollo the Viking towards the end of the tenth century and had settled in Normandy, following Rollo's treaty with the French king, Charles 'the Simple'. Rollo married the king's daughter to seal the bargain, and left his Møre cousins to hold the region which bordered King Charles' lands against any future French attack. Within a few years of their arrival in Normandy, the Møre family changed their name to Saint-Claire. And the reason for this change shed another small beam of light upon the mystery of the head of God, and confirmed my belief that the Sinclairs had been privy to the secret of the cult of the head from a very early stage.

The Headless Hermit

The tale goes that the family took its new name from a holy hermit, a Scottish divine named St William Sancto Claros, who had travelled to France and who lived out his days in prayer and meditation in a simple

247

hut by a healing well on the river Epte. This was the same river where Rollo the Viking had come to terms with the French king, and which became part of the Møre estates. Why the hermit was called Sancto Claros, meaning Holy or Clear Light, is unknown, nor is there any concrete information as to why the Møre family appropriated this title. The answer, however, seems to lie in the story of the hermit's death.

The holy man, William Sancto Claros, was apparently scandalised by the loose morals of a lady of the region. Nor was he tardy in letting her know his feelings and to what a bad end he predicted that she would come. He could not be persuaded to hold his tongue and the lady, rather confirming his view of her as a child of Satan, had the old hermit murdered. But it was the manner of his death that caused me to sit up and take notice. The loquacious hermit had been beheaded. And because of this, St William Sancto Claros is normally represented as a headless figure, holding out his severed head in his hands.[2] Knowing the story of the sacred head cult and the Sinclairs' apparent connection to the holy heads, this all seemed to be too much of a coincidence; once again the motifs of a holy man and decapitation had surfaced. The Møre family had deliberately taken its new name from a headless man of great sanctity. Was this, I wondered, a symbolic reference to the ritual decapitation of that other holy man who had shown himself to be filled with the spirit of God, that is, to Jesus, the holiest of men? When I also recalled that Catherine Saint-Claire had married the founder of the Knights Templar, Hugues de Payens, whose own coat of arms portrayed three severed heads (which was itself, I believed, a symbolic reference to the ancient line of sacred heads), I became more and more convinced that this explanation was the only one that could adequately explain the strange combination of symbols and events. Even before the Templar excavations beneath the temple were complete, certain families intimately connected with the Poor Knights had chosen names and symbols for themselves which appear to confirm their knowledge of the cult of the sacred head and the ritual that had been performed on the body of Jesus.

Guardians of the Holy Relics

In Scotland the Sinclairs prospered and, intriguingly, they were given a significant title by the Scottish crown. For long centuries they were known as the Guardians of the Holy Relics of Scotland. This role had begun in the early eleventh century when Margaret, and her brother Edgar Atheling, had fled England for Hungary. As grandchildren of King Edmund Ironsides of England, they were close to the succession and were forced to flee to escape the byzantine plots that surrounded King Edward the Confessor in his final days, as claimants vied for the succession to the English crown. A St Clair youth, William, was a member of Margaret's entourage and he chose to go with her into political exile. Despite the fact that Edgar Atheling, as Edward the Confessor's first cousin, had a stronger claim on the English crown, it was Duke William of Normandy, 'the Conqueror', (and only a first cousin once removed to King Edward) who eventually took the English throne.

While Edgar Atheling lost his right to rule, his sister was eventually given a royal crown. The Scottish King Malcolm III, after the death of his first wife, chose Margaret Atheling as his bride. In or around 1069, following lengthy negotiations, Margaret and her faithful cupbearer, William St Clair, made the arduous journey from Hungary to Scotland. While she had been in exile, Margaret had come under the influence of the stern Christianity of King Stephen of Hungary. She brought with her to Scotland a gift from the Hungarian monarch, a piece of the true cross, a length of wood from the very cross upon which Christ had been crucified. This relic, surrounded by a reliquary cunningly wrought of gold and silver, and studded with precious stones, became known as the Holy Rood.

Upon his arrival in Scotland, William Sinclair had been knighted, and he had taken up a very special and very significant role for the Scottish crown – Keeper of the Holy Relics. Why the Sinclairs were given this prestigious position has never been explained, but Sir William became custodian of all Scotland's religious treasures, including the Stone of Destiny and the Bethel Stone. The Holy Rood was added to these relics and from that time forward the Sinclairs guarded the sacred objects for the Scottish nation. In their hands the Sinclairs now held three objects that embodied most of the key 'characters' in the story I had been attempting to trace: the throne of Akhenaten, the reputed keystone of the Temple of Solomon (the Bethel Stone), and the Holy Rood, a relic of Christ's time on earth.

There was also yet another link to the severed head. On being knighted, Sir William was given the lands of Roslin, which lie to the south of Edinburgh. Here, a healing well was said to have gushed from the earth when Queen Margaret poured a phial of the blood of St Katherine of Alexandria, the Sinclairs' patron saint, upon the ground.[3] The queen ordered that a chapel should be built over the well and it became famous as a healing well of great power, especially in curing skin ailments.[4] By a strange quirk of fate, Sir William St Clair was made a keeper of a holy well, a striking echo of St William Sancto Claros, from whom the St Clairs took their name. However, fate may not have had much to do with this intriguing coincidence: when it came to Roslin, I was to find that most of the legends concerning this place were far more complex than the simple surface story. Queen Margaret's holy well had been flowing long before the arrival of Sir William Sinclair and the queen he served. It seems that the story of Queen Margaret, St Katherine's blood, and the miraculous upwelling of healing waters, was a cleverly crafted piece of propaganda. The tale was obviously a construct, designed as a vehicle to point up the parallels with the headless hermit St William Sancto Claros and his holy well; and to emphasise the link between the Sinclairs of Roslin and the holy man who stands holding his severed head in the palms of his hands. Later, as I researched the famous Rosslyn Chapel of the Sinclairs, I discovered that there was more to the choice of St Katherine as the saint to whom the well is dedicated, and patron of the St Clair family. In the National Gallery in London there is a painting by Stephen Lochnar, completed just one year before the founding of Rosslyn Chapel, in 1445. It depicts St Matthew (Rosslyn Chapel's formal title is the Collegiate Church of St Matthew) and also the Sinclair's patron saint, St Katherine, holding in her hand the sword with which *she was beheaded*.

I sat back to consider what I had just learned. The Sinclairs were the Guardians of the Holy Relics of Scotland, objects whose history was intimately linked to the religion of Akhenaten and the cult of the sacred head. The Sinclairs were named after a hermit who guarded a holy well and who is depicted holding his severed head in his hands, and they had dedicated a second holy well on their new estates in Scotland to another saint who had also been beheaded. Added to this, Lady Margaret Saint-Claire, on whose lands near Roslin the first Templar preceptory outside Palestine was built, had married a knight who had founded the Templars, and upon whose shield three severed heads were depicted.[5] This was, I felt, pushing coincidence a little too far. I had to conclude that these events were connected, and that they were linked in quite a direct manner to the cult of the sacred head.

The Declaration of Arbroath

Although Templar troops ensured a Scottish victory against the English at Bannockburn, confirming Robert the Bruce as King of Scotland, the new monarch was still excommunicate. Thanks to the wiles of the English envoys at the Holy See, the pope was to excommunicate King Robert, and almost everyone else connected with him, on no fewer than three occasions.[6] In 1320 (following the initial interdict of 1309) the pope commanded that on each Sunday and feast-day, the Archbishop of York and the bishops of London and Carlisle were to repeat the notice of excommunication made upon the king and his followers. Shortly thereafter, the same command was issued to the bishops of Aberdeen, Dunkeld, Moray and St Andrews. Rather than weakening Robert's position, however, the Scots lords closed ranks behind their beleaguered king and together agreed a common declaration of their rights, and the rights of the free and independent nation of Scotland. This document, the Declaration of Arbroath, has rung down the centuries as a clarion-call to Scottish independence (and indeed the freedom of all men). It is hard not to be stirred by its ringing eloquence and its implacable avowal of nationhood. Something of its flavour can be grasped in the following lines.

... for so long as there shall be but one hundred of us remain alive we will never give consent to subject ourselves to the dominion of the English. For it is not glory, it is not riches, neither is it honour, but it is freedom alone that we fight and contend for, which no honest man will lose but with his life.[7]

This text comes towards the end of the declaration, and it is the final part of the document that is most quoted. The beginning of the declaration has tended to excite far less interest as it simply documents the history of the Scottish people. But it was while reading this section that I stopped in amazement, and the ancient text ceased to be simply an historical document and became yet another piece in the puzzle, a piece which confirmed the provenance of the Scoti. This section of the declaration is often glossed over by scholars, as it does not fit their preconceived notions of who or what the Scots are. However, it was written to the high pontiff of Rome by Scotsmen proud of their independence, and equally proud of their heritage, and it states:

We know, most Holy Father and Lord, and from the chronicles and books of the ancients gather, that among other illustrious nations, ours, to wit, the nation of the Scots, has been distinguished by many honours; which passing from the greater Scythia through the Mediterranean Sea and the Pillars of Hercules, and sojourning in Spain among the most savage tribes through a long course of time, could nowhere be subjugated by any people however barbarous; and coming thence one thousand two hundred years after the outgoing of the people of Israel, they, by many victories and infinite toil acquired for themselves the possessions of the West which they now hold...

In this historic affirmation of nationhood, a document that has been compared in importance to the Declaration of Independence of the United States, the Scots confirm the story of an immigration from the eastern Mediterranean to the British Isles, and state, as a principal point, that their ancestry derives from Scythia. Gaythelos, the husband of Akhenaten's daughter, was according to most accounts a Scythian. By the 1300s, the once maternalistic Scoti had evolved into a paternalistic society, so it is natural that they should emphasise their lineage as deriving from the male line. That the Declaration of Arbroath refers to the ancient story of Gaythelos and Scota is confirmed by the route the Scots say their ancestors took: across the Mediterranean, through the straits of Gibraltar, with a stay among the savage tribes of Spain, before the final leg of their journey to the British Isles. This is exactly the same itinerary that the refugees from Egypt are said to have followed.[8] It is also important to note that the time of their arrival in the British Isles is given in terms of the 'outgoing of the people of Israel', that is, from the time of the Exodus. It was immediately after the Exodus that Scota and Gaythelos are said to have departed Egypt to begin their long sea journey to the West.

The Templars Disappear

The stirring contents of the Declaration of Arbroath softened even the pope's stern heart and he renewed diplomatic pressure for new negotiations between the two warring nations. Bruce pursued a policy of reconciliation with England, but the English king wanted none of it. Negotiations between the two countries broke down once more, and the English ambassadors were again able to persuade the Vicar of Christ that the blame lay with the Scots' intransigence. The result was that, in February 1321, the high pontiff again excommunicated the Scottish king, dooming him to the fiery torments of hell, and any Scot who invaded England with the Bruce was warned that they would suffer the same fate.[9]

Although these fulminations were given as little credence as the earlier interdicts, King Robert was becoming uneasy. A 'heretic' nation, under an excommunicated king, was very vulnerable in the Middle Ages. He became afraid that the pope would call a holy war, a crusade, against him and his nation, as an earlier pope had done in the Languedoc against the 'heretic' Cathars. The torments and terrors of that war, which had ended less than eighty years before, were still fresh in the collective psyche of Christendom. If King Robert was not extremely careful, the whole of Christian Europe might join against him, and those scenes of horror could be replayed within his own nation of Scotland. The pope had to be mollified, and crown and nation returned within the pale of the Roman Church, and that meant reaching an accommodation with the English as soon as possible. This was difficult enough to achieve, but Bruce's task was made far more complicated by the presence in his nation of a heretic military order, the Knights Templar, whose existence had been formally suppressed by a papal bull nine years before. And yet Bruce was indebted to the Templars for his crown, for assuring victory at the Battle of Bannockburn and for giving Scotland its independence. How could King Robert turn on the very men who had saved him from death and his country from enslavement?

Robert the Bruce solved this seemingly intractable problem with his usual sureness of touch. The Order of the Temple of Solomon would not be suppressed in Scotland, but neither could it be allowed to continue as an overt military order. It had to go underground and become a secret organisation. One tradition states that Robert the Bruce founded another order, the Royal Order of Scotland, as a way of, as it were, compensating the Templars for their loss.[10] Although the two orders remained separate, many Scottish Templars were inducted into the Royal Order of Scotland including, it is said, the Templar grand master in Scotland, Sir William St Clair. It therefore came as no real surprise to discover that the hereditary grand master of this new order was to be chosen solely from the ranks of a single family – the ubiquitous St Clairs. This same family also became the hereditary grand masters of the Crafts and Guilds and Orders of Scotland, and later of another secret fraternity that arose out of the destruction of the Order of the Temple – the Freemasons.

This does not seem to have been the only way in which the St Clairs benefited from the dissolution of the Templar Order. After the victory at Bannockburn, a grateful King Robert granted the family both a bishopric and extensive lands. And in the years following the Templar flight from France, extensive rebuilding and fortification took place at the main stronghold of the Scottish St Clairs, Rosslyn Castle. Begun in the twelfth century, the castle was refurbished and extended at great cost during the early part of the fourteenth century. It was as if the St Clairs had received an unforeseen influx of wealth and building knowledge from an unknown source; and the most likely provenance of such resources was the refugee Templars.

Rosslyn, Roslin, and the Rose-Line

The present-day name for the Sinclair castle is Rosslyn, and it has been spelled this way for well over a hundred years. Prior to this, the name of the area was Roslin. I decided to try to trace the meaning of Rosslyn/Roslin, and it was here that, quite unexpectedly, I met with yet another strong confirmation of my theory.

Rosslyn is quite obviously derived from the older name for the area, Roslin. It is possible that this title is an amalgamation of two Celtic words, *ros*, meaning a ridge or promontory and *lin*, a waterfall. However, I discovered that the Sinclairs (who should, after all, know the true meaning of the title of their own estates) favoured a second explanation. They saw Roslin as meaning Rose-Line, which in turn symbolised the blood (or perhaps the bloodline) of Jesus. The name Rose-Line, or Roseline, struck a chord in my mind – I had seen this name before and I knew that it was important but, try as I might, I could not remember where. After a long search through my notes I discovered two references to the Rose-Line, both of them linked to our story. The first was Sainte Roseline de Villeneuve, a female divine whose feast-day is, intriguingly, 17 January. This was an important date for the Merovingian kings, and some authorities have suggested that the saint's name itself symbolises the Merovingian bloodline.[11] As I knew that the Merovingian bloodline continued the lineage of Jesus, this made the interpretation of Saint Roseline's name identical to that of the Sinclairs' derivation for Roslin. Both are symbolic references to the bloodline of Jesus.

The second reference to the Rose-Line proved to be even more illuminating. That enigmatic and shadowy order, the Priory of Sion (which is reputed to have been the *eminence grise* behind the setting up of the Order of the Temple) has, over the past two decades, made repeated reference to a Rose-Line. And they have linked the name to the location of a great treasure or secret. Pierre Plantard, a past grand master of the Priory of Sion, has referred on several occasions to lines of longitude or meridians said to be connected to the 'Secret' the Priory of Sion guards, the site where the earthly remains of Jesus have been hidden. On one occasion, M. Plantard named one of these meridians as the 'Rose-Line'.[12] But this information is given in the context of so much conflicting information, in which Plantard seems purposefully to confuse two French meridians for the sake of emphasising the one he has named 'Rose-Line', that we are justified in suspecting that, in fact, it is the Rose-Line to which he wishes to draw our attention. This would mean that the Priory of Sion (while deliberately confusing the issue by seeming to indicate a French location) is essentially indicating that the 'Rose-Line' demarcates the site of the secret, and that this site is outside France. It came as no surprise when, on delving further into M. Plantard's background, I discovered a direct connection with the Scottish Roslin. M. Plantard's full name is Pierre Plantard de Saint Clair.

This really did seem to clinch matters. A French St Clair, grand master of an order closely connected with the Templars, states that the secret, the earthly remains of Jesus, are to be found on the Rose-Line. The Scottish St Clairs were strongly associated with the Templars and with the warrior-monks' arrival as fugitives in Scotland; and moreover, Sir William Sinclair had been named as the grand master of the Templars in Scotland. More-over, the family's ancestral home was the Rose-Line. Added to this, as I had discovered, the Sinclair family had been the hereditary Guardians of Scotland's Holy Relics. What could have offered greater security, what could have been more natural, than that the Sinclairs should also be entrusted with the most sacred relic of the Order of the Temple, following that order's escape from persecution in France? If the 'Templar Treasure' was in Scotland, if the secret was 'on the Rose-Line', it seemed that the Sinclair lands, and especially Roslin, would be the place to look.

18

A Second Temple of Solomon

I made my first trip to Rosslyn Castle and Chapel in the spring of 1995. I was on my way to Dunsinane to research the history and possible whereabouts of the Stone of Destiny and, as I was passing close to Rosslyn, I decided to drive over to take a look at the place. It was not possible to gain entrance to Rosslyn Castle but, externally, the view was uninspiring: the vast buttresses and crumbling stone towers of a medieval fortress left to wind, rain and the ravages of time. But Rosslyn Chapel was different. It was, quite literally, a revelation.

Rosslyn Chapel sits on a small knoll on the outskirts of a sleepy Scottish village which retains the older name for the area, Roslin. It is quite a modest structure, not much more than twenty-one metres long, and no larger than an ordinary village church, but what it lacks in size it makes up for in the sheer exuberance of its spires and flying buttresses, and in the elaborate carvings that adorn its external stonework. But if the outside of the chapel is impressive, it was the interior that set my pulse racing with excitement. There were figures and symbols everywhere; hardly a square centimetre of the place was without its quota of intricate carving. When I looked up, I could see that the whole of the roof (constructed of stone and up to a metre thick) was adorned in five sections with daisies, lilies, flowers, roses and stars. All around the chapel were symbols in such exuberant and immoderate profusion that their myriad images were overwhelming: Moses, Jesus and Mary stared with mute serenity from the walls; grails and engrailed crosses were carved across pillars; angels held hearts or fell headfirst towards the earth, bound by strong ropes; devils issued from hell, while kings, bishops and common folk gyrated madly, each paired with a skeleton in a *dance macabre*, the Dance of Death. The whole edifice was covered in a superabundance of the most intricate symbolic carvings, but what intrigued and excited me most was that almost every carving contained motifs of Templar, masonic, Judaic or Celtic origin. I could see Templar symbols such as the Agnus Dei (the Lamb of God), the five-pointed star and the floriated cross on the walls and pillars of Rosslyn, interspersed with figures demonstrating a variety of masonic signals, which themselves stood cheek-by-jowl with an assortment of Judaic figures from the Bible, such as David, Isaac, and Samson. And at every turn there were numerous examples of that most Celtic of motifs, the Green Man.

But what did it all mean? Why had so much effort, such overwhelming care and attention, been showered upon this small chapel, hidden in what was then a remote and inaccessible part of western Christendom? Who had built this remarkable edifice, and why?

The 'Prodigus'

The founder of Rosslyn was the third and final Sinclair to hold the title Jarl (Earl) of Orkney and he was named, like his Templar predecessor, William. The repetition of William as a Christian name is carried to almost ludicrous lengths in the Sinclairs – no fewer than eleven of the first twenty Sinclairs to hold Rosslyn have been Williams.[1] This may be yet another means of emphasising the Sinclair link with the 'headless hermit' Guillermus (William) Sancto Claros, and through him their connection with the cult of the severed head. Earl William was known by his contemporaries as the 'Prodigus', a student of hermetic knowledge and steeped in occult lore. Moreover, he was the hereditary grand master of all Scottish masonic lodges. According to Father Richard Hay, who compiled *A Genealogie of the Saintclaires of Rosslyn*, published in 1835, as Sir William grew older:

> his age creeping upon him, made him consider how he had spent his time past, and how to spend that which was to come. Therefore ... it came into his mind to build a house for God's service, of most curious work, the which, that it might be done with greater glory and splendour, he called artificers to be brought from other regions and foreign kingdoms...[2]

Sir William began the building of Rosslyn Chapel in 1446 according to Father Hay, or some six years earlier if we believe another chronicler, Slezer.[3] He took great pains to oversee every aspect of the chapel's construction, from the blueprint for the whole edifice to the smallest feature of the stonework. Father Hay is at pains to describe the attention to detail that Sir William lavished upon the carvings:

> And to the end the work might be the more rare; first he caused the draughts to be drawn upon Eastland boards, (wooden boards of Norway pine) and made the carpenters to carve them according to the draughts thereon, and then gave them for patterns to the masons, that they might thereby cut the like in stone.[4]

It was obvious from this that Sir William knew exactly what he wanted – he insisted on specific designs which accorded exactly with his own requirements, and every stage of the process was under the supervision of his own keen eye. He did not simply cover his chapel with motifs chosen at random from the Bible and elsewhere. Every figure was there to tell a story. The old *illuminatus* was leaving a message in stone, to be read by those who came after. But I was to find that it was not simply the carvings that carried a message – the building itself was also part of the intricate cypher Sir William Sinclair had devised.

Sacred Geometry

It appears that the chapel was intended to be merely the nave of a much larger church built, like most medieval churches, to the plan of a cross. The foundations for this larger edifice are said to have been uncovered twenty-eight metres to the west of the present chapel early in the nineteenth century. A radar scan of the grounds is planned to confirm this report, but it is obvious that this larger part of the building was never completed. If, indeed, there was ever an intention to complete it; for the foundations may have been merely a 'blind' to cover the building of what is essentially a mystical temple. For Rosslyn Chapel is constructed to a most exacting plan that incorporates esoteric and occult symbols from far more ancient cultures than medieval Christendom.

The layout of the chapel has been shown very convincingly to incorporate, in cross-section, the Templar cross pattée, the foliated rose and the double-triangle within the circle, the so-called Seal of Solomon, all symbols used by the Order of the Temple.[5] In similar fashion, the ground plan of the chapel also contains a sacred geometry based on the main walls of the chapel, and the pillars that mark out its aisles. The pillars at the eastern end of the building form the triple tau, three tau crosses joined together with their bases centred on a single pillar. This pillar links with other pillars and with points on the north and south walls to reveal once again the Seal of Solomon.[6] All these signs are emblematic of a specifically non-orthodox Christianity: the tau cross (and indeed the cross pattée) can be traced back to ancient Egypt.[7]

It seems that this 'heathen' symbolism was not lost on the elders of the Scottish Church. In 1589 William Knox, the brother of the Calvinist preacher John Knox, was taken to task for baptising one of the Sinclair infants in Rosslyn Chapel. The presbytery records of Dalkeith, which report this 'offence', describe the chapel as a 'house and monument of idolatrie, and not ane place appointit for teaching the word and min-istratioun of ye sacrements'.[8] Three years later excommunication was threatened upon Oliver Sinclair should the altars remain in place after 17 August 1592. On 31 August of that year George Ramsay reported that 'the altars of Roslene were haile demolishit', and Rosslyn ceased to function as a place of Christian worship. It was not until 22 April 1862, when the chapel was rededicated by the Bishop of Edinburgh, that Sunday services were once again heard beneath the chapel's barrelled roof.[9]

A Second Temple of Solomon

There is a further link between Rosslyn Chapel and the Temple of Solomon, the building revered in both Templar and masonic tradition. The positioning of the two most ornate pillars in the east of the chapel (the so-called Master and Apprentice Pillars) mimics that of Jachin and Boaz, the pillars of brass cast by the master architect Hiram Abif as one of the centrepieces of the temple built by King Solomon in Jerusalem (I Kings 7: 15–22). This theme is emphasised on the stone bosses which stud the chapel roof – one of the most frequent carvings on these suspended blocks of stone is a representation of the Temple of Solomon. In addition, as authors Christopher Knight and Robert Lomas have shown, one of the meanings of the ancient sign of the triple tau is 'The Temple of Jerusalem'.[10] Intriguingly, the sign also means 'A Place Where a Precious Thing is hidden (deponitur?)' or 'A Key to a Treasure'. Less convincingly, Knight and Lomas also claim that the ground plan of Rosslyn is an exact match for that of Herod's Temple (the final temple of Jerusalem that was destroyed by the Romans in AD 70). Unfortunately, there is no convincing evidence to show the exact layout of Herod's Temple and this assertion, though it may possibly be true, must be regarded as speculation at the present time. However, although its construction as an *exact* replica of a specific temple of Jerusalem is by no means proved, there does seem little doubt that Rosslyn Chapel is intended as a *substitute* temple of Jerusalem. Above the southern aisle is an inscription that actually points to the rebuilding of the first temple. Carved in stone are the words:

FORTE EST VINUM. FORTIOR EST REX. FORTIORES SUNT MULIERES. SUPER OMNIA VINCET VERITAS.
Wine is strong, the king is stronger, women are strongest, (but) truth conquers over all.

Knight and Lomas assume that this quote is from the hypothetical Nazorean scrolls which they believe were discovered beneath the temple of Jerusalem by the Templars. In fact, the words are from the Jewish book of Esdras (I Esdras 3: 10–12), and concern the period in Jewish history when the House of Judah was held in exile in Persia, ruled at that time by King Darius. One of Darius' three bodyguards was a Jew named Zerubbabel. Darius gave a test of wisdom to each of the three young warriors, and was so pleased by Zerubbabel's words praising truth above all that, as a reward, he permitted him to ask for anything that he wished. Instead of choosing riches or land or position, Zerubbabel begged that Darius should fulfil an old decree of an earlier Persian monarch, King Cyrus. Cyrus had promised to release the Jews from their captivity and allow them to return home to Israel and rebuild the Temple of Solomon at Jerusalem. Darius granted Zerubbabel's request. He made Zerubbabel king over the Jews and gave him responsibility for the reconstruction of the temple, which was begun around 520 BC and stood for three hundred and fifty years, until it was overrun, as we have seen, by the Syrian King Antiochus Ephiphanes in 170 BC. Darius and his three guards can be seen in a separate carving at Rosslyn, which lies close to the carved lettering of Zerubbabel's maxim.

This reference to the rebuilding of the first temple of Jerusalem almost certainly indicates that Rosslyn is another rebuilding of the temple. The Templars' dream of a Christian Jerusalem had been irrevocably lost when the last coastal castles fell to the Muslims. Unable to complete their vow of rebuilding the temple there, they appear to have decided on a new stratagem. Sir William Sinclair, a masonic grand master and almost certainly a covert Templar himself, had constructed in Scotland an alternative Temple of Solomon, an elaboration of the ruined Jewish temple in which the Templars had discovered their most sacred treasure, the head of God.

If, as now seemed likely, the Templars had located the sacred relic beneath the Jerusalem temple, and had carried it with them to Scotland, I could think of no more fitting place for the head of God to reside than in this medieval reconstruction of the Jewish House of God. The words of

260

Pierre Plantard de Sainte Claire, grand master of the Priory of Sion, had proved to be true. The secret did reside on the Rose-Line. I felt sure now that the head of God was here; somewhere in Rosslyn Chapel.

A Message in Stone

But the carvings at Rosslyn reveal far more. Interlinked with the Templar and masonic stonework, the chapel contained an almost equal number of Celtic symbols. I had been led to the conclusion that a cult of the head existed in both Judaic and Celtic cultures. If true, these two separate strands would have co-mingled when the Templars brought the treasure, both 'Grail' and gold, to Scotland. And here, in Rosslyn Chapel, the carvings told the same story, an interlinking of Judaic and Celtic symbolism. For me it was a confirmation in stone of my hypothesis.

What was especially interesting was the choice of Celtic motif. By far the most prominent was the ancient figure of the Green Man. Often drawn or carved as a powerful human figure covered in leaves and with shoots and tendrils sprouting from his mouth, the Green Man symbolises the fecund power of nature, the force that lies behind the procreative and regenerative forces of the natural world.[11] But what intrigued me most was that here, at Rosslyn, the Green Man was represented only by his head, scores of which can be seen peering out from behind the foliage, the vines and leaves growing from their mouths and attesting to their powers of fertility. I could not find a single full-length or even half-length figure of this symbol at Rosslyn. There are more than one hundred images of the Green Man carved inside the chapel, yet every one of them shows only the head. Why, of all Celtic symbols, was the Green Man's *head* chosen by Sir William Sinclair as the most ubiquitous of all Rosslyn's carvings? The answer led me once again to the cult of the head. As an emblem of fruitfulness, the head of the Green Man finds obvious parallels in the head of Bran, which was also a fertility symbol, and in the head which the Templars worshipped, Baphomet, 'Father of Wisdom', which was also said to 'make the trees flower' and 'make the land germinate'. Given Sir William's deep knowledge of occult lore and his connections with the Templars, it seemed too much to believe that this motif was chosen simply by chance (indeed, as we have seen, when it came to Rosslyn's carvings, absolutely nothing had been left to chance). This was, I was convinced, yet another subtle clue left by the founder of Rosslyn to indicate the true nature of the treasure that the chapel contained.

The Passion of Christ?

Along with the straightforwardly pagan and Celtic symbol of the Green Man are carvings which, at first glance, seem far easier to interpret as orthodox Christian. They appear to be uncomplicated vignettes of important scenes from the passion of Jesus, and his resurrection. These images are commonly believed to show:

Pontius Pilate in the act of washing his hands to indicate that he took no responsibility for the crucifixion of Christ.

St Veronica, holding a cloth with the head of Christ imprinted on it. (This image was miraculously left on the cloth after Veronica, in an act of compassion, had handed it to Christ to use as a face cloth as he carried the cross to Calvary. Veronica was beatified by the early Christians, and the cloth with its head of Christ became known simply as the Veronica.)

The crucifixion of Jesus.

Two angels rolling the stone away from the sepulchre.

The carvings are around three metres above ground and not more than thirty centimetres tall. It is difficult to obtain a clear view of the stone images and most people rely on, and take as accurate, a series of drawings made of the carvings some time before. However, closer inspection of the actual carvings reveals discrepancies with the artist's (orthodox Christian) portrayal of these images, and shows a number of anomalies in the composition of each carving that serve to cast doubt on the orthodox interpretations.

In the first, Pontius Pilate is shown as a long-haired and heavily bearded man. This is at odds with what we know of first-century Roman habits, where men were, almost without exception, clean shaven, whereas the Jewish elders retained their beards and long hair. Of course, it can be objected that medieval man could not be expected to know as much as we do concerning the styles and fashions of Romans at the time of Christ. However, it is noticeable that most of the figures in these carvings are clean shaven, whereas the hirsuteness of 'Pontius Pilate' seems to have been deliberately emphasised.

With 'the Veronica' carving, two aspects immediately stand out. The image of the person holding the cloth has been badly damaged. The head has been removed and it is impossible to know whether the image represents St Veronica, or even if it is female. Robert Bryden, the Templar archivist and one of the most knowledgeable of all Rosslyn researchers, has examined the chapel in detail for his book *Rosslyn – a History of the Guilds, the Masons and the Rosicrucians*.[12] He told me that he is convinced the damage in the chapel is 'very specific, not done by accident ... Someone has deliberately damaged parts of it for a reason.' This puts a new slant on the removal of the head of 'St Veronica'. Everyone assumes that the head of the person holding the towel is female; however, if the head was that of a man, this would change the meaning of the image utterly. Such musings are supported by a very solid piece of evidence. What is commonly shown in drawings of this carving as a two-dimensional image of Christ on the cloth, is in fact an incised bas-relief of Christ's head. This is an extremely odd representation. There seems to be no good reason for the depth of carving around the head; a two-dimensional image on the cloth would have been easier to execute and would certainly have represented the miraculous image of the Veronica far more accurately. As it stands, what the carving actually seems to show is an unidentified figure holding a cloth which contains a head of Jesus.

The crucifixion scene is just as problematical. Jesus is shown hanging from a tau cross, not the usual *crux immissa*, the intersecting cross of normal Christian iconography. Although one of the men by the cross *may* be holding a hammer (the image is too heavily eroded to be certain), there is no sign of nails. Moreover, the arms are held against the tau cross with bonds, wrapped around the horizontal beam of the cross and the arms of Jesus. In addition, Jesus is not held with his body off the ground; on the contrary, he appears to be actually standing with his feet on the earth. This, of course, would have completely negated the main purpose of any crucifixion, to cause a most painful death as the full weight of the victim's body hung from the nails that had been driven through his hands and feet. This image is ambiguous in the extreme: it may show a crucifixion but, equally, it corresponds closely to the Jewish practice of displaying the dead body of a man stoned to death for 'having seduced Israel and estranged them from God'.[13]

The final scene, of two 'angels' rolling away the stone of the sepulchre, also raises serious doubts. To begin with, the angels are possessed of no special distinguishing marks that reveal them as heavenly messengers. Because everyone knows (from Christian tradition) that angels rolled away the stone this interpretation has gained acceptance. In fact, the image portrays two men rolling away the stone. Are these two figures meant to represent Joseph of Arimathea and Nicodemus, or does the carving show the secret removal of Jesus' body by members of his entourage?

Although Christian interpreters organise the order of the carvings to correspond to the passion of Christ, these powerful images are scattered between the areas over the north and south aisles and are quite definitely not set out in any discernible order. Devout orthodox Christians see the carvings as telling first the story of Pilate, then the tale of the Veronica, which leads ineluctably to the crucifixion and so finally to the resurrection. However, it is perfectly possible to construct another chain of events, with a completely logical sequence, and one, it must be said, that is fully in accord with the evidence of the *Evangelicum Nicodemi*, and with the sequence of events given by Jewish writers in the Talmud and Mishnaic tracts (as reviewed in Chapter 10). In this scenario, the sequence would show:

Jesus before the bearded Jewish elders on a charge of seducing the Children of Israel away from orthodox Judaism (hand-washing to demonstrate innocence was an established Jewish tradition).[14]

The body of Jesus tied to a tau cross after death by stoning, his feet trailing on the ground.

Removal of the body from the tomb by two members of Jesus' entourage.

The sacred relic, the head of God, displayed after being removed and embalmed.

Given the discrepancies between the carvings at Rosslyn and the version of events as promulgated by orthodox Christianity, I am convinced that this explanation is far more likely to reveal the true intention behind these images, inscribed at the express command of Sir William Sinclair.

We must remember that we are talking about images carved when the power of the Catholic Church was enormously strong. Anyone commissioning unorthodox carvings ran the risk of torture and death. It is a similar situation to that of the poet writing a Grail romance or a troubadour composing a song which might contain forbidden teachings. In each case, the work had to be given a patina of Christian respectability which would permit the poem, song or carving to be heard, sung or displayed openly, and at the same time allow the underlying secret teaching to be made manifest to the *cognoscenti*.

It seems that Sir William Sinclair took a similar line to that of the troubadours and the Grail poets, using a variety of symbolism to hide his true intentions. The crucifixion scene was there in stone – it proved to the ecclesiastics of Sir William's day that Rosslyn and its builder were Christian. What did it matter if Jesus' feet trailed the ground, and that he was tied to the cross? Similarly, a figure holds the Veronica, a patently Christian icon; the fact that the head is rather too deeply incised for it to be a representation of marks on a cloth would probably have been explained away in medieval times as the result of an over-enthusiastic stone mason. But as we now know that each figure was scrupulously assessed by Sir William himself prior to carving, this explanation simply will not do. There was no leeway given to the artisans, no examples of a stone mason deciding to extemporise on his subject. Everything was carved exactly as Sir William demanded. It is no mistake that these strange discrepancies occur in the stone images. They are there for a purpose, and should not be ignored.

Nor is it an artistic accident that other characters from our story figure prominently in Rosslyn's decorations. Sampson (whose name, Man of the Sun, I have shown to be linked to the Sampsaei, the Nazarite subsect that followed a religion identical to that of Akhenaten) is shown on three occasions at Rosslyn in various guises such as rending the lion's jaw, and pulling down the Philistines' House of Dagon.

The Aten at Rosslyn

Sir William's chosen medium, stone, was probably the safest of all the several methods used by medieval adepts to transmit the mysteries. It allowed him to say more than anyone else, to intimate more clearly the secret teachings. He could afford to take some chances and, on at least one occasion, it seems that he did.

It was the recorded intention of Sir William Sinclair to build Rosslyn as a Grail chapel.[15] The Grail romances, as we have seen in Chapter 11, are redolent with non-Christian and heretical Christian symbolism – and replete with severed heads, the 'Grails' which I have identified as a 'cover name' for the sacred heads of Akhenaten's mystery religion. In particular, I believe that the 'head of the cousin' in the Grail romances refers specifically to that of Jesus. If my hypothesis is correct, and there was a secret associated with sacred heads (including that of Jesus), which devolved from the time of Akhenaten and his worship of the Aten as a sun disc, then we might hope to find an intimation of this in the images that cover Rosslyn Chapel. In fact, we find much more. I was astonished to discover that this association is written openly in stone on the westernmost part of the roof of the building.

Here, when facing south, one can see four images lying close together in the star-studded firmament that covers the roof. The first is, astonishingly for a Christian chapel, the symbol of the Aten, an image of the sun, its life-giving rays spreading from the central disc. The sun disc is placed in the top right corner, the highest point on the structure. Below this, unbelievably, is carved the head of Christ, long-haired and bearded, and beside the head is the *manus dei*, the hand of God. To the left and above is a dove carrying in its beak the host of the eucharist. This is a direct reference to the *Parzival* Grail romance, where the dove is said to bring the host and lay it upon the Grail.[16] Below the dove and the host, lest the Grail connection has not been made, Sir William has caused to be carved an actual Grail, out of which pours 'God's grace and bounty, seen as waves or flow'.[17] How much clearer can the message be? Apart from literally spelling out these connections openly in writing (which would of course have exposed Sir William to the accusation of heresy and his family to ruin), it is hard to see how the builder of Rosslyn could have made the connections any more plain. The Aten sun disc of Akhenaten, the head of Jesus, and the Grail are all specifically linked in this series of carvings, and set into the roof at Rosslyn Chapel.

The Cross of the Head of God

As if in confirmation, on my third visit to Rosslyn Chapel, in 1997, I happened upon an object that set my heart racing. It was at the back of the building, on one of the small stone shelves that function as altars for the 'chapels' along the east wall. And it was so strange that I had several photographs taken. The object was a crucifix, but unlike any other I had ever seen. There was the usual cross, made of dark wood, but the crucified body of Jesus was missing. Instead, on a light-coloured cruciform board set in the centre of the cross where the horizontal and vertical arms met, the bearded head of Jesus stared out into the chapel. Nothing more, just the head. The head of God on a crucifix.

I had to control my excitement at seeing this strange cross. Perhaps, I told myself, I was making too much of the image. I found it unusual, unique even, but did that really mean a great deal? It was true that I had never seen such a crucifix before, but I was certainly no expert on this particular aspect of Christian iconography. Nor could I claim to have visited the majority of British churches and places of worship, let alone those of Europe. It might be that the design was far more common than I supposed, and could be found in churches the world over. In which case I was perhaps overreacting. But if it was not a common image ... The subject cried out for additional research. I needed to find out more about the crucifix in general and this design in particular. Was the head of God crucifix unique?

I left my other researches and immediately began a study of the crucifix. What I discovered was that for the first three centuries after the birth of Christ, his followers had made no attempt to portray him on the cross. The cross was certainly used as a sacred sign, to an almost obsessive degree. In the second century AD, Tertullian, the Carthaginian theologian, wrote, 'In every undertaking, on coming in and going out, on dressing or washing, at the beginning of the lights, going to bed, on whatever occupation we are engaged, we imprint our foreheads with the sign of the cross.'[18] The cross as a sign was one thing, but to represent Jesus on the cross was quite another. As the most feared and terrible of all punishments, the small sect of the Christians would have been inviting persecution had they worn the sign of a crucified god as a sacred talisman. In the catacombs and underground chambers where the early Christians worshipped, there are early symbols of Jesus as the Lamb of God, as the Good Shepherd or as a fish or vine, but there are no representations of Jesus on the cross. Even the cross alone was a relatively rare motif during this early period of Christian evolution.

When, in the fourth century AD the Emperor Constantine decided that Christianity should be encouraged, much of this danger receded. A few years later, St Helena, the empress mother, 'fortuitously' discovered the remains of the true cross in the Holy Land. It was found in a pit close to the sepulchre of Jesus and, lest anyone should suggest that the relic was fake, the upright beam miraculously (and one might say conveniently), still had nailed to it the inscription, INRI, 'Jesus of Nazareth [or more properly, the Nazarite], King of the Jews'. Less than one hundred years after these two events, crosses had begun to be carried in Church processions, and during the reign of Justinian (527–65) it was decreed that every church built should have a cross at its highest point.[19] Later, the crusades gave a great impetus to the carrying and wearing of the sign of the cross.

The tradition that finally culminated in the crucifix proper began in the sixth century AD when Jesus as the Agnus Dei, the Lamb of God, was placed at the base of the cross with the five wounds of the Saviour represented on its body. Later, the lamb was placed at the centre of the cross, where the two beams intersect. It was but a short step from here to representing Jesus as a man upon the cross. This was formalised in AD 692 at the Council of Trullo, with a decree that stated, 'We order that, instead of the Lamb, our Lord Jesus Christ shall be shown hereafter in His human form in the images; so that, without forgetting the height from which the Divine Word stooped to us, we shall be led to remember His Mortal Life, His Passion, and His Death, which paid the ransom for mankind.'[20]

Following this the image of the crucifix flourished in greater and greater profusion and complexity. At first, no attempt at realism was made, and the image was starkly triumphalist, Jesus as *Christus victor*: Jesus stood in regal grandeur on a small platform on the cross, with arms outstretched along the horizontal beam, eyes open and staring straight ahead, fully robed and sometimes with a crown of kingship upon his head. Later, as Anselm of Canterbury preached his doctrine of atonement, elements of realism were introduced with Jesus portrayed as *Christus patens* (the patient Christ), a trend which culminated in the powerful and harrowing images of the late Middle Ages and the Renaissance where, as *Christus mortuus*, the Saviour is shown suffering death upon the cross in all his vulnerable humanity.[21]

However, despite the volumes and volumes of Christian iconography that I consulted, I could find no reference to a crucifix showing Christ's head alone. The closest I came was the discovery that early Irish crucifixes (from the 8th century AD) showed a figure of Christ which strongly emphasised the head, while still showing the rest of the body. The reason for this odd motif was worthy of note. Intriguingly, this stressing of Christ's head was said to derive from a surviving tradition of the ancient druidic cult of the head.[22] This was confirmation indeed. It demonstrated that for the druids and their descendants (and for other heirs of Akhenaten's mystery religion), Christ's head would have been of supreme importance.

As astonishing as this was, its significance could not compare with the fact that, try as I might, I could find no example of Jesus' head upon a cross. There is simply no tradition in Christian iconography that places Christ's disembodied head upon the cross at the intersection of the arms. The importance of this discovery dawned on me only slowly. The cross of the head of God was unique to Rosslyn. Here, in the chapel where I suspected the embalmed head of Jesus was hidden, was the world's only crucifix upon which Jesus was depicted as a disembodied head.

I found the whole thing so astounding that I spent long hours studying photographs of this crucifix. Three other aspects of the object seemed significant to me. The first concerned the image of the disembodied head itself. Christ was shown not with a crown of thorns, but with a cloth or leather headband round his head. Why had the artist (or the person who commissioned the artist) decided to omit this potent symbol of Christ's passion and death on the cross? Might it be to indicate that the story of the crucifixion did not occur exactly as it is portrayed in the Bible? The second attribute was both intriguing and suggestive. The crucifix was set on a stepped plinth, which mirrored the steps on the grave slab of the Templar Sir William Sinclair (and many others), and must, like them, symbolise the Temple of Solomon. And, as this 'chapel' had been built by a hereditary grand master of the Masons, and a descendant of a grand master of the Templars (who was almost certainly a covert Templar himself), the steps also linked the crucifix to the Order of the Temple itself. And there was confirmation of this in another aspect of the crucifix on which the head had been placed – the arms of the cross had been splayed in conscious emulation of the cross pattée of the Templars.

Soon afterwards, the link with the Order of the Temple was confirmed to me in a quite remarkable way. The Templar archivist Robert Bryden informed me that the image of a head on a cross was a specifically Templar symbol, used in their higher degrees of initiation.[23] He was able to obtain for me two pieces of Templar regalia – one showing the sun at the centre of a red cross, the other with a head similarly positioned. It is very telling that the head is said to represent Apollo – the sun god. So, placing Jesus' head in exactly the same position on the Rosslyn crucifix not only intimates the existence of the head of God in the chapel, it symbolises both Jesus' link with the Aten (whose symbol was the sun) and with the bloodline of the pharaoh, who was the offspring of the sun god.

I discovered another intriguing clue outside the chapel, at a grave in the southwest corner of the grounds, an imposing structure over three metres tall. It was the last resting place of the Fourth Earl of Rosslyn, who had specifically requested this site for his interment. This lord of Rosslyn was also a poet, and the choice of one of his poems for the gravestone contained two lines that set my pulses racing. In this couplet the earl said that he was:

> Safe, safe at last from doubt, from storm, from strife
> Moored in the depths of Christ's unfathomed grave

Christ's unfathomed grave? But according to orthodox Christian teaching, Christ had no grave. Unless of course, as the Gnostic Christians declared, the dogma of bodily resurrection was a myth, a worldly misrepresentation of a mystical truth, the reality of spiritual resurrection derived from Gnosis, union with God. In which case, the body of the holy teacher known as Christ would have to have remained on earth when he died, hidden in some unknown location. The earl's poem pointed to the existence of just such an unfathomed or unknown grave and asserted that he, the earl, was now 'moored' there. The body of the earl was quite certainly buried in the chapel grounds. The words of the poem had to mean that the bodily remains of Jesus were also here, that both Jesus and the earl had been interred beneath the earth of Rosslyn Chapel.

I was now more convinced than ever that the head of God was at Rosslyn. If the 'Grail' was anywhere, it would be here in this magnificent medieval chapel constructed under the instructions of a Templar master mason, in accordance with sacred geometry, to be a second Temple of Solomon. What more fitting place could there be for the sacred relic? But where within the fantastic cornucopia of carvings that comprised Rosslyn Chapel could the sacred relic lie hidden? The most obvious place was underground, especially as both tradition and recent research had pointed to the existence of numerous vaults and stone stairways beneath the chapel floor.

The Hidden Vaults

The crypts below Rosslyn, and the bodies they contain, have never really been secret. Slezer, writing in 1693, says the barons of Rosslyn 'lie in a vault so dry that their bodies have been found entire after four score years, and as fresh as when they were buried'.[24] Even the point of access to the vaults was known. In 1897 the Reverend John Thompson published a guide to Rosslyn, in which he states that the vaults are 'built of polished ashlar ... are divided into compartments and run east to west'. He also accurately identifies the point of access into the vaults, naming a large slab on the floor of the chapel near the north door that 'emits a hollow sound' when struck.[25] My studies had revealed that another researcher, a Sinclair himself, had recently been given unique permission to run a radar scan on the floor of the chapel. The scan vindicated the old legends and revealed numerous hidden vaults, of unknown depth. Radar reflections registering as metal (and stimulating thoughts of treasure in some minds) were found in several areas.[26] The radar scans also indicated the presence of two flights of steps beneath the floor of the chapel, leading to the vaults. Andrew Sinclair, who organised the work, was allowed to raise the stone slabs above the first set of hidden steps: '... and, indeed, three steep stone steps led to a vault below ... It was small, the space between the foundations of two pillars. It was arched with stone, but access to the main vaults beyond had been sealed by a thick wall of stone masonry, perfectly shaped beneath the arch'. The second stairway (found exactly where the Reverend Thompson had described it in 1897) was far deeper and filled with sand and earth. For some reason the excavation was discontinued at this point, and instead an attempt was made to drill through the roof of the vault from the surface, the intention being to lower an endoscope with a fibre optic lead, and to film the interior of the vault remotely. Unfortunately, this proved impossible and the research was abandoned. The vaults of Rosslyn still hold their secrets, and their contents remain unknown.

Despite the disappointingly slim results of this research, it had established beyond doubt the existence of underground vaults. It was obvious that Sir William had not only conceived Rosslyn Chapel as a very well thought out edifice above ground – the structure below ground was quite as important and he had lavished just as much attention on this aspect of the building. There was no doubt that there were ample places beneath the chapel where the head of God, and much else besides, could safely be hidden away.

But interesting though this undoubtedly was, it did not really advance matters very much. In fact in one sense it made things worse. I would have been happier with just a single vault, a place where 'X' marked the spot, one area where I could have concentrated my energies. Instead, like everything else at Rosslyn, we had a superabundance of vaults, and apparently no way of determining which one might hold the relic. It would hardly excite the confidence of the trustees of Rosslyn Chapel to inform them that the embalmed head of Jesus lay below their chapel floor but, unfortunately, its exact location was unknown. One can hardly dig up the whole of the chapel in the hope of stumbling upon the relic. And besides, at the back of my mind there was the sneaking suspicion that Sir William Sinclair would not have made the task of finding the holy of holies so easy. If there were so many vaults, the possibility of an eventual chance discovery of one of them was high; in which case, there was a high degree of probability that a search would be carried out and that the remaining vaults would soon be discovered and broken into. I could not believe that a family as subtle and shrewd as Sir William and his ancestors would have been so transparent. They would not have gone to so much trouble to maintain the occult nature of the relic over the centuries, and then have deposited it in so obvious a 'secret hiding place'. I was convinced that I was overlooking something. And knowing the meticulous temperament of Sir William Sinclair, and his love of symbols and riddles, I felt sure that he would have left a clue. There had to be something above ground in the chapel, well hidden and no doubt difficult to decipher, some arcane sign or pointer that would irrevocably mark the location of this, the most sacred of all Christian relics.

There was, and the key was provided by a remarkable piece of serendipity (or perhaps synchronicity), a chance remark that gave me the final clue to the last resting place of the head of God.

19

The Final Clue

While I was sure that the head of God was somewhere in or under Rosslyn Chapel, I had as yet no idea of the exact location of the sacred relic. But I felt certain that the erudite and inventive genius of its architect, Sir William Sinclair, could not resist leaving a clue as to its hiding place. Sir William delighted in symbol and allegory; the solution to the puzzle had to lie in the carvings that adorned the wall of this second Temple of Solomon.

But that got me precisely nowhere. The place was quite literally covered with carvings, each one with symbolic and mythological allusions. To follow the labyrinthine symbolism incorporated in just one figure might take weeks; to attempt to research the meaning of each and every carving would be a labour of several lifetimes. Nor was I confident that a chance find might bring about a breakthrough. Looking at the walls and ceilings of Rosslyn Chapel I was reminded of the strategy used by herd animals to escape predators such as lions. In a large herd there are so many choices that the lion, instead of making for a single beast, becomes confused by the multiplicity of opportunities around him and, spoilt for choice, makes half-hearted attempts at several beasts, never catching a single animal. I felt a grudging respect for the old Templar: Sir William had filled his 'chapel' with so many figures that one became confused, hopping this way and that but never being able to settle for long on one object or to decide which was most important. Defeated by the plenitude of figures that seemed to leap from the walls and ceilings, I had no hope that I would be fortunate enough to pick the single clue from among so many figures simply by chance. Where was the answer to the riddle? *Was* there an answer?

It was while I was sitting quietly on a rough wooden bench near the east of the chapel that I was given the clue I needed, and from a most unlikely source. I was staring aimlessly about, hoping for inspiration, when a group of tourists trudged in, wrapped up warmly against the bitter spring weather. A short, sprightly man in his fifties was at the head of the group, his face all but covered by a huge scarf. 'The Apprentice Pillar's next', he said in a loud Liverpudlian voice, peering round earnestly. 'It's one of the eastern columns, but which one is it?'

'*Which one is it?*' His words struck home like a thunderbolt! I had said the same thing when I first visited the chapel, and during the many days I had spent in the place I must have heard that or similar phrases, on numerous occasions. The Apprentice Pillar is one of the glories of Rosslyn Chapel. It is a 'must see' for anyone visiting the chapel, and in fact Rosslyn is 'marketed' on the tourist circuit as being 'home to the world famous Apprentice Pillar'. And yet: '*Which one is it?*' It suddenly became clear to me that, at first sight, most people cannot see any unique artistic merit in the 'world famous' column that would justify setting it apart from the other columns in the eastern row. And I believed I knew why. If a stranger was somehow dropped into Rosslyn Chapel without ever seeing or reading any of the propaganda about the Apprentice Pillar, he would see the column for what it really is. Shorn of our preconceptions, the Apprentice Pillar is, on the surface, just another column holding up the chapel's roof, slightly more ornate perhaps, but certainly no more so than the northeast column, the Master's Pillar. The arguments that legitimise this particular column as 'special' do not really hold up. The Apprentice Pillar is important because tradition says it is, not for any intrinsic superiority in its structure or design.

And yet the man who built Rosslyn Chapel did want us to believe that the Apprentice Pillar was, in some occult fashion, very special. The pillar depicts an apprentice mason murdered by his master in a fit of jealous rage; but the story is so obviously false that one can only conclude that it has been deliberately fabricated in order to give the pillar a degree of notoriety and make it stand out from the others. It is the choice of this particular story that points the way towards the true, hidden reason for the pillar's importance.

Hiram in Disguise

The story goes that, during the building of the chapel, the master mason had, according to Sir William's instruction, completed the column that lies in the northeast corner of the building, and is known now as the

Master Mason's Pillar. Sir William then revealed the style that was to be carved for the southeast column. The master, studying the model, decided for some reason that its completion would require him to go to Europe to study and become more proficient in his art (some versions say to study the 'original pillar'), before he attempted this piece of sculpture. Sir William gave him leave, and the master duly departed for the continent.

While he was away, the master's own apprentice had a dream in which he saw himself carving and completing the southeast column. On awakening, he rushed to Sir William Sinclair and pleaded with him for the opportunity to do all the work on this particular pillar. Whether it was because of the dream, or simply because Sir William was by then past fifty and eager to finish his masterpiece, we do not know, but permission was granted and the apprentice set to work. Several months later the master returned to Rosslyn from Europe, to discover that the column had been completed in his absence, finished with a degree of subtlety and skill that he could not hope to match and, adding insult to injury, it had been carved by his own apprentice. Driven to fury by pride and jealousy, he seized a mallet and struck the young man such a blow to his forehead that he died. And since that day, it is said, the column that was the cause of this tragic murder has been called the Apprentice Pillar.

The story, with its account of the twin pillars and murder within a holy place by a blow, struck with a maul, to the head of the victim is quite obviously an (intentionally) garbled account of the Hiram Abif legend. Indeed, the *Encyclopaedia of Freemasonry* concurs with this assessment, stating that, 'There can be little doubt that this legend referred to that of the Third Degree [that is to the death of Hiram Abif by the three conspirators].'[1] And as if to silence further doubt, in the southwest corner of Rosslyn Chapel, tucked beneath a plinth, the face of the Apprentice-Hiram looks out, complete with the head wound which is identical in both legends.

If, as seems certain, the Apprentice story is a concealed attempt to connect the Apprentice Pillar with Hiram Abif, some very interesting conclusions follow. As we saw in Chapter 8, the Hiram Abif legend is itself a cover story, a legend that carries within it other information, secret knowledge that points to an occult tradition concerning Akhenaten's Aten religion and (from the story of Hiram Abif's burial with head removed) to the cult of the severed head. So, by using the story of the Apprentice Pillar, someone is both drawing attention to this one pillar among the fourteen that exist in the chapel, and connecting it to the cult of the severed head.

There can be no other explanation: the pillar and the severed head are linked in some way. And there is a second connection. As both Hiram Abif and Jesus are known under the appellation Son of the Widow, it seems reasonable to assume that the pillar is also linked to Jesus.

Robert Bryden, whom I was fortunate to meet, was again able to offer confirmation of this identification.[2] He told me that the face of the Apprentice is not what it seems to be. An American Templar, on a visit to Rosslyn, had examined the face of the 'Apprentice' in detail. The carving has been very carefully altered: it originally possessed a beard and moustache, but these have been painstakingly removed (I was able to confirm this myself later, with the aid of high-power binoculars). This was a highly significant discovery. In medieval times an apprentice stone mason was not allowed to sport a full beard and moustache. Facial hair was reserved for those who had completed their initiation into the mysteries of the craft. In other words, the head on the plinth at Rosslyn was not the head of the Apprentice, but the head of the Master. And according to the New Testament, 'Master' is the name often used by the disciples for Jesus. With mixed emotions, I sensed I was finally close to understanding the meaning of the Rosslyn column, that I was at last getting very, very close to the end of my search. Could it be that the Apprentice Pillar in some way marked the site of the head of God?

It was at this point in my research that I stumbled across a second legend connected with the Apprentice Pillar. In Chapter 10 I conclude that the Grail was a cover name for a sacred embalmed head. Sir William Sinclair had constructed Rosslyn as a Grail chapel. I now discovered that another tale told of the location of the Grail at Rosslyn – it was said to lie deep within the Apprentice Pillar. This story was believed by the writers Trevor Ravenscroft and Walter Johannes Stein.[3] Ravenscroft was so convinced of the truth of this story he requested permission from the Earl of Rosslyn to conduct a radar scan of the pillar. When the earl declined to allow such a survey, Ravenscroft's wife protested this refusal by fastening herself to the column with chains. As we have seen, the earl eventually relented and allowed one of his own clan members, the writer and author Andrew Sinclair, to conduct a radar scan of both the chapel floor and the Apprentice Pillar. The results were, unfortunately, disappointing in the extreme. Unlike the many vaults, steps and metal 'reflections' discovered under Rosslyn Chapel, a detailed scan of the Apprentice Pillar failed to find any indication of a hidden cavity within the column holding a Grail or anything else.

However, perhaps the legend that the column hid the Grail meant something other than that the Grail was inside the column. Given that all the other secret hiding places in Rosslyn are below ground, it seemed to me that the meaning of the legend was that the Grail, the head of God, was underneath the pillar.

There are two compelling reasons for believing this. At the top of the Apprentice Pillar is a carving, with the central section broken off but, despite the vandalism, its meaning is clear enough. There is a young man lying by an altar and, a little way off, a ram with its horns trapped in a bush. The central figure is now unrecognisable but, according to Bishop Forbes, who saw the carving complete in 1774, there was a man standing with arms raised as if praying to God.[4] The stonework quite certainly represents the biblical story of Abraham's attempted sacrifice of Isaac, in which God intervened at the last moment, and for which, as a substitute for Isaac, God provided the ram entangled in the bush. It took a while for the import of this carving to sink in. Here, at the top of the column, below which I believed lay the embalmed head of Jesus, was a representation of the beginning of the whole story: that Abraham had wished to immolate Isaac because he was not his own natural son, but the son of the pharoah, Tutmosis III, to whom Abraham's wife, Sarah, had for a time been big-amously married. I remembered Robert Bryden's words, that the damage to Rosslyn's carvings is 'very specific, not done by accident ... Someone has deliberately damaged parts of it for a reason.' Might, I wondered, the central figure in the Isaac-ram tableau have been someone other than Abraham? Or was there perhaps a clue on the figure of Abraham which pointed to an Egyptian origin?

As we have seen, it was Isaac's descendants, including Joseph and Moses (as Akhenaten) who continued to carry the pharaoh's bloodline, a line that had culminated in Jesus ben Pandera, Jesus Son of Ra who was indeed of the line of David and a rightful king. Whether or not the damaged 'Abraham' figure had carried an esoteric clue, I was utterly astonished to find this story indicated in stone at the top of the very pillar I had identified as hiding the embalmed head of Jesus ben Pandera, Jesus the Christ. If the head of God was under the base of the Apprentice Pillar, then the symbolism was perfect. The top of the column represented the beginning of the story (Abraham, and his 'foster-son' Isaac descended from pharaoh), and the base its culmination (Jesus and his bloodline descended from the same pharaoh).

In addition to this unique carving, there was a whole constellation of symbolism connected with the Apprentice Pillar that linked the column with Jesus. As mentioned above, it is one of the two pillars of freemasonry,

Jachin and Boaz, with its story of Hiram Abif. But this enigmatic column is also something else – according to the official guide to Rosslyn Chapel, the pillar, with its carved leafy spirals encircling the column, represents the Tree of Life.[5] This was extremely telling: the Tree of Life being an acknowledged synonym for Christ; it was no less a person than St Augustine who had identified Jesus in exactly those terms. This led me to an inevitable conclusion: Christian iconography depicts Jesus as the Tree of Life, and the Apprentice Pillar is also said to symbolise the same motif. It follows, then, that the Apprentice Pillar is, or in some way represents, Jesus.

The author Andrew Sinclair has uncovered a further level of symbolism. He has shown that Sir William Sinclair alluded to his Viking ancestry by having the pillar carved as the Tree of Life of Norse mythology, as Yggdrasil, the World Ash.[6] The present Earl of Rosslyn has confirmed this association.[7] It was upon the World Ash that Odin, in a remarkable parallel to the story of Jesus' crucifixion, hung for nine days as a voluntary sacrifice. As an old poem says:

> For nine nights, wounded by my own spear, consecrated to Odin, myself consecrated to myself, I remained hanging from the tree shaken by the wind, from the mighty tree whose roots men know not.[8]

The Final Clue

It was to be something dwelling in these roots 'that men know not' that was to provide a final, even more compelling reason for believing that the Apprentice Pillar marked the location of the head of God. Around the base of the column coils a motif of eight serpents. With the Apprentice Pillar in its guise as one of the two pillars of the Temple of Solomon, Jachin and Boaz, this snake motif may stand for the Shamir, the rock-splitting serpent of Jewish myth that helped King Solomon to build his House of God without the use of iron to work the stones used in its construction. But if the Apprentice Pillar is regarded as the World Ash, Yggdrasil, the creature on the column becomes the Nordic serpent, Nidhögg. Even more than the Shamir, this is a curious device for any Christian chapel and, oddly, it is neither Celtic, nor Judaic, nor masonic, nor Templar in origin. In fact, as far as I could tell from an exhaustive study of the chapel's carvings, these serpents are the only motif of Nordic origin in the whole fantastic edifice (apart, of course, from the pillar itself). It seemed obvious to me that old Sir William had placed this bizarre symbol here for a reason. He had after all designed and supervised every carving himself; nothing in the chapel had been left to whimsy or chance. In Norse mythology the serpent Nidhögg lived beneath the great World Ash, Yggdrasil, ceaselessly gnawing at its roots. So, by using this incongruous symbol, Sir William Sinclair was once again drawing attention to the tree-like Apprentice Pillar as different from the other thirteen columns, and he was signifying its occult identity as the World Ash. He was also indicating that the important region of Yggdrasil, as far as he was concerned, was the place where Nidhögg dwelt, in the tree's roots. But why, I wondered, was this important?

Obviously, Sir William Sinclair was pointing to an object below ground, in the earth, which confirmed my belief that the 'Grail' was hidden not inside, but under the Apprentice Pillar. However, there was another reason for indicating the roots of the World Ash, and for using the Nordic serpent as a symbol. Apart from the serpent Nidhögg, there was something else that dwelt underground, among the roots of Yggdrasil, something that indicated the identity of the Grail with almost unbelievable clarity and precision – the head of Mimir.

Mimir is another character from Norse mythology, and he lived in such close communion with the Norse gods that he was often regarded by the Nordic peoples as a god himself.[9] According to their mythology, Mimir was decapitated in battle while helping the gods against their enemies. When Mimir's fate was reported to him, Odin, king of the gods, had the head embalmed, and it became his most sacred relic, for it continued to talk and prophesy. This discovery so convincingly confirmed my theory that for a moment I felt I was dreaming. Below ground, with Nidhögg, was the embalmed head of a man who was regarded as a god. The parallels with the Gnostic concept of Jesus as a man whom the Roman Church mistakenly regarded as a god were uncannily strong.

This was astonishing enough, but when I looked up the myth of Mimir I discovered another stunning correspondence. Mimir's head was famed for its sagacity, and it was used by Odin as his most trusted counsellor to speed his plans and protect him from the wiles of his enemies, just as the head of the Templars was said to 'save them' and 'make them rich'. But it was another comment on Mimir that proved almost too much for me – unbelievably, Mimir's embalmed head was known as the 'Father of Wisdom'. This phrase set my head spinning – it was almost too much of a coincidence. I had seen this term before, and in only one context: the trial of the Templars. The severed head the Templars worshipped, the embalmed head of Jesus, was also given the title Father of Wisdom (Baphomet – *bufihimat* in the dialect of the Moors).[10]

It was the final confirmation. Standing in Rosslyn Chapel the day after my discovery, I stared at the base of the Apprentice Pillar with a dazed feeling of awe and reverence. I was certain now that the 'Grail' was in the Grail chapel, hidden beneath its pillar. The chapel was busy that day. Visitors walked the aisles, stopping to gaze vacantly at the carvings on the Apprentice Pillar, before moving away with that aimless, half-bored gait of tourists the world over. And beneath them, the embalmed head of Jesus lay hidden in its secret vault. I had finally accomplished what I had set out to achieve, to discover the location and the identity of the Baphomet, to know the name of the Father of Wisdom. The dead Templar's message, carved in stone and calling out across the centuries, could not have been clearer: *'Here, beneath this column, lies the Head of a God.'*

Appendix I *Articles of Accusation*

12 August, 1308

These are the articles on which enquiry should be made against the Order of the Knighthood of the Temple.

Firstly, that although they declared that the Order had been solemnly established and approved by the Apostolic See, nevertheless in the reception of the brothers of the said Order, and at some time after, there were preserved and performed by the brothers those things which follow:

Namely that each in his reception, or at some time after, or as soon as a fit occasion could be found for the reception, denied Christ, sometimes Christ crucified, sometimes Jesus, and sometimes God, and sometimes the Holy Virgin, and sometimes all the saints of God, led and advised by those who received him – Item, [that] the brothers as a whole did this. – Item, that the majority [of them did this].
Item, that [they did this] also sometimes after the reception.
Item, that the receptors said and taught those whom they were receiving, that Christ, or sometimes Jesus, or sometimes Christ crucified, is not the true God.
Item, that they told those whom they received that he was a false prophet.
Item, that he had not suffered nor was he crucified for the redemption of the human race, but on account of his sins.
Item, that neither the receptors nor those being received had a hope of achieving salvation through Jesus, and they said this, or the equivalent or similar, to those whom they received.
Item, that they made those whom they received spit on a cross, or on a

representation or sculpture of the cross and an image of Christ, although sometimes those who were being received spat next [to it].

Item, that they sometimes ordered that this cross be trampled underfoot.

Item, that brothers who had been received sometimes trampled on the cross.

Item, that sometimes they urinated and trampled, and caused others to urinate, on this cross, and several times they did this on Good Friday.

Item, that some of them, on that same day or on another of Holy Week, were accustomed to assemble for the aforesaid trampling and urination.

Item, that they adored a certain cat, [which] sometimes appeared to them in their assembly.

Item, that they did this in contempt of Christ and the orthodox faith.

Item, that they did not believe in the sacrament of the altar. – Item, that some of them [did not believe]. – Item, that the majority [of them did not believe].

Item, that nor [did they believe] in the other sacraments of the Church.

Item, that the priests of the Order by whom the body of Christ is consecrated did not speak the words in the canon of the mass. – Item, that some of them [did not]. – Item, that the majority [did not].

Item, that the receptors enjoined this upon them.

Item, that they believed, and thus it was told to them, that the Grand Master could absolve them from sin. – Item, that the Visitor [could]. – Item, that the preceptors [could], of whom many were laymen.

Item, that they did this *de facto*. – Item, that some of them [did].

Item, that the Grand Master of the aforesaid Order confessed this, in the presence of important persons, before he was arrested.

Item, that in the reception of the brothers of the said Order or at about that time, sometimes the receptor and sometimes the received were kissed on the mouth, on the navel, or on the bare stomach, and on the buttocks or the base of the spine. – Item, [that they were kissed] sometimes on the navel. – Item, [that they were kissed] sometimes on the base of the spine. – Item, [that they were kissed] sometimes on the penis.

Item, that in that reception they made those who were being received swear that they would not leave the Order.

Item, that they regarded them straightway as professed brethren.

Item, that they held these receptions secretly.

Item, that there was no one present except the brothers of the said Order.

Item, that on account of this vehement suspicion had, for a long time, worked against the said Order.

Item, that it was generally held.

Item, that they told the brothers whom they received that they could have carnal relations together.

Item, that it was licit for them to do this.

Item, that they ought to do and submit to this mutually.

Item, that it was not a sin for them to do this.

Item, that they did this, or many of them [did]. – Item, that some of them [did].

Item, that in each province they had idols, namely heads, of which some had three faces, and some one, and others had a human skull.

Item, that they adored these idols, or that idol, and especially in their great chapters and assemblies.

Item, that they venerated [them].

Item, that [they venerated them] as God.

Item, that [they venerated them] as their Saviour.

Item, that some of them [did].

Item, that the majority of those that were in the chapters [did].

Item, that they said the head could save them.

Item, that [it could] make riches.

Item, that it gave them all the riches of the Order.

Item, that it made the trees flower.

Item, that [it made] the land germinate.

Item, that they surrounded or touched each head of the aforesaid idols with small cords, which they wore around themselves next to the shirt or the flesh.

Item, that in his reception, the aforesaid small cords or some lengths of them were given to each of the brothers.

Item, that they did this in veneration of an idol.

Item, that it was enjoined on them that they should wear the small cords around themselves, as is set out, and wear them continually, and they did this even by night.

Item, that the brothers of the said Order were generally received in the aforesaid manner.

Item, that [it was done] everywhere.

Item, that [it was done] by the majority.

Item, that those who were not willing to do the aforesaid at their reception or afterwards were killed or imprisoned.

Item, that some of them [were].

Item, that the majority [were].

Item, that they enjoined them, on oath, that they should not reveal the aforesaid.

Item, that [this was done] under punishment of death, or of imprisonment.

Item, that nor should they reveal the manner of reception.

Item, that neither should they dare speak about the aforesaid among themselves.

Item, that if they were found to have revealed [these things], they were punished by death or prison.

Item, that they enjoined them not to confess to anyone except a brother of their Order.

Item, that the said brothers of the Order, knowing the said errors, neglected to correct them.

Item, that they neglected to inform Holy Mother Church.

Item, that they did not retreat from the observance of the aforesaid errors and the community of the aforesaid brothers, although they had the opportunity for retreating and for doing the aforesaid.

Item, that the aforesaid things were done and preserved beyond the sea, in places in which the Grand Master and chapter of the said Order were at the time staying.

Item, that sometimes the aforesaid denial of Christ was done in the presence of the Grand Master and the chapter of the aforesaid.

Item, that the aforesaid things were done and observed in Cyprus.

Item, that [they were done] on this side of the sea in all kingdoms and in other places in which receptions of the aforesaid brothers were made.

Item, that the aforesaid things were observed in the whole Order generally and communally. – Item, that [they were] of long and general observance. – Item, that [they were] of ancient custom. – Item, that [they were] from the statute of the aforesaid Order.

Item, that the aforesaid observances, customs, ordinances and statutes were made and observed in the whole order, beyond the sea and on this side of the sea.

Item, that the aforesaid were from points of the Order, having been introduced by their errors after the approval of the Apostolic See.

Item, that the receptions of the brothers of the said Order were made generally in the aforesaid manner in the whole Order aforesaid.

Item, that the Grand Master of the said Order enjoined that the aforesaid be thus observed and done. – Item, that the Visitors [did]. – Item, that the preceptors [did]. – Item, that other leaders of the said Order did.

Item, that these self-same men observed this, and taught that it be done and preserved.

284

Item, that others of them [did].

Item, that the brothers did not preserve another mode of reception in the said Order.

Item, that it is not within the memory of anyone of the Order who is living that there has been observed in their time another mode [of reception].

Item, that the Grand Master, the Visitors, the preceptors and the other Masters of the said Order, having power in this, punished gravely [those] not preserving nor willing to preserve the aforesaid manner of reception and the other things above, when a complaint was brought to them.

Item, that charitable gifts in the said Order were not made as they ought, nor was hospitality offered.

Item, that they did not reckon [it] a sin in the said Order to acquire properties belonging to another by legal or illegal means.

Item, that it was authorised by them that they should procure increase and profit to the said Order in whatever way they could by legal or illegal means.

Item, that it was not reckoned a sin to commit perjury on this account.

Item, that they were accustomed to hold their chapters in secret.

Item, that [they were held] secretly, either at the first sleep or in the first vigil of the night.

Item, that [they were held] secretly, since all the other *familia* of the house had been sent out and the house had been closed, as they sent out all the *familia* on those nights when they held chapters.

Item, that [they were held] secretly, because in this way they shut themselves up when a chapter was held, as all the doors of the house and church in which they were holding the chapter they fortified so firmly that no one might nor could gain access to them or near them, nor could anyone see or hear what they were doing or saying.

Item, that [they were held] so secretly that they were accustomed to place a guard on the roof of the house or church in which they were holding the chapter, in case anyone approached the place in which they were holding the chapter.

Item, that they observed and were accustomed to observe similar secrecy, as was usual in the receiving of brothers.

Item, that this error flourishes and has flourished in the Order for a long time, since they hold the opinion, and held in the past, that the Grand Master can absolve the brothers from their sins.

Item, that the greater error flourishes and has flourished, that these hold and have held in the past that the Grand Master can absolve the brothers of the Order from sin, even [sins] not confessed which they omitted to confess on account of some shame or fear of the penance to be enjoined or inflicted.

Item, that the Grand Master has confessed these aforesaid errors before capture, spontaneously, in the presence of ecclesiastics and laymen dignified in the faith.

Item, that the majority of the preceptors of the Order were present.

Item, that they hold and have held the aforesaid errors, not only through the opinions and beliefs of the Grand Master, but from other preceptors and especially from leading Visitors of the Order.

Item, that whatever the Grand Master, especially with his chapter, made, ordained and legislated, the whole Order had to hold and to observe and also was observed.

Item, that this power appertained to him and has resided in him from of old.

Item, that the aforesaid depraved habits and errors had lasted for such a time that the Order could have been renewed in personnel once, twice or more from the time of the introduction or observation of the aforesaid errors.

Item, that ... all or two-thirds of the Order, knowing the said errors, neglected to correct them.

Item, that they neglected to inform Holy Mother Church.

Item, that they did not retreat from the observance of the aforesaid errors and from the community of the said brothers, although they had the opportunity to retreat and do the aforesaid.

Item, that many brothers of the said Order, because of the filth and errors of their Order, departed, some transferring to another Order and others remaining in secular life.

Item, that on account of each of the aforesaid, great scandals have arisen against the said Order in the hearts of elevated persons, even of kings and princes, and have been generated in almost the whole of the Christian population.

Item, that all and each of the aforesaid have been observed and manifest among the brothers of the said Order.

Item, that concerning these things there is public talk, general opinion and repute both among the brothers of the Order and outside. – Item, that [there is] concerning the majority of the aforesaid. – Item, that [there is] concerning others.

Item, that the Grand Master of the Order, the Visitor and the Grand Preceptors of Cyprus, Normandy and Poitou, as well as many other preceptors and some other brothers of the said Order, have confessed what is written above, both in judicial enquiry and outside, in the presence of appointed persons and also before public persons in many places.

Item, that some brothers of the said Order, knights as well as priests, also others, in the presence of our lord pope and of the lords cardinal, have confessed the aforesaid or a great part of the said errors.

Item, that [they have confessed] through the swearing of oaths by them.

Item, that also they have certified the aforesaid in full consistory.

J. Michelet, *Proces des Templiers*, I, pp. 89–96.

Appendix II *The 'Lobineau Document'*

ONE DAY THE DESCENDANTS OF BENJAMIN LEFT THEIR COUNTRY, SOME REMAINED, TWO THOUSAND YEARS LATER GODFREY VI BECAME KING OF JERUSALEM AND FOUNDED THE ORDER OF SION – From this wonderful story which adorns history, in the same way that the architecture of a temple whose pinnacle is lost in the immensity of space and time, of which POUSSIN wished to declare the mystery in his two pictures, the 'Shepherds of Arcadia', there is without doubt the secret of the treasure before which the descendants, countryfolk and shepherds, of the proud Sicambrian Franks reflect on *'et in Arcadia ego'*, the [hexagram appears here] and King *'Midas'*. Before 1200 BC, an important event is the arrival of the Hebrews in the Promised Land and their tardy installation in Caanan. In the Bible, Deuteronomy 33: it is said of BENJAMIN: This is the beloved one of the Eternal, he shall dwell in security by him, the Eternal shall shelter him always, and reside between his shoulders. • It is moreover stated in Joshua 18 that the lot given as inheritance to the sons of BENJAMIN included among the fourteen towns and their villages: JEBUSI, these days JERUSALEM with its three points of a triangle: GOLGOTHA, SION and BETHANY. • And finally it is written in Judges 20 and 21: 'Not one of us shall give his daughter as wife to a Benjamite – O Eternal, God of Israel, why has this occurred in Israel for one tribe to be missing today in Israel.' From the great enigma of Arcadia VERGIL who was in the secret of the gods, lifted the veil in the Pastorals X – 46/50: 'You far from your homeland (let me not believe such). Without me, you gaze upon the snow-clad Alps and the frosty Rhine. May you not be injured by frostbite! May the soles of your delicate feet not be cut by sharp ice!' [hexagram appears here] SIX DOORS or the seal of Destiny, here are the secrets of the parchments of the Reverend

Saunière, priest of Rennes-le-Château, and which before him the great initiate POUSSIN knew when he realised his work to the order of the POPE, the inscription on the tomb is the same.

Notes

NB for clarity and ease of reference all biblical and talmudic references appear in the text.

1: The True Nature of the Templar Treasure
1. Lizerand, G., 'Le Dossier de l'affaire des Templiers', (1923), p.15ff.
2. *La Regle du Temple* (1886).
3. Barber, M., *The Trial of the Templars* (1978), p.12.
4. William of Tyre, *A History of Deeds Done Beyond the Sea* (1943).
5. Ben Dov, M., *In the Shadow of the Temple* (1985).
6. This connection is made implicitly in the Grail romance *Perlesvaus*, and overtly in von Eschenbach's Grail story, *Parzifal*.
7. See Appendix I.
8. Finke H., *Papsttum und Untergang des Templerordens* II, p.386.
9. Oursel, R., *Le Proces des Templiers* (1959), p.208.
10. I assumed: (i) that the hypothetical tradition had continued unbroken in one form or other; (ii) that embalming of the head had occurred throughout; and (iii) that on average, two persons 'worthy' of the embalming ceremony had arisen each century. This gave me a time span of (very roughly) 2900 years. Working back from 1307 gives a date of 1593 BC. The time of the establishment of the Eighteenth Dynasty in Egypt, the era of Moses and the Exodus, and (it later turned out), other major characters in the early part of our story.

2: Moses the Pharaoh
1. Freud, S., *Moses and Monotheism* (1937).
2. See also William Stein on 'mystical beheading': 'Waking man is beheaded to bring about supersensible experience. In waking the etheric body, which permeates the organism with life, is beheaded'. Ritual beheading could

therefore symbolise the achievement of a high level of spirituality during the lifetime of the person whose head is removed. Stein, W., *The Death of Merlin* (1990), p.157.

3. White, J. E. M., *Ancient Egypt* (1970), p.15.

4. Osman, A., *Moses, Pharaoh of Egypt* (1991). See also Ranke, H., (1902).

5. Freud, *Moses and Monotheism*. 1937.

6. See, for example: Graves, 1948 and 1986, and the New Larousse *Encyclopaedia of Mythology* (1984), p.173.

7. Herodotus, *The Histories* (1954).

8. Jordan, P., *Egypt the Black Land* (1976).

9. Osman, A., *Moses, Pharaoh of Egypt* (1991).

10. New Larousse *Encyclopaedia of Mythology* (1984), p.48.

11. Redford, D. B., *Akhenaten, the Heretic King* (1984).

12. van Seters, J., *The Hyksos* (1966).

13. Devi, S., *Son of the Sun* (1981), p.40ff.

14. Petrie, F., *A History of Egypt*, II, 215–18 (1899).

15. Barton, G. A., *Semitic and Hamitic Origins* (1934).

16. Özbeck, M., *Anatolica*, XV, 127–32. 1988.

17. See, for example: Kenyon, K., *Digging Up Jericho* (1957). Yakar and Hershkovitz, 'Atiquot, 18, 59–63 (1988). Rollefson, G., Simmons, A. H. and Kafafi, Z., *Journal of Field Archaeology*, 19 (1992).

18. Ferembach, D., *L'Anthropologie*, 74, 247–54 (1970).

19. Kenyon, K., *Archaeology in the Holy Land* (1970).

20. Cauvin, J., *Religions Néolithiques de Syro-Palestine* (1972).

21. Aldred, C., *Akhenaten* (1968).

22. Osman, A., *Moses Pharaoh of Egypt* (1991), p.130.

23. Redford, D. B., *Akhenaten, the Heretic King* (1984).

24. Carter, H., *The Tomb of Tutankhamun* (1933).

25. Abdalla, A. B. and Harrison, R. G., *Antiquity*, 46, 9 (1972).

26. Carter, H. and Mace, A. C., *The Tomb of Tutankhamun* (1923), Vol. 1, pp.x–xi.

27. Gardiner, A. H., *Journal of Egyptian Archaeology*, 24 (1938).

28. Reford, D. B., *Akhenaten, the Heretic King* (1984).

29. Osman, A., *Moses Pharaoh of Egypt* (1991).

30. Josephus, F., *Works* (1926).

31. van Seters, J., *The Hyksos* (1966).

32. Manetho's writings are now lost, and can be reconstructed only from references by other authors to his works.

33. Osman, A., *Moses, Pharaoh of Egypt* (1970).

34. Hamza, M., *Annales du Service des Antiquities de l'Égypte*, 40 (1940).

35. Pendlebury, J., *Annales du Service des Antiquities de l'Égypte*, 3 (1931).

36. Gunn, B., *The City of Akhenaten* (1923).

37. Seele, K. C., *Journal of Near Eastern Studies*, 14, 168–180 (1955).

38. Fairman, H. W., *Journal of Egyptian Archaeology*, 46 (1960).

39. Gunn, B., *The City of Akhenaten*. (1923).

40. Redford, D. B., *Journal of Near Eastern Studies*, 25 (1966).

41. Derry, D. E., *Annales du Service des Antiqités de l'Égypte*, 3 (1931).

42. Osman, A., *Moses Pharaoh of Egypt*. (1991).

43. Helck, W., *Untersuchungen zu Manetho und den ägyptischen Koniglisten* (1956).

44. Polano, H., *Selections from the Talmud* (1894), p.132.

45. Osman, A., *Moses Pharaoh of Egypt* (1991), p.171–2.

46. Petrie, W. M. F., *Researches in Sinai* (1906). Sir Flinders Petrie was one of the prime movers in the discovery of ancient Egypt. Intriguingly, when he died in the Holy Land, he left instructions that his head was to be removed from his body and taken back to England. This was done, but the head was apparently 'lost' *en route*, and, to this day, has never been found (J. Zias, pers. comm.).

47. Kitchen, K. A., *Ramesside Inscriptions* (1975).

48. Gaballa, G. A., *The Memphite Tomb Chapel of Mose* (1977), p.23ff.

49. Freud, S., *Moses and Monotheism*, (1937).

50. Josephus, F., *Contra Apionem III*. In *Works* (1926).

51. Osman, A., *Moses Pharaoh of Egypt* (1991), p.165.

3: Druids and the Cult of the Head

1. Nennius, *British History and Welsh Annals* (1980).

2. Eusebius/Jerome, *Eusebius Werke* (1956).

3. *Scotichronicon* (1993).

4. Randall-McIver, D. and Wilkin, A., *Libyan Notes* (1901).

5. Watkin, I. M., *Genetic and Population Studies in Wales* (1986).

6. Poloni, E. S., *et al.*, *American Journal of Human Genetics*, 59, 185–203 (1997).

7. Bryden, R., personal communication (1998).

8. Helck, W., *Untersuchungen zu Manetho und den ägyptischen Koniglisten* (1956).

9. *Calendar of Documents Relating to Scotland*, ii, 840 (1881–8).

10. *The Works of Robert of Gloucester* (1810).

11. *Documents Illustrative of the History of Scotland*, ii, 25 (1870).

12. *Morning Chronicle*, 2 January, 1809.

13. *The Stone of Destiny*, BBC TV Scotland (1997).

14. Chadwick, N., *The Druids* (1966).

15. Ross A. and Robins D., *The Life and Death of a Druid Prince* (1989).

16. Suzuki, B. L., *Mahayana Buddhism* (1981).

17. Campbell, J., *The Hero With a Thousand Faces* (Meridien Books, New York, 1968).

18. Ross A. and Robins D., *The Life and Death of a Druid Prince* (1989).
19. Diodorus Siculus, *World History*, vol. V: 31.
20. Caesar, J., *De Bello Gallico*, vi. 14.
21. Diogenes Laertius, *Vitae Philosophorum* (1964).
22. *Posidonius*, Cambridge University Press (1972–88).
23. Diodorus Siculus, v.31.
24. Strabo, *Geography*, iv.4.
25. Ammianus Marcellinus, *The Late Roman Empire* (1986).
26. Caesar, J., *De Bello Gallico*, vi. 12.
27. Valerius Maximus, *Factorum Libri Novem*, ii.6.10.
28. Chadwick N., *The Druids* (1966), p.15.
29. Caesar, J., *De Bello Gallico*, vi. 13.
30. Livy, Book xxiii, 24, 12.
31. Merrifield, R., *The Archaeology of Ritual and Magic* (1987).
32. London *Times*, 7 October, 1963.
33. *The Mabinogion* (1963).
34. Jobes, G., *Dictionary of Mythology, Folklore and Symbols* (1961–2). Intriguingly, the head of Eurytheus (of Mycaenae) was also said to have been buried in a pass guarding the approaches to Athens.

4: The Bethel Stone

1. Dunstan, V., *Did the Virgin Mary Live and Die in England?* (1985).
2. O'Connor, R., *The Chronicles of Eri* (1822).
3. Capt, R., *Jacob's Pillar* (1977).
4. Capt. R., *Jacob's Pillar* (1977).
5. Sinclair, A., *The Sword and the Grail* (1992), p.73 and p.217.
6. Brown, P. H., *History of Scotland* (1971).

5: Sacred Hair, Sacred Heads

1. Abelson, J., *Jewish Mysticism* (1913), p.147.
2. Ginzberg, L., *Legends of the Jews*, 1946–55 p.354.
3. In the light of what has been said (and what follows), it is interesting to note that the members of the tribe of Dan were accustomed to swear oaths 'by the Head of Dan', their forefather.
4. Budde, E., 'Samson'. In Hastings, J., *Dictionary of the Bible*.
5. Epiphanius's major work is the *Panarion*, composed sometime between 374 and 377 AD. In it he attacks 'the poison of the hydra-headed serpents of error', by which he means any heterodox Christian belief which does not accord with the orthodox account of Jesus and his religion which followed the Council of Nicea some fifty years before. His treatment of the 'heresies' is

heavy-handed and considerably coloured by his own prejudices and miscon-
ceptions. However, occasionally in what he calls his 'antidote' to error, he lets
slip information about the heretical sects which can be found in no other
source.

6. Epiphanius, *Panarion*, Haer. xviii ff. (1987).
7. Epiphanius, *Panarion*, Haer. liii ff. op. cit.
8. Mead, G. R. S., *Did Jesus Live 100 B.C.?* (1903).
9. Eusebius, *Ecclesiastical History*, ii.23.
10. Routh, G., *Reliquae Sacrae*, p.208–9 (1846).
11. Mead, G.R.S., *Did Jesus Live 100 B.C.?*, p.350 (1903).

6: The Heretic Tribe
1. New Larousse Encyclopaedia of Mythology, pp.18–19 (1984).
2. New Larousse Encyclopaedia of Mythology, p.19 (1984).
3. Lobineau. See Appendix II.
4. Graves, R., *Greek Myths*, Vol 1. p.203, n 1, (1948).
5. Michell, H., *Sparta* (1964), p.173.
6. Bridge, A., *Suleiman the Magnificent* (1983), p.114.

7: The Magician Kings
1. Baigent, M., Lincoln, H. and Leigh, R., *The Holy Blood and the Holy Grail* (1982), pp.249–50.
2. Wallace-Hadrill, J. M., *The Long-Haired Kings* (1962).
3. Gregory of Tours, *The History of the Franks* (1977).
4. Wallace-Hadrill, J. M., *The Chronicle of Fredegar with its Continuations* (1960).
5. In addition, as David was chosen by the Nazarite Samuel, there is a strong possibility that, as king, the Nazarite teachings would have been made available to him. There are hints in the Old Testament (e.g. Amos 2: 11ff) that at certain times in the history of Israel the Nazarites were as organised and powerful as the prophets.
6. Dondane, A., *Archivum Fratrum, Praedictadorum* (Rome), 29, 228–76, (1959). This anti-heretical tract states that the 'Albigensians' (i.e. Cathars) had a secret teaching that Mary Magdalene was the wife of Jesus. It is of interest that, although the Cathars are generally considered to have had their origins in the Balkan Bogomil sect (see Ch 13) the teaching that the Magdalene was the wife of Christ appears to have arisen *de novo* in the Cathars (see Stoyanov (1994), p.223). So, this belief was a product of the Cathar Languedoc, the area in the south of France to which, tradition relates, the Magdalene fled after the death of Jesus.

7. Baigent, M., Lincoln, H. and Leigh, R., *The Holy Blood and the Holy Grail* (1982), p.346ff.
8. Wilson, A. N., *Jesus* (1993), p.83.
9. Mead, G. R. S., *Did Jesus Live 100 B.C?* (1903), p.141.
10. Phipps, W. E., *The Sexuality of Jesus* (1973), p.4.
11. Taylor, J. W., *The Coming of the Saints* (1969).
12. Other medieval tracts also agree with this account, see for example: Bockenham, O., *Legendys of Hooly Wummen* (1447).
13. Baronius, C., *Annales Ecclesiastici* (1735–46).
14. Hoyoux, J., *Review Belge*, XXI (1942).
15. Gregory of Tours, *The History of the Franks* (1977).
16. Wallace-Hadrill, J. M., *The Long-Haired Kings* (1962), p.203.
17. Frazer, Sir J., *The Golden Bough*, Penguin (abridged version, 1996), p.279–80.
18. Wallace-Hadrill, J. M., *The Long-Haired Kings* (1962), p.244.
19. Rabinowitz, J. J., *Speculum*, 22 (1947).
20. Dumas, F., *Le Tombeau de Childeric*, n.d.
21. Wilson, E. O., *Sociobiology*, (1975), pp.42–3.
22. Montet, P., *Lives of the Pharaohs* (1974).
23. Wallace-Hadrill, J. M., *The Long-Haired Kings* (1962).
24. Digot, A., *Histoire de Royaume d'Austrasie* (1856), vol 3, p.220ff.
25. Lanigan, J., *An Ecclesiastical History of Ireland* (1829), p.101.
26. Chadwick, N., *The Druids* (1966).
27. Digot, A., *Histoire de Royaume d'Austrasie*, vol 3, (1856).
28. Wallace-Hadrill, J. M., *The Long-Haired Kings* (1962).
29. It is interesting to note that, whereas the remains of most of the Merovingian dynasty were cast together in a single 'pit grave' during the French Revolution, (and are consequently unidentifiable) the head of Dagobert II *had already been removed* and held as a relic.
30. Baigent, M., Lincoln, H. and Leigh, R., *The Holy Blood and the Holy Grail* (1982), p.272.
31. Zuckerman, A. J., *A Jewish Princedom in France* (1972).
32. Sinclair, A., *The Sword and the Grail* (1992).
33. Baigent, M., Lincoln, H. and Leigh, R., *The Holy Blood and the Holy Grail* (1982).

8: The Thrice Built Temple

1. Barker, M., *The Gate of Heaven* (1991).
2. Barker, M., *The Gate of Heaven* (1991), p.7.
3. In *The Apocrypha and Pseudepigrapha of the Old Testament* (1913).

4. Josephus, F., *Jewish War*, I. 148.

5. Josephus, F., *Antiquities of the Jews*, XV, 390–1; 394–6; 421; 425.

6. Josephus, F., *Jewish War*, V, 225.

7. Jagersma, H., *A History of Israel From Alexander the Great to Bar Kochba* (1986).

8. Barker, M., *The Gate of Heaven* (1991).

9. Solomon's Temple was a Sun Temple, and it was built on Jebusite land conquered by the Israelites and belonging (initially) to the tribe of Benjamin. 'It was the Jerusalamites' (i.e. Benjamites') conception of Jahweh as Sun-God which long held the centre of the stage and only gradually retreated into the background' (F. J. Hollis: 'The Sun Cult and the Temple at Jerusalem', in *Myth and Ritual* 1933). In addition, in the Davidic cults, Jahweh is known to have played the part of a Sun-god (see A. R. Robinson, *The Labyrinth*, 1935).

10. Ward, J. S. M., *Freemasonry and the Ancient Gods* (1926).

11. Josephus, F., *Jewish War*, V. 193–4.

12. Barker, M., *The Gate of Heaven* (1991), p.24.

13. Adoniram is said later in the bible to have been stoned to death. However, as Hiram Abiff is given three different versions of his life (and death) after the building of the temple, we can place very little reliance on this account.

14. Knight, C. and Lomas, R., *The Hiram Key* (1996).

15. Ward, J. S. M., *Freemasonry and the Ancient Gods* (1926).

16. Michelet, J., *Le Procès des Templiers*, I, p.645.

17. Loomis, R., *The Grail* (1963).

18. Roger de Howden, *Chronica*, III, pp.158–9 (1870).

19. Michelet, J., *Le Procès des Templiers*, II, pp.223–4.

20. Reinach, S., *La Tête Magique de Templiers* (1911).

21. Gervais of Tilbury, *Des Gervasius von Tilbury Otia Imperialia*, secunda decisio, XII, p.11 (1856).

22. In *The Apocrypha and Pseudepigrapha of the Old Testament* (1913).

23. Jagersma, H., *A History of Israel From Alexander the Great to Bar Kochba* (1986).

24. Josephus, F., *Jewish War*, VI, 299.

25. Bilde, P., *Josephus Between Jerusalem and Rome* (1988).

26. Josephus, *Jewish War*, VI, 232–3.

27. Josephus, *Jewish War*, VI, 252–3, 259.

28. Josephus, *Jewish War*, VI, 387–9.

29. Josephus, *Jewish War*, VI, 390.

30. Allegro, J. M., *The Dead Sea Scrolls* (1959).

31. Barker, M., *The Gate of Heaven* p.55, (1991).

32. Vilnay, Z., *Legends of Jerusalem: the Sacred Land*, Vol 1, p.123, (1973).

33. Byers, G., *Association for Biblical Research*.

9: The True Bloodline

1. Peet, T. E., *Egypt and the Old Testament* (1922).
2. Osman, A., *Stranger in the Valley of the Kings* (1987).
3. Bakir, A. el-M., *Annales du Service des Antiquités de l'Égypte*, 18 (1952).
4. Yahuda, A. S., *The Language of the Pentateuch in its Relation to Egypt* (1933).
5. Davis, T. M., *The Tomb of Iouiya and Touiyou* (1907).
6. Weigall, A., *The Life and Times of Akhenaten* (1910).
7. Naville, H. E., *Funerary Papyrus of Iouiya* (1908).
8. Naville, H. E., *Funerary Papyrus of Iouiya* (1908).
9. Weigall, A., *The Life and Times of Akhenaten* (1910).
10. Schwantes, S. J., *A Short History of the Ancient Near East* (1965).
11. Hayes, W. C., *The Sceptre of Egypt*, pp.116–17, (1959).
12. According to Biblical genealogies, Seth the son of Adam (and Eve) produced (via a line of eight descendants) Noah. Noah, in turn, sired three sons: Japeth, Ham and Shem. From the latter arose the Shemites or Semites (which of course included the Hebrews). Ham's descendants were the Canaanites, (and very probably the Egyptians also).

10: Jesus, Son of Ra

1. See, for example: Brandon, S. G. F., *Jesus and the Zealots* (Manchester, 1967); Hengel, M., *Was Jesus a Revolutionist?* (Philadelphia, 1971); and Sweet, J. P. M., 'The Zealots and Jesus'. In *Jesus and the Politics of his Day* (E. Bammel and C. F. D. Moule (eds), Cambridge (1984).
2. Mead, G. R. S., *Did Jesus Live 100 B.C.?* Ch IV, p.70ff. (1903).
3. Popper, W., *The Censorship of Hebrew Books* (New York, 1899).
4. In the Apocryphal Gospels, it is said that Jesus visits Pharaoh, which does not seem a very plausible event for the son of a carpenter, but which, as we shall see, may not be as incredible as it sounds.
5. See, for example, A. N. Wilson, (1993), pp.87–8.
6. Wilson, A. N., *Jesus* (1993), pp.82–3.
7. Mead, G. R. S., *Did Jesus Live 100 B.C.?* (1903), p.180.
8. This quote is taken from the Toldoth rescension of the Strassburg MS, which preserves numerous Aramaic traces and therefore links it to the earliest Toldoth forms. Part of the Strassburg MS. Toldoth (including the passage quoted) is identical with Raymund Martini's account in *Pugio Fidei*, proving that this version goes back to at least the middle of the thirteenth century.
9. Osman, A., *House of the Messiah* (1992), p.170.
10. Origen, *Contra Celsum* (1953).
11. Mead, G. R. S., *Did Jesus Live 100 B.C.?* (1903).
12. Knight, C. and Lomas, R., *The Hiram Key* (1996), p.191.

13. Mead, G. R. S., *Did Jesus Live 100 B.C.?* (1903), p.141.
14. Davis, C., *The Observer*, 28 March 1971, p.25.
15. Baigent, M., Lincoln, H. and Leigh, R., *The Holy Blood and the Holy Grail* (1982), p.355.
16. Dondaine, A., *Archivum Fratrum, Praedicatorum*, 29: 228–76 (1959).
17. Bockenham, O., *Legendys of Hooly Wummen* (1992).
18. This intriguing information appears in the Toldoth recension of the Strassburg MS., the same tract that contained the Ben Pandira information (see n 8).
19. Josephus, F., *Jewish War*, I, 4.
20. In the Gospel of John the Jews try to stone Jesus to death for blasphemy, but he is said to escape from them (John 10: 31ff).
21. Bockenham, O., *Legendys of Hooly Wummen* (1992).

11: The Holy Grail
1. Loomis, R., *The Grail* (1963).
2. Baigent, M., Lincoln, H. and Leigh, R., *The Holy Blood and the Holy Grail* (1982), p.314.
3. Goetinck, G., *Peredur* (1975).
4. *The Epic of Gilgamesh*, Sanders, N. K. (trans), 1960.
5. Brown, A. C. L., *Origins of the Grail Legend*, Ch 1 (1966).
6. Joyce, R. W., *Old Celtic Romances* (1920).
7. 'Cath Maige Tured . . .', *Anthropos*, XXVI, 435–60 (1931).
8. Borron, de R., *Roman de l'Estoire dou Saint Graal* (1927).
9. *Mabinogion*, T. & G. Jones (trans), 1963.
10. Waite, A. E., *The Hidden Church of the Holy Grail* (1909).
11. *Mabinogion*, T. & G. Jones (trans), 1963.
12. Michelet, J., *Le Proces des Templiers* I, pp.89–96.
13. Chretien de Troyes, *Le Roman de Perceval ou Le Conte du Graal* (1959).
14. Brown, A. C. L., *Origins of the Grail Legend* (1966).
15. Loomis, R., *The Grail* (1963), p.279, n.7.
16. Taylor, A., *Romantic Review*, IX, 21–8 (1918).
17. Goetinck, G., *Peredur*, p.2 (1975).
18. Goetinck, G., *Peredur*, p.79 (1975).
19. Bryant, N., *The High Book of the Grail* (1978).
20. Goetinck, G., *Peredur*, p.287 (1975).
21. Loomis, R., *The Grail*, p.120 (1963).
22. von Eschenbach, W., *Parzifal* (1961).
23. Michelet, J., *Le Proces des Templiers* I, pp.89–96.
24. Rowbotham, G. F., *Troubadours and the Courts of Love* (1895).
25. Borron, de R., *Roman de l'Estoire dou Saint Graal* (1927).

26. One possibility is that the head is that of John the Baptist, who is said in the New Testament to be Jesus's cousin. However, this is unlikely for the reasons concerning the Cult of Relics given in Chapter 14.

27. *Continuation of the Old French 'Perceval'*, W. Roach (ed), pp.480–8 (1952).

28. Lea, H. C., *A History of the Inquisition of the Middle Ages* (1888).

12: The Templars and the Sacred Head

1. Forey, A., *The Military Orders: from the twelfth to the early fourteenth century*, (1992), p.7.

2. Forey, A., *The Military Orders: from the twelfth to the early fourteenth century*, (1992), p.8.

3. Smaragdus, *Commentaria in regulam sancti Benedicti* (1844–55).

4. Bonizi de Sutri, *Liber de Vita Christiana*, (1930), VII, 28, pp.248–9.

5. Guibert de Nogent, *Gesta Dei per Francos*, I.1. (1844–95).

6. Barber, M., *The New Knighthood: a history of the order of the temple*, (1994).

7. William of Tyre, *A History of Deeds Done beyond the Sea* (1943).

8. *La Règle du Temple*, H. Curzon (ed), 1886.

9. *In Praise of the New Knighthood*, C. Greenia (trans), 1977.

10. See for example, *Cartulaire General de l'ordre du Temple*, Marquis d'Albon (ed), no. 9, p.6; no. 7, p.5.

11. Paris, M., *Chronica Majora*, H. R. Luard (ed), 1880.

12. Barber, M., *The New Knighthood: a history of the order of the temple*, (1994).

13. *Papsturkunden für Templer und Johanniter*, R. Hiestand (ed), 1972 and 1984.

14. *University History of the World*, J. A. Garraty and P. Gay (eds), pp.286–7.

15. Barber, M., *The New Knighthood: a history of the order of the temple*, 1994.

16. Forey, A., *The Military Orders*, 1992, p.116.

17. *Emprunts de St-Louis en Palestine et en Afrique*, G. Servois (ed), 1858.

18. Forey, A., *The Military Orders*, 1992, p.119.

19. Barber, M., *The New Knighthood: a history of the order of the temple*, 1994.

20. *Flores Historianum*, H. R. Luard (ed), 1890.

21. *Regesta Regni Hierosolymitani*, R. Röhricht (ed), 1893–1904.

22. Barber, M., *The New Knighthood* (1994).

23. *Gestes de Chiprois*, G. Raynaud (ed), 1887.

24. Seward, D., *The Monks of War*.

25. Seward, D., *The Monks of War* (1972), p.84.

26. Seward, D., *The Monks of War* (1972), p.85.

27. *Gestes de Chiprois*, G. Raynaud (ed), 1887.

28. William of Tyre, *A History of Deeds Done Beyond the Sea* (1943).

29. Saewulf, *The Pilgrimage of Saewulf to Jerusalem and the Holy Land in the Years 1102 and 1103*, Palestine Pilgrims' Text Society, vol 4, pp.8–9 (1892).

30. Barber, M., *The New Knighthood: a history of the order of the temple*, (1994).
31. Barber, M., *The New Knighthood: a history of the order of the temple*, (1994).
32. The Count of Anjou joined in 1120, and the Count of Champagne four years later (Baigent, M., Leigh, R. and Lincoln, H., 1982). In addition, the *Cartulaire général de l'ordre du Temple 1119?–1150* (p.2 Charter III 1125, and p.3 Charter IV 1125), cites two men Roberto and Henrico as members of the Order, making a total of four additional knights recruited before the nine year 'deadline' of 1127.
33. *Receuil des historiens des Gaules et de la France*, M. Bouquet (ed), Vol 15, p.162, no. 245.
34. *Theoderich's description of the Holy Places circa 1172*AD, Palestine Pilgrims' Text Society, vol 5 (1891).
35. Ben-Dov, M., *In the Shadow of the Temple* (1985).
36. Silberman, N. A., *Digging for Gold and Country* (1992).
37. Bryden: personal communication, December, 1997.
38. Daniell, C., *Death and Burial in Medieval England* (1997), p.44.
39. Darragh, J. T., *The Resurrection of the Flesh* (1921).
40. This seems not to apply to the bodies of saints and holy men: as we'll see in Chapter 14, their bodies were divided *ad libitum* to provide holy remains for as many places as were lucky enough to secure a piece.
41. Finke, H., *Papsttum und Untergang des Templerordens*, II, pp.364–76.
42. Michelet, J., *Procès des Templiers*, II, pp.364–76.
43. Shah, I., *The Sufis* (1969), p.225.
44. Wilson, I., *The Turin Shroud* (1978).
45. Michelet, J., *Procès des Templiers*, II, p.364.
46. Michelet, J., *Procès des Templiers*, II, pp.361–3.
47. Finke, H., *Papsttum und Untergang des Templerordens*, II, p.336.
48. Currer-Briggs, N., *The Shroud and the Grail* (1988).

13: The Cathar Connection

1. Rudolph, K., *Gnosis* (1983).
2. Stoyanov, Y., *The Hidden Tradition in Europe* (1984), p.xiv.
3. Holmes, E., *The Holy Heretics* (1948).
4. Stoyanov, Y., *The Hidden Tradition in Europe* (1994), p.154.
5. Gospel of Philip, *In The Nag Hammadi Library in English* (1977), p.153.
6. Stoyanov, Y., *The Hidden Tradition in Europe* (1994), p.155.
7. Duvernoy, J., *Cahiers du Sud*, nos: 387–8, (1966).
8. see Appendix I.
9. Shahar, S., *Juifs et Judäisme de Languedoc* (1977).
10. Stoyanov, Y., *The Hidden Tradition in Europe* (1994), pp.159–60.

11. Scholem, G., *The Origins of the Kabbalah* A. Arkush (trans), 1987.
12. Stoyanov, Y., *The Hidden Tradition in Europe*, (1994), p.130.
13. *Le Traité Contre le Bogomils de Cosmas le prêtre*, H. C. Puech and Availlant (trans), 1945.
14. Stoyanov, Y., *The Hidden Tradition in Europe* (1994), pp.133–4.
15. See *Les Lettres de Gerbert*, J. Havet (ed), 1889, no. 180, pp.161–2.; Runciman, S., *The Medieval Manichee* (1946); and da Milano, *Studi Gregoriani*, 2: 44–6.
16. Eckbert of Schonau, *Patrologia Latina*, 195, cols. 11–102.
17. Anselm of Alessandria, *Archivum Fratrum Praedicatorum*, 20, (1950), pp.308–24.
18. Ivanov, I., *Bogomilski knigi I legendi* (1925), pp.50–51.
19. Stoyanov, Y., *The Hidden Tradition in Europe* (1994), p.133.
20. *Bulgarian Apocryphal Chronicle*, quoted in Ivanov, I., *Bogomilski knigi I legendi* (1925), pp.273–87.
21. Stoyanov, Y., *The Hidden Tradition in Europe* (1994), pp.281–2.
22. Theiner, A., *Vetera monumenta historica Hungariam sacram illustrantia* (1859–60), p.20.
23. Strayer, J., *The Albigensian Crusade* (1971).
24. Stoyanov, Y., *The Hidden Tradition in Europe* (1994), p.173.
25. Aimery, *Patrologia Latina*, Vol 216, Col. 139.
26. *La Chanson de la Croisade Albigeoise*, Guillaume de Tudèle. E Martin-Chabot (ed & trans). Vol 3, 208–9, 1931.
27. *The Song of the Cathar Wars*, Guillaume de Tudele. J Shirley (trans), 1996.
28. Lea, H. C., *A History of the Inquisition of the Middle Ages*, 3 Vols, 1888.
29. Oldenbourg, Z., *The Massacre at Montségur* (1961), p.335.
30. Oldenbourg, Z., *The Massacre at Montségur* (1961), p.336.
31. *The Song of the Cathar Wars*, Guillaume de Tudele. J. Shirley (trans), 1996.
32. Stoyanov, Y., *The Hidden Tradition in Europe*, 1994, pp.181–3.
33. Oldenbourg, Z., *The Massacre at Montségur*, 1961, p.356ff.
34. Stoyanov, Y., *The Hidden Tradition in Europe*, 1994, p.183.
35. Niel, F., *Les Cathars de Montsegur* (1973).
36. Durrel, L., quoted in Stoyanov, Y., *The Hidden Tradition in Europe* (1994), p.xiv.
37. Sinclair, A., *The Sword and the Grail* (1992).
38. Stoyanov, Y., *The Hidden Tradition in Europe* (1994).

14: The Forbidden Relic

1. Rattray, R. S., *Religion and Art in Ashanti* (1927).
2. Bentley, J., *Restless Bones* (1985), p.193.
3. Kahn, I., *Reliques of the Quais-I-Azam* (1980).
4. Wilson, S., *Saints and their Cults* (1983), p.4.

5. Bentley, J., *Restless Bones* (1985).

6. Bentley, J., *Restless Bones* (1985).

7. Bentley, J., *Restless Bones* (1985).

8. Wilson, S., *Saints and their Cults* (1983), p.130.

9. Baynes, N. H., *Analecta Bollandiana*, tôme 67, (1949), pp.165–7.

10. Bentley, J., *Restless Bones* (1985).

11. Butler, J., *The Quest for Becket's Bones* (1995).

12. Geary, P. J., *Furta Sacra: thefts of relics in the Central Middle Ages* (1978).

13. Bentley, J., *Restless Bones* (1985), p.94.

14. Herman-Mansard, N., *Les Reliques des Saints* (1975).

15. Brooke, R. and Brooke, C., *Popular Religion in the Middle Ages* (1984).

16. The seamless robe is itself a suggestive mystery. Why the robe of Jesus is emphasised as being 'seamless' in the Fourth Gospel (the only time in the entire bible that the word seam is used) makes more sense when it is recognised that the sacred robe of the Manichees and other gnostic was emphatically *not* seamless. It was an absolute requirement that the robe was made of two pieces with a seam on either side of the body. The writer of the Fourth Gospel is making clear that this 'was not the robe of a Sun-Cult initiate as – it may be legitimately inferred – the gnostics were, at the time of his writing, already contending that it was'.

17. Wilson, I., *The Turin Shroud* (1978).

18. Bentley, J., *Restless Bones* (1985).

19. Runciman, S., *Analecta Bollandiana*, tôme 68, (1950), pp.197–204.

20. Chaucer, G., *The Canterbury Tales*, N. F. Blake (ed), 1980.

21. 'The Gospel of the Infancy of Jesus Christ', 2:4. In *The Lost Books of the Bible*, R. H. Platt (ed), 1974.

22. Wilson, I., *The Turin Shroud* (1978).

15: The Templars Suppressed

1. Barber, M., *The New Knighthood: a history of the order of the temple* (1994).

2. Dupuy, P., *Histoire de la differend d'entre le pape Boniface VIII et Phillipe le Bel, Roy de France*, (1655), p.518.

3. Dupuy, P., *Histoire de la differend d'entre le pape Boniface VIII et Phillipe le Bel, Roy de France*, (1655), p.643–4.

4. Strayer, J. R., in *Medieval Statecraft and the Perspectives of History*, (1971), pp.239–47.

5. Boutaric, E., *La France sous Phillipe le Bel* (1861), pp.302–3.

6. Barber, M., *The New Knighthood: a history of the order of the temple* (1994), p.39.

7. *Speculum Ecclesiae*, J. S. Brewer (ed), Vol IV, 554 (1861–91).

8. quoted in E. J. Martin, *The Trial of the Knights Templar*, (1928), p.20.

9. Song of the Second Crusades. In *The Making of the Middle Ages*, (1953), p.55.

10. de Bartholomaeis, V. *Poesie provenzali storiche relative all'Italia*, ii, (1931), pp.222–4.

11. Meyer, P., *Bibliotheque de l'Ecole des Chartres*, sixth ser., v, pp.484ff. (1869).

12. Lea, H. C., *A History of the Inquisition of the Middle Ages*, 3 Vols, (1888).

13. Finke, H., *Papsttum und Untergang des Templerordens*, II, pp.83–4.

14. Baluze, E., *Vitae Paparum Avienonensium*. G. Mollat (ed), Vol III, pp.58–60 (1914–27).

15. Barker, M., *The Trial of the Templars*, (1978), p.53.

16. See Appendix I.

17. Robinson, J. J., *Dungeon, Fire and Sword: the Knights Templar in the Crusades* (1992).

18. Robinson, J. J., *Dungeon, Fire and Sword: the Knights Templar in the Crusades* (1992).

19. de Nangis, G., *Chronique latine de Guillaume de nangis, de 1113 a 1300 avec les continuations decette chronique de 1300 a 1368*. H. Geraud (ed), 1843.

20. Delisle, L., *Memoires sur les operations financieres des Templiers* (Memoires de l'Institut National de France, Academie des Inscriptions et Belles-Lettres, Vol 33). Paris, 1889.

21. Michelet, J., *Procès des Templiers*, I, pp.169–71.

22. Seward, D., *The Monks of War* (1972), p.203.

23. Seward, D., *The Monks of War* (1972), p.207.

24. This example, and this argument, was used by the Templars themselves., see Michelet, J. *Procès des Templiers*, I, pp.169–71.

25. Von Calusewitz, K., *On War*, 1982.

26. Pauwels, L. and Bergier, J., *The Dawn of Magic* (1963), p.200ff.

27. Stoyanov Y., *The Hidden Tradition in Europe* (1994).

28. de Nangis, G., *Chronique latine de Guillaume de nangis, de 1113 a 1300 avec les continuations decette chronique de 1300 a 1368*. H. Geraud (ed), Vol 1, pp.402–3, 1843.

29. Seward, D., *The Monks of War* (1972), pp.212–13.

30. de Nangis, G., *Chronique latine de Guillaume de nangis, de 1113 a 1300 avec les continuations decette chronique de 1300 a 1368*. H. Geraud (ed), Vol 1, p.404, 1843.

31. Begg, E., *The Cult of the Black Virgin* (1985), p.14.

32. de Nangis, G., *Chronique latine de Guillaume de nangis, de 1113 a 1300 avec les continuations decette chronique de 1300 a 1368*. H. Geraud (ed), Vol 1, p.404. (1843).

33. Villani, G., *Cronica*, Vol 2, p.127 (1845).

34. Cadet de Gassicourt, C. L., *Les Initiés anciens et modernes, suite du Tombeau de Jacques Molay.* n.d. (1796?).

35. See, for example, Barber, M., *The Military Orders* (1994); *The New Knighthood* (1994); Forey, A., *The Military Orders* (1992). Seward, D., *The Monks of War* (1972).

36. Baigent, M., Lincoln, H. and Leigh, R., *The Holy Blood and the Holy Grail* (1982), p.72.

37. Finke, H., *Papsttum und Untergang des Templerordens*, II, pp.337–9.

16: To the Extremity of the World

1. Fordun, J., *Scotichronicon*. F. S. H. Skene (trans), p.330, 1872.

2. *Liber Pluscardenensis*. F. H. Skene (ed), p.174, 1880.

3. Sinclair, A., *The Sword and the Grail*, (1992), p.35.

4. Mackenzie, A. M., *Robert Bruce, King of Scots* (1934), p.220.

5. Sinclair, A., *The Sword and the Grail* (1992), p.42.

6. Baigent, M., Lincoln, H. and Leigh, R., *The Holy Blood and the Holy Grail* (1982), p.75.

7. Sinclair, A., *The Sword and the Grail* (1992), p.45.

8. Sinclair, A., *The Sword and the Grail* (1992), p.45. See also Bothwell-Gosse, A., *The Knights Templar*, London (1912).

9. Baigent, M., Lincoln, H. and Leigh, R., *The Holy Blood and the Holy Grail* (1982), p.80. Robert Graves has revealed arabic wordplay linking 'black' and 'wise' (see Shah, I., *The Sufis*. p.xix., 1969). Graves believes such an allusion is contained in Hugues de Payns coat of arms, making the heads, Heads of Wisdom, a title close to the arabic *abufihimat* 'Father of Wisdom', which is almost certainly the derivation of the Templar 'Baphomet'.

10. Sinclair, A., *The Sword and the Grail* (1992).

11. Dupuy, P., *Histoire de la differend d'entre le pape Boniface VIII et Phillipe le Bel, Roy de France*, pp.182–6 (1655).

12. *Calendar of Documents Relating to Scotland*, J. Bain (ed), ii, (1881).

13. All were executed. At Westminster, the assembled peers demanded that the captured Earl of Atholl, being of royal blood, should be treated as befitted his high station. With grim humour, Edward I demonstrated the earl's exalted status by having him hanged on a gallows thirty feet higher than the normal and, after the headsman had done his work, by exhibiting the earl's head on London Bridge on an exceptionally tall pole.

14. Tout, T. F., *Edward I* (1872). Also *Flores Historiarum*, II, 595 (1890).

15. *The Brus*, G. E. Todd (trans) (1907).

16. *The Brus*, G. E. Todd (trans) (1907).

17. Christison, P., Scot F. S. A. and Taylor, I. C. *Bannockburn, the story of the battle* (1962).
18. Sinclair, A., *The Sword and the Grail* (1992), p.46.
19. Sinclair, A., *The Sword and the Grail* (1992), p.48.

17: Guardians of the Sacred Light

1. The Earl of Rosslyn, *Rosslyn Chapel* (1997), p.41.
2. Sinclair, A., *The Sword and the Grail* (1992), p.28.
3. Hay, R. A., *Genealogie of the Saintclaires of Rosslyn* (1835).
4. Lesley, Bishop, *History of Scotland* (1578).
5. See Chapter 16, note 9.
6. Scott, R. McN. *Robert the Bruce, King of Scots* (1982).
7. Fergusson, J., *The Declaration of Arbroath*, n.d., p.9.
8. Scotichronicon, J. and W. McQueen (eds), ch 12 ff., (1993).
9. *Calendar of Documents Relating to Scotland*, J. Bain (ed), iii, (1881), p.725.
10. Sinclair, A., *The Sword and the Grail* (1992), p.49.
11. Begg, E., *The Cult of the Black Virgin* (1985).
12. Delaude, J., *Le Circle d'Ulysse* (1977).

18: A Second Temple of Solomon

1. Hay, R. A., *Genealogie of the Saintclaires of Rosslyn* (1835).
2. Hay, R. A., *Genealogie of the Saintclaires of Rosslyn* (1835).
3. Slezer, J., *Theatrum Scotiae* (1693).
4. Hay, R. A., *Genealogie of the Saintclaires of Rosslyn* (1835).
5. Sinclair, A., *The Sword and the Grail* (1992).
6. Knight and Lomas, *The Hiram Key* (1996), p.417.
7. Ward, J. S. M., *Freemasonry and the Ancient Gods* (1926).
8. The Earl of Rosslyn, *Rosslyn Chapel* (1997), p.4.
9. The Earl of Rosslyn, *Rosslyn Chapel* (1997), p.5.
10. Knight and Lomas, *The Hiram Key* (1996), p.144.
11. Frazer, J., *The Golden Bough* (abridged edition) (1922), p.152.
12. Bryden, R., *Rosslyn – a History of the Guilds, the Masons and the Holy Cross* (1994).
13. Mead, G.R.S. *Did Jesus Live 100 B.C.?* (1903), p.180.
14. The Apocryphal writings specifically mention the Jews as refusing to wash their hands which (as we saw in the example of the 'seamless robe' – Chapter 14, note 16) may be a deliberate inversion of the true circumstances by the early Christian writers.
15. Sinclair, A., *The Sword and the Grail* (1992), p.77.
16. von Eschenbach, W., *Parsival* (1961).

17. Sinclair, A., *The Sword and the Grail* (1992), p.84.
18. Tertullian, *Opera*. G. Wissowa *et al.* (trans), 1890–1939.
19. Hunt, J. E., *English and Welsh Crucifixes, 670–1550* (1956), p.2.
20. Hunt, J. E., *English and Welsh Crucifixes, 670–1550* (1956), p.3.
21. Apostolos-Cappadora, D., *Dictionary of Christian Art* (1995).
22. Dr C. P. Groves, personal communication, 1998.
23. R. Bryden, personal communication, 1998.
24. Slezer, J., *Theatrum Scotiae* (1693).
25. Thompson, J., *The Illustrated Guide to Rosslyn Chapel and Castle, Hawthornden, etc.* Third Edition (1897).
26. Sinclair, A., *The Sword and the Grail* (1992), p.86ff.

19: The Final Clue

1. MacKey, A. G., *Encyclopedia of Freemasonry* (1946).
2. R. Bryden, personal communication, 1998.
3. Stein, W. J., *The Death of Merlin* (1990), p.157 and Ravenscroft, T. and Wallace-Murphy, T., *The Mark of the Beast* (1990).
4. Forbes, Bishop, *An Account of the Chapel of Rosslyn* (1774).
5. The Earl of Rosslyn, *Rosslyn Chapel* (1997).
6. Sinclair, A., *The Sword and the Grail* (1992), p.5.
7. The Earl of Rosslyn, *Rosslyn Chapel* (1997), p.27.
8. *Poetic Edda*, 'Hovamol', 139.
9. *New Larousse Encyclopaedia of Mythology* (1984).
10. Shah, I., *The Sufis* (1969).

Bibliography

A Source Book of Scottish History. W. C. Dickinson, G. Donaldson, I. A. Milne.

Abdalla, A. B. and Harrison R. G., 'The remains of Tutankhamen', (*Antiquity*, 46. 9, 1972).

Abelson, J., *Jewish Mysticism* (G Bell & Sons Ltd., London, 1913).

Aimery, Arnold, *Patrologia Latina* (Vol 216).

Aldred, C., *Akhenaten* (Abacus, London, 1968).

Allegro, J. M., *The Dead Sea Scrolls* (Penguin Books, 1959).

Ammianus Marcellinus, *The Later Roman Empire* (W. Hamilton (trans.), Penguin, 1986).

Andrews, R. and Schellenberger P., *The Tomb of God* (Little Brown and Company, 1996).

Anselm of Alessandria, *Tractatus de hereticus* (A. Dondaine (ed.). 'L'Hiérarchie cathare en Italie', *Archivum Fratrum Praedicatorum*, 20, 1950).

Apostolos-Cappadora, D., *Dictionary of Christian Art* (Lutterworth Press, 1995).

Aristotle (p.53).

Bakir, A el-M., 'Slavery in Pharaonic Egypt' (Supplement to *Annales du Service des Antiquités de l'Égypte*, 18, 1952).

Baluze, E., *Vitae Paparum Avienonensium* (G. Mollat (ed), 4 vols, Paris, 1914–1927).

Baigent, M., Leigh R. and Lincoln H., *The Holy Blood and the Holy Grail* (Jonathan Cape, 1982).

Barber, M., *The Trial of the Templars* (Cambridge University Press, 1978).

——*The New Knighthood: a history of the order of the temple* (Cambridge University Press, 1994).

——(ed) *The Military Orders* (Variorum, 1994).

Barker, M., *The Gate of Heaven: the history and symbolism of the Temple in Jerusalem* (SPCK, London, 1991).

Barton, G. A., *Semitic and Hamitic Origins* (University of Pennsylvania, Philadelphia, 1934).

Bautier, R-H., 'Diplomatique et histoire politique: Ce que la critique diplomatique nous apprend su la personalité de Phillipe le Bel' (*Revue Historique*, 259, 3–27, 1978).

Baynes, N. H., 'The Supernatural Defenders of Constantinople' (*Analecta Bollandiana*, tôme 67, pp165–167, Société des Bollandistes, Brussels, 1949).

Baronius, C., *Annales Ecclesiastici* (19 Vols, G. D. Mansi and D. Giorgi (eds), 1735–46).

Barron, E. M., *The Scottish War of Independence* (Second edition, 1934).

de Bartholomaeis, V., *Poesie provenzali storiche relative all'Itaia* (Rome, 1931) ii, pp222–224.

Bede, *The Comlete Works of the Venerable Bede* (J. A. Giles (ed), 6 Vols, London, 1843).

Begg, E., *The Cult of the Black Virgin* (Arkana, 1985).

Begg, E. and Begg D., *In Search of the Holy Grail and the Precious Blood* (Thorsons, 1995).

Ben-Dov, M., *In the Shadow of the Temple* (Trans. Ina Friedman, Harper & Row, 1985).

Bentley, J., *Restless Bones* (Constable and Co. Ltd., London, 1985).

Bilde, P., *Josephus between Jerusalem and Rome: his life, his works and their importance* (Sheffield Academic Press, Sheffield, 1988).

Borron de R., *Roman de l'Estoire dou Saint Graal* (or *Joseph d'Aramathie*) (W. A. Nitze (ed), Paris, 1927).

Bockenham, O., *Legendys of Hooly Wummen* (1447?) in 'A Legend of Holy Women' (Trans. S. Delaney, University of Notre Dame Press, Indiana, 1992).

Bonizi de Sutri, *Liber de Vita Christiana*, (E. Perels (ed), Berlin, 1930) VII, 28, pp248–249.

Bordier, H., 'Une Satire contre Phillipe le Bel (vers 1290)' (*Bulletins de la Société de l'Histoire de France*, Second ser., 1, 197–201, 1857–58).

Boutaric, E., *La France sous Phillipe le Bel* (Paris, 1861).

Bridge, A., *Suleiman the Magnificent* (Granada, London, 1983).

Britton, J., *Archîtectural Antiquities of Britain*.

Brooke, R. and C., *Popular Religion in the Middle Ages* (Thames and Hudson, London, 1984).

Brown, A. C. L., *Origins of the Grail Legend* (Russel and Russel, New York, 1966).

Brown, P. H., *History of Scotland* (Octagon Books, 1971).

Bryant, N., *The High Book of the Grail* (D. S. Brewer, Cambridge, 1978).

Bryden, R., *Rosslyn – a History of the Guilds, the Masons and the Rosy Cross* (Rosslyn Chapel Trust, 1994).

Bulgarian Apocryphal Chronicle, The, 13. In Ivanov, I., *Bogomilski knigi i legendi* (Bogomil Books and Legends, Sofia, 1925). pp273–287.

Burton, J. H., *History of Scotland* (second edition, 1873).

Butler, J., *The Quest for Becket's Bones* (Yale University Press, 1995).

Caesar, J., *Caesar's War Commentaries: de Bello Gallico and de Bello Civili* (J. Warrington (ed and trans), London, Dent, 1953).

Calendar of Documents Relating to Scotland (J. Bain (ed), 1881–1888).

Capt, R., *Jacob's Pillar* (Artisan, California, 1977).

Carter, H. and Mace, A. C., *The Tomb of Tutankhamun* (London, 1923).

Carter, H., *The Tomb of Tutankhamun* (Cassel, London, 1933).

Cartulaire général de l'ordre du Temple 1119?–1150 (Receuil deschartres et des bulles relative à l'ordre du Temple, Marquis d'Albon (ed), Paris, 1913) No. 9, p.6 and No. 7, p.5.

Cath Maige Tured an scelsa sisocus genemain Bres maic Eladhain ocus a righe (G. Lehmacher (trans), *Anthropos*, XXVI, 435–460, 1931).

Cauvin, J., *Religions Néoloithiques de Syro-Palestine* (Publications du Centre de Researches d'Ecologie et de Préhistoire, St André-de-Cruzieres I, Paris).

Cavalli-Sforza, L. I., 'Genes, Peoples and Languages' (*Scientific American*, 265 (5), 72–78).

Chadwick, N., *The Druids* (University of Wales Press, Cardiff, 1966).

Chretian de Troyes, *Le Roman de Perceval ou Le Conte du Graal* (W. Roach (ed), Second edition, Paris, 1959).

——*Lancelot ou Le Chevalier de Charette* (J. C. Aubailly (ed), Flammarion, Paris, 1991).

——*Erec und Enide* (W. Foerster (ed), 1909).

Christison, P. and Taylor, I. C., *Bannockburn: The Story of the Battle* (Scottish National Trust, 1962).

Cornélius, H. et al., *La Résurrection de la chair* (1962).

Continuation of the Old French 'Perceval' (W. Roach (ed), Philadelphia, 1952).

Cotton MS Titus.

Currer-Briggs, N., *The Shroud and the Grail: a modern quest for the true grail* (1988).

Daniell, C., *Death and Burial in Medieval England* (Routledge, 1997).

Darragh, J. T., *The Resurrection of the Flesh* (SPCK, 1921).

Davis, T. M., *The Tomb of Iouiya and Touiyou* (London, 1907).

Davis, C., *The Observer* newspaper, (London, 28 March 1971) p.25.

Delaude, J., *Le Circle d'Ulysse* (Priory of Sion Document, Toulouse, 1977).

Derry, D. E., 'Note on the Skeleton hitherto Believed to be that of King Akhenaten' (*Annales du Service des Antiquités de l'Égypte*, 31, 1931).

Deutsch, I., *What is the Talmud* (The Quarterly Review, London, 1867, 417–464).

Devi, S., *Son of the Sun* (Grand Lodge of AMORC, Inc., 1981).

Digot, A., *Histoire de Royaume d'Austrasie* (Vol 3, Nancy, 1856).

Diodorus Siculus (C. H. Oldfather, R. M. Geer, F. R. Walton, C. L. Sherman and C. B. Welles (eds), Loeb Classical Library, 12 Vols, Cambridge, Mass, 1933–1967).

Diogenes Laertius, *Vitae Philosophorum* (2 vols, H. S. Long (ed and trans), Oxford, 1964).

Documents Illustrative of the History of Scotland (J. Stevenson (ed), 1870).

Dondaine, A., 'Durand de Huesca et la polémique anti-cathare' (*Archivum Fratrum, Praedicatorum*, Rome, 29, 228–276).

Dumas, F., *Le Tombeau de Childeric* (Paris, No date).

Dunstan, V., *Did the Virgin Mary Live and Die in England?* (Megiddo Press, 1985).

Dupuy, P., *Histoire du différendd'entre le pape Boniface VIII et Philippe le Bel, Roy de france* (Paris, 1655).

Duvernoy, J., *Albigeisme ou Catharisme* (Cahiers du Sud, Nos 387–388, 1966).

Eckbert of Schönau, *Sermones tredicum contra Catharos* (Patrologia Latina, 195).

Emprunts de Saint-Louis en Palestine et en Afrique (G. Servois (ed), Bibliothèque de l'Ecole des Chartres, 19, 1858).

von Eschenbach, W., *Parzival* (A. Lefevere, New York, Continuum, 1991).

Epiphanius of Salamis, *The Panarion of Epiphanius of Salamis* (2 vols. F. Williams (trans), E. J. Brill, New York, 1987).

Eusebius, *Ecclesiastical History* (G. A. Williamson (trans), Penguin, London, 1989).

Eusebius/Jerome, *Eusebius Werke, Siebenter hand: Die Chronik des Hiernonymus* (*Hieronymi Chronicon*, R. Helme (ed and trans), Berlin, 1956).

Evangelium Nicodemii, *The Gospel of Nicodemus: a late Middle English version*, (B. Lindstrom (trans), 1974).

Fairman, H. W., 'The Supposed year 21 of Akhenaten' (*Journal of Egyptian Archaeology*, 46, 1960).

Ferguson, J., The Declaration of Arbroath.XXXXX

Ferembach, D., 'Étude Anthropologique des Ossements Humains Néolithique de Tell-Ramad, Syrie (Compagnes 1963–66)' (*L'Anthropologie*, 74: 247–254, 1970).

Finke, H., *Papsttum und Untergang des Templerordens*, Vols I and II (Münster, 1907).

Flores Historiarum, H. R. Luard (ed), Vols I–III (London, 1890).

Forbes-Bishop, *An Account of the Chapel of Rosslyn* (Edinburgh, 1774).

Fordun, J., *Scotichronicon* (F. S. H. Skene (trans), W. F. Skene (ed), 1872).

Forey, A., *The Military Orders: from the twelfth century to the early fourteenth century* (Basingstoke, Macmillan, 1992).

Frazer, Sir J., *The Golden Bough* (London, Macmillan, 1911–1915).

——*The Golden Bough* (abridged edn), Penguin, 1966.

Freud, S., *Moses and Monotheism* (The Hogarth Press, 1951).

Gaballa, G. A., *The Memphite Tomb Chapel of Mose* (Aris and Philips, Warminster, 1977). pp23ff.

Gardiner, A. H., 'A Later Allusion to Akhenaten' (*Journal of Egyptian Archaeology*, 24, 1938).

Cadet de Gassicourt, C. L., *Les Initiés anciens et modernes, suite du Tombeau de Jacques Molay* (Paris, 1796?).

Geary, P. J., *Furta Sacra: Thefts of relics in the Central Middle Ages* (Princeton University Press, New Jersey, 1978).

Gervais of Tilbury, *Des Gervasius von Tilbury Otia Imperialia* (F. Liebrecht (ed), Hanover, 1856).

Gestes de Chiprois, (G. Raynaud (ed), Geneva, 1887).

Ginzberg, L., *Legends of the Jews* (Philadelphia, The Jewish Publication Society of America, 1946–55).

Goetinck, G., *Peredur: a study of Welsh Tradition in the Grail Legends* (University of Wales Press, Cardiff, 1975).

Graves, R., *The White Goddess*, (Faber and Faber, London, 1986).

——*The Greek Myths* (2 Vols, Penguin Books, Harmondsworth, 1978).

Gregory of Tours, *The History of the Franks* (Lewis Thorpe (trans), Harmondsworth, 1977).

Guibert de Nogent, 'Gesta Dei per Francos', I.1 (in *Receuil des historiens de croisades: historiens occidentaux*, Paris, 1844–95).

Guillaume de Tyr, *Chronique*, (R. B. C. Huygens (ed), *Corpus Christianorum, Continuatio Mediaevalis* 63 and 63A, Turnhout, 1986).

Gunn, B., *The City of Akhenaten* (Egypt Exploration Society, London, 1923).

Hmaza, M., 'The Alabaster Canopic Box of Akhenaten' (*Annales du Service des Antiquités de l'Égyptie*, 40, 1940).

Hay, R. A., *Genealogie of the Saintclaires of Rosslyn* (Edinburgh, 1835).

Helck, W., *Untersuchungen zu Manetho und den äegyptischen Königlisten* (Berlin, 1956).

Herman-Mansard, N., *Les Reliques des Saints. Formation coutumière d'un droit* (editions Klincksieck, Paris, 1975).

Herodotus, *The Histories* (A de Selincourt (trans), Penguin Classics, Harmondsworth, 1954).

Holmes, E., *The Holy Heretics* (Watts, London, 1948).

Hoyoux, J., 'Le Collier de Clovis' (*Rev. belge*, XXI, 1942).

Hunt, J. E., *English and Welsh Crucifixes, 670–1550* (London, SPCK, 1956). *In Praise of the New Knighthood* (in *The Works of Bernard of Clairvaux*, vol VII, Treatises, 3, C. Greenia (trans), Cistercian Fathers Series 19, Kalamazoo, Michegan, 1977).

Ivanov, I., *Bogomilski knigi i legendi* (Bogomil Books and Legends, Sofia, 1925).

Jagersma, H., *A History of Israel from Alexander the Great to Bar Kochba* (Fortress Press, Philadelphia, 1986).

Jobes, G., *Dictionary of Mythology, Folklore and Symbols* (3 Vols, Scarecrow Press, 1961–62).

Jordan, P., *Egypt, the Black Land* (Phaidon, Oxford, 1976).

Josephus, F., *Works* (includes *Antiquities of the Jews; Jewish War; Against Apion*) (H. St J. Thackeray, et al. (eds), Heinemann, London, 1926).

Joyce, P. W., *Old Celtic Romances* (London, 1920).

Kahn, I., *Reliques of the Quais-l-Azam* (F. Quadir and M. M. Daig (eds), Karachi, 1980).

Kenyon, K., *Digging Up Jericho* (Benn, London, 1957).

——*Archaeology in the Holy Land* (London, 1970).

Kitchen, K. A., *Ramesside Inscriptions* (Blackwell, Oxford, 1975).

Knight, C. and Lomas R., *The Hiram Key* (Century, 1976).

Kuryluk, E., *Veronica and her Cloth* (Blackwell, Oxford, 1991).

La Chanson de la Croisade Albigeoise, Guillaume de Tudèle (Martin-Chabot, E. (ed & trans) 3 vols, 1931–61, Paris).

La Règle du Temple (H. de Curzon (ed), Paris, 1886).

Le Traité contre les Bogomils de Cosmas le prêtre (H-C. Puech and Availlant (trans), Paris, 1945).

Lea, H. C., *A history of the Inquisition of the Middle Ages* (3 Vols, New York and London, 1888).

Les Lettres de Gerbert (J. Havet (ed), Paris, 1889) No 180, p.161–162.

Lesley, Bishop, *History of Scotland* (Edinburgh, 1578).

Letter of Aristeas, 83, 88–91 (in *The Apocrypha and Pseudepigrapha of the Old Testament*, R. H. Charles (ed), Vol 2, Oxford, 1913).

Liber Pluscardenensis (F. H. Skene (ed), 1880).

Livy, *Works* (B. O. Foster et al. (trans), Loeb Classical Library, Heineeman, London, 1919–1959).

Lizerand, G., *Le Dossier de l'affaire des Templiers* (Paris, 1923).

Lobineau, H., *Dossiers Secrets d'Henri Lobineau* (Paris, 1967).

Loomis, R., *The Grail* (Cardiff, 1963).

The Times (London, 21 October 1968).

Mabinogion, (T. and G. Jones (trans), Dent, London, 1963).

MacKenzie, A. M., *Robert Bruce, King of Scots* (1934).

Mackey, A. G., *Encyclopaedia of Freemasonry* (2 Vols, Chicago, 1946).

Magna Glastoniensis Tabula, p.182.

Marjanen, A., *The Woman Jesus Loved* (E. J. Brill, 1996).

Martin, E. J., *The Trial of the Knights Templar* (London, 1928).

Martin, G. T., *The Royal Tomb at el-Amarna* (Egypt Exploration Society, London, 1974).

Mead G. R. S., *Did Jesus Live 100* BC? (Theosophical Publishing Society, 1903).

Merrifield, R., *The Archaeology of Ritual and Magic*. Batsford. 1987.

Meyer, P., 'Les derniers troubadours de la Provence' (*Bibliothèque de l'École des Chartres*, 1869), sixth ser., v, pp484ff.

Michelet, J., *Le Procès des Templiers* (2 vols, *Collections de Documents Inédits sur l'Histoire de France*, Paris, 1841–1851).

Michell, H., *Sparta* (Cambridge, 1964).

da Milano, I., 'Le eresie populari' (*Studi Gregoriani*, 2, 44–46).

Montet, P., *Lives of the Pharoahs*, (Spring Books, London, 1974).

Morning Chornicle, (2 January 1819).

Nag Hammadi Library in English, The (Leiden, 1977).

De Nangis, G., *Chronique latine de Guillaume de Nagis, de 1113 à 1300 avec les continuations de cette chronique de 1300 à 1368* (H. Géraud (ed), Paris, 1843).

Naville, H. E., *Funerary Payrus of Iouiya* (London, 1908).

Nelli, R., *La Vie Quotidienne des Cathares* (Hachette, Paris, 1969).

Nennius, *British History and the Welsh Annals* (J. Morris (ed), London, 1980).

New Larousse Encyclopaedia of Mythology (Guirand, F. (ed), R. Aldington and D. Ames (trans), Hamlyn, 1984).

Niel, F., *Les Cathars de Montségur* (Paris, 1973).

O'Connor, R., *The Chronicles of Eri* (printed for Sir Richard Philips & Co., London, 1822).

Oldenbourg, Z., *Massacre at Montségur* (London, 1961).

Origen, *Contra Celsum* (H. Chadwick (trans), Cambridge University Press, Cambridge, 1953).

Osman, A., *Moses Pharaoh of Egypt* (Paladin, 1991).

——*Stranger in the Valley of the Kings* (1987, London).

——*The House of the Messiah* (HarperCollins, 1992).

Oursel, R., *Le Procès des Templiers*, (Paris, 1959), p.208.

Ozbeck, M., 'Culte des cranes humains a Cayonu' (*Anatolica*, XV, 127–132, 1988).

Papsturkunden für Templer und Johanniter (R. Hiestand (ed), Vorarbeiten zum Oriens Pontificus, vol I, Abhandlungen des Akadamie der Wissenschaftenin Gottingen 77, Gottingen, 1972, and Vol. II, 135, Gottingen, 1984).

Paris, M., *Chronica Majora* (H. R. Luard (ed), London, 1880).

Partner, P., *The Murdered Magicians: the Templars and their myth* (Oxford University Press, 1982).

Pauwels, L. and Bergier J., *The Dawn of Magic* (R. Myers (trqans), Anthony Gibbs and Phillips Ltd, 1963).

Peet, T. E., *Egypt and the Old Testament* (London, 1922).

Pendlebury, J., 'Report on the Clearance of the Royal tomb at el-Amarna' (*Annales du Service des Antiquités de l'Égypte*, 3, 1931).

Perlesvaus, The High History of the Holy Grail (S. Evans (trans), London, Dent, 1910).

313

Petrie, W. M. F., *A History of Egypt*, (Vol II, London, 1899) pp215–218.

——*Researches in Sinai* (John Murray, London, 1906).

Phipps, W. E., *The Sexuality of Jesus* (New York, 1973).

Polano, H., *Selections from the Talmud*, (Fredrick Warne, London, 1894) p.132.

Poloni, E. S., Semino, O., Passarino, G., Santachiara-Benerecetti, A. S., Doupahlou, I., Langaney, A. and Excoffier, L., 'Human genetic affinities for Y-chromosom P49a,f/Taq1 haplotypes show strong correspondence with linguistics', *American Journal of Human Genetics*, 59, 185–203, 1997.

Popper, W., *The Censorship of Hebrew Books* (1899, New York).

Posidonius (L. Edelstein and I. G. Kidd (eds), Cambridge University Press, Cambridge, 1972–88).

Rabinowitz, J. J., 'The Title *De Migrantibus* of the *Lex Salica* and the Jewish *Herem Hayishub*' (*Speculum*, V 22, Cambridge Mass, 1947).

Randall-MacIver, D. and Wilkin, A., *Libyan Notes* (London, 1901).

Ranke, H., *Die äegyptischen Personennamen* (Münster, 1902).

Rattray, R. S., *Religion and Art in Ashanti* (Clarendon Press, Oxford, 1927).

Recueil des historiens des Gaules et de la France (M. Bouquet (ed), Paris, 1738).

Redford, D. B. 'On the Chronology of the Egyptian Eighteenth Dynasty' (*Journal of Near Eastern Studies*, 25, 1966).

——*Akhenaten, the Heretic King* (Princeton University Press, 1984).

Regesta Regni Hierosolymitani (R. Röhricht (ed), 2 Vols, Innsbruck, 1893–1904).

Reinach, S., *La Tete Magique de Templiers* (Revue de l'Histoire de Religions, 1911), 63, 25–39.

Robert of Gloucester, *The Works of Robert of Gloucester* (T. Hearne (ed), Printed for amuel Bagster, 2 Vols, 1810).

Robinson, J. J., *Dungeon, Fire and Sword: the Knights Templar in the Crusades* (M. Evans & Co., 1992).

Rollefson, G., Simmons, A. H., and Kafafi, Z., *Neolithic 'Ain Ghazal, Jordan,* (Journal of Field Archaeology, 19, 1992).

Rowbotham, G. F., *Troubadours and the Courts of Love* (1895).

Roger de Howden, *Chronica* (W. R. Stubbs (ed), III (Roll series LI), London, 1870) pp158–159.

Ross, A. and Robins D., *The Life and Death of a Druid Prince* (Rider, 1989).

Routh, G., *Reliquiae Sacrae* Second Edition, Oxford, 1846) p.208–9.

Rudolph, K., *Gnosis* (R. McL. Wilson (ed & trans), Edinburgh, 1983).

Runciman, S., *The Medieval Manichee: A Study of the Christian Dualist Heresy* (Cambridge, 1946).

——'The Holy Lance Found at Antioch' (in *Analecta Bollandiana*, tôme 68, 1950) pp197–204.

Saewulf, 'The Pilgrimage of Saewulf to Jerusalem and the Holy Land in the Years

1102 and 1103' (W. R. B. Brownlow (trans), Palestine Pilgrims' Text Society, Vol 4, London 1892).

Scholem, G., *The Origins of the Kabbalah* (A. Arkush (trans), Princeton, 1987).

Schwantes, S. J., *A Short History of the Ancient Near East* (Baker Book House, Michigan, 1965).

Scotichronicon (J. and W. McQueen (eds), The Mercat Press, 1993).

Scott, R. McN., *Robert the Bruce* (Hutchinson and Co. Ltd, 1982).

Seele, K. C., 'King Aye and the Close of the Amarna Age' (*Journal of Near Eastern Studies*, 14, 1955).

Seward, D., *The Monks of War* (Eyre Methuen, 1972).

Shah, I., *The Sufis* (London, 1969).

Shahar, S., 'Écrits cathares et commentaire d'Abraham Abulafia sur "Le Livre de la Crétion", Images et Idées Communes', (I, *Juifs et Judaïsme de Languedoc*, Toulouse, 1977).

Silberman, N. A., *Digging for Gold and Country* (Alfred A. Knopf, 1992).

Sinclair, A., *The Sword and the Grail* (Crown Publishers Inc., New York, 1992).

Slezer, J., *Theatrum Scotiae* (London, 1693).

Smaragdus, 'Commentaria in regulam sancti Benedicti' (in J. P. Milne, *Patrologiae cursus completus, Series latina*, Paris, 1844–55).

Song of the Cathar Wars, (J. Shirley (trans), Aldershot, Scolar Press, 1996).

Song of the Second Crusades (R. W. Southern (trans), in *The Making of the Middle Ages*, London, 1953).

Speculum Ecclesiae (J. S. Brewer (ed), in *Giraldi Cambrensis Opera* (RS No 21, 8 vols. IV, 554), London, 1861–91).

Stein, W., *The Death of Merlin* (Floris Books, 1990).

Stoyanov, Y., *The Hidden Tradition in Europe* (Penguin Arkana, 1994).

Strabo, *The 'Geography' of Strabo* (H. L. Jones (trans), Heinemann, London, 1918).

Strayer, J. R., *The Albigensian Crusade* (New York, 1971).

——'Italian Bankers and Philip the Fair' (in *Medieval Statecraft and the Perspectives of History* J. F. Benson and T. H. Bisson (eds), Princeton, New Jersey, 1971).

Suzuki, B. L., *Mahayana Buddhism* (1981).

Taylor, A., 'The Motif of the vacant Stake in Folklore and Romance' (*Romanic Review*, IX, 21–28, 1918).

Taylor, J. W., *The Coming of the Saints* (Artisan, 1969).

Tertullian, *Opera* (4 Vols, G. Wissowa et al (trans), 1890–1939).

Tout, T. F., *Edward I* (1872).

The Apocrypha and Pseudepigrapha of the Old Testament (Vol 2, R. H. Charles (ed), Oxford, 1913).

The Brus (G. E. Todd (trans), and J. Barbour (ed), 1907).

The Earl of Rosslyn, *Rosslyn Chapel* (Rosslyn Chapel Trust, 1997).

The Epic of Gilgamesh (N. K. Sanders (trans), Penguin Classics, Harmondsworth, 1960).

The Five Books of Maccabees in English (H. Cotton (trans), Oxford University Press, Oxford, 1832).

The Lost Books of The Bible, R. H. Platt (ed), New York, 1974.

'The Throne of Destiny' (BBC TV Scotland, 1997).

Theiner, A., *Vetera monumenta historica Hungariam sacram illustrantia* (2 Vols, Rome, 1859–60).

Theoderich's description of the Holy Places circa 1172 AD (A. Stewart (ed and trans), Palestine Pilgrims' Text Society, Vol 5, London, 1891).

Thompson, J., *The Illustrated Guide to Rosslyn Chapel and Castle, Hawthornden, etc* (Third edition, MacNiven and Wallace, Edinburgh, 1897).

Tout, T. F., *Edward I* (1872).

University History of the World, J. A. Garraty and P. Gay (eds), New Orchard Editions, 1985.

Valerius Maximus.

Van Seters, J., *The Hyksos* (Yale University Press, London, 1966).

Villani, G., *Cronica*, Vol 2 (*Collezione di Storici e Cronisti Italiani*, Florence, 1845).

Vilnay, Z., *Legends of Jerusalem: the Sacred Land* (The Jewish Publication Society of America, Philadelphia, 1973).

Van Seters, J., *The Hyksos: a new investigation* (London, Yale University Press, 1966).

Von Clausewitz, *On War* (Penguin, 1982).

von Eschenbach, W., *Parzival* (H. E. Mustard and C. E. Pasage (trans), New York, 1961).

Waite, A. E., *The Hidden Church of the Holy Grail* (London, 1909).

Ward, J. S. M., *Freemasonry and the Ancient Gods* (London, 1926).

Wallace-Hadrill, J. M., *The Long-Haired Kings* (London, 1962).

——*The Chronicle of Fredegar with its Continuations* (Thomas Nelson & Sons Ltd., London, 1960).

Walter of Heminborough, *Chronicon Domini Walteri de Heminburgh, De Gestis Regum Angliae*, (H. C. Hamilton (ed), Vol 2, London, 1868).

Watkin, I. M., 'ABO blood group distribution in Wales in relation to human settlement' (in P. S. Harper and E. Sunderland (eds), *Genetic and Population Studies in Wales*, Cardiff, University of Wales Press, 1986).

Weigall, A., *The Life and Times of Akhenaten* (London, 1910).

White, J. E. M., *Ancient Egypt* (Allen & Unwin, 1970).

William of Tyre, *A History of Deeds Done Beyond the Sea* (2 vols), E. A. Babcock and A. C. Krey (trans), New York, 1943).

Wilson, A. N., *Jesus* (Flamingo, 1993).

Wilson, I., *The Turin Shroud* (Gollancz, London, 1978).

Wilson, E. O., *Sociobiology: the new synthesis*, (The Bellknap Press of Harvard University Press, London, 1975).

Yahuda, A. S., *The Language of the Pentateuch in its Relation to Egypt* (Oxford, 1933).

Yakar, R. and Hershkovitz, I., 'Nahal Hamar Cave. The Modeled Skulls' ('*Atiquot*, 18: 59–63, 1988).

Zuckerman, A. J., *A Jewish Princedom in Feudal France* (1972).

Index

318